MW00927851

Shinken

Kaiyuh Rose Cornberg

Outskirts Press, Inc.
Denver, Colorado

This is a work of fiction. The events and characters described herein are imaginary and are not intended to refer to specific places or living persons. The opinions expressed in this manuscript are solely the opinions of the author and do not represent the opinions or thoughts of the publisher. The author has represented and warranted full ownership and/or legal right to publish all the materials in this book.

Shinken
All Rights Reserved.
Copyright © 2010 Kaiyuh Rose Cornberg
v2.0

Cover Photo © 2010 JupiterImages Corporation. All rights reserved - used with permission.

This book may not be reproduced, transmitted, or stored in whole or in part by any means, including graphic, electronic, or mechanical without the express written consent of the publisher except in the case of brief quotations embodied in critical articles and reviews.

Outskirts Press, Inc.
http://www.outskirtspress.com

ISBN: 978-1-4327-5281-1

Outskirts Press and the "OP" logo are trademarks belonging to Outskirts Press, Inc.

PRINTED IN THE UNITED STATES OF AMERICA

To My Parents,
Without whom I would never have
been able to make this journey.

Clouds clear from the sky, dispersing as if being pushed by some invisible hand. The sun shines through the atmosphere and onto the grassy plains where a rabbit nibbles at grass. Far from the other side of the moon and never directly visible from Earth, Asthekia is still shrouded in clouds. Like a damp gray blanket, the ceiling of massive condensation looms over a nearly deserted meadow. In the middle of the meadow sits a small mammal, much like a rabbit, but with shorter ears, and a long tail, swishing in a cat-like manner. It also nibbles grass.

Contrary to the belief that Earth is the only planet with intelligent life, there is actually another planet inhabited by creatures much like humans. When the Earth formed, a meteor collided with the young and seething planet. A significant piece of the Earth disconnected and was left floating in the abyss of space.

Soon after the separation, the small chunk of matter collided with another, larger piece. Debris from Earth's great divide, over time, those pieces fused by their collision became a nearly spherical mass. Over the next many eons, the rock was shaped by gravity and meteorites into a larger and larger ball. Asthekia is about a two and a half times smaller than Earth, or approximately the size of Mercury. A myriad of scientists have made this hypothesis—not that many people have believed them. Of course it could have happened in some other way, but then how would we explain the life on Asthekia that is so similar to the life on Earth?

The geography of Asthekia is so similar to Earth that when scientists on Earth sent a satellite to take pictures of Earth from near the moon, the satellite sensed Asthekia, was confused, and took pictures of it instead of Earth. This is precisely how Earth discovered Asthekia. Just like Earth, life on Asthekia evolved over time, and at about the same rate as that of Earth. The atmosphere around Asthekia is identical to that of Earth's, with oxygen to breathe, and thus water to drink, and animals, grains and fruit to eat. Humans evolved from earlier creatures, except that instead of having five toes on their feet, they have four, with four fingers and a thumb on each hand. Other than that, they are as human as you and I.

Six land masses formed on the planet of Asthekia, which make up Asthekia's six main continents. The largest city and the most populated area on the small planet is Starling City. Five of the continents were named in an age that the Asthekians no longer can remember. The sixth continent, Elder Islands, was named in English when the Asthekians learned that their planet had come from Earth. The five are: Thron Avaykwathorel, Thous Avaykwathorel, Sekamorathai, Kovraantic, and Bancrûptia,

One of the most beautiful places in all of Asthekia is the Mortmier Swamps. However, it could hardly be called a swamp; it is really just a massive lake that is only knee deep all around its edge. The water always shows a placid blue on its crystalline surface. As the lake stretches out from the western shore of Thron Avaykwathorel, it deepens into vast and treacherous oceans. Oceans make up about seventy-five percent of the entire planet. Towering mountain ranges in Asthekia stretch up to the sky, snow capped or bare. Plains of tutfer grass stretch for hundreds of miles in the fields below the mountains. Tutfer grass grows wild on Asthekia and cannot be grown on Earth because of the unique soil conditions that the plant requires to thrive.

Soil on Asthekia has special minerals, such as Aphedine, Torgadal, and Doihum. These minerals make the grass a dark green, and cause it to give off a scent that resembles cinnamon. Before they knew better, Earthlings tried to eat the grass, after which they fell into a deep coma from which they could be revived only by highly experienced Asthekian Medicine People. All attempts to grow specimens of Tutfer grass on Earth have proven futile.

Weather in Asthekia is mild for most of the summer, but harsh and icy in the winter months. Flowers and plants bloom all over the hillsides and on the mountains in the spring time. Small pink flowers cover the green mounds that make up the Asthekian hills. On the sides of roads grow long stalks of purple flowers; in the direct sun and moonlight of Asthekian summers, the flowers appear to be on fire. Hence they have been named Flambourd weeds. The water of the oceans and the lakes is warm in the summertime, and the air is balmy and breezy.

Because Asthekia is farther away from the sun than Earth, it does not get nearly as hot. Highs never exceed seventy five or eighty degrees Fahrenheit. Fall brings a bite to the air and the leaves of the Firlon trees fall in succumberance to the cold. The majority of the planet goes a shade of golden brown. But the extreme northern regions stay their normal snow washed white throughout the entire year. Winter goes from fall's bite to an icy chomp. The air becomes frigid, and snow falls over most of the small planet; while only a few desert regions close to the equator of Asthekia stay warm and uncovered by the blanket of winter.

Surprisingly, Earth and Asthekia have had absolutely no history of war. When Asthekia was discovered, people were astounded. Asthekia had known about Earth much longer before Earth caught on, but Asthekians had made no attempt to contact Earthlings. Earth sent a space expedition to Asthekia; the trip took around three months, and when they finally reached Asthekia, they couldn't figure out where they were going to land. Below them they saw only mountains, forests, and large bodies of water. The crew on the spacecraft scoured the planet for days before finding a desert-like region that they could safely set down in. Upon landing, the crew was terrified, and so were the Asthekians, who had tracked them from the ground but had never encountered living beings from off their planet.

People from all over Asthekia hurried and gathered around the ship. For a full week, the crew did not leave the ship, and finally, on the eighth day of their stay, the Captain mustered enough courage and set foot onto Asthekian soil. When he stepped out, fully clad in his space suit, he saw the Asthekians. They were human just as he was, so he took off the suit. The first breath of Asthekian air was inhaled into the lungs of Captain J.R. Molbern, Captain of the Starstretch 11. The Asthekians watched attentively as the crew stepped forward form the ship. The Earthlings and the Asthekians stood, silent and still for at least five minutes, all of them speechless with surprise.

"Hello," said the Captain, raising his right hand in a gesture of salute. The Asthekians did not speak English, or any Earth language for that matter. At first, the Asthekians nearest the Captain moved back quickly from his gesture. Then, after the Captain had understood the negative result of his gesture, he greeted them again with no hand motions. The Asthekians stood still and listened.

Communication was the first road block. It took much reassurance from the head of the Asthekian council, who was present, for the people to relax in the presence of the Earthlings.

The Asthekians brought the Earth people food, beautiful food. Many things were just like the food on Earth, such as potatoes, meat and vegetables of all sorts. Though no one could actually speak to one another, they could all point and smile. Like the Earthlings, the Asthekians also smiled and frowned. But they did not use the gesture of nodding and shaking their heads, so the Asthekians all broke up in laughter and consternation when one of the crew members nodded in acceptance of a dinner dish. The Earthlings didn't understand the Asthekians reaction, but interpreted it as part of their food sharing customs, and proceeded to laugh with them. Mutual laughter during exchange of gifts, especially food, lasted until certain members of each group began to master each other's languages and understand each other's customs. However, the common people outside the scholarly circles of Earthlings and Asthekians liked the sharing of laughter so much that the new knowledge did not entirely remove the practice. In villages farther from urban centers it is still common practice between Earthlings and Asthekians.

Asthekian people don't dress extravagantly. Most wear a simple shirt and pants or shorts, while some prefer skirts. Asthekians use a range of colorful dyes, and enjoy painting designs on the originally white cloth that is made from native Asthekian cotton. A silvery thread made of refined Aphedine and Torgadal sparkles and shines when sewn into cloth, so most people like to sew it into clothes to make them shimmer in the bright Asthekian sunlight and moonlight.

Their buildings are usually made out of stone, and their language is extremely complicated. Over the next three months, the crew members learned the rudimentary ways of the Asthekians, and were housed with volunteer Asthekian families. Every week, the Captain would send messages back to Earth about the amazing discovery of a new people and the extraordinary events that took place on Asthekia. He also assisted the geologists, biologists, and doctors who had accompanied him in collecting and transmitting a large amount of data back to Earth. Responses from Earth were full of excitement, astonishment, and eagerness for further information. Slowly, the Asthekians also became used to the sophisticated audiovisual recording equipment that was employed by the scientists. Data sent back to Earth soon included interviews with and videos of many aspects of Asthekian life.

The crew members slowly picked up basic words and phrases in the language, mastered everyday customs of interaction, and were widely accepted by everyone in Asthekia. A year after the landing of the Starstrech 11, all the crew members had achieved a basic fluency in Sdrawkcab, the most commonly spoken language in all of Asthekia. Some of the crew members even began to form closer relationships with Asthekian males and females who were willing to introduce the newcomers to possibilities for long term residence on the newly found planet.

After long reflection, during which he considered the possibility of bringing Earthlings to Asthekia to live, or vice versa, the

Captain made a proposal to allow ten ships from Earth to fly one hundred people each to Asthekia to live. One thousand people from Earth would move onto the planet and become residents. At first, the Asthekians were confused and dubious. Cautiously, they found all of the Earthlings and escorted them with the Captain back to their ship, and requested that they stay there for three days while the Asthekian council debated the proposal. Unlike Earthlings, the Asthekians see no need for a centralized, world government per se. Instead, each city, village, and community of Asthekia has an elected leader, and when a global issue arises, all of the leaders meet to discuss it and work to resolve it. Otherwise, each community makes its own rules and keeps its own counsel.

The three days turned into three weeks, and then three months. Anxious and cabin-feverish, the astronauts came out of their spaceship on the third day of the third month of their time in the spaceship. The Asthekians accepted them back into the community, but did not disclose any information about their decision. The weather was fair. On Earth, people would have called it spring, but the Asthekians didn't have names for the different seasons. They found no point in that; they simply dressed warmly in cool weather, and dressed more lightly in warmer weather.

Weeks later, the special Asthekian council called for a meeting with the Earthlings. The council in which the astronauts and the Asthekians gathered was buzzing with excitement and apprehension. Captain Molbern and his crew were anxious about the decision that the Asthekian council would deliver, but excited because they had waited months to hear the final answer. The captain and his crew found themselves in an awesome environment. In the center of Starling city stands a massive circular meeting hall, used for the most important of mass meetings. In a great circle of chairs sat all of the representatives for the Asthekian villages and cities. In the center of the circle stood the leader of the entire group, whose elegant white meeting robes were wrapped immaculately around him. Curly gray hair was tied back into a tight bun, and deep green eyes scanned the audience of the council members and the nervous astronauts. His name was Nayek Elebron. Captain Molbern smiled up at him, impressed by the presence that he carried with him like a neon sign.

Nayek looked positively regal. Respectfully, the group of astronauts greeted him in the most common and simple manner, as their skills in Sdrawkcab weren't quite polished enough for formal salutations.

"Ollehi" they chorused solemnly.

Immediately Nayek broke into a slough of cascading tongues. Never before had the group heard this language, and assumed that it was part of the whole meeting ceremony. What they didn't know was that Nayek did not speak English, nor did he speak Sdrawkcab very fluently. Instead he spoke the older language, Nectliclas, a dialect known by few, and employed by even fewer. It was because he was fluent in this seldom used but highly regarded language that he was elected to be the head of the entire council, for many of the older and more remote villages of the planet still used it, and needed to be communicated with in their own tongue. A female translator quickly translated the flowing speech into Sdrawkcab, and a male translator then repeated it in English for the astronauts. The latter translator was one of those who had taken it upon themselves to become as fluent as possible in English.

"You stand before us today, Earth people, because you wish for a merger. A merging of two similar peoples from across the void. Contemplated have we your plea. Many a time did we nearly bury your request with negative possibilities, but every time it was unearthed by the positives that ring so strongly, like a pealing bell in the hearts and imaginings of our people. For your Earth friends to join the Asthekians would be a great risk. A great unknown, and sure were we not that we would allow for it to actually happen.

But still, the possibilities for peaceful co-existence and the blending of the two human groups would spring forth a myriad of creative and developmental possibilities, as well has helping to ensure the everlasting union between our two planets. So I, Nayek Elebron stand before you on behalf of the council of Asthekia, on behalf of the people of Asthekia, and I tell you that nothing would please us more than for an allotted number of Earthlings to join us on our great planet, and to live and become one with our global community."

The male translator spoke slowly and clearly, and the astronauts beamed wider and wider as they realized the direction that the speech was taking, until finally they burst into joyous cries and embraced one another. The Asthekian council members grinned as they watched the Earthlings rejoice loudly. Finally the Earthlings re-gathered themselves and returned to their group order in front of Nayek, surrounded by a pleased circle of council members. Captain Molbern looked to the translators inquisitively, non-verbal communication taking place all the while. The translators nodded for him to speak, and readied themselves for another flow of words ready to be translated.

"I thank you from the bottom of my heart, council head Nayek, on behalf of my crew and on behalf of our fellow people of Earth who will be ever so lucky to join us on this great planet," his palms sweated and his heart fluttered with relief and a new and fast blooming anticipation. "I will send word immediately to Earth, telling them of your gracious decision, and we will begin the process of setting up the transport of the people and scientists who will come to Asthekia. Truly—truly we cannot thank you enough."

With that, and to further demonstrate their acceptance of the Earthlings and their culture, Nayek and the council members used the new gesture of applause which then spread from the surrounding circle. The council also nodded in the Earthlings' way to show approval of the captain's impromptu speech. And that was it. The Earthlings would come to Asthekia.

Right away the crew sent a message to Earth. The first 1000 people to register would be the ones going, no more, no less. Thus began a long and tedious process of choosing and registering the lucky people and families who would be making the voyage across thousands of miles of empty space to live on an entirely new planet. One hundred spots aboard the ship were already reserved for some of the world's top scientists. Biologists, medical doctors, archeologists, oceanographers, anthropologists, teachers, and certain government diplomats would be occupying one hundred spaces, for their knowledge and data gathering would be much needed to rightfully educate the people back on Earth about the new sister planet whose inhabitants were so similar to them. Aside from those one hundred specialists, the other nine hundred people going would be determined by a lottery system, to make sure that the process was as random and unbiased as possible. Surprisingly enough, there were not a great number of people who actually wished to leave Earth. Only about three million people in the world's entire population actually signed themselves up for the great lottery draw. Families that wanted to stick together would obviously register under one family name, and if one of the family members was chosen, then they would all go. The process took about three months, including the entire health examination process. Asthekian health officials had insisted politely but definitely that no one be allowed to come to their planet carrying any kind of disease.

Eventually, the ten ships were stocked with ice blocks to supply water, and special bacteria to eat (one bacterium is the protein equivalent of a rack of ribs). The ship also contained filtration systems that continuously cleaned and recycled air and gathered and purified urine to recover usable water. The trip took a long three months. Out of 1000 people, 54 passengers died. Some deaths were caused by extreme disorientation and confusion that led to refusal to eat or drink; others succumbed to a bout of meningococcal meningitis that spread among the passengers. One man also went so crazy that he killed three other innocent passengers and then himself. After the latter incident, the passengers and the crew were given daily doses of the tranquilizer Hemitone to calm their nerves and worries.

When the ship reached Asthekia, the same captain of the first voyage found the large desert in which they had landed the first expedition. When the people landed, the Asthekian health regulators insisted upon a six week quarantine for all passengers who were on the ship affected by the meningococcal meningitis. Asthekian planners had worked out a system in which they would dole out the new comers to all the different continents, cities, and villages. The Earth people had been given many lessons and information on the Asthekians so they would know what to expect, and have a basic mastery of the every day language. The

Asthekians had also taken the time to learn about the new arrivals and their cultures, and more Asthekians had taken it upon themselves to learn English, which was the common tongue of the new arrivals, even though they had come from many different Earth cultures.

Over the next year, the Asthekians lived in close harmony with the Earth people. Both groups forgot their differences, and English and Sdrawkcab became the two main languages of communication. As the Earth people learned Sdrawkcab more fluently, the children all went to the same schools and the adults all worked together. Asthekians and Earthlings had children together. At first the people were tentative about this crossing of the two human kinds, but when a healthy baby girl was born to a mixed couple, the initial worries abated.

When Earthlings moved onto Asthekia, Asthekians adopted calendars and dates because it made a positive addition to their society. Clothing from Earth was also introduced when the Earth people came, as well as building designs and ideas for government (though all suggestions for a change in government were completely vetoed). The Earth people and the Asthekian people blended easily, and to this day, no wars have ever broken out; certainly there have been conflicts, but they have not divided people of Earth and the Asthekians. Peace is a focus of Asthekia, and people have always been capable of coexisting harmoniously with neighboring communities; large or small.

After the 1000 Earthlings came, the Asthekian council drew the line and banned any more Earth people from coming to Asthekia. But that did not mean that contact was eradicated. Earth and Asthekia decided to establish regular satellite communication: if ever either planet had a problem, the other one would give it advice via a communication satellite that NASA sent out from the space center in Florida. This satellite also picks up Earth TV channels that are transmitted to Asthekian viewing devices. They are not called televisions, and are only used to transmit a few select programs from Earth. Certain channels are used solely for scholarly and scientific exchanges. Entertainment on Asthekia is similar to Earth's. They read books and music is an important part of the culture. Though people in Asthekia do not listen to much Earth music, they make their own beautiful melodies with native instruments and their own voices.

Money is not of great importance on Asthekia, but in order to buy something, one must pay the required sum of small white rocks. These particular rocks are exclusive to the exchange system, and are mined from an undersea quarry that was formed during the period when the sea bottom was an active volcanic area.

Chapter 1

Daniel's Invitation

Sagel walked out of the cottage in the early hours of the morning. The weather had turned colder since she last went down to the creek, so she bundled up in her coat and her warm hat. The winter winds had picked up a great deal in the past week or so. Great drafts of cold air blew from mountain to mountain, carrying everything that was caught in the wind onto the neighboring peaks. Snow hadn't laid its blanket on the mountain yet. But Sagel knew it was on its way.

The town of Shinken was situated on the lush side of Mt. Aarotte. The other side of the mountain was barren, rocky, and unpopulated; Mt. Aarotte was the largest mountain in the Seuthsai mountain range. A winding creek snaked down the slope of the terrain about three miles away from Sagel's family house. She enjoyed walking down to the creek on her days off from school to play on the rocks, watch and listen to the water and occasionally read a book.

Sagel had always lived on Mt. Aarotte with her mother and father and her brother and sister. Her father owned a flourishing pottery business in the town of Shinken and buyers from all over the planet of Asthekia ordered his beautiful work which he usually shipped to Starling City for distribution. Her mother stayed at home; gardening in the warmer months and selling the fruits of her labor at the market.

Sagel and her brother and sister attended the school on the far side of town. Sagel's brother Nigel could be extremely inquisitive at some times, and utterly excitable at others. He had a very small build, but was the fastest kid in the village. Sagel's smallest sibling was Nova. She had dark brown hair that fell straight down on her shoulders, her blue eyes shining like a baby blue sky above. Sagel looked just like her younger siblings, with straight brown hair that fell like a waterfall and was unruly when she wanted to tie it up. Her eyes were a cool shade of gray, but her emotions pulsed through them like a ringing wind. As Sagel walked down the path to her favorite little river, she hummed to herself.

"Sagel! Hey Sage!" called a voice from the path behind her. Sagel spun around, almost tripping over her own skirt.

"Don't do that, Dan!" Sagel cried, clutching her chest and sighing theatrically. Dan was "Sagel's Shadow", as Nigel had put it one day. Daniel was a sweet boy who was the same age as Sagel, and in her class at school. Dan had dishwater blonde hair, fair skin, and high cheek bones. His hair was cut to the middle of his neck, and he had short even bangs. Hazel eyes shone form behind thin eyelashes, thin, but long. Despite the fact that Sagel bristled any time a girl from school called him good looking, she would never admit her special affection for him. Sagel and Daniel had been friends since they could recognize faces, and intended to keep it that way.

"Sorry, Sage, just wanted to tell you the good news!" said

Dan, his eyes bright.

"You're moving to the other side of the mountain?" Sagel asked sarcastically.

"Very funny! Actually, my family and I get to go on vacation to Starling City!" Dan exclaimed, pretending to clap for himself.

"Even better!" Sagel laughed, giving him a playful shove. "Just joking, maybe...," Sagel said, continuing down the path.

"Oh, hahaha...," Dan said, putting his hands in his pockets sheepishly. Sagel turned back to him and smiled to let him know she wasn't serious. Daniel was a tender soul, and often took things literally. Dan had an Earth name, and this was simply because both of his parents were from Earth. When they found out that Louise, Dan's mother, was pregnant with a boy, Daniel seemed like a nice name for him while reminding him of his origin planet. If it had been up to Daniel, he would be named something purely Asthekian. Even though his parents told him that being from Earth wasn't a bad thing in the slightest, Daniel still pined to be like every other child in the village.

"So, my family was wondering if your family wanted to come on a little road trip. You could pack up your station wagon, and we could all drive to Starling City," Dan said, a little less enthusiastically.

"Dan, you can't expect me to answer that—I'm not my parents!" Sagel said. Sometimes, Dan could be so silly about these things, as if his excitement got in the way of his logic.

"Then you can ask your parents about it," Dan said simply.

"If I remember," Sagel said irritably.

"Very good," Daniel said, pretending not to notice Sagel's mood.

"Oh yeah, how's Gordon?" Sagel queried.

Gordon was Daniel's family's horse. Though Shinken was on a mountain, and the terrain did not exactly suit horses, a few people in town owned them. Several weeks before, Daniel's father, Michael, had been riding Gordon on the mountain road when the horse stumbled and cut his leg open on a fallen branch. He had not been able to walk on it, and Daniel had been in a state, scared that he would never be ridden again. Fortunately, Michael had a real way with horses, and was able to fix him up with bandages and poultices.

"Yeah, he is. We were lucky he survived an infection. I have to go—my mom wants me to help her around the house today, but maybe we can hang out tomorrow!" Dan said, as he turned and ran back up the dirt path.

The path was packed dirt with rounded rocks sticking out. The landscape surrounding it was rocky and grassy, and very, very steep. The path was so steep that if Sagel had lain down, she would almost be looking straight out at the peaks of the smaller mountains below. The road up to Shinken was just as steep and rough as the mountain path. That is why it was so rare for anyone to come and go on a regular basis. Trucks of imported goods, including food from Starling City, made the perilous journey every month. Because Shinken had a grocery store, Starling City distributors would drive in trucks of food, wait until the store was completely sold out, and then bring more. When the grocery store ran out of food, Shinken residents would have to wait a few days before more food arrived. Families usually just ate what they had in their freezing units in the meantime. Asthekia has refrigerators and freezers that operate on solar and wind generators. Villagers would occasionally have to hunt or kill some of their own animals. Shinken families especially liked making meals out of Churkeys, a large bird that is native to Asthekian mountains. In Earth terms, it is a cross among a grouse, a turkey, and a chicken.

Sagel was about five minutes away from the creek when she saw it coursing down the hill. This was a dangerous part of her little hike. The path came to an abrupt cliff, and she had to climb down on jagged rocks, slippery and prickly with violet and chartreuse lichen, to where the land flattened out. Thankfully, if she did fall, an old shepherd woman would be walking this path at about ten in the morning with her flock of Churkeys. But Sagel didn't fall; she made it safely to the creek, climbed up on her favorite boulder, and hunkered down in a small rock crevice to relax.

Chapter 2

The Medicine Woman

"Nova, get outta my room!" fumed Nigel, rushing up from his bed and grabbing his little sister by the arm and pulling her to the door.

"Let go of me, Nigel. MMMMMAAAAAA!" hollered Nova from the hallway outside of Nigel's room. No answer. Displeased with the lack of immediate penalization of her brother, she stormed through the house and outside into the chilly, fall air.

Nigel breathed a sigh of relief when he heard the front door slam. He had been drawing his dreams of the previous night, and didn't like his little sister seeing them. Dreams in Asthekia, and especially in Shinken, are vitally important. The Asthekian culture in general values dreams as messages from the psyche and sub-conscious; to ignore a dream would be a ridiculous thing to do. It would be like declining assistance from someone who is trying to teach you to pluck a Churkey for the first time.

This dream of Nigel's was particularly strange; he was bargaining at a night market in Starling city, when people started dying around him. Nigel had sobbed for the people in the dream, and then, in desperation, threw himself from the top of a building.

He had awakened with a headache from crying. Never before had Nigel experienced a dream with that magnitude of death. On occasion there would be a dead relative or friend haunting his nighttime world, and sometimes the friend or relative that was dreamt of would be faced with a crisis in the real world. Any time this happened Nigel went to his parents, usually frightened and excited at the same time.

Nigel's mother, Lorel, was out in the garden at the edge of their property, toward the cliff that defined the west edge of the town. Their house was far away from the center of Shinken, which was quite spread out. If all the buildings were combined in closer proximity, the town would actually be quite small.

Nova would probably be going down to the bending rock face behind the school to play and pretend with her other friends. Nigel's father, Torren, was in the shed behind the house, working on his latest pottery project.

Every time he let his mind replay the previous night's dream, an icy flutter wisped through his stomach. He decided not to tell anyone, because no one he knew perished in the dream. No one but himself. Something else kept him from disclosing the dream; he could feel it, but he could not put it into words.

Finished with his drawing, Nigel abandoned his sketchpad and walked out into the living room to ponder his plans for the day. He could go to the stream like Sagel had, but she would be irritated to have him show up there and bother her. All of his friends were free that day, but Nigel didn't really feel like putting energy into a visit. He decided to stroll down the village path to the center of town and get lunch at the only restaurant on the mountain. Interestingly enough, that was the name of the restaurant; "The only Restaurant on the Mountain". Nigel got cold easily, so he put on his jacket, buttoned it up, put on his shoes, and set out.

"Nigel, where are you going?" Lorel called from the garden, where she was trying to coax up a particularly stubborn plant from its grip in the soil. It was a Bulbousdock with a large, edible, fuchsia tuber just beneath the surface. The tuber keeps well when attached to its stalk, but rots quickly if the stalk is broken off. She hadn't much time to collect the last crops of the year until winter set in. Like on Earth, most Asthekian flora flourishes until the first frost of winter.

"I'm heading down to the restaurant—I'm starving," Nigel called.

"Why can't you just eat something from the refrigerator?" Lorel said, adjusting her scarf. "We have plenty of good food, you know."

"Please, Ma? I really want to get one of their sandwiches—please?" Nigel begged.

Lorel looked at her son with raised eyebrows, and then smiled.

"Go on."

Nigel smiled at his mom, blew her a kiss, and then set off down the road, feeling in his pocket the pebbles to pay for his food. There was a particular stretch on the road to town that was surrounded with thick trees; to Nigel, the dark evergreen trees looked menacing. The air was always still in this stretch; as though not even the wind would dare to blow through it. Nigel tried as usual to talk pleasantly to himself through the Stretch, but again managed to scare himself. Sometimes he imagined Shadow Shades, fabled creatures that are believed to live in the mountains of Asthekia, coming out from the woods to spirit him away. This time through the Stretch, however, Nigel was particularly edgy. He didn't know why, but for some reason, the hairs on the back of his neck prickled and his palms grew clammy and white.

Only half way through the Stretch, he attempted to draw attention away from his fear. Nigel tried to name everyone in Shinken by first and last name. That worked pretty well, but soon he ran out of people to name. He could see the end of the Stretch, where the trees receded and the ground became smooth and open. He was so close, and wanted to run, but he knew that that would frighten him even more. Suddenly, he heard someone not far behind him. No one usually walked this road other than their neighbors. But Nigel had seen them all go to town earlier that morning. He had no idea who it could be.

Nigel had had enough; he was shaking, not daring to look behind him. His foot hit a rock and made a small noise. That was enough for him. He sprinted as fast as he could all the way out of the Stretch to the hill above town. Finally, he mustered enough courage to look behind him. There was nothing, but strangely, he could still hear far away footsteps that were gaining on him. Nigel ran down the hill and onto the town's main road that led to the restaurant.

As he walked briskly up the street towards the restaurant, he realized that he had been throwing rapid glances back over his shoulder and up toward the Stretch, even though the trees were not visible from where he was. Not being able to remember having been so frightened by a walk to town before, he stopped and made an effort to slow down his breathing and calm his heart. It made it easier that a few people he knew greeted him as they passed. Finally he was able to keep a reasonable pace both in his steps and his breaths as he neared the restaurant.

Nigel was relieved that he was safe in the restaurant with other people, but he was still jumpy as he settled himself in a booth by the window. It wasn't an extravagant restaurant; it was more of a cozy diner where you could order serving after serving of mashed potatoes without the serving people becoming irritated.

"Hello, Nigel. What are you having today?" said Marillay, a very pleasant waitress who had worked there since the restaurant had been established.

"Um...I'll have a cheese and bitter sap sandwich, and some creamy mashed potatoes, and I'll have some apple cider—please."

"All right, coming up," Marillay responded with a smile.

The restaurant was well lit and heated. The seats were cushioned in dark red. The walls were painted a creamy, warm beige; there were humorous and cute pictures of Asthekian animals on the walls, and an occasional vase hanging from the ceiling by silvery wires. Small white flower bloomed from vines that grew out of the vases. Soft music played continuously in the background; it seemed tuneless, but beautiful all the same.

Nigel gazed out the window and replayed the Stretch experience in his mind until his mashed potatoes and cider came. He sipped his apple cider, and took a bite of mashed potatoes. Then someone else came into the restaurant. It was a cloaked figure; when the person took down the hood of the black and shimmering cloak, Nigel saw a woman with high cheekbones, full lips and skin that could have been ageless.

"Oh! Elenry! Oh, sit, sit down, I'll get you something hot to drink," said the male waiter whom Nigel knew to be Arin. Then Nigel remembered who the strange woman was. Nigel's father had told Nigel that a girl from next door named Gwenoth Jones had come down with a very serious illness a week before, and that her parents had decided to call a Medicine Woman. Nigel had no idea what Gwenoth's symptoms were, but the presence of a Medicine Woman had brought him a sense of severity.

Elenry was a healer who traveled the northern regions of Thron Avawkwathorel, riding on her horse, and delivering specialized medical treatment to those who could not or chose not to use a hospital. Nigel had never seen her before, but had always wondered about her mysterious work. The elders of the village spoke with great reverence about Medicine People, though Nigel had not been alive when the last healer graced their village.

The Medicine Woman was tall and muscular. Her dark brown hair shimmered and shined all the way down to her lower back. She flashed him a serene smile and sat down a couple of booths in front of him, with her back to him. Her eyes had had a strange glint to them, and Nigel could not really tell what color they were. They could have been green, they could have been blue, or they could have been gray. Even pure Asthekians do not have eyes that change color; the only unique feature relative to Earthlings is the four toes on their feet.

The waiter brought her a steaming mug of what smelled to Nigel like coffee bean, a rarity on the mountain. She thanked Arin and then he sat down in front of her. They were talking in hushed voices, ensuring that no one, not even a curious boy like Nigel, could hear their dialogue. Nigel wasn't the type to snoop, but he also wasn't the type who was satisfied to just sit around not knowing what was going on. The bathroom was at the back of the restaurant, and if he walked slowly enough, he would be able to catch a few words on the way there, and on the way back. He took a bite from his plate of mashed potatoes, and walked toward the bathroom.

"Very strange, very strange. But they don't…" said Elenry. But that was all that Nigel caught as he walked by. Once in the confines of the bathroom walls, he pondered the meaning of that. What was very strange? But they don't—what? They could be talking about anything! He would have to try to hear more. On his way back, he walked more slowly.

"Three days was all it took, then she was pretty much gone…" he heard the Medicine Woman mutter. Nigel sat back down, still trying to encode what had been said: "Very strange, very strange. But they don't…three days was all it took, then she was pretty much gone…"

None of it made any sense. But then again, maybe it was nothing important, and furthermore, it was probably none of his business. So, Nigel returned to his sandwich and mashed potatoes, and took some more sips of his cooling apple cider. Once again he let his mind drift and daydream as the village day unfolded outside the window before him. He was so immersed in his own thoughts that he did not notice a figure approach him, and started when it tapped him lightly on the shoulder.

"Oh, sorry," said a sweet and flowing voice from his left. Nigel regained his composure and looked up into the face of the Medicine Woman.

"Oh, hey-hu-hello!" Nigel said, looking up at her curiously.

"What's your name, child?" she asked. Her breath smelled sweet, like the scent of mountain flowers that bloomed in the warm months.

"Nigel Bleudry," he answered.

"Nigel, I was wondering, where does Gwenoth Jisna live?" she asked quietly.

"Oh! Yeah, she's my neighbor, she's been sick for a while,

though," Nigel said, and suddenly, his insides tightened, as though a ball of acid was building in the recesses of his stomach. "Three days was all it took, then she was pretty much gone…" What if Gwenoth was sick with whatever that person had? But he was getting ahead of himself. Maybe the person that the Medicine Woman had been talking about wasn't even sick; all the same, Nigel was good at jumping to conclusions.

"Yes, she's quite ill, so, I was wondering if, after you finish your meal, you could take me to her house," she finished.

"Sure, she lives really close to me," Nigel said.

"I'll wait for you outside."

Over his forkfuls he watched her tall frame stride towards the door. Her head was always upright, and her steps sure. Once she was outside, he could see her standing with something, though the window frame blocked from his view whatever it was she was stroking.

A few minutes later, Nigel took the final bite of his sandwich, and finished the remains of the cider.

He stood up, pulled four white rocks out of his jacket pocket and left them just above his empty plate. Once out of doors, Nigel could see what Elenry had been petting. An enormous black horse stood stoically beside her. He figured it was Elenry's, for he had never seen another horse like it in Shinken. When Nigel looked carefully, the horse appeared almost brown in the overcast light but its true color was not distinguishable. Of course the Medicine Woman owned a horse—how else could she get around? He suddenly remembered hearing from his father that her horse had been bred in Asthekia, was a full Asthekian breed, and was able to keep a fast gait for long periods of time. Nigel could hear the horse's steady breathing, and see the white steam puffing from its wide, warm nostrils into the cold fall air.

"This is Arros, my horse, my baby, and my companion," said Elenry, smiling up at Arros and stroking his nose lovingly. Arros snorted softly and looked inquisitively at Nigel.

"He wants to know your name," Elenry explained to Nigel.

"You-what-you can understand him?" Nigel starred at Elenry, astonished.

"Well, I've been with him for so long, I have learned his language, and how he communicates," Elenry added. "Go on, tell him your name."

"Nigel, my name is Nigel," Nigel said, staring into the horses full black eyes. He could see the same sort of glint in Arros's eyes as he had seen in Elenry's. It was as though the horse could see deeply into the crevices of his soul, soaking in everything, and every secret that Nigel had ever possessed in his short life. He felt very awkward talking to this animal.

"Good, now, up you go!" exclaimed Elenry, picking Nigel up by his shoulders, and throwing him up onto the massive horse.

"Wha-woah!" Nigel landed up on the horse's rump, but the force of Elenry's throw sent him over the other side. Nigel hit the icy ground with a harsh thud. A searing pain in his head made him nauseous. He put his hand to his pounding head, and felt liquid. Red blood was dripping from his forehead onto his hand.

"Oh, oh Nigel! I'm so sorry!" Elenry knelt down next to him, examining his wound. When he had fallen, he had hit the frozen, hard-packed road and knocked his head on a rock in the ground. There was a gash at his hairline that was streaming blood down his face. Elenry immediately went to work, but Nigel felt like throwing up, and while Elenry was rummaging around in her rucksack, Nigel rolled over on his side and vomited onto the road. Elenry knelt by his side and put her hands on his shoulders, holding him while he finished retching. She drew a rough blue cloth from her bag, wiped his mouth and chin, and then folded it to press the clean side against the wound.

"Nigel, you need to lie still."

But Nigel could hardly hear her, and then everything went black.

When Nigel woke up, he was staring up into the face of Elenry. Without thinking, he put his hand to his forehead, except this time he felt a white bandage and ointment spread around his forehead and not a slough of blood.

"How are you feeling?" Elenry asked, helping Nigel to his feet.

"Alright I guess. How long was I out?" Nigel asked in a trembling voice.

"About three minutes at most. Come on, let's try this again," Elenry picked Nigel up by the shoulders, and gently pushed him up onto the horse's back. Arros's back was warm and broad. Nigel patted the horse timidly on his withers, feeling the soft, fine hair of his mane. Elenry pulled herself up next, behind Nigel, reached around him to take the reins. She turned Arros away from the restaurant and towards Nigel's side of town, then clicked gently.

"You're going to have to give me directions. Just tell me which road to follow," Elenry said.

"Alright, just go down the main street, and turn when I tell you," Nigel said.

"Alright, hold onto his mane. We really need to move," Elenry said, and Arros stepped up into a fast trot.

As they traveled down the center street of Shinken, people on both sides stared, whispering in rapid Sdrawkcab and waving at Elenry. She was truly a living legend.

After they had cleared the last of the buildings in the center of the town, Nigel said, "Turn down that road on the left and then take the road up the hill," thrilled that he was actually telling a famous person what to do, and she was listening to him. Nigel had forgotten all about his fall and wound. All they had to sit on was a saddle blanket; it was soft, warm, and woven of a fine, black thread that he did not recognize. Arros started cantering, and Nigel held on tighter. Nigel was a little frightened when they rounded a tight corner, so intent on holding on, that he hardly noticed that they were now galloping through the Stretch. As the once foreboding trees blurred by, he felt secure and strangely powerful up on the great steed behind the mysterious Medicine Woman.

"Elenry, we need to turn up ahead, on that next road to the right," Nigel spoke over the clatter of hooves.

"Okay," Elenry said, and after a few strides, Arros turned down their road and slowed to a trot.

"That house up there, at the very end of the road, that's my house," Nigel pointed, "And that's Gwenoth's house, that one there," Nigel said, as Arros slowed to a stop outside his house.

"I think I should come in and explain the state of your forehead," Elenry said, checking her timekeeper. Asthekians do not use watches. But they do use devices like watches that display the movement of the sun and the moon. When the sun and the moon are aligned on the dial of the device during the day, it is noon, and when they are aligned in the dark, it is midnight.

"I thought you needed to get to Gwenoth's house," Nigel

said, worried that he was keeping her from something far more important than a little cut on his head.

"I was told that her condition was stable, so I have time enough to explain to your parents what happened," Elenry said, dismounting from Arros, helping Nigel off, and walking with the boy up the path to his front door.

"Ma! I'm home!" Nigel called as he opened the door. He could smell the familiar scents of his favorite dinner. It smelled like Churkey meat with onions and potatoes. Nigel loved his mother's cooking; every meal seemed to taste better than the last.

"Oh, Nigel! What happened?" making a bee line to her son and taking his gently face in her hands. After a moment of maternal examination, her gaze flickered up to Elenry.

"Hello, I'm Elenry. You probably know about me," Elenry said smoothly, smiling at Nigel's mother.

"It's a pleasure to meet you," Lorel replied, standing up. "What happened?"

Elenry explained everything that had happened. Lorel turned a shade whiter when Elenry got to the part where she threw Nigel over her horse, cracking his head open. Elenry apologized profusely, and offered to change the dressings on his forehead.

"Elenry, why don't you stay and have dinner? My husband is just painting some pottery, but he'll be in soon, and we can all eat together," Lorel offered.

"I'm so sorry, but I really must be getting to an appointment— it's urgent. Another time, perhaps?" Elenry replied.

"Oh, of course, silly me, I'm not surprised that you have something to do," Lorel said, opening the door for her. "You come by whenever you need anything!"

"Thank you, and sorry about injuring your son," Elenry said, smiling. "Goodbye, Nigel."

Elenry walked down to Arros, and together they made their way to Gwenoth's house. Elenry couldn't imagine how she was going to save a girl from a disease that she had never encountered before.

Chapter 3

Dinner

Sagel walked into the kitchen, where her mother was asking Nigel to repeat the details of his accident while taking the Churkey meat out of the oven. Lorel was a master preparer of Churkey. Her favorite and most frequent recipe was sap-sprinkled Churkey meat. She would bake the Churkey meat in the oven while freezing the sap she bled from trees. Then she would crush up the sap and sprinkle it over the hot Churkey. The melted amber sap added a much needed flavor to the rather bland Churkey meat.

The kitchen was large and bright, with its walls covered by white tiles with small blue flowers painted by her father many years before Sagel was born. The stove was old, but easily used. A circular wooden table was the centerpiece of their kitchen, with five differently colored chairs pushed under it. Sagel's favorite chair was the blue one with three old legs and one new one. She had sat in this chair since she was coordinated enough to sit up on her own. She still remembered the day when she had been standing on the chair reaching for a cup for water, and the leg had just snapped. Her father had fixed it but the new paint continued to look fresher and brighter than the paint on the old legs.

"What happened to you?" Sagel asked.

"The Medicine Woman threw me over her horse, and I hit a rock," Nigel replied, a certain pride in his voice.

"Oh sure she did. Are you sure you didn't fly off the mountain into a large willow tree and then were abducted by fairies?" Sagel prodded.

"I'm serious! Ma, tell her!" Nigel said angrily, stabbing a piece of raw vegetable aggressively.

"It's true, unfortunately," said Lorel, dishing potatoes and onions around the Churkey and then moving the platter to the table.

"Wait, so you are telling me that the Medicine Woman is actually here? In Shinken?" Sagel asked, her eyes growing wide.

"Yes, she came to the village to treat Gwenoth. Apparently she is really sick," Nigel affirmed, pleased with the extent of his knowledge.

"Wow, so…where's the part when she threw you over the horse?" Sagel teased, her eyebrows raised.

Nigel took a deep breath and told her everything about the day, right up until his sitting down for dinner.

"Oh, Sagel, guess what happened in the Stretch?" Nigel asked.

"What, a ghost popped out and said 'Boo'?" she threw out sarcastically. She had always pretended not to believe in the paranormal scariness of the Stretch, but Nigel knew that she was a little spooked.

"I heard these creepy footsteps, almost like…wait a minute!" Nigel broke into a smile. "Those must have been the Medicine Woman's horse's footsteps!"

"See, I tell you children that there is absolutely nothing in that stretch or whatever you call it!" Lorel said, pouring water into drinking glasses. Their mother had never believed in anything out of the ordinary, but when she wasn't around, they would ask their dad to tell them ghost stories that would come back to haunt them every time they walked through the Stretch.

"Sagel, go out to the workshop and tell your dad to get in here for dinner," Lorel said. "And where in the world is Nova?"

"I saw her in her room about an hour ago," Sagel said, "Nigel, go get her."

"Why me?" he groaned.

"Because Ma cooked dinner, and I'm getting Dad, now do it," Sagel said calmly.

"Fine…" he grumbled, walking out of the kitchen to retrieve his youngest sister.

Sagel walked to the back door and pushed it open. A wave of chilly air washed over her prickling face. Tomorrow she was sure there would be a thin coat of frost on the grass, and on her bedroom window.

"Where is Sagel?" Lorel asked, after ten minutes.

"Didn't you send her out to get dad?" Nigel said, a worried look settling in his eyes.

"I'll go out and check. He's probably just having her help paint," Lorel sighed irritably. She walked to the back door and pushed open the screen, letting it slam behind her.

Nova walked into the kitchen, wearing a long white dress with silvery sparkles embedded into the fine fabric.

"You're going to mess up your dress—drop food all over it," Nigel said.

"No I won't! Where's Ma? And Sagel and Dad?" Nova demanded, climbing into her chair and smoothing her dress.

"She went out to get Sage—" Nigel stopped abruptly when Lorel, Sagel, and Torren walked through the door. Sagel looked rather surly, the kind of look certain kids acquire after a parent has told them off. Lorel walked over to the stove where the Churkey meat and potatoes were cooling. Torren kissed each of his children on the forehead, ruffling Nigel's hair, his hand brushing the bandage. Nigel winced.

"Whoa, what is that, Nigel?" Torren's eyes flooded with concern.

Nigel happily recounted everything that had happened that afternoon. By the end of Nigel's tale, Sagel, Lorel, and Nova were all dished up, and Torren was already chewing a piece of Churkey.

"Well, that was quite an experience..." Torren smiled. "You said that Gwenoth is sick? Yes, I did hear that the other day from her father. He was over to visit and he said that she had come down with something...." Torren thought a moment.

"I don't want you children going in or even too close to their house until she's one hundred percent better. It's getting into the season of illness, and I don't want us to start off the winter with runny noses," Lorel explained. Torren nodded his head in agreement, sputtering as a bit of potato went down the wrong pipe.

"So, Dan was wondering if our family wanted to go with his family down to Starling City," Sagel said.

"When were they thinking of going? It's the main pottery season again. I don't know if we're going to have enough time for a trip."

"But it's not like you're working all the time. You said just last week we had loads of time on our hands," Sagel pressed.

"I know, but in the last couple of days I have gotten three orders for very complicated designs. I'm sorry, Sage, but I'll finish them off as soon as possible," Torren said.

Sagel sighed and returned to looking surly again.

"I wanna go to Starling City!" Nova cried, almost spilling her water on herself.

"Yeah, I remember the last time we went, the time where we got to go to that big restaurant and pool thingy," Nigel recalled.

"That was a good trip, wasn't it?" Lorel asked, more to herself than her family.

Torren smiled, "You know, I was thinking, after this schooling season ends for the year, we should go on a little trip."

"I thought you just said that we hadn't the time!" Sagel cried, not knowing whether to smile or scowl.

"I meant that we don't have time this schooling season, I didn't say that after the season we wouldn't do something fun."

There are five schooling seasons in the Asthekian school systems. Each of them lasts for thirty days. On Earth, they would be considered a month: the Asthekian months for school are February, March, May, August, and November. The other seven months are vacations. School had been out for almost a month, and the Bleudry children were looking forward to school starting again in a few days.

Schooling in Asthekia differs greatly from that on Earth. In Asthekia, there are five main studies: reading and writing, a question and answer class, where all students do is ask teachers questions and discuss their answers, a survival and wilderness information class, a studies of Earth class, and a fitness class. Classes always start in the morning as the sun is rising, and stop at noon. No homework is given. The main purpose of schools in Asthekia is to teach young people how to live in the world, to answer their questions on life, and to help them learn what they want to learn.

"So, are you kids excited for school?" Torren asked, breaking into the sounds of chewing and swallowing.

"Yes!" Nova piped, before anyone else could say anything. "In Earth studies, we're going to learn about children like us. They have dolls and play games like we do!" Nova's eyes grew wide and excited. "They even look like us! They showed us pictures last school season."

"You didn't think they looked like us? We're all human!" Nigel scoffed, surprised at his little sister's ignorance.

"Well, I didn't know!" Nova said, pushing her empty plate away.

They all sat back in their chairs, and Nigel burped, sending Nova into a bout of hysterics.

"Sagel, Nigel, Nova, please help me with the dishes so we can relax for the night," Lorel said, and the clearing and washing began.

When the dishes were done, dried, and put away, Sagel went alone to the backyard of the house, where she lay down on the grass that was drying and turning brown. Her dark hair sprawled against the prickly spears. Sagel soaked in the sweet smell of mountain mist, a shiver went down her spine, and a small smile peeled across her face. Sometime later, when Sagel sat up, the sun and the moon were resting on the far horizon. Because of Asthekia's position behind the Earth's moon, both the sun and the moon can be seen next to each other at certain times in the year. The air was crisper than before, and Sagel's skin raised to the chill.

"Sagel, you need this," Lorel walked across the grass, holding a silvery robe for her daughter.

"It wasn't this cold when I first came out," Sagel replied, letting her mother wrap the robe around her shoulders and sit next to her.

"You know, you really look much older these days," Lorel said, slipping her arm around Sagel's broad shoulders.

Sagel blushed. She had noticed that she had grown in height in the last month or so. Her thin, childhood frame had filled out a bit, making her curvier and sturdier. She liked her body. She looked like a young woman, strong, healthy, and lean.

"What do you think I'll be like when I become an adult?" Sagel asked her mother.

"There is no telling, dear," Lorel smiled and shook her head. "But you will certainly be an amazing person. I can tell that already."

"Thanks," Sagel beamed, resting her head on her mother's shoulder.

Lorel and Sagel sat side by side for the next ten minutes or so, both basking in the silence that enveloped the yard. Words seemed unwarranted.

"We should get inside…it's getting late," Lorel said, climbing to her feet.

After helping her daughter up, the two made their way back into the house where their warm beds awaited them.

Chapter 4

Winter's Scream

A scream filled the mountain. It battered the leaves and buffeted them from their trees. Shouts of cold rang through awakening rocks, lashing them with icy breath. A cry churned the river, shivering the water with cold. The voice of winter clambered over Mt. Aarotte.

Then, another voice rang through the streets of Shinken, not as strong as the winters, but just as shocking. Strangled cries pierced the village peace. Sagel sat bolt upright in her nest of warm blankets. She scrambled out of bed and ran out into the house's sitting room where her parents were already donning their coats. Nigel and Nova ran out after Sagel. Nova whimpered and groped for Sagel's hand.

It was colder outside than before, and Nigel shivered and took Sagel's other hand, something he rarely did.

Out in the middle of the dirt road lay Gwenoth Jisna, writhing and shrieking. Her parents were trembling, her mother bawling to the point of choking.

"HEEEEEELLPPPPPPP!!! Elenry, help!" cried Gwen's father, searching the growing crowd of townspeople for the Medicine Woman.

Nigel heard the familiar hoof beats of the horse, Arros, carrying the Medicine Woman at frantic speed up the road. The Bleudrys stood on their doorstep, watching helplessly. A crowd of cloaked villagers huddled together holding lanterns and some even weapons in case the screaming had been some sort of mountain beast. Those who had brought their knives and stone mallets lowered them. A few braver souls broke away from the group and started to walk towards the distressed family on the road.

"Stay back! She's very sick, stay back," Elenry shouted, hoisting her bag over her shoulder and trotting over to where Gwenoth lay, quieter now.

Hushed whispers ran through the crowd as everyone obeyed Elenry and drew back. Keeping a tight hold on her siblings' hands, Sagel was suddenly aware of how the sound of Elenry's command echoed through the night. Nigel counted, or at least tried to; it looked as though the entire town had showed up. Nova gripped Sagel's hand with both of hers as tears filled Nova's eyes. The entire family moved closer together.

Elenry pulled flask after flask out of her bag, chanting in a language Sagel had never heard as she searched for the right one. Finally, she uncorked a brownish mixture, performed a complex gesture with the bottle around Gwen's entire body and then poured what she could down Gwen's throat.

"How did she get out here? I told you to keep her inside. Now the whole town could be infected!" Elenry raised her voice at Gwenoth's parents. They were stepping timidly up to their shuddering daughter.

"We were bringing her to you. She suddenly got worse," responded Gwen's father.

Elenry snapped back, "You should have sent for me."

Her mother cried, "She looked like she was dying!"

"Well, she's not, not yet," Elenry replied, more quietly, and then added, "She's calmed down and she's stable. She needs to be inside your house and away from everyone else."

Gwen's father scooped his daughter up without hesitation and began to run her back towards the house, his wife on his heels. Gwen's head lolled from side to side and then slumped back as her father jogged inside.

"Everyone please go home and go to sleep," Elenry called over her shoulder, "You cannot do anything for her."

Lorel and Torren led their children into their house and shut the door quickly.

"Alright, let us all go back to bed and try not to worry," Torren soothed, his children gazing up at him, their faces wrought with shock.

"Will she be okay?" Nigel asked, voice trembling.

"I don't know, but we cannot do anything for her," Torren answered. "Go on, children. Go to bed and try to sleep."

Sagel and Nigel obeyed and walked to their rooms, but Nova ended up sleeping in her parents' bed.

A hinge of her door creaked as Sagel closed it, her heart still racing. She climbed into bed after shutting her normally cracked window so nothing unwelcome could slip in during the night.

"What was wrong with her? What was it?" Lorel whispered to Torren. Nova had fallen asleep sprawled across their bed, and they had decided to drink some relaxing tea in the dimly lit kitchen before trying to sleep again.

"Whatever it was, I hope no one else gets it," Torren said, shaking his head. "Poor Renald...when I spoke to him he sounded a bit worried, but I never thought that his daughter was suffering with something that serious."

"I do hope the Medicine Woman can heal her," Lorel sighed, clearing their empty mugs and washing them tiredly. "She looked confident, didn't she? A person of that power will surely be able to help Gwenoth."

"I don't know," Torren said, "Gwenoth looked gone when her father picked her up."

Sagel woke up to the sound of the wind against her closed window. As she had expected, there was frost on the window pane, and a thin layer of snow on the ground. Sagel smiled. She loved the first snow fall.

Stretching, she climbed out of bed and opened her window a crack to let the cool air kiss her face. She heard her mother turn on the generator, and soft yellow glowed through the crack under her door as the living room and kitchen lights came on. Everyone in Shinken had a generator with a fan that blew the outside air into the small machine to create electricity for the houses. For heat at night they burned wood or kept the generator on for electric heat. Torren and Lorel preferred wood heat while they were sleeping.

The wooden plank floor was cold, so Sagel put on her thick socks and stepped lightly out of her room. Lorel was in the kitchen puttering about. Bread and berry jam were already on the table, the bread plate almost empty except for three pieces that had been saved for Sagel. Sagel walked to the table, settled herself down in her old blue chair, and took a piece of bread and some fruit juice.

"Sleep well, Ma?" Sagel asked.

"Surprisingly, I slept pretty well, considering last night," Lorel said, joining her daughter. Most adults on Earth would be sipping their morning coffee at this time, but coffee is one of the items that do not mimic Earth's menu. Occasionally, shipments of coffee are sent over from Earth, but towns as remote as Shinken rarely receive any of it. Up until then Sagel had not remembered all that had transpired the night before. Her stomach tightened unpleasantly.

"Have you heard anything about Gwenoth? How are her parents?" Sagel queried quietly, not wanting to break the comfortable mood between her and her mother.

"I'm sorry, Sagel, Gwenoth passed away in the early hours of the morning," Lorel said, turning slowly from the sink where she was washing the dishes from the early risers.

"Oh," Sagel breathed.

"They're planning for her death ceremony—nothing extravagant, I think they'll just be laying her to rest in the forest and letting nature care for her," Lorel continued, taking her mug of hot tea from the counter and joining her daughter at the table.

Death ceremonies on Asthekia are quite different from those on Earth. There aren't any fussy funerals or hearses. The bodies are stripped naked and then put in a place where the deceased would want to be, and then left there. Some families consider wild animals to be guardians and guides of all living things, so they entrust the bodies of their deceased members to the forests and mountains. The bodies are not buried and no one deliberately visits the places where they are last put.

"Oh. Gwenoth always liked the ocean, I thought they would've taken her down to Mordre Beach…she always talked about her visits there," Sagel said solemnly.   Gwenoth's accounts of her vacations to the warm beaches of the south always used to irritate Sagel, especially since the Bleudrys usually spent their vacations in Shinken or occasionally Starling City. Now she became a bit sad remembering how excited Gwenoth used to become when she spoke about playing in the waves and the sand.

"Do you think whatever she had will spread?" Sagel asked after a silence.

Lorel's jaw tightened and she picked at an old gardening callus, "I don't know. We do not even know if it is contagious, sweetheart. The truth is, we do not even know what was wrong with her. You need to protect yourself, wash your hands, send good energy, and think good thoughts. That's all we can do right now."

"Will you tell me more if you or Dad finds out more?" Sagel wondered quietly.

"Sagel, have your father or I ever kept anything of importance from you?" Lorel raised her eyebrows and touched her daughter's shoulder.

"No. I suppose not," Sagel answered, nibbling away the last bit of her bread.

"And nor do we plan to. We will tell you more if we find out anything else," Lorel said, nodding to her daughter and resting her hands on the table.

"Where are Nigel and Nova?" Sagel asked. The house was strangely quiet without their playful quips and banter.

"They ate and are outside playing," Lorel said, her face relaxing, "It's the first snow of the winter. Your dad is delivering some pottery down the mountain. There is a truck waiting to bring it down to Starling today."

"Ma, I'm gonna go find Dan—can I hang out with him a little

today?" Sagel asked, looking up at her mother.

"Of course. I'm going to town to buy some groceries and to drop off some preserves to a friend. Let your siblings come, if they want. Dan doesn't mind them, does he?"

"Ma!" Sagel cried.

"Only joking!" Lorel laughed as she playfully pushed her daughter towards the front door.

Nigel and Nova tore through the yard at their older sister, barraging her with snow and slush.

"Stop!" Sagel yelled at them, sending handfuls back at them.

Their battle lasted only a few seconds before Sagel ran into the road, leaving her siblings laughing and rolling happily in the white powder.

"Where are you going?" Nova called, running to the edge of their yard.

"I'm going to a friend's house," Sagel answered quickly, hoping her little sister would leave it.

"Can we come?" Nova implored, her wide eyes sparkling.

"No. Ma said I could go by myself today. You guys stay here," Sagel threw back over her shoulder.

"Oh. Okay, bye!" Nova shrieked, showering her older sister with some more snow before giggling and running back to make snow-mountains with Nigel.

Sagel hummed as she walked down the road. Dan's house was in the dead center of town, right on the main road. Sagel had many other friends in the village, but she felt like being with Dan today. The air was frigid. The cold from her cloak that had been dampened by the snow and slush, made Sagel shiver as she walked on the dust of snow. She kicked her feet, billowing up little flurries of snow that rained back onto the ground behind her. This made her smile. She had always loved the winter—the way the snow piled up in pristine whiteness that covered up the dirt, grass, and trees. Snow covered the impurities of the land. Winter was the renewing season with the snow wiping the slate of the land that started over fresh in the spring.

Drifting in and out of her memories of past winters, Sagel hadn't realized where she was until she spotted a familiar tree that was not bare of leaves, but still dark jade green with needles. She was in the Stretch. Though she pretended to be indifferent while in the company of her siblings, the Stretch always made her a bit nervous. Sagel became aware that she was unconsciously holding her breath and letting her eyes dart from tree to tree. She breathed evenly again and looked around more carefully, walking steadily. The shadows on the ground stretched to the center of the road, their owners creaking and bending in their wooden forms towards her. Looking closely at one trunk, she saw a topaz bead of sap bleeding from a crack in the bark. Elenry's face bending over Gwenoth's body flashed through her mind, and her hands felt sticky. She picked up her pace, looking at her hands which were warmed and covered by her dark green gloves.

She let out a shuddering sigh when she cleared the Stretch, and jogged down the final hill to the center of town, putting the Stretch from her mind. Daniel's cottage was quite small, but warm and nicely decorated by his parents. Sagel rang the bells hanging beside the front door, announcing her arrival. Almost immediately, Dan opened the door. His hair was brushed—a rarity for Dan.

"Wow, Dan! You clean up nice!" Sagel joshed. "What's the occasion?"

"Why thank you, Sage. No occasion," Dan bowed. "Do you wanna hang out?"

"No, Daniel, I just walked all the way into town not to hang out with you!" Sagel rolled her eyes.

Dan laughed as he motioned Sagel into the warm living room.

Sagel and Dan usually hung out at his house, or down by the creek, but not usually at her own house. Sagel liked Dan's house; it wasn't grand, but it was a work of art. Dan's mother, Louise, was an artist, and enjoyed painting circular designs on large rocks and then selling them to people in the larger cities of Asthekia. Louise kept her favorite pieces, hanging them in the living room and hallway of the house.

Dan led Sagel back to his room, where they sat on his rug. Both of them waited silently, willing the other to bring up Gwenoth.

"So, that was pretty scary last night," Dan finally sighed.

"Yeah, I know. Did you come up after you heard the scream?" Sagel asked, trying to recall seeing Dan's face in the crowd the night before.

"Yeah, my parents told me to stay in bed, but I snuck out after they had left the house. It was crazy. Everyone in the town all ran up there at once. I've never seen the town like that..." Dan trailed off, his eyes lost in the memory of the unsettling experience.

"Was she screaming outside? Because I have no idea how everyone heard it. It was like she was screaming into a microphone, it was the loudest thing," Sagel said, swallowing the knot of fear in her throat.

They sat in silence on Dan's floor for what seemed like a very long time.

Sagel asked quietly, "Have you heard anything...I mean,

about—what was wrong with her?"

Daniel shook his head. "No one seems to know anything. And the Medicine Woman hasn't been in town since last night. She's camped in the woods up on the other side of town."

Sagel continued curiously, "The clinic? Has anybody been down there to ask about it?"

"I don't know. My parents said nothing about it."

They sat pondering the possibilities.

"So…what did your parents say about the road trip?" Dan finally asked, breaking the uncomfortable silence.

"Oh, they said not until next school season is over, because my dad's pottery business is really busy this time of year, so we are going to wait until people are taking a break," Sagel said.

"Oh, okay," Dan said, trying valiantly to hide disappointment.

"Dan, it's not like they said no, we just can't go in the next week or so!" Sagel said, pinching him lightly, trying to cheer him up. She hated seeing Dan sad. Dan smiled and tried to pinch her back, but she scooted away.

"Wanna go to the other side of the mountain? I've heard there are huge tutfer fields. I bet it's really cool to see them after the first snow," Dan urged, standing up and stretching.

"We wouldn't be able to see through the clouds. The mountain is totally packed in with clouds! Besides, it would take a long time, maybe days, and it's cold," Sagel countered, shaking her head.

"Then what do you want to do?" Dan asked, sighing, disappointed that Sagel wasn't more enthusiastic about his plan. "What do you want to do today?" Dan insisted.

"We could go to the stream" Sagel suggested.

"Yeah, but that's just the stream, it's not a real adventure!"

Dan exclaimed, waving his hands like a restless wind.

"Alright, we'll do something *adventurous*, just not the other side of the mountain," Sagel compromised, smiling at Dan.

"But someday we'll go to the other side, right, Sage?" Dan added quickly, raising an eyebrow at Sagel, who was looking dubious.

"Yeah, Dan, someday in twenty years," Sagel laughed. "Just kidding, yeah, we'll go sometime soon."

"You know, if you roll your eyes too much they might freeze up in your head," Dan teased, laughing as Sagel rolled her eyes again. He continued, "So, the big question is, where do you want to go?"

"No idea," Sagel said, standing up and leading them out of Dan's room towards the front door. Daniel followed her out. The front door seemed like a good place for them to start, and it would at least get them out in the cold where their decision would likely be made faster.

"Oh, how long can you stay?" Dan asked, putting on his coat and snow boots.

"As long as I want," Sagel said.

The two walked out into the street. It was snowing ever so lightly. They walked up the road, towards Sagel's house, not knowing exactly where they were going.

"Do you wanna just head down to the creek? We could follow it down the mountain a ways and jump from boulder to boulder, like we did last time," Sagel said, not wanting to disappoint Dan with a lack of adventure.

"Sure!" Dan agreed heartily, and then stopped. "Wait, my parents say we shouldn't do that in the winter, because the rocks are so slippery."

"We'll be careful," Sagel coaxed, "unless you want to just hang out inside all day."

"Alright, we'll go," Daniel said quickly, "but if one of us splits our head open on an icy rock, it's not my fault."

"Well, of course it would be your fault if you split your own head open," Sagel giggled, setting off down the road towards the head of the creek trail. Dan huffed and set off after her.

Sagel often wondered if they were too old to be doing this. She remembered when she and Daniel couldn't have been more than seven, and all the children of the village would race and play on the rocks by the stream. Now it was just she and Daniel, with the occasional exception of the bored schoolmate who agreed to accompany them. They were both fourteen years old, and most children their age would've rather been at home or hanging out in the village with friends; not rock hopping. She realized that she didn't care, and she didn't need to figure out why. It was good fun, and she was thrilled that Daniel didn't think it was boring or silly.

Down they went on the hoary path, laughing whenever either of them slipped or slid. As soon as they got out of the steep danger zone, they ran down the snow dusted bank to the water's edge. The swift, narrow stream had not yet frozen, so they could still leap from rock to rock without worrying too much about falling into ice. On the way down the mountainside, before they reached the stream, Dan had pointed out a mound of brown material. It looked like a burlap sack with legs. Dan and Sagel hadn't left the path to take a closer look.

"I know what that was!" Sagel exclaimed, rubbing her cold, gloved hands together.

"What? What are you talking about, Sage?"

"That burlap back on the mountain. It's the old Churkey herding woman's bag of clothes!"

Daniel nodded and shrugged.

"Let's go!" Sagel hoisted herself up on to her favorite high, white rock and dusted the snow off of it.

"Okay, how far are we gonna go down?" Daniel asked, craning his head as he looked down the stream.

"Until one of us breaks a leg on a rock," Sagel said, trying hard not to smile so as to seem serious.

"But seriously, be careful, the rocks are kind of snowy," Daniel warned, dusting off a gray boulder that sat half in the water and half out, and then pulling himself up onto it.

"Daniel, relax. I'm a pro."

"It's not you I'm worried about," Daniel joked, leaping to the closest rock in front of him. He landed with flat feet and bent knees, surprised that it was not slippery. He gave Sagel a nod and they continued jumping.

The duo bounded from rock to rock, sometimes even jumping across the narrower parts of the stream to a rock on the other bank. Once they got enough momentum and speed going, they leaped further and faster between the rocks. Sagel had a near miss when she leaped onto a particularly slick rock with some old leaves remaining from fall. Just as she was about to tumble into the icy, rushing water, Daniel grabbed her by the back of her cloak and steadied her.

They decided then to just run on the side of the stream and avoid any more close calls. Wind and heavier snowfall chased them as they ran all the way down into a small cave-like shelter between two large, overhanging rocks. Both of them were panting. They caught their breaths as they marveled at how far down the stream they had come so quickly. Neither of them had ever been this far down the water's path. They had both gotten so into the rhythm of leaping and landing that they had lost track of the distance.

"That was great," Sagel puffed, "and look—no broken bones."

All of a sudden, Dan reeled around, gasping quietly.

"What? What is it?" Sagel gasped jokingly, resting her hands on her knees. "Mutant Churkeys?"

"No Sagel, I'm serious. There was something back there, deeper under the rock, let's go back," Dan whispered quickly.

"Of course there's something back there, it's probably a mutant Churkey! It must've gotten down here before us!" Sagel said, trying to elude her slowly surfacing apprehension. Daniel did not sound like he was joking at all.

"No, Sagel! Stop, I'm not playing, please let's g—", Dan stopped, staring wide eyed towards the back of the cavern.

At the back of the grotto was a small figure crouching, dry heaving on the ground.

Fear knotted in Daniel's stomach and his legs wouldn't unlock. He felt like he had plunged into a horrible dream where no matter how much you will yourself to move, you stay paralyzed.

"Whu-whu-what is it?" he stuttered, standing jelly-legged next to Sagel, one hand forward as though trying to grab something for stability.

Sagel could feel her skin prickling and her eyes widening as she looked at the small being crouched at the back of the cave. It looked like a small child. Just then, it stopped heaving and turned towards them. The thing looked human, like a little boy. It—he was wrapped in a thick, brown cloth that covered up everything except his feet. His skin looked like aged wax; it was almost colorless but weakly tinged with yellow. Matted, unkempt black hair hung in front of sunken, black eyes. Something was off about the whites of his eyes. Instead of being a normal white color, they were the same light, milky yellow as his skin.

"Ma?" he whispered, starting to crawl laboriously towards them.

Both Sagel and Dan breathed sharply and cringed back towards the mouth of the cave. The boy stopped, whimpering, and curled up into his cloth. Sagel felt pity for him; his tatty cloth could not be keeping him very warm.

"Who are you?" Sagel finally managed to ask.

Dan stood stalk still, not able to move a muscle.

"Ebin," the child whispered.

"What are you doing here—Ebin?" Sagel continued, swallowing her fear and confusion in great writhing lumps.

"Ma said we had to come here to escape the disease," he answered, rasping out the words with difficulty.

"Disease? What disease?" Dan asked, suddenly aware of a frightening possibility.   "The disease that killed my sister," he said, choking on tears.

Sagel moved down towards the boy, ignoring her stomach as it threatened mutiny. Stopping a few feet from him, she asked gently, "Can you walk?"

Ebin tried to stand up. It took him a few tries, as his knees kept buckling, but when he had finally gained his balance, she saw that he wasn't much taller than Nova.

"Where do you come from, Ebin? Which village?" Sagel pressed on, stepping forward and helping Ebin wrap the cloth tightly around him after it had slipped off his meager frame in his struggle to stand. Under the cloak he wore only a pair of shorts. Sagel was careful not to touch his skin.

"We come from Deagial," he murmured, hacking again.

Daniel and Sagel knew where Deagial was, though neither had ever been there. It was a neighboring community on a nearby mountain in the Seauthsai Mountains. Deagial shared a similar culture with Shinken but was much more remote and closed off from the outside world. There were no connecting roads to Deagial, and it was about a four day walk on foot from Shinken. During particularly harsh winters, Shinken would often send food and medicine to them, for the land that Deagial was settled on was much harder to live on due to its severe rockiness. Deagial relied almost completely on hunting and gathering techniques that had been refined over thousands of years.

Sagel took a step back. "Where is your mother?"

"She left to walk up to Shinken last night. She said she was getting help, so we could be saved. She said she would come back for me..." Ebin trailed off and began to cry softly as he sank back down onto the ground. One dull tear dragged down his cheek, but that was all that his dehydrated body could produce.

Sagel's stomach knotted. It was a sick and twisted knot that was doing slow and oozing somersaults in her abdomen. This kind of knot made her squirm and sweat, hot and freezing almost simultaneously. Sagel now knew what was wrapped in that unexpected cloth a ways up the mountain.

She turned slowly and looked at Daniel, who had already made the same connection. He nodded to her gravely.

Chapter 5

An Upward Battle

Sagel sighed softly, her eyes widening further. Dan walked towards her finally, and stood beside her and Ebin.

"Ebin, what was your mother wearing when she left?" Sagel asked, her palms clammy.

"A brown robe, like mine," Ebin said softly, dragging his arm across his nose. It was Dan's turn to squirm when he heard this confirmation of what was lying under the bag beside the trail.

"That means…" he trailed off, and then he turned and vomited. Sagel bent down beside Dan, helping him sit down. Daniel waved her away, wiping the back of his hand across his mouth and cleaning his hand with some snow from the floor of the cave's mouth.

"Are you alright?" Sagel asked Daniel, hoping that his vomiting was a result of sickened nerves and not a sickened body.

"I've never seen a dead person before," Daniel mumbled, looking queasy and embarrassed. Sagel nodded knowingly, her own stomach menacing her. She quickly pushed the image of Ebin's mother from her head.

When she turned around, she was staring down into Ebin's

yellow eyes; she recoiled slightly. Ebin had crawled over to Sagel and was now watching the two older children anxiously.

"What happened in your village?" Sagel asked gently, helping Ebin to bundle himself up as much as she could.

"Everybody got sick, lots of people died, like my sister, so Ma said we had to go to Shinken to get help…we were the only ones in the village that could walk…we didn't get as sick," he rasped, his eyes glowing thinly at the fact that they had survived the illness. Or at least, he had.

Sagel turned to Dan, her hands buried deep in the pockets of her cloak. She stood stiffly, braced by a sickening fear of this little boy and his affliction. Part of her wanted to hold him and bring him health. Another part wanted nothing to do with him or his illness.

Dan finally spoke, "Is anyone…alive in your village?"

"Yes, but they are really sick…only me and my ma can walk around," Ebin whispered.

"Ebin, where are your clothes?" Sagel asked.

"Ma burned them, said they were dirty, and sick, so she got these brown robes…." He whimpered, "Where's my Ma?"

"Ebin," Sagel was never good at breaking bad news, but she wasn't about to lie in this exceedingly complicated situation.

"Ebin, your Ma is dead. We found her on the mountain, by our village of Shinken." She said, reaching a hand toward him and then drawing it back. She felt Dan move closer beside her.

Ebin's eyes changed. Instead of the apprehensive flicker of anxiety there was now shock. Ebin gasped, and mumbled something.

"It's okay Ebin, we'll get you help," Sagel assured, watching the child attempt to rise and then fall, his trembling howls of sorrow filling the cave. Dan moved back toward the mouth of the cave, trying to diminish the grating din of the boy's sorrow in his ears.

Ebin's body bucked and rocked as he heaved dry sobs of anger and torment. He held his knees and cried at the dark, cave ceiling. His frail body shook so hard Sagel worried it would break apart. Finally, he became lax as he succumbed to exhaustion.

"Dan, we have to get him up to Shinken," Sagel said, turning to her best friend.

Daniel said nothing for a moment, as if he had forgotten how to speak in the trauma of the afternoon. He finally simply nodded, and walked slowly towards the little boy. Stopping short of the crumpled body, he asked, "How are we gonna do it, Sage?"

Sagel took a deep breath; the air in the cave was cold, and it stung her nose with the chill. The sweat from their boulder hopping had dried cold on her skin, making her teeth chatter an icy beat.

Dan whispered in her ear, "He's really sick. We shouldn't touch him."

Sagel whispered back, "But he'll never make it on his own. We have to carry him."

They looked at each other for a long moment, as if trying to draw the answer from each other's eyes. Almost simultaneously, they both said, "Between us."

Sagel moved first, positioning herself at Ebin's feet. Daniel followed suit, going to the boy's shoulders. They slid their arms under him, Sagel holding his legs and feet, and Daniel supporting the head and torso. Ebin made no movement but to cast one wary gaze at them both before closing his eyes and going limp.

They walked out of the cave and began the ascent to their village. Out of nowhere, Sagel was angry; angry at the abrupt end to their carefree afternoon. She felt frightened and embarrassed by her resentment. Here she was, in the company of a child who was dying in their arms, and she was angry about it! *Ridiculous!* she thought, shaking her head to herself. Fear took another stab at her gut. The proximity of the events of Gwenoth dying of her illness, the boy's dead mother, and finding this sick little boy was far too close for comfort.

The journey up the steep incline took longer with Ebin, but, sooner than she thought possible, they came to the spot where his mother lay. Dan stopped and looked sideways at Sagel. His face was pinched, and sweat ran down his temples even though it couldn't have been more than five degrees Celsius. Sagel shook her head, and nodded her head upwards to keep walking. Her back ached and her stomach twisted. Every so often Ebin would stir in their arms, coughing or whimpering. The bearers would stop and turn their faces away from the boy, holding their breaths.

About a half hour later, the trail leveled out. Sagel smiled to herself with stiff, chapped lips; they were almost there. The air was colder at this altitude, and Sagel noticed that it was snowing lightly. Dan noticed it too, and they unanimously picked up the pace.

A short time later, the trail widened into the town's road. Dan's house sat comfortably beside the street, smoke pouring from its chimney as if nothing in the world could phase it. Sagel envied its peace.

"Dan, I'll run ahead to the clinic to warn them, you know, so they have time to get ready to treat him," Sagel said, beginning to transfer all of Ebin's weight to Daniel.

"No," Daniel breathed, stopping, "I won't carry him alone. I'll wait with him here."

There was no time to argue. Sagel and Daniel scanned the surrounding area and found a tree with thick, low hanging branches that created a dry space beside the trunk. They trotted to the tree, laid Ebin on the bed of needles and dirt, and stepped back. Sagel took off up the road.

Sagel ran as fast as she could on her weary legs. They solidified from their jelly state a while ago, but they were still a little shaky. She ran down the road and through the center of town, past the restaurant and the food co-op, and turned onto the road that led to the clinic. A few people walked the roads, but most were indoors. The town seemed much longer in her fearful rush. Finally, she reached the clinic steps. Sagel took them two at a time to the door, burst in, and a warm wave of air washed over her numb face.

Galah, the head nurse, was staffing the front desk. Launching without hesitation, Sagel began a run-down of what had happened. Galah listened, her green eyes widening and her full mouth puckering. As soon as Sagel ended her recount of the events, Galah was already barking orders to the two nurses on duty about preparing baths and beds; Sagel had no space in her occupied mind for any more details and did not bother listening.

"I'll take my horse. You said they were under the large tree where the creek trail flattens to come into town?" Galah asked sharply, donning her coat and beginning to put her gloves on.

"Yes, I can show you—"

"No. You'll stay here and be treated. You've been out in the cold for far too long, you are exhausted, and you have been exposed. Ava will take good care of you while I fetch them,"

SHINKEN

Galah's word was final as she left the clinic and went for her horse. Freida, the other nurse, was busy in the examination room; Ava was at Sagel's side as soon as Galah had left. The nurse before Sagel was plump and endearing. Her sleek brown hair was braided and then twisted around itself to make a tight bun at the back of her head.

A cloth mask wrapped her round face and she wore white rubber gloves on her thick hands.

"You'll need to get out of those clothes, dear. They are contaminated and need to be burned. You can do that in the examination room." Ava handed her a dark plastic bag. "Put your clothes in this and tie the top tightly. I'll dispose of the bag. You'll need to be bathed, too," Ava finished, leading Sagel toward one of the smaller of the two examination rooms. Before Sagel had reached the entrance to the room, she burst into sobs.

"What is it, child?" Ava gasped, turning to Sagel but not going to her.

"M-my c-cloak belonged to m-my grandmother," she cried, covering her face with her freezing hands.

"I'm sure that your grandmother would have chosen your health over a cloak, dear," Ava reassured, walking to the girl and taking the hand-sewn garment off her and putting it in the plastic bag. Ava said firmly, "You do the rest."

Taking the bag, Sagel stepped into the small room and closed the door behind her. She shuddered and sobbed as she stripped off the rest of her clothes. Ava stepped in and handed her a disposable gown for cover while she filled a large washtub in the corner with steaming hot water. The temporary garment would have to be burned as well. Ava poured in a disinfectant soap and stirred the water with a wooden paddle.

"This is going to feel hot, but it has to be. In you go, now," Ava said, her eyes smiling above her mask.

Sagel climbed into the tub, letting the gown fall from her into Ava's hands. The hot water felt wonderful on her aching muscles and frayed nerves. Ava scrubbed the girl with odiferous soap. It made Sagel's skin tingle and burn unpleasantly.

The nurse hummed as she scrubbed.

By the time Sagel was dried and clothed in a billowing clinic dress, Galah had returned with the boys. Sagel had no idea what had become of Ebin, but she heard running water in the neighboring examination room.

"Can you call my parents so they can pick me up?" Sagel asked quietly, her eyelids drooping and her cheeks blotchy.

"I shall call your parents to inform them that you are safe and being looked after, but you will not be able to go home tonight," Ava said as she led Sagel across the hall to the recovery room. This particular room had a large glass window in its hallway wall through which nurses could observe patients. Sagel stopped in the doorway, tears welling up in her spent eyes.

"W-why not?" she asked, brushing away the fresh tears in vain.

"Because you have been exposed to a possibly deadly illness and you need to be observed over night to make sure that you are not symptomatic," Ava said, her wide-set blue eyes filling with empathy, and maybe even a fleck of fear. "You need to rest now. I will bring you water and some hot tea to drink. Are you hungry, dear?"

"No. But tea would be good." She smiled weakly, "That's what my mother would give me."

Patting her on the shoulder and guiding her into the room,

Ava said, "Then I'll bring you tea, and after that you can sleep."

"Will you call my parents?" Sagel asked again, walking to the third bed on the far side of the recovery room.

"Of course, dear, and I'll tell them to bring you some new clothes when they come to fetch you tomorrow," Ava patted the pillow and Sagel climbed into the bed, pulling the covers up to her chest.

"Where is Dan?" she gasped, remembering her companion in the other room, "And Ebin?"

"Daniel is receiving the same treatment as you and will be lying in the bed next to you in a short time," Ava said, as she walked towards the door.

"What about Ebin?" Sagel pressed, swallowing a lump in her throat.

"I do not know, but I believe he will be taken to Starling City for evaluation and treatment." Ava closed the door behind her.

The door clicked closed and Sagel let her tears wash down her face. Her body unwound but her mind whirred uncomfortably. The ordeal played over and over again in her mind, infused with worries about the illness and a painful longing for her parents.

A short time later, the door to the recovery room opened for Freida and Daniel. Dan was clad in a matching white robe that made his pale face look even chalkier. Freida wore an identical mask to Ava's. Behind them bustled Ava herself, holding a tray with two mugs of water and two mugs of steaming tea. Daniel needed no prompting as he lay down on the bed, not bothering with covers.

"Drink the water first, children. You need to rehydrate your bodies. We'll be checking on you every thirty minutes or so. We'll bring you dinner in about an hour if you're still awake. Ava will contact your parents now," Freida rattled, watching Ava as she hurried from the room to the phone at the front desk. Freida's voice was not nearly as smooth and welcoming as Ava's, but its confidence was reassuring to the children. "We commend you for your bravery." With that she nodded, left the room, and turned right outside the door towards the operating room where they had Ebin.

"Are you alright?" Sagel asked, after she had taken a long sip of water.

"Yeah," Dan sighed, sitting up to drink his water. After he swallowed, he started laughing; Sagel didn't know what to make of it and just stared at the ceiling. His laughter turned to silent tears and Sagel sat up.

"I'm sorry, Daniel," she whispered thickly, tears of her own cascading down her face.

"For what? You didn't do anything," Daniel said, sniffling and wiping his eyes with the back of his hand. His voice was low and embarrassed.

"I should have let us go to the other side of the mountain. Then we wouldn't be in this mess. I'm so stupid…."

"You're not stupid, Sage. Ebin would have died if we hadn't found him," Daniel consoled, sitting up in his bed and turning his whole body towards Sagel.

"So what? He's going to die anyways!" Sagel cried, burying her face in her pillow. Daniel watched her helplessly and then lay back in his bed.

They both fell asleep.

Dan was running, he was running away from something. Sagel looked around helplessly, she was just a bystander in this chase. Dan was running into the Stretch, the cold, still Stretch. Nigel hated the Stretch and she did too. Elenry was there, she was just walking away. Sagel called out to Dan, trying to warn him about the things that would get him if he entered the Stretch. Elenry turned around, crying about something unimportant. Sagel was angry; she wanted Elenry to DO something, to help her friend. Dan was still running, whatever was chasing him was gaining on him. Sagel looked back to see what Dan was running from. It was Gwenoth. Sagel cried out with joy, but then she was flooded with fear. Gwenoth was screaming, a bloodcurdling, earsplitting scream. A scream so horrible that it would melt ice, and untwist barbed wire. Gwenoth was yellow, a sickly decaying yellow. Gwenoth launched herself at Dan, and then....

Gasping, her eyes flew open. Sagel grimaced at a sour taste in her mouth. She was curled up in a web of blankets, sweat dripping down her face. She rolled her tongue around in her mouth, tasting a musty, sour flavor. Slowly, she took in the room she was in. Daniel slept as still as a stone in the bed next to her. The lights were on, but they had been dimmed. Her tea had long since cooled on the bedside table between their beds. As she drew long drinks from her water and her tea, her thirst quieted. Through the window she could see the door on the opposite side of the hallway, but not much else.

A small foggy window above her bed gave her a partial view of the street outside, but she could see enough through the clouded glass to know that it had to be early evening. Beyond the road she could see a single street lamp casting an ocher glow onto the ashen ground, disturbed only by the shadows of the occasional person, horse, or car.

"Evening," the door swung open to Galah's deep voice. Her tall, slender figure glided through the doorway, holding a tray with two bowls on it. "How are you, Sagel?"

"I'm fine," Sagel croaked, trying to shake the sleep from her head.

Galah set the tray down on a small set of shelves by the door and pulled from the top drawer a long, silvery instrument.

"I'll need to take your temperature," she said, walking to Sagel and holding the shiny apparatus up to Sagel's mouth. Sagel obliged and wrapped her mouth around the tool. As she felt the cool metal, she remembered that her mother had a temperature reader of her own; fortunately, no one was sick very often in the Bleudry family, so they hadn't had to use it for the past two years or so.

A few moments later Galah removed the device from Sagel's mouth, holding up the end that Sagel had had in her mouth. The wet tip of the utensil glowed a dull indigo.

"No fever," Galah said happily, moving to Daniel's bed. Sagel stretched her arms, wincing as her wrists and elbows crackled and groaned. Daniel started awake when Galah prodded his mattress with her foot.

"Amisick…am…I…?" he mumbled, sitting up quickly and fumbling with his blankets.

"Easy does it, Daniel," Galah said, stepping back slightly.

"Oh…," Daniel yawned deeply, his eyes focusing. "Hello."

"Good evening," Galah answered, popping the thermometer into Dan's mouth. He sat still and waited for her to remove it. Dull indigo. Sagel released her breath in relief.

"Wonderful," Galah commented, placing the apparatus in the pocket of her robe for sterilization. "Now, you'll both need to eat a nice hot dinner. We have soup from your mother, Daniel, and a sap and petal sweetened bread from your mother, Sagel." Galah strode to the cabinet and fetched the tray, bringing Sagel her large bowl of food first and then giving Daniel his.

"Our parents were here?" Sagel asked anxiously, cradling her warm bowl in her lap.

"Yes—well, not *in* the clinic. They left the food on the door-step and I brought it in, but they both told me by phone to tell you that they send their love from both your mothers and your fathers, and Sagel's younger siblings." Galah stepped briskly to the door and paused. "Assuming all goes well with you two to-night and tomorrow morning, your parents will be here at midday to pick you up and take you home."

"What if things, you know, don't go well?" Sagel queried timidly.

"We shall deal with that if it happens, but let us put our stock in your full recovery," Galah answered, nodding her head to ac-cent every word she spoke.

"But we aren't sick, are we? I mean, I don't feel sick," Daniel said nervously, surfacing from his bowl of soup. "Do you, Sage?"

Sagel shook her head, but looked intently at Galah.

"No, probably not, but you have both suffered from exhaus-tion and mild hypothermia. Fret not children, just eat well and sleep well and all should be well tomorrow. I'll be back in a bit for your bowls." With that, Galah turned on her heel and left the room, her snaking red pony-tail twisting energetically across her back as she shut the door behind her.

"We forgot to ask about Ebin," Sagel blurted.

"We can ask Galah when she comes back for the dishes," Daniel assured, swallowing his bread.

"Is it bad that I'm not hungry?" Sagel wondered aloud,

pushing her soup around with her spoon.

Daniel appraised Sagel, his hazel eyes searching and fretful, "I dunno. You're probably just too tired still. Or you're in shock or something. But we need to eat, Sage. Really, we do."

Sagel nodded and forced herself to have two spoonfuls. Daniel relaxed a bit. The soup burned her tongue and warmed her stomach. After two more spoonfuls she felt ravenous for more. She ate until her bowl was empty but for the hard little flavoring spices in the bottom.

"I guess you're not in shock anymore," Daniel smiled broadly, standing from his bed and bringing his bowl to the tray, and then going to Sagel's bed. "Here, I'll take it."

"Thank you," she said, handing him her bowl and lying back against her pillow.

Daniel walked with steadiness, but Sagel could see from the way his back drooped and his feet dragged that he was still drained.

"I really want to go home," Sagel sighed, when Daniel was back in bed and they were both studying the ceiling.

Daniel nodded, "Mm-hm."

Galah came in some time later to take away their dishes. She took their temperatures again; both indigo. Before turning out their lights, she patted them both on their shoulders and bade them goodnight. Neither of them remembered to ask her about Ebin.

"I'll be here all night, in the front room. Knock if you are feeling sick or if you need anything," she smiled comfortingly through her mask. "Sleep well, brave children."

They did.

The next morning raised an optimistic sun that streamed a wakeup call through the recovery room window. Sagel was again the first to stir. Daniel slept easily, one of his arms crossed over his rhythmically rising chest. Sagel swung her legs from the bed, feeling a strong need to use the bathroom. In her hurry to get to a facility, she forgot Galah's request to knock before exiting the recovery room. The hallway of the clinic was quiet, but Sagel could hear the familiar voices of Ava and Galah in the operating room. Freida was in the larger examination room sterilizing equipment, and jumped when she saw Sagel up and about.

"Oh, dear, you're up," she said, her hand going to her mask and adjusting it higher on her face, "What do you need?"

"The toilet," Sagel smiled sheepishly.

Freida showed Sagel to a small door beside the operating room and waited outside until she was done.

"How do you feel?" Freida asked, walking Sagel back to the recovery room and stepping inside with her. Dan sat blurry eyed in his bed.

"I feel fine," Sagel answered, casting an unconscious look down at herself and stretching her arms. "Just a little sore."

"Yes, well, that would be expected," Freida replied.

The nurse took their temperatures again and found the same peaceful blue. Daniel used the toilet while Freida brought them breakfast.

"How is Ebin?" Sagel asked quickly, just before Freida closed the door behind her to leave.

"Not so well. I will call your parents and have them come and pick you up. I'll clear it with Galah first, just to be sure, but you two should be home by midday today." Then Freida shut the door.

Sagel and Nigel exchanged a glance.

"I wish they'd tell us more," Sagel sighed, taking a sizeable bite of her scrambled Churkey eggs.

"I'm not sure if I want to know…you know, if he dies or not," Daniel pronounced quietly. They spoke no more of Ebin, but proceeded to distract themselves by discussing their return home. Freida poked her head in with the good news that they would be going home that day. She left before Sagel could enquire about Ebin.

The morning rolled on as the sun and moon climbed high and higher in the crisp winter sky. Lorel and Torren showed up when the celestial bodies sat directly above the mountains, passing each other before they began their downhill slides. Sagel threw herself into her mother's embrace, and then flung her arms around Torren's neck. Lorel looked a bit pale, but relieved. Torren held his wife and daughter close, muttering grateful words to the cosmos.

Daniel's parents, Louise and Michael, arrived shortly after Sagel's. Louise did not look as if she would ever let go of Dan, and when she finally did, he was claimed by his father. Both families thanked Freida copiously, though neither Galah nor Ava was present to receive their proper thanks. Freida said that they were tied up at the moment and that she would pass the kind words on to them.

A twisting in Sagel's stomach began when she tried to imagine what they were busy with.

Before Sagel could climb into the car after her parents, Dan called to her, "Hey Sage!"

"What?" she called back at him.

"Great adventure!" He called back, and then followed his parents up the street towards their house.

"Great adventure…," she whispered.

Chapter 6

The Churkey Woman

Three days later, Sagel awoke in her own bed after a pleasant evening spent relaxing with her family. Nigel had sat in silent awe on her first afternoon home as he listened to Sagel narrate the events of the day before. Lorel and Torren had sent Sagel to bed early that night, saving her from having to describe every gruesome detail to her curious little brother, though she appreciated his interest. It was rather nice to be the center of attention in the world of her siblings. Nova had fretted over her big sister, saying that going to the creek alone was dangerous and that she could have slipped and fallen into the water. Sagel assured her sister that she had been careful and that it was by chance that they had ended up in their situation.

The brief warmth of the previous few days had been overtaken by a cold front that grayed the sky and drove the temperature down to nearly freezing. New layers of snow had packed onto the ground. Stepping out into the cold made Sagel's heart wrench in her chest when she remembered what had become of her Grandmother's cloak. Fortunately, Lorel had been informed by whatever nurse had called her parents, saving Sagel from another painful recount. The news of Ebin's death had whistled through the town like the glacial northern wind. Even though she had expected it, Sagel's stomach clenched every time it intruded on her mostly pleasant thoughts.

Breakfast was porridge with sap and berries, much to Sagel's delight.

Torren did not rush out to his pottery shed after breakfast, but stayed at the table with Sagel as she sipped her mug of sap tea that Lorel had made for her. She looked into the clear, amber liquid as she stirred it with her spoon. The tea was still too hot to drink from the mug, so she took a spoonful, blew on it and sipped.

"How do you feel today, Sagel?" Torren asked, placing a loving hand on his daughter's shoulder.

"Very well," Sagel smiled at her parents. The past three days had consisted primarily of rest and relaxation for Sagel. She had not gone to town, or even beyond their yard, for that matter. They sat in comfortable silence, finishing their drinks while Nigel drew in his room and Nova tried to decide whether or not she wanted to pester her older brother or make snow-mountains outside.

"Do you think I could go see Daniel today?" Sagel asked a while later, when her parents were cleaning up after breakfast.

"I don't see why not," Lorel said, "As long as you two take it easy. I do not want you leaving the village or being outside too much. You are both still recovering from that ordeal."

"Agreed," Torren said, as he dried the dishes that Lorel handed him.

"Don't worry, we will definitely be taking it easy," Sagel smiled, kissing both of her parents on the cheek and then heading for the door.

It felt strange stepping out into the cold wearing her brown, button-up coat, rather than her beloved cloak. Trying to put the cloak completely out of her mind, she strolled to Daniel's house, her hands jammed into her coat pockets and her chin buried in the neck of the jacket. It felt good to be outside again, but she knew that Shinken would never feel the same again.

Louise opened the door after Sagel knocked, smiling at the bundled girl.

"Good morning, Miss Sagel," Louise smiled, pulling Sagel into the warm house by her hand.

"Hey Sage!" Daniel exclaimed, turning from his post at the sink.

"Daniel, please finish the dishes before you two head off," Louise said, clearing the table of the rest of the breakfast dishes. Michael had already left for work.

Sagel helped Daniel finish off his morning chore and then they headed for their usual rug in Daniel's room down the hall.

When the door was closed and they were out of earshot from Louise, Sagel said, "I want to go to the clinic and see if anything else has happened with the disease."

"But we can't go in, can we," Daniel pointed out.

"No, but we can knock and ask them at the door."

Daniel mulled it over and then agreed. They bundled up warmly against the deepening freeze. Louise asked them where they were going.

"I don't think it's such a good idea for you to go back there," she said.

"But we just want to know if anything else has happened," Daniel replied, "We'll just get an update and come back."

"We would have known if something else happened," Louise countered.

"All we want to do is check in," Daniel sighed.

"And I doubt that there are any sick people since nobody's heard anything," added Sagel, hopefully.

Louise thought a moment, finally agreeing on the condition that they come straight home after receiving their update.

To the clinic they went, crunching on the frozen earth. People on the street stared at them, smiling warily when they made eye contact. News spread quickly in small villages.

Elenry walked out of the restaurant. She had become quite fond of the little café. The food was always well done and warm, and they brewed her cinnamon and sap tea with more cinnamon than sap. Cinnamon was in high demand on Asthekia, as Asthekians knew of the healthful properties of cinnamon. She had arrived at the clinic only minutes after Sagel and Daniel had left, but Galah had given her a full rundown. Though Galah and the other nurses had handled the whole situation very well, Elenry was concerned that she had not been summoned. Galah apologized and assured her that in the future she would be called immediately, and that it was just hard to break her habit of doing everything in the clinic with her own staff. Elenry understood.

Elenry paused and let Galah gather her energy. "Galah, how did Ebin die?"

Galah was puzzled, "How—do you mean?"

"What were his symptoms?"

"High fever, dehydration, fatigue, yellowing of the skin...."

"None of those is fatal."

"You're asking then, what killed him."

"Exactly. What happened just before he died?"

Galah responded slowly, "I was the only one in the room. He had stopped talking or moving, and appeared to shrink down into the bed."

"How long was he like that?"

"About twenty minutes."

"And then," Elenry continued.

"And then...his breathing suddenly became labored. He didn't seem to be able to get enough air. I put one arm behind his back and held him up to open his windpipe. Then, his breathing stopped completely and he was limp in my arms. That's how he died."

"Heart failure."

"I don't know what else could have killed him that quickly," Galah concluded.

"Have you ever heard of an influenza causing heart failure?"

"Possibly in someone who is very old or weak, but not in a boy who was normal and strong before he got the illness."

"I agree. There is certainly something unusual about this illness."

After further conversation with Galah, they had decided that Elenry would stay one more night and leave the next morning if no one else fell sick. The nurses had put Ebin in a burlap sack and then buried him at the edge of the forest far behind the clinic, not knowing what else to do with the probably contagious body. Galah was exhausted and had been ready to leave the clinic, so Elenry suggested that she and the other nurses take an hour or two break at their homes while Elenry covered for them.

That was early in the morning, and as soon as Galah and the nurses had returned, Elenry left for lunch. Before she left, Elenry informed Galah that some villagers had come to enquire about the situation and that she had told them the basic facts. She and Galah agreed that they did not know what had killed the boy.

Arros stood outside the restaurant, waiting for her. Translucent steam puffed from his gaping nostrils. His saddle blanket was made from the pelt of a Manks, a common lynx-like mammal in the southern hill country of Thron Avaykwathorel. It has a large bear-like head, with long pointy ears and a long, slender body. Long legs that bend at small, flexible knee caps help it run down its prey of Churkeys and small rabbit-like creatures. Gray is the most common Manks color, but occasionally white and brown ones are spotted and often killed. Before Elenry had been summoned to Shinken, she had been in a small hill village where she had been gifted with the saddle blanket after curing the father of the village's wealthiest hunter. Carefully descending the icy restaurant steps, she mused to herself that she would not likely receive a tribute for her skill from this village.

Elenry gently patted Arros, talking to him quietly and asking his advice as to what she should do. Arros blinked his round, black eyes a few times, tossed his head in the direction of the road, and snorted, then nuzzled her with his velvety nose.

"Thank you, Arros," Elenry crooned to him, resting her forehead on his black, glistening neck. "Let's leave."

Elenry loved no being more than Arros; if the time called for it, she would have been prepared to die for her horse. Adroitly, she swung her leg up over Arros, settling comfortably into the long arc of his back. The Medicine Woman used only silver reins attached to his bridle to guide Arros. He was an extremely intelligent horse, did not need to be told a command twice, and often anticipated Elenry's direction. They rode away from the café; Elenry steered him up the schoolhouse road that would lead them to a small off-road clearing where she had set up her tent. She always carried her canvas tent when she traveled. It was large and held heat well. Arros slept outside with a heavy blanket draped over his back, his winter coat helping to keep him warm. Tomorrow she might have to take it all down and leave.

People they passed on the street watched her with disappointment and even resentment.

Shinken had only called on a Medicine Person for help once in its recent history. About twenty years before, a young family had called for the help of a Medicine Woman named Diann. The family had seven year old twins who were ailing with a horrible lung condition. They coughed so hard sometimes that they brought up blood into their shaking, clammy palms. Alas, Diann was not able to do anything for the twins, and they died within a few hours of each other on the second night of her stay. From that day forward, Shinken's inhabitants associated a feeling of dread and foreboding with Medicine People. That morning Galah had shared the story with Elenry so as to explain why she might not get the warmest send off.

She smiled to the people; sending them waves of apology and good energy, all the while suppressing the gnawing parasite of premonition that plagued her.

These last few days had taken their toll on Elenry. The night before, she had dreamed of a dark and nameless fear, which disappeared every time she turned to catch it, hanging just behind her shoulder.

After gathering wood and putting out dry grass and water for Arros, Elenry lit a fire, and started boiling water for a much needed hot drink. She was on the far side of town, up behind the school, on a ledge of the precipitously ascending Mt. Aarotte. Thick fog was creeping down the slopes and had already begun to obscure the rock face above her. A ceramic mug of hot sap and leaf tea was soon cupped between Elenry's cold hands as she sat on a stump close to her fire. This was her favorite tea. Every sip brought back memories of childhood. Her mother used to brew sap and leaf tea for her when she was sick and when she wasn't, because she believed strongly that sap was the best thing for keeping away colds and flues. Elenry had drunk a cup every morning since her childhood.

She had told Galah that if anyone else fell sick and came to the clinic, she was to send someone up to her camp to fetch her.

All the time she was at her camp she sent energy to the cosmos, focusing on no one else falling sick in Shinken. Though she knew this technique was effective, she also knew that her ignorance of the nature of the disease strongly limited its effectiveness. Elenry let more water boil, and pulled assorted grains out of Arros's food pack. Arros always thinned down a little in the winter, but she had to keep him strong in case they had to go somewhere in an emergency. Arros gobbled down the oats and warm water in the blink of an eye. He then went over to a snow covered tree to scratch his back on the frozen branches.

Footsteps. Crunching snow. Elenry tensed, instinctively reaching for her medicine bag. She had many rare herbs and serums that she had brewed and collected over the years. Elenry took the pot of melting snow off the fire, and smothered the flames with her boot. Suddenly, she knew that she wasn't going to need the fire. She called Arros over and quickly put on his bridle after pulling on her cloak and gloves. Now she was ready to go.

She started down the hill to meet the person, but no one appeared. Elenry walked further down. She wasn't imagining this—there was someone walking on the hill. She was sure. More footsteps. She wheeled around, realizing that the sound was coming from behind her. Something was coming down the mountain.

She gazed up into the damp fog that now completely obscured the mountain. Her heart was racing. Something wasn't right. She had been told by Galah that no one lived up the mountain from Shinken; no one inhabited the other side of Mt. Aarotte. Was there someone else out there? Someone that no one had known about? There was a shape coming out of the fog. A cry shattered the enveloping silence, a cry from the emerging being.

"Plevy! Plevy em! Eshaelp! Daedla, lla daedla," it cried. Elenry listened to what the voice was saying. Fluent in Sdrawkcab, Elenry felt her stomach clench in horror when she realized what the person had said. *Help! Help me! Please! Dead, all dead.* Dead, who—what was dead? Who else was on this mountain? Elenry ran up the snowy incline, dropping Arros's reins. Arros followed her trail of footsteps, drawn by his master's sudden actions.

Elenry ran up to the tree line, where a person stumbled out of the fog and completely into view.

It was an old woman. Grasped tightly in her wrinkled hand was a dead Churkey; blood was dried on the feathers around its beak and nostrils. Its eyes were open, but they were a bleak yellow. They looked just like Gwenoth's eyes. Elenry grabbed the woman's hand and shook the Churkey from it; apparently animals were just as vulnerable as people.

Realizing that this was a very serious sign, Elenry spoke quickly, calming the old woman as best she could, but to little avail. Elenry told her that she was alright, and that she needed to come with her so they could help her at the clinic. Elenry did not touch her again, but let all the good energy that she could summon flow through her and out to the old woman. Despite the Medicine Woman's soft words, the Churkey woman wailed incomprehensibly, waving her hands about like an angry blizzard.

Finally, Elenry decided that she was going to have to take matters into her own hands. Telling the old woman to wait for her, she ran back down the hill to her medicine bag by the dead fire, rummaging until she found the desired item. It was a silvery mask that had been designed and sewn by Elenry's old teacher many years ago. It was said to be able to filter almost any disease from the air and keep its wearer healthy and strong. Deftly, her fingers tied the mask over her face, and then she went back to the old woman. In the snow sat the withered woman, her face distant and drenched with tears while she muttered and sniffed. Elenry bent down and gently picked the woman up, despite her rekindled howls, and walked to the remains of her fire.

Elenry set the woman down on the stump, and then turned to her medicine bag. She took from the bag a small flask full of light green liquid. The green liquid was more commonly known as Bromidomine, a natural tranquilizer used by doctors all over Asthekia. Bromidomine is derived from a red fern that grows in the swamps of Asthekia. Before people realized that they had to extract the medicine from the plant, they tried to eat the fern, only to die a fast but painful death.

Elenry popped the cork from the bottle and held the woman's jaw; the woman tried to bite her, but Elenry had already poured the fast acting liquid into her open mouth. Placing her hands on the old woman's shoulders, Elenry soothed and waited until her patient's head lolled forward as she fell into the Bromidomine-induced stupor. Once Elenry had stocked and organized her medicine bag, and hoisted the old lady up onto Arros's back. Then she climbed on herself, and began the short ride to the clinic.

Knocking was getting them nowhere. The duo had been rapping away at the door for the past few minutes, and still no one had answered. They exchanged a glance and Sagel shrugged. At first Daniel shook his head, pointing to the new sign on the clinic's door.

"No entrance unless there is an emergency," he read aloud.

"Daniel, we've already been exposed, and we're both fine. Galah will understand since we've been knocking for so long."

"Okay," Daniel breathed after a moment's thought, sniffing from the cold. He knew there was no use arguing with her.

Daniel and Sagel pushed open the door of the clinic, their noses tingling as warmth rushed back into their faces. Galah wasn't at her usual post at the front desk. Sagel and Dan started to walk quietly back to the recovery rooms, hoping to get word on any new development with the disease. They heard the frantic voices of one of the nurses and Galah coming from the recovery room.

"What do you mean, quarantined?" the nurse said, though they could not tell which one.

"Just what the letter said!" Galah hissed desperately, "I'll be right back."

Sagel and Daniel glanced at each other, both feeling a knot of worry form in their stomachs. They heard the softer nurse's voice say something they could not understand.

Galah stepped out into the hallway, her long red hair in a messy bun.

"What are you children doing here? Are you sick?" she snapped, stepping backwards and fumbling with the mask that was hanging around her neck.

"W-we were here to see if anything else has happened—with the illness," Sagel spoke up.

"And we're not sick," Daniel added.

"Nothing, children. I'm sure you two have heard about Ebin," she said, smoothing her hair and wiping the sweat from her brow. "I'm happy that you are fine, but you both need to go home."

Sagel and Daniel left the clinic without another word. As they closed the clinic door and started to walk away, they were shocked to see a great black horse trotting straight for them. Sagel gasped and they both stepped back under the eve of the clinic's doorway. When Elenry leaped off the horse, they realized immediately that she was not traveling alone. The Churkey-herding woman, who lived alone on the mountain, was lying limp in Elenry's arms.

"Move back and don't touch," Elenry barked as Sagel and Daniel moved quickly away from the door, their hearts fluttering.

Balancing the old woman in one arm, the Medicine Woman thrust the door open and strode in, then slammed the door shut behind her. Arros walked to the side of the building, stamped his feet, then settled.

"What does that mean? Quarantine?" Sagel asked, though she knew exactly what that foreboding word meant.

"What else could it mean? Shinken's quarantined. No one can leave and no one can come," Daniel said, his voice shaking.

"That doesn't make sense, though! You heard what Galah said, we have had only two sick people. They can only quarantine us if three people fall sick with a disease we can't cure," Sagel countered. "That's the law! We learned about that in school."

"Maybe we could wait, Elenry might be out soon, she might tell us what's going on," Daniel offered, "and, we don't even know if Shinken really *is* quarantined. We didn't hear the whole story."

"Why would *she* tell us anything?" Sagel asked skeptically.

"And we shouldn't wait out in the cold like this. *And*— Galah told us to go home."

Daniel chewed his lip and heaved a sigh, "What do we do?"

"I don't think we can do anything but go home."

They unanimously turned and set off for Daniel's house.

Chapter 7

Quarantine

Galah put her Churkey sandwich down on the desk when Elenry walked in.

Elenry was carrying the thin, flaccid woman in her arms; the old woman was still unconscious from Elenry's sedative.

"What in the name of Mlack?" Galah gasped. "Another one?"

"I'm not sure, get a bed ready. She's been exposed to sickened animals," Elenry said, keeping her voice low and level as she brought her burden into the first examination room.

"Is she sick?" Galah asked.

"I don't *know*," Elenry said, still clutching the old woman.

Galah called in the other nurses in Sdrawkcab, ordering them to build a fire in the yard behind the clinic.

"What did you do to her?" Galah asked, helping Elenry lay her onto the bed.

"I had to give her a sedative because she was hysterical. She was walking down to my camp holding a dead Churkey. The Churkey looked sick with the disease," Elenry replied flatly, following Galah's lead and stripping the old woman of her clothes.

"The Churkey? The bird?" she puzzled. "How——?"

"Obviously, if it *is* the same illness, this illness can be contracted by animals as well as by humans." Elenry added, "She kept saying 'Lla daedla', over and over again."

"All dead—her birds?" Galah asked.

"What birds? She only had one," Elenry asked, relaxing her knitted brow.

"We know this woman. She herds Churkeys and other animals on the mountain and has a small hut down the south side a ways," Galah explained. "We've offered to bring her into the village, but she fishes and hunts, and refuses to move into Shinken."

"So she lives with no one else?" Elenry asked, feeling relieved.

"No, she lives alone, except for her animals," Galah said, tossing the old woman's clothes into a bag that was tied up and taken away by Ava. "I believe her name is Magda Dasiol," Galah finished.

Before they did anything else, Elenry stopped and pulled a second shimmering mask from her medicine bag, and handed it to Galah, pointing to hers and nodding. Though Galah wanted to examine the strange, new mask, she knew that Elenry wanted her to put it on right away, and she wasn't about to question a Medicine Woman.

"What is it made of?" Galah asked, as the two women bathed Magda in hot water and medicinal soap.

"The material is referred to as Saskageadal by the Asthekian Medicine People," Elenry answered quietly, rubbing the pungent soap over the patient's tough, wrinkled skin.

"Where is it from?" Galah continued, her voice mirroring Elenry's smooth cadence.

"It is sewn by the expert hands of the oldest and most experienced Medicine People," the words rolled off Elenry's tongue in clouds of palpable peace. "Though I myself do not know the precise technique, I do know that the main thread is from the dead body of the Silken ferns that grow on the Moonery Hills in Kovraantic."

Galah just nodded, her eyes focused but soft. Elenry breathed in and out, and soon both Galah and Magda were breathing in time with her. As they finished washing Magda, Elenry let her energy pulse between the three of them. In the air before her she could see with second sight a golden band connecting them through their abdomens.

After the tub was drained and Magda was ready to be dried and dressed, Elenry let the energy flow fall away. It took considerable effort to align the energies of three separate entities in a work situation, and she needed to conserve her strength for what was yet to come.

While they dried her off, the old woman began to stir, mumbling something indecipherable. Once they had her dressed and in a recovery bed, she seemed to focus. Galah spoke to her slowly, milking the old woman's memory for every fuzzy detail she could recall. Five minutes of probing and listening allowed them to gather that the old woman had woken up that morning to find her entire flock of Churkeys dead in their pen next to her hut. She could not remember any more than that. Galah had consoled her and had Freida bring her a steaming mug of tea. After sipping at it, Magda lay back on her pillows, her aged eyes crinkling and sagging.

"Well, while she rests, I have something I need to show you," Galah said tiredly, leading Elenry from the recovery room, pulling a piece of paper out of her pant pocket and handing it to

Elenry. The knot that had been slowly tying itself tugged suddenly in Elenry's chest. This was it.

It read:

Dear Inhabitants of Shinken, Mt. Aarotte,

It has come to our attention that an unknown and incurable illness has been circulating through your community. We gather that one child has actually died from it, and another, though not from your community, has passed through and even stayed over night, only to die the next day. The ABHR states that only if three people fall sick with an unknown illness, that the affected area must be quarantined. This is, however, a special case. Two children, Daniel Richard Carson, and Sagel Mahaylu Bleudry were in close contact with one of the afflicted children. This is cause for concern, and since the two children were in such close contact with the sick child, the ABHR hereby quarantines your village until this illness has passed. Food and medical supplies will be delivered at their regular times, but will be left at the base of the mountain; it will be your village's responsibility to retrieve them. Under no circumstances can anyone living in Shinken leave the mountain, or send out Lobands. The best of luck from everyone here at the ABHR.

Sincerely,
Waira Migtand.
Director of ABHR.

Elenry stood silently, re-reading the letter. Her heart sank to the soles of her feet. They could no longer send Lobands with messages to the city or other villages. Lobands are an exceptionally intelligent species of bird that, over the years, has been trained by Asthekians to carry messages. The letter that the clinic received was sent by a Loband from Starling City, the base of the ABHR. That Loband now had to stay in Shinken.

"What are we to do now?" Elenry asked to no one in particular, frustration trying to pry its way into her core. She said a silent spell and relaxed herself. Galah did not answer, but retreated to the examination room to help Freida clean up and disinfect. Through a side window, Elenry could see the smoke from the fire that Ava had set in the pit in the backyard. Elenry resolved that she would stay at the clinic for the rest of the day to monitor and, if possible, treat the old lady.

Before opening the door to the recovery room, she tightened her mask. Her stomach dropped to her feet to join her heart. The old woman lay on the bed, drenched in her own vomit. Blood ran from her nose and her chest heaved and wretched a few more times before deflating as death finally relieved her. Elenry called for Galah.

"What do you think will happen now?" Daniel asked as he and Sagel sat on his familiar rug.

"What do you mean 'now'?" Sagel enquired quietly, picking at a loose thread on her sleeve.

"Like…what do you think will happen with the illness—and Elenry?" Daniel pursued.

"I don't know. I think Elenry will have some answers if she's as great and powerful as Medicine People are supposed to be. She's probably come across something like this before and will know how to cure it," Sagel said to herself as much as to Daniel.

"Is it our fault?" Daniel murmured, staring at the pattern on the rug before him.

Sagel said nothing, but fought to hold back an onslaught of hot tears.

"Well, I suppose Gwenoth was sick before Ebin was, but Shinken is quarantined because of our bringing him here," Daniel answered himself, drumming his hands incessantly on the floor.

"We don't even know if Shinken *is* quarantined. We didn't hear their whole conversation," Sagel insisted, getting a grip on her tear ducts.

Daniel nodded in agreement, but Sagel spoke before he could answer.

"I should get home, Dan," she said, standing up. "My parents will be worried."

"Okay," Daniel said, standing with her and walking her out.

"Are you going home already, Sagel?" Louise asked from the kitchen table where she read a book and drank her tea.

"My parents will be waiting for me," Sagel answered briefly. "Thank you for having me."

"You're always welcome, hon," Louise answered, returning to her book.

"See you later," Sagel said to Daniel, opening the front door and stepping out into winter.

Before she could close the door, Daniel put his hand out, "Stay healthy, please."

"You, too," Sagel answered. Despite her common sense, she hugged Daniel. He warmed her even in their brief embrace.

"See you later," they said together, smiling as they parted.

Glistening stars of snow drifted and danced on the wind.

Elenry's hair tossed and played with the icy breeze as she sat before her fire that night. With Arros and herself fed and watered, she meditated before the gentle blaze. Ever since Magda had died that afternoon, Elenry's premonitions had burgeoned with unpleasant connotations. She could not quite put her healing finger on it, though she had probed and searched for the better part of the evening before starting her meditation. The only thing that felt sure in her heart was the fact that she would not be leaving the town the next day, or the day after that, if she couldn't solve this in a timely fashion.

Foreboding questions thundered and poured within her as she began to clear her mind. Firelight twinkled in her eyes, joining with her interior light to burn the storm clouds of doubt and negativity from her psyche. She loved the flames. As she watched, they danced lower and more steadily, matching her breath. Her heart quickened at any rogue drop of off-putting thought, sending the flames spewing upwards.

Unwaveringly, she watched the little conflagration. A few minutes later, she brought the flames down to a slow blaze; not an inch from the charcoaled pile of sticks beneath it. At last, her mind stopped, frozen like the creek far below, now that the temperatures had dropped and stayed below zero.

The fire went out, and she went to bed.

Chapter 8

Groaning Trees

Sagel climbed into bed after a small dinner of leftover Churkey sandwiches. Sleep eluded her; every time she began to drift off, an instant replay of the past few days invaded her resting mind. It was like having an endless movie reel playing in her head, and just when she paused it, someone would press play again. At last, a fitful sleep crept into her wearied consciousness.

Sagel awoke to a scream. Not a dreamlike scream, but a real scream. She bolted from her bed, not bothering to pull on her cozy slippers. She ran across the cold, wood floor to the front of the house, where her mother was standing in the entryway, gazing out the open door. Nigel, Nova, and Torren were running up behind her, but she saw it first. The evergreen trees outside their house stayed green all winter, summer, spring, and fall. Their needles were tough against the freezes of the winter months. But now, every tree across the dirt road from the house was bare; their brown, shriveled needles littering the ground below them. As the wind swept through the surrounding forest, the trees creaked and groaned arthritically. A sharp gasp escaped Sagel's throat. Air from the outside swirled inside, little cold fingers running up her legs to her body and then up to her tingling scalp.

Sagel took a step forward and stood in the doorway, scanning the strange scene. "What's wrong with them?" she whispered, her voice cracking.

"I don't understand it, the trees…," Torren muttered, in one swift movement, he took Sagel's arm, pulled her inside, and slammed the door.

"Something is clearly wrong around here," Torren began.

"You think?" Sagel groaned, regretting her words immediately.

"Excuse me, but if you are going to be sarcastic and rude, you can go to your room. What'll it be?" Torren looked steadily at Sagel.

"Sorry, Dad. I'm sorry," Sagel muttered, her face flushing with anger. Lorel was sitting on the coach with her face in her hands; she wasn't crying, but she looked as if she was about to.

"No one leaves this house unless it's on fire," Torren said, hugging his children toward him. "We don't know what's wrong with those trees, and if we don't find out something positive by tonight, I'll drive to town and see what's going on down there."

"Why can't we go outside?" Nova whimpered, running to a window and pressing her face up against the glass to look.

"Because the trees are sick, sweet one, and we don't want to be exposed to it until we know what's wrong with them," Lorel replied, touching Nova on her shoulder and then pulling her away from the window.

Sagel sighed to herself. Having no choice but to hide out in their warm house made her feel horribly claustrophobic. More than anything, she wanted to talk to Dan, but something told her that things weren't going any better in town. Torren, Lorel, and

Nova gathered in the living room, but Sagel pulled her brother into the kitchen before he could join them.

"Nigel, just listen to me and don't talk. I must go to town, I need to talk to Daniel, and I need you to tell Ma and Pa that I'm resting in bed," Sagel whispered.

Nigel glanced uncertainly from her to the doorway into the living room. He heard the low voices of the rest of his family. Finally, he looked up at Sagel. "Sagel, no, I won't let you!" Nigel whispered angrily. "Please don't go outside." His face softened into pouty fear.

Taking both of his shoulders in her hands and holding him squarely in front of her, she whispered intensely, "I need to talk to Elenry, I need to ask her something. I think I know something."

"No you don't! You're just saying that so I'll let you go," Nigel retorted, puffing his cheeks out and making himself as large as possible in front of his older sister.

Just then there was a knock at the door, sending the two of them running to the front room. Torren opened the door to the man outside.

"Hello Torren, Lorel, kids," greeted Haykyel Madrih, the Town Head. He helped facilitate all the town meetings, and mediated discussion about any important decisions that the village needed to make.

"Hello Haykyel. What's going on?" Torren asked quickly.

"We're calling a town meeting, the trees are too much," he said, sweeping his hand behind him. "I recommend that you walk to the town meeting. I know it's cold and a bit of a walk, but I don't think being so close in a car is a good idea. There may be something contagious." And then he was gone, jogging across their yard to alert the next house, before Torren could question further.

Relieved to be going to town, Sagel dressed quickly and was the first one in the entryway, ready to go. The walk was heart wrenching. All the trees had contorted in on themselves. Their trunks had curved and bowed, their branches twisted and bare. They groaned eerily.

"Why are they groaning, Pa?" Nova asked shakily.

"I'm not really sure—maybe they're hurt or sick," Torren answered, pulling his youngest daughter closer and tightening his grip on Lorel's hand.

All the trees were like that, except for those in the Stretch. The family stopped walking. Standing in the stretch was like standing in another dimension entirely. The needles on the healthy branches were as green as could be underneath the powder of snow. As usual, the Stretch was perfectly still, no wind, no sound—perfectly quiet. The only noise to be heard was the rhythmic breathing of the five family members admiring the healthy trees.

Torren shepherded them on. The scene in town wasn't much better than it was at their house, with the forest line full of aggrieved trees. The snow on the road was not powdery anymore but hard; it crunched and squeaked under Sagel's boots. Normally these sounds of winter would have brought a smile to Sagel's face, but now they grated like tiny echoes of the trees' agony.

The Village Hall had always been Sagel's favorite building in Shinken, besides her own home, of course. The outside of the building was built with the same beige bricks as the other buildings of the village, but into the plain stone were etched beautiful carvings of trees, leaves, birds, waterfalls and mountains. It was a feast for the eyes, and Sagel had spent much time with Daniel making up stories to go with the pictures in the stones.

Sagel and her family entered the hall, a low ceilinged, one

roomed building. The inner walls were painted a soft cream color, with only one decoration hanging on the front wall. This decoration was the Shinken Crest, a circular plate with an "S" painted in silver on blue porcelain. In the curves of the "S" were enameled blue eyes; the eyes of the town, watching over all, taking in everything, but saying nothing. Out of a desperate imagination, Sagel pictured the "S" sprouting a mouth and telling the town exactly what they needed to do to fix the present quandary.

Villagers had already packed into the hall. Her family found seats next to Dan's family, but before she and Daniel could talk, the meeting was called to order. The audience fell into a tense hush, all eyes trained anxiously to the front of the room.

Haykyel stepped forward and smiled, but his mouth was tight and his eyes were troubled. "First of all, I thank you for braving the cold weather and the strange trees to be here. I'd like to start today's meeting with a story."

Not only was Haykyel the Town Head, but also a master story-teller. It was said that no matter what language he used to tell the story, he could be understood, because he spoke so beautifully. It was a customary gesture of unity and peace to open village meetings with stories of Shinken, or Asthekia. Though Sagel had not been many places on Thron Avaykwathorel, she felt that she had personally experienced every setting that Haykyel had brought to life in his many stories.

"Can we leave after the story?" Nova whispered to Lorel.

"We must stay for all of the meeting, Nova," Lorel whispered back, patting her youngest child's leg.

"Many a tale has been told within these walls. The story I will tell you today is one that has been passed down from Town Head to Town Head. I am aware that the story I am about to tell is usually reserved for our annual village celebration, but in light of the events of the past few days, I think we all need to hear this story."

As he began, his mouth softened and the clouds left his eyes. "In the long forgotten language of Nakitik, Seuthsai means *Wild Ocean*. Long ago, the mountain range was named for its furious storms and volatile conditions. Hasty travelers often came to the mountain range, and opted to go over it instead of all the way around it, only to be caught in rain, snow and hail storms. Some did not make it over the mountains, and those who did usually arrived in the South with harrowing stories. Most of these travelers came from the North, leaving behind the arid soil of the grasslands for the fertile plains and beautiful forests and hills of the South. The great Seuthsai range extends like a reaching arm across the middle of Thron Avaykwathorel, much to the inconvenience of travelers. Safer, though it was, to trek around the mountains, some travelers went over them. It was because of one of these travelers that our village was born. Seahn Naen, a man from a small village in the far North, led a band of his people south.

They traveled in the summer, when the Mayer Grasslands swished and swelled with green. The group numbered nine: Seahn, Seahn's wife, Ecelia, Leolo, Leolo's wife and son, and Lessa, Ecelia's sister, and three neighbors.

"On the horizon, Seahn," pointed Leolo, Seahn's friend and traveling companion. "A wall."

They stopped and appraised the mountains that rose before them. Seahn smiled to the snowcapped Seuthsai, his straight, white teeth glimmering in the moonlight, and his light hair shimmering in the sun's rays.

"We'll climb," Seahn said to his group. "The mountains welcome us, and it's only a wall."

Seahn was a well-built man, strong from his work as a hunter and builder for his old village. In fact, all of the travelers were sturdy and lithe, and agreed that the best thing to do was to go over the mountains. Oh, how they sang songs of travel as they walked. The grasslands rang with their vigorous tunes. Lessa wanted to sing ballads from their village, but Seahn forbade her to.

"It is a village left behind, Lessa," he said, stopping and turning to her. "It pays us no virtue now."

It took them a little over two days to cross the grasslands. Under a star-dappled sky, they made camp, right at the base of the mountain range. Seahn told the others that they would start up the wall of the peaks at the first light of day. Lessa slept restlessly, for fears of the towering mountains above them loomed in her dreams all the night long.

"Wake, everyone," Seahn said, rousing them with a loud clap of his hands. "Eat with me, and then we shall climb."

They ate quickly, speaking little to one another. The day settled with a warm breeze, and light clouds streaked the intensely deep blue sky. As Seahn looked up at their impending climb, he was happy to see that the slope was mostly rock and dirt as far as he could see.

"Let us say a prayer," Lessa offered when they had finished packing up to go.

"A prayer for what?" asked Leolo.

"For peace and safety," Lessa said, glancing at Seahn, who only nodded and joined the rest of the group in a circle.

They chanted and raised their heads to the sky above.

Finally, they broke their circle, and Seahn took the head of the procession.

"I wish not to climb," Lessa blurted.

"It is our only way, Lessa," Ecelia said to her sister. "We'll be fine."

"We won't," Lessa cried, starting to sob. "I have a feeling!"

Seahn walked to his wife's sister, and placed his hand on her shoulder. She tried her best to stop crying.

"If you do not wish to climb, then you may go around the mountains—or back to the village."

"We never should have left!" Lessa sobbed.

"Then you may return. But you will not hinder the rest of our journey," Seahn said firmly, turning away from the woman.

Ecelia went to her sister and spoke in a frantic whisper, "You must come, Lessa. Please. Put your feeling aside, and see that this is our path."

After coaxing and reassuring by Ecelia, Lessa finally agreed to go with them. Up they climbed; their pace steady and their eyes trained on the ground before them. A warm wind blew at their backs, strong enough so that they had to pull back their hair to get it out of their faces. The mountains steepened and the dark, jagged rocks that made up the ground became rougher and larger.

Leolo's son, Albero, wandered ahead, his long, nimble legs and his youthful energy propelling him upward. The boy stopped hiking and turned around, for all of a sudden, his shadow had disappeared. A massive, rumbling storm cloud blocked both the sun and the moon in their high perches at the top of the sky. He called down to his people, pointing up at the darkening atmosphere.

"Walk on, boy. Rain will only make us wet," Leolo called back, and Albero continued walking. Heavy rain drops wetted the stone and pelted the travelers. Fortunately, the stone was rough enough to provide adequate traction, and they could climb on without fear of slipping. Lessa, at the back of the party, shook her head and watched the sky. Her hair was sopping wet, and her arms raised goose bumps against the cooling wind.

"Are we going to stop and lunch?" asked Grogia, one of Seahn's neighbors.

Seahn kept walking, but spoke to her over the din of the wind and rain, "We will stop when we are at that cliff."

They scanned upwards for the cliff, and saw a shelf jutting from the mountainside. At last, they reached their rest spot, an overhang of the shelf beneath which was enough dry ground for all of them to sit. As the rain continued, they dug into their packs for food and water. The rain had subsided, and was now a meager drizzle that came and went with little gusts of wind.

"You see, Lessa? No more than a feeling," Seahn said happily, taking a long draw if water from his bottle.

"My feeling has not subsided, Seahn, no matter how hard you try to ignore it," Lessa said through clenched teeth. "I am frightened, and I do not know why."

"You're just tired," Ecelia said to her younger sister. "When we make camp for the night, and you get a good sleep, you will see things differently."

After a short lunch, they set off again up the mountain. One particular peak loomed high above them. They gazed warily at what we now know as Mt. Aarotte. None of them, not even Seahn, could see how they could safely summit it. The mountain steepened until it was eventually a sheer face below an impossibly sharp pinnacle. Appraising the mountain was getting them nowhere, and Seahn finally decided that they would climb up and to the right of the peak, in hope of finding a pass of some sort, or at least a scalable summit. More rain began to fall as thick gray clouds stormed the summer sky. The group bundled more clothes on, for as the altitude rose, the temperature dropped. Albero was still in the lead when he stopped cold.

"What is it, Albero?" Seahn called. "What was that?"

Something shifted in the ground.

"Stay still," Seahn called to his group.

Lessa's breath grew short, and her doom-ridden premonition peaked. The surface ground pulled them away from the subsiding land beneath. Lessa fell backwards with the rock and dirt after the three neighbors had disappeared into the slide. Leolo's wife, Beatril, clung to the mountain, but her husband fell at the same time as Lessa and was swiftly smothered by dirt and rock. The entire slide traveled hundreds of feet down the route they had come up, roaring and blasting up clouds of dust. As suddenly as it had begun, it stopped, leaving no trace of a human being on its broken, jumbled surface.

Seahn and Ecelia stood in shocked silence. Beatril fell back onto the ground, holding her injured foot. The fine rain cleared the air of dust as they scanned the slide for their companions. Nothing was visible but rock jutting out of freshly turned soil. Seahn and Ecelia searched the slide, but could not walk far on it because it was still too loose. They found no sign of their lost companions.

"We must continue…," Seahn whispered to his sobbing wife. "We need to get up this mountain."

"No! She was right…she was right," Ecelia cried, falling into Seahn's arms.

"There is nothing we can do for them now," Seahn sighed, holding his wife gently. "We hav—"

"Help! Mother?" Albero suddenly cried from above them.

"Albero?" a voice croaked. Beatril stood up beside Seahn and Ecelia.

"Oh, what virtue that we have survived," Seahn said. The three adults went to Albero, who sat shaking on a large boulder.

The group of four slept there that night, mourning their losses and nursing their cuts and scrapes. Beatril's foot was not badly wounded, and Seahn bandaged it after smearing it with a poultice from his rucksack.

"It smells like home," Beatril sighed, stroking her son's hair.

"That is not our home anymore," grunted Seahn, the light from their little fire casting dark shadows above his eyes as he glared at Beatril. "We will find a new one, and you can talk about that one all you like."

Ecelia patted her husband's shoulder and said, "Really, Seahn, they are just tired, and pine for something familiar, what is the harm of—"

"I see them floundering in their sorrows as if caught in a deluge. You all need to get out of the past. Stop hindering yourselves. We made a choice. A choice to leave that village. Have you left?" he demanded.

"Of course I've *left*," Beatril cried. "I just haven't *arrived* anywhere. I think it's better to have somewhere to talk about than to just float across the land."

"Then have the mountain! You are on the mountain, why not actually be here?" Seahn said.

"This place killed my husband and almost killed my son. It killed half of our party! Why would I want to be here?" Beatril cried, pulling Albero close to her and stifling a sob.

"This mountain did not kill them, a landslide did. And there is nothing that any of us can do to change that."

Ecelia stood and smothered the fire with dirt and rocks, "Let us all go to sleep. Tomorrow will be different."

And it was. Four weary travelers navigated their way up the mountain, speaking little after the confrontation of the previous night. Seahn was determined to find a way over the mountain, and could finally see a route that might be possible. Only a few hundred feet above them jutted another cliff. It was large, and looked stable. The left side of the cliff, from their angle, merged with the ascending mountain, but Seahn thought that if they could climb to that cliff, they might find an easier summit behind it. The morning came and went, with nothing in the sky but the sun and moon floating through the sea of dark blue. Wind stirred the air and their hair, cooling their necks and pushing the hair from their tanned faces.

Albero supported his mother in the back of the small procession, so it was Seahn who topped the cliff first. He cried out, throwing his hands to the sky and beaming at the mountain.

"Trees!" he shouted. Before them were the fringes of a forest. After days without foliage, the tall, emerald-needled trees filled them with happiness. Here, the land began to slope downward, much to Seahn's relief. The ground of the forest was more dirt and less rock. Small deer-like animals ran through the trees before them, frightened and intrigued by the strange visitors. Fat, short-winged birds crouched behind rocks and trees, their gray feathers fluffed and their eyes bugged out at the travelers.

Seahn sent Albero to kill one such bird, and they found that, once cooked, it was mild, white meat. Little mountain springs gurgled around them, and they delighted at the fresh, icy water. They bathed for the first time in days in a stream that flowed from a particularly large spring. Sweet was the water that they drank and lay in. They slept in the forest that night, exhausted, but thrilled at the beautiful, friendly land.

Jade green light filtered through the thick trees and into their little camp the next morning. They moved slowly, taking their time as they ate and conversed.

"It is beautiful here," Ecelia said, as they sat for breakfast.

"And safe," Beatril sighed, patting the ground next to her.

All were rather reluctant to move on from the forest, but curious as to what lay beyond the trees. Ahead of them shone light through the forest. Albero jogged ahead, as Beatril walked with Ecelia.

He ran back over the bare forest ground to the adults.

"What did you see?" Seahn asked immediately, after seeing the excitement on the boy's face.

"It is a pocket in the land," Albero said happily. "Come, it's right ahead."

Breaking through the last of the trees, the four of them gazed down. The land sloped gently downwards to a very large pocket in the mountain. The ground flattened onto a massive shelf that stretched for a few miles until finally reaching another ridge of the mountain. More forest stretched around the pocket, and grew almost clear to the end of the shelf. The pocket of land lay against the mountainside, as if the land had rested here before continuing up to the summit of the mountain. Berry bushes grew here, as well as smaller trees. Little mountain pools shimmered in the light of the ethereal spheres.

"Here," Seahn said.

"Here…what?" Beatril asked.

"What is it, Seahn?" Ecelia enquired.

"We will stop here, in this restful place."

None of them argued, for there were fresh water, edible plants, and an abundance of animals. Later they would find a creek that ran down the mountain, only a small hike away, where they could fish. They built the first structures of the little village out of fallen branches, but later, as more and more travelers found them in their safe pocket, they used tools to build wooden housing. It was only much later, when roads were built, and larger cities were established, that they brought clay to the village for the dwellings.

Seahn named the village in his language of Nakitik, and his fellow travelers could not agree with the name more. *Shinken.* To rest."

Silence hung in the hall as the story faded from the air. The crowd burst into applause, and Haykyel bowed low to the villagers.

Once the clapping had died away, Haykyel spoke, "We will keep you here for the shortest amount of time possible. Now, I turn things over to Elenry." The audience murmured as the Medicine Woman stepped forward.

"I'm going to cut right to it. We have received news from Starling City," Elenry took another breath as the audience sat in expectant silence. "In light of the recent events, Shinken is officially quarantined." A gasp was taken in unison, and then, like a string of furious fire crackers, conversation exploded between every adult and child in the room.

Elenry stood, breathing calmly and letting the shock talk itself out. As people realized that she was still standing, watching them and not speaking, they quieted down. A restless silence spread through the audience. Lorel took Torren's hand and sighed, her face pinched with dread. Torren took her hand and put his arm protectively around Nova, who was seated next to him.

"What does quarantine mean, Pa?" Nova whispered, her blue eyes widening in a mix of curiosity and fear. But before Torren could answer his daughter, Elenry proceeded.

"I don't mean to frighten you, but I must be truthful to keep you safe," Elenry gripped her black skirt with one hand. Unlike stages on Earth, stages in Asthekia are not raised. They are on the same level as the rest of the theater or conference room. Also, unlike on Earth, speeches are not given behind podiums; they are simply out in the open, with nothing to cover up or shield the speaker. Elenry's palms were sweaty, and waves of icy anxiety washed through her chest as she stood exposed before the restive villagers.

"As you probably know, Shinken has been exposed on more than one occasion to an unknown illness—" Elenry was interrupted.

"So what does Starling expect us to do about it?" someone called out from the audience. Others muttered nervously.

Elenry addressed the interrupter directly, "They do not expect anything of you but to stay healthy. It is I who must try to resolve this. Even though I do not have a solution for you yet, I will be encouraging new precautions that will change your everyday routines, but hopefully keep you from contracting whatever it is that killed Gwenoth and the little boy from a neighboring mountain village," Elenry finished, swallowing. The audience shifted and whispered. A stab of guilt took aim at Sagel's gut at the mention of Ebin.

"There are five main precautions that should be attended to at all times." Elenry continued. Her speech had gone almost perfectly so far, and the waves of anxiety that had been sweeping through the room were not coming as close together as they had been.

"First, no one in the entire village can leave the mountain until this illness is identified and under control." Elenry took a shallow breath, "Secondly, residents should not enter anyone else's house for more than an hour at a time so as to prevent the possible spread of the illness."

"Can we go to the public buildings? What about the co-op?" Daniel's father asked. More people chimed in with their questions.

"Yes, you need to enter public buildings such as the food co-op and the clinic, but only for as long a time as absolutely necessary," Elenry went on. She felt calmer and clearer than she had upon beginning the speech.

"Thirdly, under no circumstances should citizens of this village share food or drink from the same drink container," Elenry continued strongly and steadily, helping the entire group to concentrate on prevention rather than fear.

"Fourthly, only medical personnel will have contact with sick patients who will be quarantined in the clinic. And lastly, if you or your family members show signs of illness—be it a runny nose or vomiting—you need to go immediately to the clinic for consultation and treatment." Finished, she turned on her heel and walked off stage.

Muttering spread through the crowd as Haykyel Madrih took

over the stage and hushed the people in a calm voice.

"I know this must be hard to accept, but the doctors of Starling City's prestigious hospital are doing what they can to properly diagnose and come up with a treatment for this mystery illness. If any of you were wondering as to how Starling came to know about our problem, I will tell you that the dedicated staff members at the clinic are obligated to report odd symptoms and any deaths to the ABHR. I implore you all to harbor no hard feelings towards the nurses, for it is for the good of Shinken and its surrounding lands that this quarantine is in place." He had a rare voice quality that could lull a baby to sleep. It was a voice as soft as freshly fallen snow, but as warm as a well-loved heart. His skin was olive, and his eyes were amber and seemed intently focused on each and every villager before him, all simultaneously. The people of Shinken listened to him, loved him, and had a kind of innocent trust that Elenry knew she would never gain from them. She accepted this reality because she was in Shinken to heal, not to live.

After the meeting, families were advised to go straight home, but questions were raised before anyone even left the hall. What about the trees? When will the disease be controlled? What about their animals? Haykyel reassured them that he knew no more than they did and that there would be another town meeting as soon as more information was available. The mood as the town of Shinken returned home was highly charged. People hardly looked at each other, and kept to their own families.

Sagel, waiting right outside the door, stood on her tiptoes and scanned the flowing crowd for Dan. She caught a glimpse of the top of his head coming out the door with his parents on either side of him. She wanted so badly to run to him and apologize for her abrupt and uptight departure the day before, but before she could act, her mother took hold of her arm.

"Sage, come on sweetie, we need to head home," Lorel said, her voice as steady as she could make it. Sagel walked with her mother. She felt poisoned somehow; it was hard for her to breathe and to not feel contaminated. Everything familiar and lovable about Shinken had left on the winds that had brought the mysterious illness.

The walk home rang with pensive silence. Torren would occasionally mutter something inaudible to Lorel, and she would mutter something back. But Sagel, Nigel, and Nova walked silently, close together, behind their parents, eyes glazed with shock. The barren trees groaned and shifted, making Sagel's spine shiver and her throat tighten as she listened to their sorrowful songs. Then they were in the Stretch. The needles were fully attached to their healthy branches, and all the trees were covered with snow. Nigel gazed slowly around him, feeling like he would in a dream, where a landscape is familiar and utterly strange at the same time.

Finally, the three children crunched through the snow, after their parents, to their front door.

"When will this end?" Nigel asked Torren as the family sat down in their small living room. Torren sat silently for a minute or two, though to Nigel it felt like a lifetime.

"I don't know," he said, his arm curving around his wife's shoulders.

Nova slipped off to her room to play with her toys. Her young mind had worked to process it all, but play in the present seemed much more appealing. Sagel went to her room and lay down on her bed to try to sort out her thoughts. The wind tapped at the window above her, tempting her to the outdoors. She turned away on to her right side and watched her bedroom door instead.

Chapter 9

Bitter Cold

"Ma, can I go outside?" Nigel asked Lorel as she cleaned up after lunch that day.

Lorel glanced out the window and thought for a moment.

"To do what?" she asked.

"I want to go to the Stretch," Nigel answered quickly. "I just want to see the healthy trees, and then I'll come home."

"I don't have a problem with it, but check with your father first," she said lightly. "And if anyone else is in the Stretch, I want you to come straight home."

"Why? We'd be outside. Don't worry, Ma," Nigel said, walking to the living room where his father read.

"That's my job," Lorel said to herself.

Torren looked up at his son and smiled, "Cabin fever?"

Nigel nodded and sighed as he sank onto the couch next to his father.

"Can I?" Nigel asked.

Torren nodded understandingly.

"But do not go to anyone's house or spend time with anyone," he told Nigel, who was already in the entryway buttoning his coat and pulling on his hat and gloves.

"Thanks, Pa," Nigel smiled, slipping on his boots and stepping out into the fresh chill.

Nigel didn't reflect or worry as he crunched down the road. He hardly even noticed the grizzled trees that ended as he walked into the Stretch. He stopped at the head of it. Walking to the first healthy tree, he dropped to his knees. Nigel crawled under the snow packed branches to the trunk of the tree; the needle covered branches hung low around him, like a protective cocoon. His blue knit cap stuck to something on the trunk of the tree, and when Nigel went to roll over, his hat was pulled off. Rolling back towards the trunk, Nigel smiled at his hat stuck to the brown, grooved bark. Something about it was comical. Nigel pulled at his hat; the sticky sap stretched into a fine thread and then broke. With his hat on his head again, Nigel curled under the tree, not knowing what else to do. He wanted to be somewhere normal, and the Stretch seemed to be the last normal place in Shinken. His usual fear of the Stretch had evaporated.

Nigel pulled off his glove and touched the sap on the tree. It glowed amber on the tip of his finger, though there was too little light to shine through it. He brought it to his nose and breathed in; it smelled of the tree—of health. Without thinking about what he was doing, Nigel brought the sap to his lips, running his tongue through the gooey substance. It was bitter but syrupy and Nigel swallowed on an impulse that he couldn't explain. It felt like a good thing to do.

Elenry paced slowly around her camp. The town meeting had gone well enough. She planned to sort through her supply bag and decide on what spells and droughts she would use to try to treat the sickness. Sitting down with her bag, she noticed Arros approaching her. His massive head lowered to hers and he brushed his nose gently on her cheek.

"Hey boy, how've you be—", Elenry stopped as she ran her hand through Arros's main. It was sticky. She parted the thick, black hair and watched it shine with a silvery sheen.

"What in the name?" Elenry sniffed her sticky fingers and the scent of sap crept up her nostrils, reminding her of her morning tea. Arros pushed his nose into her shoulder gently, and then a little harder. Elenry stood from her bag and turned to her horse curiously. He tossed his head in the direction of the forest.

Surprised at the sap in her horse's mane, because he rarely walked into the forest without her, Elenry laid the blanket over Arros's back, and swung herself up onto his back. Arros was perfumed with sap.

"Show me, Arros," Elenry said, settling into her horse's gait. He snorted with contentment and began a purposeful trot away from their camp and onto the road to town. Arros wanted to pick up the speed, and Elenry let him. Instead of riding into the town center, Arros turned and cantered up the path towards Gwenoth's house. Before the horse stopped, Elenry could feel a new energy around them. Arros slowed to a walk as he entered the Stretch. Elenry sat still on his back as he walked to the far end of the area. Without warning, Arros started to throw his head and rear up off his front legs.

"Arros, what is it?" Elenry asked, leaning and patting his neck to try and calm him. Arros whinnied and snorted strongly. Then, for the first time in his life, Arros reared up onto his back legs, and threw Elenry from his back. The road provided little cushion for her fall.

Arros trotted over to a healthy tree of the Stretch and started to rub his shoulder and neck up against the snow covered branches. *So that explains the sap...* Elenry thought as she stood up and examined herself. She had slid off easily with the blanket under her and she was not injured.

"Whoa! Hey, stop!" a frantic, young voice sounded from beneath the tree. Elenry walked closer and bent down. Under the tree cowered Nigel, his hands over his head to protect himself from the shower of snow and needles. "Nigel! What are you doing here?" Elenry inquired, pulling Arros away from the tree so that Nigel could climb out from under it.

"I was—I was just here to see the trees," Nigel explained, standing up and watching Arros warily.

"He won't hurt you—he was just trying to show me something. Please explain to me what exactly you were doing under the tree," she pressed.

"I wanted to get out of my house, and—and, I dunno, the Stretch just seemed like the best place to go," Nigel said nervously.

"Why the Stretch, Nigel?" Elenry asked, surprised that they had both come to the same place.

"You wouldn't believe me if I told you," Nigel looked down, speaking softly.

"I might, you never know, I just might," Elenry said, mentally willing Nigel to disclose.

"No, you wouldn't," Nigel said again, turning away from Elenry.

Elenry looked at the back of his hat.

"Nigel, what's that on your hat?" Elenry asked, keeping her voice calm.

"Sap. I leaned against the tree and the sap stuck to my hat, I—I even tasted some," he continued. "What's wrong?" he asked, suddenly worried.

"Nothing at all. Nigel, please, you need to tell me what you are doing here, please, I won't be angry," Elenry coaxed.

Nigel sighed, and looked at Elenry, assessing in his own way whether to explain himself. He took a deep breath and began.

"When we got home from the meeting, I just felt like I needed to be here," he said.

Elenry waited patiently for him to continue.

"I had this weird feeling. I didn't even really think about it, I just came here. Is that bad or something?"

"No, Nigel, not at all, and I'm happy you told me," Elenry replied. She stopped and looked at Arros. The sticky patch on his mane shown dully in the pale daylight.

"Nigel! Have you felt sick lately?" Elenry asked abruptly.

"Uh…no, I've felt fine," Nigel answered, fiddling nervously with his gloves.

"Do you ever eat sap in anything? Like in tea, or sprinkled on meat or something?" Elenry asked. Rising above the dark mountains in her mind was a light of realization.

"Yes. My ma freezes it, grinds it up and cooks it with our Churkey meat. She says it spices the flavor," Nigel answered.

"Is that all? Does she give it to you in any other way?"

"Sap tea."

"How often?"

"A few times a week…," Nigel said after a moment's thought.

"Does all your family use it the same way?"

"Yes."

"Has any of your family been sick?"

"No."

"The sap…," Elenry whispered.

"What about it?" Nigel asked.

The Medicine Woman stepped from the road and walked between the trees. She found a place where she could reach a trunk. Nigel was right behind her. With a knife from her belt loop, she stabbed the tree; fresh amber sap seeped out of the wound, clotting like blood.

"Nigel, I have an idea," Elenry said.

"What do you mean?" Nigel asked, looking from Elenry to the wounded tree.

"Now, I want you to go home, get warm, and eat a good dinner tonight," Elenry instructed, placing her hand firmly on his shoulder. "Tell your mom to use sap in whatever she cooks."

"But she usually does."

Elenry smiled, "Good. Tell her to keep doing it."

Without another word, Nigel nodded and started back towards his house.

Turning to Arros, Elenry grinned, "Thank you!" She whispered to him, "You knew all along, you knew, you always knew…," Elenry hugged Arros around the neck, and led him by his reins to the tree that she had maimed. How she wished that she had brought a vial to collect the sap. She dug through her cloak pockets hopefully, pulling out a long, glass tube of herbs. The herbs were for the headaches she sometimes got after she did a particularly intense healing. Fortunately, they were easily replaceable and not essential to her work in Shinken.

Arros watched as she uncorked and emptied the tube into one of her pockets. From the oozing gash, she scooped as much sap as she could.

Before she mounted Arros, Elenry walked from the Stretch to the roadside where a forest of ailing trees unfolded before her. With her knife, she stabbed the wood. The knife delved easily into it as if it were old bread. The bark itself fell away easily to expose naked, ivory skin. Once more she drove the knife into the wood, finding no amber trickle. It was as if she had stabbed a dry bone.

Chapter 10

Vision

Elenry dismounted from Arros, and led him to the front door of a small dwelling. Haykyel's house was not like the others in town. Most of the Shinken dwellings were made of simple, small beige bricks; the roofs laid with tiles. Haykyel's house was made from the regular bricks, but was painted in vibrant colors that displayed the solar system. His door was round, and painted a silvery white, to display the moon, the closest and most important celestial body to Asthekia. His windows were also all circular, to portray the planets like the Earth, and stars like the sun. Elenry couldn't help smiling at the beauty of the house. Elenry wondered why other houses in town weren't like his.

She knocked on the silver door, and waited until it was finally opened. Haykyel stood there looking worn by the recent events. His silver beard was untrimmed, and his shoulder length grey hair was uncombed and tousled. This was only the second time that she had met him. The first time was when he had come to her camp that morning to speak with her before the meeting.

"Elenry, what is it?" he asked, his eyes livening.

"I need to speak with you," Elenry answered calmly.

"Has something happened?" Haykyel asked, his eyes searching nervously.

"Yes. I might have a cure," Elenry said.

His face lit up as his down-turned mouth stretched skyward, "That's wonderful. Wonderful news! Come in, come in and tell me about it," he said, stepping sideways to allow her entry.

Haykyel's house was as interesting on the inside as it was on the outside. Pictures and diagrams of space and planets hung on every possible bit of wall. His living room had five bookshelves and only one seat, so they ended up sitting at his kitchen table.

Elenry began her recount of the events in the Stretch as soon as they were seated. Haykyel listened intently, occasionally stroking his beard thoughtfully.

"But there is no proof?" he asked, after she had fallen silent.

"No, but I wanted to inform you before I go to the clinic and start treating people with it," Elenry said. She could feel his energy tightening.

"Well, please do whatever you feel is best to do," he finally said, resting his hands on the table.

"Thank you, Haykyel," Elenry said softly, "And I know that this is difficult for you."

Haykyel's eyes froze on the table, "I am at loss as to what to do. The people here trust me. They turn to me in times of hardship. In the past I have been able to come up with answers for everything." He paused to take a shuddering breath, "One child has already died—two if you count the boy from Deagial. And here I am at a loss for what to do."

Elenry waited for him to say anything more, and then spoke when he did not.

"You are doing what you can. Supporting me in trying the sap on patients is a good decision. And you handled the meeting this morning marvelously," Elenry conciliated. "The people of this village trust you, and they will continue to trust you so long as you take care of them. They may not trust me, but I can see and feel that they have the utmost trust and respect for you. You are doing everything you can."

After a silence, Haykyel looked Elenry fully in the eyes.

"Please, help us."

Nodding, Elenry said, "I will. Now, I must go to the clinic to discuss this possible treatment with your health personnel."

"Of course, of course. Thank you," Haykyel stood from the table and went to open the door for Elenry.

She swept after him and passed out into the cold.

"And Elenry?"

"Yes?"

"I trust you," he nodded, and closed the door.

Upon returning to the clinic, she found the opportunity that she dreaded but needed. Two more people had fallen ill, and were in the quarantine rooms.

"Oh, there you are," Galah said, "I sent Ava to call for you but you weren't at your camp."

"I was at Haykyel's, discussing a possible cure," Elenry began. "I have reason to think that the sap from the trees in the Stretch will cure this illness. I would like to try it out on the patients."

Galah stood surprised, "What are your reasons for believing it will help?"

"All of my evidence is circumstantial. I know that my horse has led me in the right direction before. I know that Sagel was exposed and has not become ill."

"Is that enough?"

"Nothing is enough until something works. None of us knows what this disease is and we have no other treatment. There are two people in there who are probably going to die if we don't do something. I think we should try."

Galah and Elenry looked into each other's eyes for a long time. Both of them were experienced healers. They had seen death, and they knew how fragile life was. They also knew that doing nothing in this situation was not acceptable.

Galah nodded, "Alright."

One of the sick was a young woman named Leskel; she was twenty three revolutions around the sun. She had come in with her husband shortly after the town meeting. Soni, her husband, stood on the far side of her bed, his face almost entirely obscured by a mask. Her symptoms were similar to Gwenoth's and Ebin's, but much milder. Her face was chalky yellow and her lips dried and cracked, like Gwenoth's and Ebin's before they died. But not so apparent was the slight slurring of her speech as she slowly narrated the details of her activities before her first symptoms appeared. Elenry noticed that she was having to exert focus to hear the young woman's words clearly.

Elenry raised a hand and stopped the girl's talking. Turning to Galah, she asked, "Was her speech slurred when she first came in?"

"Actually, I hadn't noticed."

"Please go to the other patient, talk to him, and listen for the slur, then come back."

Galah turned without a word and left the room.

Elenry returned her attention to Leskel, who had slumped

back flat on the bed. Even the small amount of talking she had done had worn her out. Elenry examined her entire body closely. The young woman's finger nails had taken on a yellow tint, and were unnaturally chipped and cracked.

Galah returned to Leskel's bedside and spoke to Elenry, "He is not as weak as Leskel, but his speech is slurred and he has trouble finding the right words."

Elenry acknowledged the information with a nod. She took the tube of sap out of her pocket. With a sterile spoon provided by Galah, Elenry fed the woman a spoonful of sap. Leskel gagged and struggled to swallow, but was able to hold it down with coaxing from Elenry and her husband.

The Medicine Woman stoppered the tube and returned it to her pocket. She then looked at Soni. She spoke quietly, "I know that the only place you want to be in the world now is by your wife's side."

Soni shifted uncomfortably and nodded.

Elenry continued, "However, we know almost nothing about this disease. We do not even know if these face masks can prevent contagion. Do you understand what I'm saying?"

Soni looked at Elenry without moving.

"Do you and your wife have children?" Elenry asked.

Soni nodded.

"If your wife doesn't make it, they're going to need you. The best place for you now is at home, not in this room. Do you understand?"

Soni was quiet for a long time. He put his hand on his wife's shoulder, careful not to touch her skin.

"You're going to be fine, okay?" he whispered.

Leskel smiled weakly at her husband and nodded.

He wiped away a tear with the back of one hand, and then walked slowly out of the room. Elenry and Galah left for the other patient's room.

Unfortunately, the other patient wasn't quite so easily dealt with. He was an older man by the name of Dean Folge, and was too frightened to admit he was really sick. He denied this, denied that—he said the only reason he was there was because his wife had made him come to the clinic. Elenry listened to him and assured him that his wife had done the best thing for him. He might have no more than one of the common flus that comes with the change of season. But he also might have something more serious. She and the clinic nurses would do all that they could for him.

Upon examination, she found that he had a fever, and that his skin had a moldy yellow tinge to it. Elenry treated him with herbs for the fever. They were a combination of concentrated tutfer grass oil, and Nigrifluy, a plant that grows in Asthekia's oceans. After crushing the herbs, she soaked them in hot water, and then made the man chew on them. When he had chewed the herbs for a few minutes, she gave him a spoonful of sap.

Before she returned to her camp that evening, Elenry took the nurses up to the Stretch to collect jarfuls of sap from the hearty trees. Galah was to give each patient a spoonful of sap every four hours.

Arros must have gone to the Stretch while she was in the clinic, for when Elenry swung herself up onto him, the smell of sap engulfed her once again. They trotted up the road and into camp, where Elenry started a fire. As her food was cooking, she packed up her camp. She was quite clear that the only safe place for her and Arros to stay was in the Stretch. After finishing a small meal, and feeding and watering Arros, she loaded her gear on his back and climbed on. They were soon at the Stretch, where she began looking for a suitable campsite.

"Arros, thank you," Elenry said as she warmed her hands by the fire in her new camp. Arros, more comfortable and relaxed, lay down near Elenry, and rolled onto his back like an enormous dog. He rolled around a little, careful not to kick Elenry, and then stood up again, shaking and snorting contentedly.

Elenry sat on her stool and gazed into the fire, deliberately breathing in deeply the aroma of the live trees around her. A familiar taste rose in Elenry's mouth. It was an acidic taste that burned her throat. The light of the fire started to dance in and out, and then dissolved into a black expanse. Elenry fell back into the snow.

She was hovering over Mt. Aarotte as she looked down on Shinken. A powerful energy was pulling her so that she had no choice but to go where it took her. She expected to swoop into Shinken, but she did not. Instead, she continued to float over the mountain. The scene changed and she was gazing down on forest. Her heart drummed in her ears when she began plummeting towards the dark green expanse. The treetops grew larger and more defined as the forest threatened to swallow her.

Then, she was standing in a forest. Enormous trees towered around a clearing of small huts. Light from the dwellings' windows soaked her face and washed through her vision until she was floating in a bright, white space. It was void except for a low voice that started indistinctly and then became clearer as it repeated itself.

"It's your time, Elenry. It's Shinken's time. They need it,

and you can get it for them. Do this for them. Come here for them…," it faded. There was nothing for a long time but a soft, silent, swirling darkness and then Elenry found herself lying in the snow beside her fire. The strong taste had faded, only to be replaced by excitement and a thumping headache. Arros stood near her, watching her intently, his ears swiveling backwards and forwards to detect any danger.

For now, she decided to meditate, but first she took some of the pain reliever form her pocket. Having chewed and swallowed it with water, she settled again on her stump. This was her way to understand and learn from her visions. In her meditation, she saw various snippets of her vision. All the time she mediated, she heard the same message over and over again: *It's your time, Elenry. It's Shinken's time. They need it, and you can get it for them. Do this for them. Come here for them….*

Instead of letting her mind jump to any conclusions, Elenry used her imagination to relive each part of her vision. In truth, she did not know what the vision or the voice had meant. She was sure that she had experienced something to do with the disease, but she could not reach any clear understanding about what the connection was. Her past experience told her that she had not heard the last of that voice. All she could do now was hope that the sap had had some kind of positive and consistent effect on her two patients.

Elenry awoke to the hush of morning. It had turned colder that night. She had no idea how long she had slept. Elenry's breath billowed from her mouth in puffs of white condensation. She was rested, but her head still throbbed a little from the last night's vision. Massaging her head and chanting softly, she was able to bring the throbbing down to a subtle pulse. Fortunately, her dreams had taken care of the loose strings that had hung in her mind after the vision. She had a plan.

After dressing in her regular apparel, she climbed out of her tent. Medicine People never wear anything elegant, no matter what the occasion. It is their custom to be modest in both manner and dress. Elenry liked to wear a simple black shirt with silver thread sewn into the thick fabric around the collar. She wore a long black skirt with the same silver zigzag pattern around the hem. This hooded robe was her means of warmth on her long rides through the mountains. Her dark, flowing hair was tied up in a low pony tail with two strands of hair tied from the front to the back of her head.

Arros was sleeping with his side leaning slightly against the tent, and Elenry spoke to him gently, easing him slowly out of sleep. The air was icy, and the sun was just rising up from behind Mt. Aarotte into the translucent, pale blue sky. Elenry watched the rays of morning creep up and spill over the snow capped mountains. Arros stretched and shook himself awake, and then stamped on the frozen ground. Elenry brought him food and water.

Elenry relied on the sun and moon to tell her what time of day it was. The sun and the moon were just coming up from their opposite positions on the horizon; that meant it was about seven in the morning.

She brushed Arros's mane and tail with his special brush that she carried in her travel bag. Arros lived for his brushing sessions. He loved the soft bristles of the brush against his skin. He especially enjoyed it in the blistering heat of summer, when the Gorder flies were out and nibbling on large mammals like Arros.

A small breakfast and a cup of sap tea later, she was ready to brave the clinic and her patients. No one had come to summon her during the night, so she had reason to think that no emergencies had taken place.

Once they left the Stretch, Arros was edgy and stayed as centered on the road as possible, away from the eerie trees that stood twisted, creaking and moaning, on both sides of the road. The clinic was brightly lit and looked almost merry. Elenry dismounted, dropped Arros's reins to the ground, and took her mask out of her bag. With her mask tied over her oval, angular face and her medicine bad hung from her shoulder, she walked into the clinic.

"Good morning Galah," Elenry greeted the nurse, who was seated behind the desk.

"A good morning it is," Galah agreed, her eyes bright and her hands moving.

"What is it?" Elenry asked, smiling as Galah grinned at her.

"They've gotten better—not one hundred percent, but neither one of them has a fever, and their appetites have improved."

Though this was wonderful news, Elenry could not help feel a slight disappointment that they were not completely well, "That's good news," Elenry replied. "How long have they been like that?"

"Both of their fevers cleared up last night, after the second dose of sap. This morning they were both hungry enough for a full bowl of porridge and sap, but nothing has changed since then."

"I want to see both of them," Elenry said, making her way down the hall and into the recovery room. Galah followed close behind.

Leskel lay calmly in her bed. Elenry said nothing as she walked to the head of the bed. The patient watched her. The Medicine Woman spoke quietly, "Please lie still and breathe evenly." Elenry closed her eyes, took several deep breaths, and then passed both of her hands, palms down, from the top of Leskel's head to the bottoms of her feet. At the foot of the bed, Elenry stood perfectly still, her hands suspended in the air, and her eyes still closed. Slowly, she lowered her arms and shook her hands gently away from her body. She then opened her eyes and stepped to the side of the bed.

"How are you feeling?" Elenry asked.

"Better."

"Have you experienced any new symptoms since you came in yesterday?"

"No. Actually, my fever went away."

"Yes, so I've heard."

"Can my family visit?"

"I'm sorry, Leskel. Not yet."

Leskel nodded and sank deeper into her pillows.

Elenry stood by as Galah gave Leskel her next dose of sap.

Dean was snoozing lightly but woke as soon as Elenry shut the door behind her. Neither patient had lost their yellow hue.

"How are you feeling, Dean."

"I feel better. Much better. When can I go home?"

"When you don't look like a faded autumn leaf."

"What are you talking about?"

Elenry took a small mirror from her bag and handed it to Dean. His wrinkled hand reached for the mirror and brought it slowly before his face. For a moment he just stared into the little reflection. The skin around his eyes crinkled and sagged as he lowered the mirror and handed it back to Elenry.

Dean looked at Elenry, "What is it?"

"We don't know. That's why you're not going home."

The old man turned to the window, his jaw clenching. He drew a shuddering breath as a tear slid down his cheek. "I've never been sick a day in my life."

After Galah had given Dean his sap, she and Elenry returned to the front room.

"Galah, I must go to Haykyel. I believe we are on to something, but we need to have a village meeting so I can keep everyone informed. We also need to help everyone focus on prevention and cure, not on fear."

"I agree, but I have a question."

Elenry stood quietly, radiating positive energy to the nurse.

"How can you be sure that it is really the sap that is keeping them stable?"

Elenry told Galah about the previous night's vision. Galah stood in cautious awe of the Medicine Woman. "I do hope that whatever is guiding you knows what it is doing."

"It's guiding everything, Galah. It *is* everything. It is energy," Elenry explained. "I will see you soon, and send for me if there is any significant change in their conditions."

The solar system enchanted her while she waited for Haykyel to answer her knock at his door.

"Hello," he smiled warmly, wearing a comfortable pair of pants and his indoor robe. "What's the news?"

Elenry wasted no time, but told him all about what had happened in her vision and with her patients. She also told him her plan.

"This means that it is a stabilizer. A preventative. Nigel Bleudry—the boy I found in the Stretch—his mother cooks with sap. Sagel Bleudry, his older sister, was in close contact with Ebin, and she did not fall ill. We need to call a town meeting and tell them about this development," Elenry finished, her eyes bright.

"Are you sure? Are you really sure that this is what you want to do?"

"Yes, I'm sure."

There was a loud knock at the door. Haykyel stepped briskly and opened it to Ava, who stood tensely. "Elenry," she said, after nodding to Haykyel, "two more villagers have come in with the disease."

Elenry told Ava, "Tell Galah I have the news, and go back and care for the patients."

Ava nodded, turned, and walked back down the road. Haykyel closed the door and stood.

Haykyel nodded a few times, processing the new information, "Give me ten minutes. You go to the town hall, and I will get dressed and be there right after you."

Chapter 11

Bitter Mule

Haykyel was in a double bind. The people of Shinken trusted him, but they did not altogether trust Elenry. He could not ignore her vision, and her knowledge, for she was a Medicine Woman, and had powers and knowledge that no person in Shinken had, including himself. And now, two more cases. Setting aside his qualms, he climbed into his car and drove to the Village Hall to sound the horn for a meeting.

Nigel had told his family everything that had happened in the Stretch. Lorel took Elenry's advice to heart and made Churkey and vegetable soup with sap in the broth, sap soaked biscuits, and sap and berry cider. On the night of Nigel's incident, Sagel and Nigel had stayed up talking about it and drawing their own conclusions. Before going to bed, Sagel decided that she would go see Daniel the next day. Sagel wished that she had known that Nigel had gone out, for she would have gone with him. It was not pleasant to be ignorant in the midst of all this. That night she kept herself up worrying about what all was going on and how she could not do anything about it. *But if I don't know what's* *going on, then I don't need to worry about fixing it. Something will happen, when it happens...*she thought as she drifted towards sleep. A quiet smile crept across her face as she realized that she could not do anything more at that point.

The next day Nigel drew his dreams and Nova played in her room most of the morning. Sagel argued with her parents in the kitchen.

"Why can't I go see him? We aren't sick!" Sagel griped.

"We don't want to take any chances," Lorel replied, sitting across from Sagel at the kitchen table. Torren sat beside his daughter.

"Let us get some more information, Sage," Torren said. "Let things calm down a bit before you go and possibly expo—do you hear that?"

"Yeah, it's the Horn of the Village Hall," Sagel said, running to the door. "It's the emergency call." Sagel said. The horn was blowing in short high blasts; this was the special sound for emergency or danger. Torren stood from the table, motioning for his wife and daughter to follow him.

"Children, get in the car now, we need to get into town," Torren said, and Sagel and Nigel hurried to get ready.

"Nova! Hurry out here now!" Lorel called, and Nova came trotting out.

"What is it, Ma? What is that noise?" Nova asked, walking to her mother.

"It's alright, it's just the meeting horn. Get your coat on and get in the car," Lorel said, as she led her youngest daughter out into the living room to get her outerwear on.

Before Torren had even started the car, his children had begun throwing questions at him and Lorel.

"What if it's the Shadow Shades?" Nova asked, her voice almost a whisper.

"There's no such thing as Shadow Shades, Nova. People only made those up to scare children and make them stay in at night so they wouldn't get lost," Torren said, as he pulled up in front of the hall.

The Bleudrys clambered out of the vehicle and joined the nervous crowd jostling through the door into the hall. There was not much conversation as the villagers quickly found seats.

As Elenry walked to the front of the hall, an expectant silence washed through the crowd.

"Hello, people of Shinken," she started. A handful of people returned her hello.

"You have been called here today to be given information, and for me to make a proposal as to what to do about the illness plaguing this town"

"Have you found a cure?" shouted a man from the back of the hall.

"I believe I have found a preventative, not a cure."

The villagers turned to each other in excited conversation. Elenry let the energy swirl as she focused on bringing the entire field of energy in the room into harmony with her attention. Gradually, heads turned back towards Elenry and silence took over once more.

"There are now four cases in the clinic. Their conditions are stable. We do not know if we can cure them. But I am sure that we can prevent more cases. Now, before I explain what the prevention is, I am going to give you some background information to support my decisions," Elenry continued, hoping the interruptions would be few.

"When young Gwenoth fell sick and her parents called for me, I assumed that it was only a temporary illness that would be cured with bed rest and liquids—nothing too serious. But, as you all know, it proved to be much more serious. Then the disease started to spread, and two more from Shinken fell ill, along with the boy from Deagial. The conditions of the two Shinken villagers continued to worsen until I gave them both the same dosage of sap derived from a healthy tree in the Stretch. Both of them stabilized. They are under the care of the nurses at the clinic, where we have observed noticeable improvements in both of them."

Frustration and fear overcame the audience: "Then what good is it? What trees would we get it from? We need a working cure," a volley of questions and assertions took aim at the Medicine Woman. Refocusing the energy field, Elenry let the flood of talk run dry before she spoke.

"Sap can be used as a preventative. However, the only trees that we will be able to take sap from are those that grow in the Stretch," Elenry paused. "The other trees are sick, and do not yield sap. I don't know why the Stretch is protected, but something about the energy and atmosphere differs from the rest of the forest. It is charged with a powerful energy similar to the energy that I experienced in a vision last night."

The faces of the audience members displayed a mixture of shock, wonder, trust, distrust, and fear as she described her vision to them. A static hush settled upon the crowd when Elenry stopped speaking.

"Where is the forest and how will we get the cure?" Nigel spoke up. Elenry smiled at him, her spirits lightened marginally.

"Thank you, Nigel Bleudry," Elenry said. "I do not know how far the forest is from Shinken, but if we cannot retrieve the cure from that forest, the village will eventually fall to the illness. Even though our sap is a preventative, there is no knowing how long your bodies can hold off the illness."

"How do you plan to find the cure and bring it back here?" demanded a woman in the middle of the hall.

"It must be found as soon as possible. I will need to leave Shinken to find it and bring it back, but I know that it is on the other side of the mountain, and a little farther."

"How much farther?" someone chimed in.

"There is no telling, but no matter how far it is, at this point, we do not have any other choice," Elenry finished.

"But how do we know that you will not leave Shinken only never to return, to trick us into letting you go?" the same woman asked. Many other people nodded their agreement.

"First, I am a Medicine Woman, not a coward. Second, you have asked me to help, and I am bound by my vows and my calling to help you. Finally, if I had wished to desert you, I would have done it long ago, before things got this bad!" Elenry replied, her eyes bright and her strong gaze sweeping the crowd.

"How do we know you aren't lying to us? What if you leave Shinken only to run and abandon this mess?" Leskel's husband asked. His voice was barely controlled, though Elenry could not be sure whether he was about to sob or scream.

"Villagers of Shinken, hear me as I say this…I am here to heal. That is my job, my responsibility, and my life work as a Medicine Woman. I know that trust is hard to muster toward a stranger, but I implore you to try," as Elenry spoke, her voice grew louder, the lights flickered, and the audience sat back in awe.

"If you need more direct proof, would you like me to levitate something, conjure a potion, or burst something?" On the word burst, a light in the back corner of the hall exploded with a crack. Many screamed in shock. Elenry sweated as a solid pounding rose in her temples.

"I am sorry. I am sorry that you don't trust me, but if you continue to distrust me, I will have a very difficult job saving your lives. I need your positive energy for you to help yourselves and me." Elenry paused and stepped away from the center of the room. She looked at Haykyel and said, "Haykyel?"

Silence grasped the audience. Elenry watched them as they seemed to draw closer together into one confused entity.

Haykyel walked slowly to the center of the room. He raised both hands and then lowered them slowly to his sides. "An outsider in a struggling village has a difficult position. I don't expect you to welcome her with open arms, but members of our village, including me, called her here, and I will do everything I can to fulfill my summoning. I need you to work with me, and I need you to accept her."

A hand rose towards the back of the hall; it was timid and wavering. Haykyel nodded at the person to begin speaking.

"Don't get me wrong, I do trust her, but, how is she going to get the cure back to the village?" It was a woman who spoke, her voice hushed.

Haykyel raised his arm to Elenry, bringing her to his side.

She nodded her head to the crowd, breathed deeply, and then answered, "I won't be going alone. Two of you will need to go with me—two strong, able bodied and able minded people will need to assist me. Together we will bring the cure back to Shinken. I will require that whoever wants to go prove their capabilities to me. I will set the tasks and I, and only I, will make the final decision."

The crowd drew back in their seats and was completely silent. Slowly, people began to mutter to each other. Silence rose and fell with the muttering. There were no outbursts. The Medicine Woman had expected more resistance and distrust, and she was relieved at the response. Sagel felt Dan tense next to her; she turned to him, but looked away from his gaze before he could make eye contact.

"I cannot force anyone to come with me. Two of you will have to volunteer, but let me make this clear—if no one volunteers, then I honestly don't know what will happen," Elenry finished. "There is no upper age limit, but there is a lower age limit," Elenry continued. Sagel heard Nigel holding his breath, waiting for Elenry to reveal the age to the audience.

"Ten years old is the lower limit. Anyone ten or younger cannot go, as they would be too small and too immature to carry such a burden."

The hush that had held the crowd burned away as they roared into life. "That's too young! No good parent would let a ten year old go," a man said, bolstered by the crowd's rumbling agreement.

"I am aware that ten years old is very young, but in my visions I saw myself walking with two people. These two people were small. A voice said this: 'Shinken, young or old, brave and bold, Shinken'. I have learned, as a Medicine Woman, to trust my visions and insights."

The chatter died away.

"If any of you decide that you want to accompany me, then you will need to come and talk to me at my camp in the Stretch, but please, make haste, we will need to embark as soon as possible," Elenry breathed out, and breathed in again. "I do not know exactly where the forest that I search for is, but I know that it is somewhere on the other side of this mountain. I will find it with the help of two of you."

A chill crept into the room and roused the people in their seats; making them restless in the silence that followed Elenry's speech.

"Sagel, what if we went? We've always wanted to go to the other side of the mountain," Daniel whispered to Sagel as everyone started to leave the hall.

"I know you want to go, Dan," Sagel whispered back as they merged with the crowd going out through the door, "and I would too, but our parents would never let us," she finished, buttoning her coat against the icy chill as they walked down the steps onto the road. Their two families were standing a little ways away, talking to each other.

"Both of us are old enough, and we're physically able, and mentally able. We proved that to everyone when we brought back Ebin," Dan continued, glancing around to make sure no one was listening in.

"You don't think it's too dangerous?" Sagel pressed him. Her heart tugged at her voice.

"Sagel, we'd be with Elenry. We wouldn't go without her."

"Even if we decided to go, how do you expect our parents to ag-," Sagel was cut off.

"Sagel! There you are," said Torren. Sagel glanced at Daniel, and then looked back to her father.

"Can I go over to Dan's house for a while? I'll be home for dinner," Sagel asked. Torren looked at Lorel who joined them with Nigel and Nova; she nodded and shrugged.

"If his parents are okay with it, but you can't stay over the time limit," Torren answered, his brow pinched in reluctance.

"She's always welcome in our house, Torren, and Daniel can walk her home when the time is up," said Louise, stepping up beside her son.

"Thank you, Louise, and you know Dan's welcome over any time as well," Lorel said to Louise. "Please don't be too late, Sagel."

"I won't," she said, waving to her family.

Dan grinned at Sagel, "Let's go, it's cold out here."

"How have you been, Sagel?" asked Dan's father, Michael, pleasantly.

"I've been good," Sagel replied, realizing that despite the drama of the past few days, she was good. Her whole family was healthy, as were her friends. She said a silent thank you to the cosmos as they walked down the main street towards Daniel's house.

Wind and snow gusted past the houses and around the street as Daniel and Sagel entered the house after his parents. Michael bustled about for a bit and then left to go back to work. He was an environmental researcher who specialized in comparing Asthekian land masses to Earth land masses. He worked in a small cabin on the edge of town where he collected samples from around the area and sent them to Starling City to be studied. Three other people from town worked with him. Dan's mother also returned to work, though hers was outside shoveling snow from the path. The two children went straight to Daniel's room, and took their regular seats on his floor.

"I think we should go," was the first thing out of Daniel's mouth.

"But what are the chances she is going to let us go with her?' Sagel shot back quickly.

"You always make things sound so difficult!" Daniel cried.

"Because it *is* difficult. Going down the creek with snow on the rocks was difficult, but we did it. I don't make it sound difficult because I don't want to do it," Sagel threw her hands into the air. "What if we got hurt, or couldn't find the cure, or got lost?!"

"We won't get lost! Elenry is a Medicine Woman! She is a powerful being, she wouldn't let harm come to us," Daniel answered, his voice becoming quieter and firmer.

"Okay, I agree with all that, but what about our parents—how can you possibly think our parents would let us accompany her?" Sagel asked, sure that this would stump Dan.

"We don't tell them. It's simple. Tomorrow, we'll go and see her, and if she already has two people, then we'll go home, no more said. If not, we'll tell her that we want to go," Daniel finished, grinning confidently at Sagel.

"What if I decided that I don't want to go?" Sagel tested.

"Then I would think that you were not the Sagel I know. How could you not want to go?"

Sagel looked at Daniel for a long time. She wanted to go, and she didn't. Part of her could see the most amazing adventure of their lives. But another part could see being without her family on a trip that could lead nowhere. She trusted the Medicine Woman, but Elenry herself had said she didn't know exactly where the forest was. Sagel voiced her next thought, "What if Elenry can't find the forest?"

"Then it would still have been an awesome adventure. What if we hadn't found Ebin? We still would have had a great time at the creek."

"I know that. But this is different."

"How is it different?"

"This is bigger. And a lot more dangerous."

"Well, it's a good thing we've got a Medicine Woman to guide us. How about if I go see Elenry by myself," Daniel asked after a moment of thought.

"You can't go by yourself!" Sagel said, caught between decisions.

"Then you have to go! Don't you want to go? Have a real adventure for once, not just a silly game we play down by the stream?" Dan exclaimed.

Sagel sighed, as much as she secretly yearned for a real adventure, an excuse to get out and about, but she was scared.

"Dan, you know I love a good adventure as much as you do, but, but I'm scared," Sagel said.

"I know Sage, I am too, but if we don't take this chance, we'll be waiting around here getting sick and watching other people get sick," Dan said.

"We won't get sick. We'll just take the preventative measures and the sap!" Sagel pushed, though not as vehemently as before.

"But Elenry said she didn't know how long the sap would work. It's not a cure—we need a cure. I told you, we just go, and test our options. If she's got two people already, we'll go home, and forget about it. If not, we'll prove ourselves worthy to her, and our parents can't force us to stay back if the Medicine Woman decides that we are the two people who can bring the cure back to Shinken!" Dan concluded.

Sagel looked at the floor in exasperation. Though she had always wished for an extraordinary adventure, now that a possible opportunity had presented itself, she wanted nothing more than to curl up in her bed. Still, if she and Daniel could prove them-selves worthy, then they could make the trip. They might even be able to bring back the cure. That could save her and Daniel's families. And what if no one else chose to go? Hot ambivalence stewed in her.

"But what about the road trip? That's an adventure!" Sagel threw out in desperation.

"Sagel, that was just an idea. A silly idea because I was bored since school let out," Dan said, blushing slightly. "Besides, we can't even leave the mountain at this point!"

"What about school?" Sagel said.

"People are getting sick and dying. We don't need school, Sagel, we need a cure!" Dan cried.

"I don't want to lie to my parents," Sagel said.

"Chances are we won't get chosen to go, so we can just go and see first," Daniel explained fervently. "And if Elenry decides that we are qualified to go, then our parents will have to let us go for the good of the village."

Sagel thought back to all of those times when she and Daniel had traipsed around the village and run along the side of the stream, hoping for something out of the ordinary. She remem-bered the instances when she had had insights, and understood things without being told about them. Maybe they really were fit to go. Ebin's death had put things in perspective. Reality was not always predictable, and was sometimes frightening.

"Okay. Okay, we can go and see," she paused, raising her eye-brow and smiling as Daniel's face lit up, "what Elenry wants us to do, and if she'll even take us. But Dan...I'm scared."

"That's okay. I'm scared too, but we'll regret it if we stay be-cause we'll just be living in a scared village with other scared and sick people. If we go with Elenry then we can actually do something for our own village."

Sagel hadn't thought about it like that. "I see your point."

"Tomorrow then, we'll meet in the Stretch?" Dan asked hopefully.

"Yeah, but what time?" Sagel countered, wanting to meet earlier, so she didn't have to wait and worry as long, "What about eight?"

"Eight? Sagel, that will look a tad suspicious if we're up that early," Dan said. When out of school, he liked to sleep in to at least nine.

"Yes, eight. What if two other people decided to go at half past eight, and beat us to the chance? Besides, we'll just tell our parents that we're going down to the brook early to pick Nuntrefurs before the other kids can get them," Sagel offered. Daniel considered, and then nodded in agreement.

Nuntrefurs are a kind of fungus that grows much like a plant, but grow from the underside of rocks. They are approximately the size of an egg, and are white with black speckles. They grow all year round, unlike most plants, and, after they have dried, they can be used to paint on, to crush up to make paints, or to throw at things. Shinken children love to paint them with vibrant colors and trade them among themselves. If she painted good enough designs, sometimes Sagel's father would offer to sell them along with his pottery. They were usually sold for three white rocks each, depending on their quality.

Thinking about the Nuntrefurs, Sagel realized that there were others in the village besides her family that she really wanted to protect. Sagel's closest female friend was named Hayden Mara, a beautiful girl with skin as rich as the night itself. Her voice was deep and slow. Hayden and her family were from the southern most country in Asthekia, called Maradiahn. Many different races of Asthekians dwell their, people of light skin, and people of dark skin. Unlike on Earth, there has never been any racial divide or discrimination on Asthekia. Hayden was considered one of the best child painters in the village, and some of the kids from school actually paid her for her work. Sagel couldn't imagine how sad she would be if Hayden got the illness and died. With all the troubling thoughts swirling in her head, Sagel longed for a distraction.

"Dan, how is your father's horse doing?" Sagel asked.

"He's good, do you want to go out and see him?" Dan asked.

"Yes. Let's get outside."

Dan's father was one of the few who owned a horse in Shinken. About ten minutes out of town was a community stable, where anyone could keep a horse. There were currently only four horses at the stable. Two belonged to the Studiar family, who had famous relatives who bred Asthekian horses. Their two horses were a brother and sister pair, and were considered by the villagers to be the most beautiful horses on the mountain. They were what the Asthekians called Morider Horses. They were both sixteen hands high, according to Earth standards, though the Asthekians do not measure their horses. Both were chestnuts, whose coats gleamed in the sun, and whose manes were a sandy blonde, and as soft as a moss-covered forest floor. Their names were Ola and Alo.

Daniel's family horse was a dapple grey gelding named Gordon. He was a riding horse that was good tempered and easy to handle. The fourth horse in the stable was a mare, an old work pony that belonged to Galah; she was almost eighteen years old.

Her name was Balan. Apart from the four horses that lived in the stable, there was also a small Asthekian mule. Unlike Earth mules, Asthekian mules are no bigger than a medium sized pony. Other than size, there are no differences. This particular Asthekian mule was named Wisle. Wisle belonged to no one in particular, for his former owner had died of old age. Now, Wisle belonged to the community, but had become barn-sour and crotchety. If another horse came close enough, he bit it, particularly Gordon, for he knew that the even-tempered grey would not bite him back.

Sagel and Daniel put on their coats and boots and started down the road. Louise approved their visit to the horses and told Daniel to walk Sagel home afterwards and then return for dinner. The wind picked up as they were walking down the road. Both of them stopped and smelled the air.

"It's going to get colder," Sagel commented.

"How do you know?" Daniel wondered, drawing in a deep breath of icy air.

"I can smell it."

They tramped along the snow washed path.

"What do you think Elenry has in mind to prove people worthy?" Sagel wondered aloud.

"I don't know, maybe she'll have us go and get some invisible herb, and only worthy people will be able to see it," Daniel joked. "She is, after all, a Medicine Woman."

"Yeah, but invisible herbs?" Sagel laughed. The road leading to the stable was flat and winding. It wound through a forest where the trees were spaced out. The snow that caked the branches made the trees seem like frosted candy sticks despite their disease.

"Will we ride Gordon?" Sagel asked.

"Yeah, if he's well enough to ride," Daniel answered.

Dan's father had stayed up for nights and nights with the horse when the wound became infected with bacteria. Gordon's leg had healed and Daniel's father had ridden him enough to assure that his limp was gone, much to Daniel's relief.

Sagel could smell the sweet and pungent scent of horses as they approached the stable. Dan ran ahead a few steps as Sagel jogged along beside him.

"What's the rush?' she asked.

"Nothing, we're just really close," Dan answered.

They ended up racing and laughing up the road until they could see the stable ahead. Kicking snow up as they ran, they both sped up. Dan was in the lead, but Sagel put her long legs to use. She pumped her legs faster, and bent her head down; she was gaining on him. She was only an arms reach behind him, and they were both flying. Dan turned onto the small road leading to the front of the building. Sagel turned too, almost slipping on an icy patch. Dan ran up to the door, Sagel right behind him. Sagel leaped forward and both of their hands touched the wood of the door at the same time.

"I won!" Sagel cried.

"Oh, c'mon, I won. I was watching—you touched the door a second after I did. Sorry, Sage," Dan laughed.

"Then we both won!"

They bantered playfully as they slid the wide door to the side, walking into the warmth of the small barn. The stable's layout was similar to that of barns on Earth, with a high ceiling, sliding doors, and individual stalls for each animal. There were six stalls, but only five were in use. The horses and mule raised their heads when the two children came in. Gordon was in the first stall on the right, and he snorted happily when Dan went up to him.

"Hey Gordon, how're you doing, boy?" Dan cooed, kissing the horse's nose.

"He's beautiful, Dan. I haven't seen him for a while," Sagel said, walking up to Gordon and letting him sniff her hand. "Is he well enough to ride?"

"Yes, he looks fine, and he's not limping anymore," Dan said, opening the gate of Gordon's stall. Dan bent down and examined Gordon's legs. They all looked fine, even the previously injured one. His father had already removed the bandage, and the wound could hardly be seen. While Dan tended to Gordon, Sagel walked down the line of stalls to the end. She patted the noses of Ola and Alo. They had matching red blankets draped over their strong backs. The old work pony, Balan, was dozing with her side leaning up against the back of her stall. All of the horses had fresh hay in their feeding troughs and their water buckets were full. Someone had come here shortly before them. Sagel stood at the last stall, which held Wisle.

Sagel kissed to Wisle, who emerged slowly from his post at the back of the stall. His long grey nose could be seen first. He sniffed at the air around Sagel, not yet trusting her presence. Sagel reached her hand into the stall, assuring Wisle that she was not a threat. Daniel approached quietly behind Sagel with Gordon on a lead rope. Wisle startled at the other horse's presence and backed away snorting. Sagel turned to Dan and shrugged.

"Wanna ride?" Dan asked smiling.

"We only have one horse," Sagel said, "and I don't think Gordon could bear two of us."

"Sure he can," Daniel assured her. "It's not like he broke a bone."

Dan smiled and handed the lead rope to Sagel. Sagel handed it right back.

"Dan, you ride him first, he's your horse. Besides, I'm not so good on horses," Sagel said.

"I know, I just wanted you to lead him out and saddle him up for me," Dan laughed, pushing Sagel playfully.

"Right," she laughed, taking Gordon's rope. Sagel led Gordon out into the front of the barn and put the rope up over his neck as Dan came struggling out carrying the saddle and bridle. Gordon's saddle was thick, black cloth that draped down his grey back. A silvery print was sewn in, and swirls spun themselves around the edges of the fabric. Sagel marveled at how royal he looked all tacked up, and forgot that she was riding, too. Daniel had to climb down to give her a boost up before climbing back on himself.

Dan took off trotting down the road, making Sagel lose her balance momentarily and grab his shoulders to steady herself.

"Sorry about that," he said.

"No worries," she said, trying to relax into Gordon's gait.

Snow glimmered in the sun's winter light. Instead of taking the stable road all the way back into town, Dan turned Gordon off left towards the forest. The trees here also sagged and twist-ed, much like the ones in town, but determined snow still hung to their wilting branches. Gordon stood tall when he was ridden, and his gaits were all smooth. Dan picked up the pace to a quicker trot as they started down a snowy path. The trees on either side were leafless and iced with snow. In summer, the path was lined with large black and white rocks that the village children gathered from the river side. But since the snow covered them up once it fell, the children, including Sagel and Dan, hung small pieces of natural crystal from the trees above the snowy path. On sunnier days, the sun would shine through the naked branches and catch the rocks, shining rainbow patches across the glimmering snow. Unfortunately for Sagel and Dan, it was not a very sunny day, and the rocks merely swayed and tinkled as they bumped up against one another. They rode in silence for another ten minutes and then slowed to walk through the denser trees. Sagel's spirit was light as they rode into a small clearing.

"We should've brought a snack," Dan said, dismounting from Gordon upon reaching the center of the clearing.

"That would've been nice," Sagel said, noticing that her hands were beginning to get cold, even with her gloves on. She slid off Gordon's back. At first she wobbled as her legs readjusted to standing.

"How far away from the road are we?" Sagel wondered aloud.

"About, half a mile or so," Dan said. He knew the mountain well in this area, and wasn't likely to get lost or lose track of time or distance. "We should probably turn around here, so I can be back for dinner."

"Dan?" She began.

"Yeah?" He answered.

"We should tell our parents," she said.

Dan didn't say anything. Instead, he stroked Gordon on the nose; she could tell he was measuring it all in his mind. Finally, he nodded in agreement.

"I was thinking about that, too. We may as well, even if we do get accepted by Elenry, they might still say no. We might as well get told no now, rather than go through her tests only to find out that we can't even go," Dan finished, nodding again.

"I still want to do it, I just don't want to lie," Sagel said finally.

"I know, Sagel, it's the better way to go about this. Let's go and talk to our parents together. We can go to your parents first," Dan said. "Why don't you ride Gordon back?"

"Dan, we need to decide when we're going to talk to them."

"Well, what do you think?"

"I think today is too soon. Everyone is still dealing with Elenry's information. It's too soon."

"Yeah—okay, I guess I agree with that. Are you sure you can wait a night?"

Sagel looked at Dan. She realized how well he knew her, how hard it was for her to put off something that she knew she wanted to do. "I'll try."

"Good. We'll do this together."

Sagel smiled with relief, and then climbed onto Gordon's back without help, scratching his neck as she settled into the saddle. Sagel was a bit awkward at first, but quickly remembered all that Dan had shown her about handling the reins. They followed the hanging rocks back through the trees.

Daniel urged her to go faster and try out a trot, but Sagel was having none of it.

"It's easier than you think!" Daniel coaxed, "Just try it."

"No, Daniel, I like walking," she said sharply.

Daniel reached around his friend and held her hands tightly to the reins.

"Wha—" Sagel gasped as Daniel kissed to his horse. Gordon obediently began to trot, but went quickly to a canter when Daniel prodded lightly with his feet.

"Just hold on and steer!" Dan cried happily, as Sagel gasped and giggled. They went like this all the way to the main road and back to the stable. By the time they got back, Sagel had a stitch in her side and her legs ached from squeezing Gordon to stay on, but she felt refreshed.

They both dismounted in front of the stable and untacked Gordon in the warm confines of the barn. The other horses snorted eagerly, ready to be ridden. All were bored in the barn, including Wisle, who brooded at the back of his stall. Before they left for town, Daniel and Sagel scratched, petted, and talked to all of the animals. Even Wisle finally came forward for some attention, especially scratching behind his long ears. They stepped from the barn into the snow. It had indeed become colder and large flakes were falling.

"It's starting to snow even harder!" Daniel said, gazing up at the darkening sky.

"It is! I hope the food delivery trucks can get up the mountain—oh, right," Sagel stopped.

Daniel grimaced, looked up at the sky again, and then at Sagel, as his light brown hair darkened in the winter light beneath his hat.

"How did all this get so bad?" Daniel asked suddenly.

"I don't know. I wish I knew—but I don't know."

They walked in silence to Sagel's house.

Chapter 12

Waiting

Elenry sat in her tent, with a fire crackling outside, and Arros dozing on his feet nearby. No one had come to see her yet. She could feel her spirit twist and turn inside her; she was anxious and restless. Two villagers to accompany her were not the only things lacking. Elenry was exceptionally hungry, and made her way out of the tent to prepare food. Snow was falling more heavily around her, and the air had grown colder. Arros awoke as Elenry crunched through the snow to the fire and began taking out jerky. Elenry was in the mood for Goka meat. Gokas are a moose-like animal that lives only on the tundra of Asthekia; they are a much lighter color than moose, almost a champagne hue. Elenry pulled Goka jerky out of her food sack and threw it in a pot of boiling water to soften it, since it had frozen in the winter weather. She made tree sap tea, wanting to prolong her health as long as she could manage.

At every sound, every creaking tree, every clump of snow falling off a snow packed branch, she looked up and around. Every sound could be a person coming to her aid, offering to help her possibly save the town. But still no one came.

Chapter 13

In the Stretch

"Dan—I don't think you'll like this, but I don't think that I can wait a night to ask," Sagel said as they walked down the snow covered road towards Sagel's house. Few people were out and about; those few who were had heavy coats and heavy faces. Sagel wrapped her cloak a little tighter around her lean frame.

"I was pretty sure you wouldn't last a day."

"You know me."

"I know we both want to do this."

"Then—?"

"You're right, I can't either. But—but what'll we say?" Dan asked, stopping and turning to Sagel. "I've imagined talking to Elenry, I've imagined going to the other side of the mountain… but I haven't been able to imagine asking my parents."

"We'll just give them the truth, that we want to go, and that we think we can help," Sagel said, her teeth chattering a little. "Let's keep walking."

"Right," Dan agreed, as they continued.

"Okay, reason one; if they do let us go, provided we pass

the tests, we will be safer away from the sickness and disease of Shinken, and less likely to get sick," Sagel said.

"Oh yeah, they'll have to agree to that," Dan said.

"Number two; No one else seems to have stepped up," Sagel continued.

"And in Elenry's vision, she said that the two people she saw with her were small," Dan added.

"Now you're doing it, Dan. We're getting what we both need to say to them."

They smiled strongly at each other.

It was twilight, and the warm lights from store fronts and houses spilled like melted butter onto the freshly fallen snow.

"Do you think they'll let us go?' Sagel asked, as they jogged up the road.

"My dad maybe…my mom, I doubt it—no, really, our reasons are good. I don't know," Daniel said, glancing around as they entered the Stretch.

"Don't worry. Once we talk to my parents, then they'll talk to yours, and we'll all talk together. Chances are, they'll let us g-," Sagel stopped short.

"What?" Dan asked, stopping a few feet in front of Sagel, who had crumpled to the icy ground.

"Sagel!" Dan cried, kneeling beside her. Her eyes had rolled up behind partially closed and trembling lids and she was lying as still and stiff as a board.

"Sagel, Sagel, wake up!" Dan cried. Sagel would not.

A cold fire licked her cheeks; she was swimming through a lake of blues and blacks. Sound like silk rubbing on silk resonated softly through the empty waters. Then she was standing in an unknown forest. She looked down at her feet. She walked further into the woods where the trees were the largest and thickest that she had ever seen. Their bark was a deep, warm brown; it radiated energy and heat through the chill of the winter air. She drifted towards the nearest trunk and put her palm flat against the bark. As she glanced around, she realized that this was the largest tree in sight. Someone behind her grabbed her shoulder and she felt a shock of energy that ran down her arm to the tips of her fingers and then jerked her hand back from the tree. A long thin strand of golden light connected her hand to the tree; she shivered as a strange prickling energy coursed through her entire body. Then with a blast of air, she saw black.

"Sagel, oh Sagel, please wake up!" Daniel moaned, rocking on his knees and shaking his friend. Sagel opened her eyes slowly; she could still feel a tingling in her chest cavity and in her hands.

"Daniel…," She said, trying to sit up. Her head swam.

"Sagel, are you okay? You just fell. Did you pass out?" Daniel asked, helping her sit up.

"I must have. All of a sudden, I wasn't here. I was in a forest, I had a vision…," she said dreamily. She rubbed her eyes and shook herself.

Relieved, Daniel asked eagerly, "What happened? What did you see?"

"I was walking in a forest, and the trees—they were massive, and beautiful," she said, calling back the memory of the vision.

"What else?" Dan asked.

"I went up to one of the trees, and it was pulsing, and when I touched it, it shocked me, so I pulled away, and there was a golden…," she trailed off as she held up her right hand and pulled her glove off. There was a sticky golden liquid running down her palm from her finger.

"Sap!" Daniel cried, "It's sap, it—it's real!"

Sagel stared at her sticky palm.

"We're going to have to tell our parents about this," Sagel said, finally rising to her feet without Daniel's help.

"And Elenry. Your vision sounded kind of like hers," Daniel said in awe.

"Yes."

"Should we go see Elenry first?" Daniel asked Sagel.

"No. We'll see her tomorrow."

"If our parents let us go," Daniel reminded her.

"Even if they don't, I'll still go and tell her."

They continued briskly through the Stretch and up the road to Sagel's house.

Chapter 14

Unconvinced

Torren and Lorel were sitting in the living room sipping tea and enjoying each other's company. Nigel was in his room reading with the door closed, and Nova was playing at the house of her friend who lived nearby.

The front door opened and Sagel and Daniel rushed in, bringing an icy draft in with them.

"Sagel, Dan, what's the rush?" Torren asked.

"We need to talk to you," Sagel stated.

"Is anything wrong, hon?" Lorel asked. "You're very pale."

"I'm fine. We're both fine. But we need to talk to you," Sagel said.

"Okay, should you sit down?" Torren asked, shifting in his chair.

"Uh, yeah, we should sit down," Sagel said, as she and Dan took seats on one of the couches.

Sagel took a deep breath and began.

"The Medicine Woman needs two capable people to go with her to get the cure," she began, and nodded at Dan.

Daniel continued, "We think that we are capable, and we

want to go see Elenry to volunteer. And we have reasons why we should be able to try and you and my parents should let us go."

Torren sucked on his upper lip and looked at Lorel, who was listening intently.

"Go ahead," Torren said.

Sagel was surprised that neither of her parents had objected outright. Then she realized that they had trusted her and Dan for years to be on their own on the mountain. She also realized again that they were threatened as much by the mysterious illness as anyone else. When she got to this thought, she remembered Nigel and Nova and felt a slightly sickening fear rise in her belly. Her whole family was in danger. Someone had to do something.

Daniel started. "Okay, our first reason is, if we stay in the village, then it is more likely for us to come down with the disease, so if we were out of the village, we would be better protected from the disease and looked after by Elenry," Dan said, and looked at Sagel.

"The second reason," Sagel continued, "is no one else that we know of has volunteered themselves, and the longer it takes for someone to volunteer, the more people will fall sick." She searched her parent's faces for possible objections. Lorel and Torren both nodded.

"Elenry also said that the two people that she saw with her in her vision were small," Sagel said. "And our last reason is that on the way up here I had a vision."

"What did you see, Sagel?" Torren asked, leaning forward.

"At first I was swimming in this black and blue space, like water, and then I woke up in a forest," she recalled. "And then I started floating through the forest until I came to a massive tree— the biggest one I could see. I went up to it. As I approached it…it started humming, and when I touched it, it shocked me."

Lorel asked, "Shocked you? Were you hurt?"

"No, Ma, I was—I don't know how to describe it. It was like I was full of one of those summer lightening storms. My whole body filled up with energy."

Torren gasped, "Amazing!"

"So I pulled away, and there was a strand of golden liquid, I think it was sap. It was between my hand and the tree. Then I woke up," Sagel finished. "And there was this," she paused, holding up her palm. The sap had begun to harden on her skin and shone topaz in the light of the room.

"But how...?" Torren gaped, standing up and walking to Sagel. She held her hand up to him. Lorel joined them, taking her daughter's hand in hers.

"Amazing," Torren said again.

Torren and Lorel returned to their seats in silence. Torren was not entirely surprised that Sagel and Daniel were considering volunteering themselves. He had almost expected it from them. Lorel was still processing the information. She understood the urgency as well as her husband did and, ever since the meeting, a fear for her family had hovered around her like a malignant spirit. She knew that she and Torren had been thinking about this possibility even though they hadn't discussed it. Now it was real and a decision had to be made.

Torren took his wife's hand in his and looked at her. "Do you want to say anything first?"

"I'll listen for now. Go ahead."

Torren stared at his hands and had a brief image of all the beautiful pottery that had passed through them before anyone fell ill. That past was now only past. He looked at the two children.

"I think you should both go see Elenry," Torren began. Sagel and Daniel beamed. "But, we need to talk to Daniel's family first, if you haven't already spoken with them."

"We decided to come to you first," Dan said. "Maybe we could go see my parents now."

"Mom?" Sagel asked hopefully.

"I guess so, but don't be extremely disappointed if Elenry turns you down," Lorel said.

"But we qualify for age!" Sagel said.

"I know, that's one of your reasons and it's a good one. But when she tests you, don't be too sad if you don't make the cut," Lorel said, as gently as she could. "I don't doubt that you two could do it, but I am no Medicine Woman, and I don't know what she is looking for."

Sagel looked from one to the other of her parents. "So you're really sure? It's a yes from both of you?" Sagel asked hopefully.

"Yes, we know that we're all in danger. Somebody has to do something, Sagel," Torren said, after exchanging a glance with Lorel.

Lorel sighed and stood straight, "Yes." She walked down the hall to Nigel's room and told him to stay home while she and Torren drove Daniel home with Sagel.

Sagel, Daniel, Torren, and Lorel made their way out and into the car. Night was closing in on the mountain, enveloping the snowy folds of land in ebony silk. On the way down to the village, no one spoke. Sagel and Daniel exchanged excited glances every so often, but did not speak. It was as if they were afraid that unnecessary talk would turn Sagel's parents back on their decision. Lorel and Torren both had their eyes fixed on the familiar surface of the road in the headlights of the car. When they reached Dan's house, the lights were all on. Sagel and Daniel walked carefully to the door behind Lorel and Torren, so as not to slip on the icy walk.

Torren stopped in front of the door, breathed deeply, and then knocked. Louise opened the door slowly, and smiled when she saw who it was.

"Hello Bleudrys—Daniel, we were just getting worried," she said, and let them in. Michael walked out from the kitchen and clasped Torren's hand. Torren and Lorel had known Louise and Michael since the Carsons had moved to the village fifteen years ago; this was before any of them had had children. Once everyone was comfortable in the cushy couches, the discussion began.

"To what do we owe this visit?" Michael asked. Just then Louise coughed loudly and suddenly.

"Are you alright, Louise?" Lorel asked at once.

"Oh yes, just a tickle in my throat," she said. "It's nothing."

"They would like to talk to all of us. They've already spoken to Lorel and me, but given the situation, they need to speak to all of us together," Torren answered.

Before Daniel's parents could question further, Sagel started to explain. Sagel tried to keep their speech to Daniel's parents as close to the one that they had given Torren and Lorel, including her vision. A burdened silence followed. Michael leaned forward with his elbows on his knees and his hands clasped before him. His mouth formed a straight line as he watched Sagel speak. At first he wanted to tell her to stop—tell them all to stop. But then he remembered all that the Medicine Woman had said at the meeting. She had used her words carefully; not aiming to make things sound dire. But still, Michael knew that this was a dire situation.

"Well?" Daniel finally asked.

"That's a very large task to take on," Michael said, rubbing his chin.

"I really don't want my son going off like that on a dangerous journey with a woman that nobody really knows," Louise said. Her face drew into a stubborn mask.

"We've all met her. She's powerful, and she's kept her word to us so far by staying here and trying to help," Sagel replied, trying not to lose respect in her insistence.

"She has hardly been here a week, and I am also not accustomed or knowledgeable in the ways of Medicine People," Louise said, sitting rigidly.

"I'm not sure this is really about the Medicine Woman. We're all in grave danger," Torren said.

Louise responded, "I see that."

"Lorel and I have agreed to let Sagel go, Louise," Torren offered.

"I don't think Daniel will be going," Louise said.

"But Mom, it is such a great opportunity. And what about Sagel's vision?" Daniel raised his voice.

"Sagel's vision does not change the fact that it would be a long and extremely dangerous journey! It also does not change the fact that you are only fourteen years old."

"Louise, let's think about this," Michael interjected. "They offered some good reasons. They do fit the profile of the people in Elenry's vision. Whatever we may think of her, Shinken doesn't have any other plan, now. I'm inclined to at least let Daniel go through the tests with Elenry."

"Someone will step up. Children should not have to go. He's

not going," Louise said.

Lorel and Torren sat helplessly. Sagel felt her mother's hand on her back.

"Please, Mom, please?" Daniel whispered.

"Daniel, it's not a matter of *please*. I don't want you leaving Shinken. I don't want to see you in the hands of someone we don't even know!" Louise said, "No, Daniel. Lorel, Torren, you can let Sagel go across the continent and back if you want, but Daniel is staying in Shinken." Louise watched her son fight indignant tears. Ever since Daniel could walk, he had been exploring. As the years went by she had slowly loosened her hold as he had earned her trust and quelled her fears by staying out of trouble and avoiding injury. He was a good boy, and he was their only child. Her heart gave a sharp pull. She was surer than ever that she did not want him leaving.

Torren and Lorel nodded understandingly; Lorel patting Sagel's back gently. Daniel tried hard not to cry. His hands balled into fists and his chest moved stiffly up and down, struggling to keep something hard and painful from getting out. Sagel was numb with anger and disappointment, but she didn't feel any tears. Louise put her arm around Dan. Sagel saw Dan stiffen. The charged silence was becoming unbearable.

"I'm really sorry, you two. I really am," Louise said. Sagel nodded at Louise, trying not to scowl. She knew in her heart that Louise only meant well.

"Well, we better go home," Torren said finally. "We've got to pick Nova up. And Nigel will be wondering."

"Dan, I'm so sorry," Sagel said quietly, as the adults made small talk on the way out of the house.

"It's not your fault, Sagel, and don't think that I'm mad at you," Dan said. "I really am angry, but only at my Mom."

"I know, but she is only trying to protect you. I can see why she wouldn't want you to leave," Sagel said, trying to console him.

"That's easy for you to say. Your parents are fine with it," Dan scowled. Sagel looked down at her feet; she didn't have the slightest clue what she could tell him.

"I don't want to go anymore," she said quietly.

"Sagel, you have to try. No one else has stepped up. You may be the village's last hope!" said Daniel. "I'm sorry. I didn't mean to snap. I…."

Sagel watched Daniel turn away from her, his cheeks reddening and his breath sharpening.

"Come on Sage, we're off," Torren said, beckoning his daughter to the door.

"Bye," Sagel said.

"See you," Daniel whispered through tears.

Sagel and her parents made their way across the icy walkway to the car. Sagel started crying as soon as they pulled out of the driveway. She felt ridiculous; she was too old to cry about something like this.

"Sagel, you're sad, you're disappointed, you're angry. We both understand. But Louise might change her mind yet," Torren said.

"But if she doesn't," Lorel said, eyeing Torren, "then you just need to accept that Daniel isn't going to go with you."

"But it isn't fair," Sagel said quietly.

"Fairs are for tourists," Torren said with a smile.

"I'm serious," Sagel said, annoyed by the familiar joke. "He was the one who wanted to go so badly! It was his idea in the first place!"

Lorel nodded understandingly, "Well, we can't change Louise's mind. Maybe you and Dan can find a new adventure, a little closer to home"

"I still want to talk to Elenry, I still want to go," Sagel said resolutely.

"Are you sure?" Torren asked.

"Pa!" Sagel cried.

"Alright, calm down, I was merely asking," Torren said quickly.

"This is where I had the vision," Sagel said.

"We're also coming to the place that Elenry found the good sap," Torren said, stopping the car.

"Torren, what are you doing?" Lorel asked, alarmed.

"I just wanted to see something," he said, and got out of the car.

"Dad, where are you going?" Sagel asked, opening her door and stepping out onto the ground. Lorel followed Sagel out of the car and around to the driver's side. Torren had walked across the road to a healthy tree and started touching and sniffing its bark.

"Torren, what are you doing?" Lorel asked, taking a step towards her husband.

"I just wanted to smell it," he said, pulling back with an intrigued grimace on his face. "I smelled a tree out by the pottery shed that was dying, and it smelled like mold. This tree smells clean, and normal, like trees are supposed to smell."

With that, he walked back to the car. Sagel didn't move yet; she was gazing at the ground a few feet behind where the car had stopped. In contrast to the shadowed, ivory snow was a splotch of dark matter. She walked quickly over to it and bent down for a closer look. Bits of deep brown tree bark were stuck in and around gold liquid that was frozen on the ground.

From her squatting position, she called, "Ma, Pa, come here. This is what I saw in my vision. It was just like this, only it was on a live tree."

Her parents walked to her side and looked down at the patch of broken bark and frozen sap. Lorel then took Sagel gently by the arm, helped her stand and the three of them returned to the car.

Chapter 15

Something

Sagel returned home, but didn't bother explaining to an overly curious Nigel, who wanted to incessantly question his older sister. She went straight to her room after a hot shower, and climbed into bed with her most comfortable pajamas. She could feel a stinging ball beginning to swell in her throat, and her eyes started to well up with tears. At that moment she put all of her energy into something happening that would let Daniel go. With furious thoughts still swimming through her head, Sagel fell into an uneasy sleep. It was dreamless, but all through the night she could feel a tension as she slept.

"Sagel, Sagel—wake up, come on, Sagel, wake up!" A distant and fuzzy voice coaxed Sagel into consciousness. Winter's morning light crept through the window, casting shades of gray upon her room. Dan was shaking her shoulder and desperately calling for her to wake up.

"What-what's up, something...," Sagel mumbled sleepily.

"Sagel, my mom's sick, she just went into the clinic!" Dan cried. Sagel saw tears beginning to form in his eyes, and his voice became choked and quiet.

"Oh, Daniel," Sagel said, sitting up in bed and reaching out to his arm. Daniel was fighting back his tears, his forehead creased in fear and tension. "How is she?" Sagel asked.

"She's unconscious. It happened last night. I heard her coughing, and then my dad came in to tell me to stay home while he brought her to the clinic. They say she's stable, but really weak," Dan said, a single tear rolling down his cheek. Lorel came into her daughter's room with mugs of hot sap tea for both of them.

"Here you are. Drink this," she said, handing them the mugs and then patting Dan on his shoulder. He took it and drank deeply.

"They say I'm not allowed in the clinic. No one is, unless they're sick or working there," Dan said.

"And you two need to stay clear of there," Lorel said. Nigel came into the room, still in his pajamas.

"Hi, Daniel," he said softly.

"Hey, Nigel," Daniel murmured, even more quietly. Nigel walked uncertainly through the room and sat in Sagel's desk chair, biting his lip uncomfortably.

"Well, I am going to go make breakfast," Lorel said, walking out of Sagel's room.

"Are you staying?" Sagel asked.

"Yeah, my dad came up and dropped me off. He doesn't want me at home alone with my mom in the clinic, and he needs to work," Daniel said. "Your parents offered to take me for the day."

"Good," Sagel said, standing up out of bed, "Can you leave for a second?"

"Huh?" Daniel and Nigel said together.

"I want to get dressed," Sagel said.

"Oh, right," Daniel said. Both he and Nigel scurried out.

Sagel chose a warm outfit, as this morning felt even colder than the last. Her shirt was black, and her pants were a deep blue. She brushed her long, dark hair back out of her face, and made her way to the kitchen. Dan and the rest of her family were seated around the breakfast table; except for her mother, who was frying some sort of meat at the stove.

"I don't want anymore sap stuff!" Nova huffed at her father, who was pouring everyone sap tea.

"Nova, we all need to keep drinking sap—it'll keep us from getting sick," Torren said, continuing to pour.

"So? Being sick isn't as bad as drinking this stuff all the time!" Nova whined.

"Nova, this illness isn't like a cold, or flu. It is extremely serious," Torren said.

"That's why we're doing everything we can to stay healthy," Lorel added, bringing the food to the table. She put a dish of meat down. Sagel saw that it was pan fried Churkey. Onions and an Asthekian breakfast sauce soaked and surrounded the strips of fried white meat. The breakfast sauce tasted much like syrup, and was a nice contrast to the salty meat. Lorel also set out a plate of sap soaked bread. Everyone dug in without much conversation. Daniel still looked in shock, his eyes wandering and vacant. Upon glancing at her parents, Sagel observed that they both looked rather tired. The usually joyful spark in their eyes was now charged with worry.

"I know where you went last night," Nigel said, after swallowing a mouthful of bread.

"So?" Sagel asked her brother, assuming that Nigel was saying that for the sole purpose of irking her.

"Are you really going to go talk to Elenry?" Nigel asked.

"How did you know?" Sagel snapped.

"Ma told me," Nigel replied.

"Ma!" Sagel cried.

"If you are serious about doing this then you will need to be mature enough to handle telling your siblings about it. Your father and I will not lie to them, just as we will not lie to you," Lorel responded, her brows tensing.

"Can I go?" Nigel asked timidly.

"Nigel, what are you doing?" Torren sighed, putting his fork down.

"I was only asking!"

"No, I'm only having one child try out, and you are too young!" Lorel said.

"No, I qualify for age! I'm eleven turns around the sun!" Nigel said, becoming indignant.

"You don't qualify for my age limit—no," Torren interjected.

"Can't I just try out?" Nigel pleaded, making one last stand.

"No! It's not like trying out for the school Alka team! It's serious and dangerous, and your sister and Dan gave this a lot of thought!" Torren said. Alka, the most popular of Asthekian sports is played on a large sloped hill. Each team has five players who all have a Seeking stone (Adiys in Sdrawkcab). They are all blindfolded, and are left to find the treasure rock that is placed somewhere at the top of the hill. The first person from either team to find it and return it to the bottom of the hill wins. Nigel was one of the best Alka players in his grade.

Nigel looked disappointed. Defeated, he spoke no more of it.

"Let's clear away the dishes for your mother," Torren said finally, when everyone's plates were clean. "Wonderful breakfast, Lorel."

"Thank you, hon," Lorel said, smiling weakly at her husband and walking into the living room. "I need to drive down to town to buy groceries. I'll be back soon—Nova, do you want to come with me?"

"Yeah!" Nova dashed out of the kitchen to follow her mother.

"I'll come with you. I have to see some one in town about a pottery order...they haven't gotten back to me since—they haven't gotten back to me," Torren said, walking towards the living room.

Daniel and Sagel finished cleaning up in the kitchen, and retreated into Sagel's room again. Nigel had helped with the dishes and then skulked to the couch to read a book.

"I didn't know he'd be so angry," Sagel said. Daniel only nodded.

"Sagel," Dan began, "I know this will sound horrible, absolutely horrible, but I still want to go help Elenry. I feel like I'm responsible somehow, like I need to get the medicine now that my mother's sick. I know she wouldn't want me to go, but—but I have to."

Sagel looked gently at Daniel, afraid to ripple his current emotional calm. "It's not your fault, Daniel. She would be happy to know that you cared enough to disobey her in order to save her life."

Daniel burst into tears.

"Dan, I'm so sorry. She'll probably live!" Sagel said quickly.

"You don't know that!" Dan retorted sharply. Sagel resolved

to let him cry, for she knew not what else to do. Dan quickly wiped his tears with his sleeve, not looking at Sagel.

"I am going to help get that medicine; I'm going to tell my dad that I am trying out. I'm going right now," Dan said. With that he stood up and started for Sagel's door.

"Wait! I'm coming!" Sagel said, and followed him out.

As they came into the living room, Torren looked up from tying his boots. Lorel and Nova were already outside.

"What's wrong?" he asked. Nigel looked up from his book.

"Torren, I need to go tell my dad something. I need to tell him that I need to see Elenry. Now that my mom's sick, I—I need to try to get the medicine," Dan said. Sagel watched her father, willing him to let them go. Torren creased his brow and sighed. He finally nodded at Sagel and Dan.

"I will let you go, but you need to come straight back once you've told him. And when do you two plan on seeing Elenry?" Torren asked.

"If my father says yes, then today," Dan said finally. Though Sagel hadn't tried to plan that step yet, she agreed that today was a good day to do it.

Sagel and Daniel were all bundled up in their coats as they trotted down the road.

"What if your dad says no?" Sagel asked.

"He won't."

Though the trees in the Stretch were thickly spaced, Sagel could make out a darker mass further back in the woods. She assumed that it was Elenry's camp. People were out and about in town, though everyone looked straight ahead or at the ground instead of making eye contact. Daniel and Sagel walked up to the office building of Daniel's father. It was a very small research building, constructed in the same manner as the other buildings in Shinken. Blue letters on a sign read: Mt. Aarotte Research Center.

Dan and Sagel walked in through the front door; Sagel recalled fond memories of her and Daniel drawing and playing in this building when they were young and the weather was too harsh to play outside. It was composed of two small rooms. The front room had two small couches. An uninhabited desk had papers scattered over it. Pictures of plants and animals gave life to the walls.

"Dad?" Dan called.

"Daniel?" Michael called back, instantly running out his office. "What's wrong?"

"Nothing, I—I just need to talk to you," Daniel said quickly.

"Oh, I'm sorry, you scared me. I—never mind," he said. "What do you need to talk about?"

"Dad, I am going to go see Elenry. I know mom doesn't want me to, but, please, I need to—for her," Daniel said.

Michael stared at his son. "But what if you don't come back, what do I tell her?" Michael asked, looking more helpless than Sagel had ever seen any adult look. "I can't lose you. I can't lose her!" Michael said, his eyes gleaming with tears.

"Dad, please, trust me. Just let me try out, please," Daniel whispered.

Michael had had a difficult time dropping Daniel off at Sagel's that morning, and did not think he could bear to spend any amount of time not knowing where he was and what he was doing. Honestly, he knew that Daniel could handle such a journey, but Michael did not think that he himself could handle his son's absence.

"Listen, Daniel—"

"No. Please, Dad. I can do this for mom. I can do this."

Michael rubbed his chin. He looked at his son's fixed jaw and determined eyes, and said, "Okay."

Chapter 16

The Plan

Daniel walked to his father and hugged him around the chest. Michael gripped him back, holding back tears. Sagel smiled and tried not to tear up. She felt a sudden wave of admiration for Daniel. He was brave, frightened, and determined. Now more than ever, she felt that they needed to be the ones to find the cure. They left the research building with Michael, who offered to drive them back to Sagel's house. From the back seat, Sagel could hear Michael's deep breathing; it sounded labored. Daniel was fidgeting, but his large liquid eyes were filled once again with his usual, determined spark. Relieved as Sagel was, they now had the trials to think about. It began to snow again as they pulled up to Sagel's house. An icy wind whistled through the sagging trees.

"They're not here," Nigel said from the couch, not looking up from his book.

"Oh—right," Sagel remembered. "Uh…I guess we wait here until they get back."

Michael, Daniel, and Sagel sat in the kitchen sipping cups of water. Michael spoke of his work for a distraction, but neither of the children heard much of what he said over the noise in their own minds.

At last, the front door creaked open, followed by the sound of heavy boots and Nova's chatter.

"Ma, Pa!" Sagel cried as they walked in the door, Michael following closely in her wake.

"Ma, Michael said he could go! Dan can go," Sagel said, beaming.

"When are you two going to see Elenry?" Torren asked, also smiling. Nigel glanced up from his book, looking curious while Nova looked a little nervous.

"Um-," Sagel muttered, looking at Daniel.

"The sooner the better," Daniel said quietly, but confidently. Sagel nodded. Something had changed in Daniel. He was no longer doing this for the adventure, but for his mother. Michael looked anxious, but Daniel's determination would not be quenched.

"Do you have a plan?" Michael asked quietly.

"Well, we don't really know what she's going to have us do, so we'll just see when we get there," Daniel said, sounding more confident than Sagel felt.

"Are you going now? Because if you are seriously going through with this, then the sooner you go the better for everyone, as Dan said," Torren said.

"I want to go," Nigel said, as soon as Torren's last words were uttered.

"No, absolutely not. This is not a negotiation, Nigel," Lorel said, her voice composed.

"Why?" Nigel snapped.

"We are not negotiating it, and if you snap at me again, you're going to spend the rest of the day in your room. The reasons we gave you are final. Your sister had carefully thought out reasons for going, and she is going, not you."

Torren added, "Now that Daniel is going, Nigel, there are two people to accompany Elenry. She saw two people in her vision, not three."

Nigel unclenched his jaw in defeat and then went to his room.

"Well, at least she's living close by," Michael said. "I can go with you."

"It's alright, you can go back to work, Dad," Daniel said.

"No, no, you two need at least one parent there, so she knows that you have our permission," Michael said, rubbing his stubbly chin. Michael was very tall, and rather plump. His dark hair and deep brown eyes made him look brooding, but anyone who knew him well knew that he had a light heart. Lorel and Torren nodded at Michael, looking relieved.

"I think I would like to go, too," Torren said.

"I better come as well," Lorel said.

"We should go now. It's still early," Sagel said hopefully.

"Ma, can I go to Olive's house?" Nova asked, as Lorel donned her winter coat.

"No, I don't want you visiting with her anymore while the sickness is still going around," Lorel said.

"Why?" Nova said, alarmed at her mother's answer. Olive was the same age as Nova, and they had been friends since the girls were quite small.

"Because her family isn't following the sap diet as strictly as we are, and I don't want you exposed in case one of them is sick," Lorel said. "You and Nigel must stay here, we will be back soon." Lorel closed the front door behind her and followed the others down the steps and onto the road towards the Stretch.

"You two must be prepared for whatever Elenry's answer

might be. For all we know, she might have changed the age limit," Torren said.

Daniel found this possibility quite disheartening. Sagel and Dan speculated about the numerous possibilities for the tests.

"Maybe there'll be a strength test, or something," Daniel suggested.

"Yeah, we'll have to wrestle a flock of mutant Churkeys," Sagel said, making Daniel smile.

The five walked the short distance to the Stretch, and then began walking through the wintery woods towards Elenry's camp. They broke through the trees into a clearing.

Butterflies wafted up through Sagel's stomach, landing and fluttering in her chest cavity as she continued toward the Medicine Woman's tent. They all stopped. Dan stood beside Sagel. Together they moved forward, approaching the canvas tent and a small crackling fire. A great black horse snorted at their arrival and a tall, slender, cloaked woman stepped out of the tent opening, smiling at the visitors. She could have hugged them.

Chapter 17

First Test

"Hello," Elenry greeted them, her voice liquid relief, with each syllable dripping like melting snow.

"Good morning," Torren responded lightly.

"What brings you to my camp this morning?" Elenry asked, her energy flickering hopefully.

"Go ahead," Lorel said to Sagel and Daniel.

"We wish for you to test us. We want to help you find the cure," Daniel spoke with confidence.

"All of you?" Elenry quarried.

"No, just my friend and me," Daniel corrected her, motioning to Sagel.

"What are your names?" Elenry asked.

"I'm Daniel Carson," Daniel said.

"Sagel Bleudry," Sagel said.

"Of course, you are the children who carried young Ebin up the mountain," Elenry said seriously.

Both children nodded in acknowledgment.

"Daniel, you possess an Earthly name," Elenry noted.

"Yes, my parents are from Earth, but I was born here," said

Daniel, hoping that he didn't have to be Asthekian to be tested. Elenry smiled and nodded. Daniel relaxed.

"How old are you two?" Elenry enquired.

"We're both fourteen sun revolutions," Sagel answered.

"Can you verify that?" Elenry turned towards the adults.

"They are both fourteen sun revolutions, and very eager to help," Lorel said, smiling at her daughter and Daniel.

"Yes, I can tell," said Elenry. "I am willing to test you, but before I do, I want you to answer me this: Why should I test you?"

Instinctively, Sagel liked the Medicine Woman and trusted her. She suddenly felt that she was where she belonged. Without hesitation, Sagel launched into their four reasons, feeling more confident and able with each one. She also added that both she and Daniel were young and strong, and had experience on the mountain. Daniel looked pleased and relieved at Sagel's explanation. He had felt confident talking to his father and Sagel's parents, but a nagging doubt had started up in him as soon as they had reached the Medicine Woman's camp. Elenry nodded her approval after each reason.

"Well, I can see you have given a lot of thought to this," Elenry said. "They are all very legitimate reasons, and I see no reason why I should not test you both."

Sagel smiled, and Daniel relaxed.

"Now, what are your names?" Elenry asked, turning to the parents once more.

"I am Torren, and this is my wife Lorel," Torren said. "Sagel is our daughter."

"My name's Michael, I'm Dan's father, his mother's name is Louise...but she's in the clinic," he finished, his voice tightening.

"I'm sorry about your wife, Michael, and it's very good to

meet all of you," Elenry said, "but I am going to have to ask you to leave, as I am going to begin testing Daniel and Sagel now. We mustn't delay our departure any longer than necessary. I can't thank you enough for coming."

Sagel and Daniel turned to their parents.

"Come home as soon as the testing is finished," Lorel said to Sagel. A film of concern dimmed Lorel's eyes, making Sagel's butterflies turn loops anxiously.

"Not to worry, Lorel, if they finish the first part of testing then they will be home by this evening," Elenry said, emphasizing the 'If'.

"What do you mean 'If'?" Daniel asked cautiously. Sagel's insides tightened and the butterflies frenzied.

"There is no certainty that you will finish the tasks I set for you, but I will bring you home whether you are successful or not," Elenry said. Her dark hair fell and shimmered like a jewel covered blanket. The day had become gloomy; the clouds veiled the sun and the moon. Sagel wondered how her hair shined so.

"Do your best, Dan. I'll be at home after work today. I'll be waiting," Michael said to Daniel, hugging his son and ruffling his hair.

The adults made their way back through the woods, looking nervous.

Despite the cold, Elenry's throat warmed with relief.

"So, now that it's just us, I want to know a little more about you," Elenry said, leading Sagel and Daniel to the sitting blocks by the fire.

"If you two could just take turns telling me your interests," Elenry prompted.

Sagel looked at Daniel and shrugged, beginning her introduction.

"I love the winter time because I love snow," Sagel began. "I like painting on my dad's pottery, and traveling. I've been to Starling City, and a few other places on Thron Avaykwathorel."

"Very good," Elenry said, and turned to Daniel.

"Well, I love the summer time, because that's when I can ride my horse most comfortably. I like school, and hanging out with Sagel," Daniel said, smiling across the fire at his friend. "I also like hiking around the mountain trails, when it's warmer, of course."

Elenry nodded and continued. "What frightens you?" she asked.

This question reduced both the children to silence, but something about Elenry made Sagel feel secure enough to divulge.

"I, well—it might sound silly, but, I really dislike the dark," Sagel said, feeling like a little girl. "And I really hate deep water, like the kind you can't see the bottom of."

Years before, when Sagel was about five, her family had visited a large vacation hotel in Starling City. It had an enormous pool, meant for the entertainment of the guests, but when Sagel fell into it without knowing how to swim, it was anything but entertaining.

Elenry contemplated what Sagel had said, her impassive eyes glowing in the fire light.

"And you, Daniel?" Elenry asked.

"Um…I really don't like not knowing how things are going to turn out," Daniel said.

"Yes, most do dislike that, but does it truly frighten you?" Elenry countered.

"Yes, it does," Daniel said.

"Good, very good. Now, I am going to show you something, well, no, actually," Elenry said, "you are going to show me something. As a Medicine Person, I must heal people; therefore, I have many tools and medicines for countering sicknesses.

Unfortunately, I don't often get to know the person in my care, either because they heal quickly and I move on to the next sick person, or they die before I can help them. I need to learn, and get to know your souls. If you want to work and travel closely with me, then you need to trust me, and I you," Elenry said, reaching into her brown bag and rummaging around. She pulled a clear container out of her bag.

Sagel tried to see the contents of the container, but Elenry put it in her lap and opened it before she could see anything. Elenry carefully took a handful of fine silvery powder that glimmered like illuminated dust in the flickering fire. Kneeling closer to the blaze, Elenry cast the powder into the flickering flames. Immediately the fire cracked loudly, and then began to hum and murmur. The flame spat and writhed, all the while humming in the voice of a small child. The tune lacked a distinct melody, but was mesmerizing. Daniel and Sagel stared into the fire, entranced by the strange and beautiful flames.

"Sagel, why don't you go first again," Elenry said, pulling them out of their trance. When Sagel looked nervously at Elenry, the Medicine Woman said, "I need you to trust me, and do as I say. I want you to place both of you hands into the fire. It is not hot, and will not burn you. I promise."

Sagel knelt down to the fire. If the fire had been a normal fire, then the flames would have been emitting heat, but this was no normal fire, and she could only feel faint warmth on her cheeks. She took off her gloves. Slowly, she stretched her arms out towards the fire. The tips of her fingers tingled pleasantly as she put them into the humming blaze. The flames felt like a dimmed and almost pleasant version of the strong shock that she had felt in her vision. A few seconds later, the small inferno sputtered, and then changed from a yellow orange to a periwinkle blue. Sagel gasped and tried to pull her hands out, but she found that she could not. It was as if they had been cemented in the flames.

"Don't struggle Sagel—this kind of fire is a soul reader. It feels your soul, and then it turns the color of your aura. Your soul's color is periwinkle blue. All Medicine People are taught to channel and read what the flames see. Now, you need to look into the fire, nowhere else," Elenry said, kneeling down beside Sagel. Staring into the flames, Sagel grew sleepy—she felt completely relaxed. Elenry put her hands into the flames, and stared at the fire. Behind them, Daniel watched in fascination. The Medicine Woman pulled her hands out again, ending the meditation, and instructed Sagel to do the same. Her hands were free, and felt light now that they were out of the fire.

"That felt, so…refreshing," Sagel said, her eyes glazed over in a dreamy stare. The fire spit again, and then returned to its normal color.

Elenry nodded knowingly, and returned to her block.

"What did you see—or feel?" Sagel asked.

"Do you mind if Daniel hears?" Elenry asked.

"No, of course he can hear," Sagel said, hoping that nothing that Elenry had experienced would be cause for embarrassment.

"Alright then, here we go," Elenry began. "I saw that you are a naturally caring soul. You are curious and very intuitive, sometimes to the point of psychic ability. You like to plan for things. Your planning helps to quell your anxiety," Elenry smiled at Sagel. "You are extremely intelligent and nurturing, but your stubborn streak can get in the way of your acceptance."

Sagel listened intently, thrilled that the Medicine Woman saw so much good in her; however, this was not the first time she had been perceived as stubborn.

"Thank you," Sagel said.

"Don't thank me, Sagel, thank who you are," Elenry replied. "Also, don't try to stand up too fast. You may experience some dizziness."

Sagel rose to her feet very slowly, stood very still for a moment while intense vertigo passed, and then went to her block.

"Daniel, why don't you step up to the fire," Elenry said, casting another handful of powder into the flames and kneeling down with him.

"Go on, put you hands in," Elenry instructed. Snapping out of his trance, Daniel hesitantly brought his hands into the flames. Just as it had done with Sagel, the fire cracked loudly, spluttered, and then glowed a soft yellow. Daniel started and tried to pull his hands out. He began panicking and squirming when the fire cemented his hands in its depths.

"Do not struggle," Elenry soothed. Her words worked, for Daniel became still with his hands still engulfed in flames. Elenry again plunged her hands in. She closed her eyes. Movement could be seen under the lids, as if she were reading Daniel's soul from writing on the backs of her eyelids. Eyes snapping open, Elenry pulled her hands from the flame; Daniel followed her lead, relieved when his hands slid effortlessly from the humming fire.

"That actually felt kind of nice," Daniel said, smiling, a little embarrassed at his initial struggle. He stood slowly, steadied himself, and returned to his seat.

Elenry laughed and nodded in agreement.

Daniel tensed, bracing himself for any criticism.

Elenry spoke, "When I first laid eyes on you, I could tell that you are a very pure soul. The fire confirmed that you are loving, compassionate, and generous."

Daniel smiled.

"But—"

Daniel's face tensed and became worried.

"Yes there are always 'buts'," Elenry said. "You can be selfless to the point that people take advantage of you. You get yourself into situations where you don't speak up when you need to in order to protect yourself, and rely on other people's emotions to dictate your own."

"You got that all from the fire?" Daniel asked in awe.

"I am able to read a lot about a person with that fire," Elenry replied. "You two passed your first test."

"That was a test?" Sagel asked, surprised and relieved.

"I had to find out the nature of the people who want to help me," Elenry explained. "If the fire revealed that you were a couple of hate filled, resentful teenagers, then I probably would have turned you away without further testing. In order for this journey to be successful, you both need to be fully committed to it— physically, mentally, and spiritually. That is not to say that you will not have doubts or fears, of course."

A warm sense of success filled Sagel's core as she looked with relief to Daniel. He nodded and smiled.

"Now, for the second test."

Sagel's stomach clenched as she was brought back to the reality of the challenges still ahead of them. Stiffening, Daniel's hands clenched and unclenched.

"Relax, children, its not like you have to wrestle a flock of mutant Churkeys," Elenry reassured them.

Sagel looked at Daniel and they both laughed, their eyebrows raised in amazement.

Elenry continued, "Your second test will be a test of physical skill and endurance. It will also involve intellectual skill, and problem solving. It came to my attention last night that the delivery truck from Starling City has made it's monthly round to Mt. Aarotte. Unfortunately, due to the quarantine rules, they were not permitted to come up the mountain to deliver the food to us. That's where you two step in. As far as I know, there are four crates full of food and other supplies sitting at the bottom of the mountain. It is your job to get those four crates up the mountain and to the food co-op. You need to have them up the mountain by sunrise tomorrow morning. After you complete this test, you are to come and see me immediately. Oh yes, and no motor vehicle assistance."

Still processing all that they had heard, Sagel and Daniel stared blankly at Elenry, worry and wonder claiming their faces.

"Go ahead, you've got work to do," Elenry said. Finality resonated in her voice.

With a hurried glance towards each other, Sagel and Dan stood and began walking quickly out of her camp toward town. Neither of them had any idea as to what they were going to do. As they hiked into town, Sagel slowed to a stop.

"C'mon Sage, we have to hurry."

"Dan, we can't get those crates up ourselves. They're too heavy," Sagel said despairingly. "We need another way!"

"What?" Daniel sighed.

"I—I don't know."

"Wait!" Dan exclaimed. "She said that we couldn't use a car, right?"

"Yeah, so?" Sagel asked desperately.

"She never said anything about horses!"

Chapter 18

Of Body

"Dan, we can't use the horses! How would we?" Sagel cried as she followed Daniel down the horse stable road.

"We'll put their bridles and saddles on, and we'll ride them down the mountain to where the crates are, and then we'll hook the crates up to their tack, and lead them back up," Daniel said, beaming.

"Yeah, but…"

"But—what?" Daniel demanded, stopping to look at Sagel.

"How?" Sagel moaned.

"Just trust me, Sagel, this is the only way. Just like you said— we can't push those crates up ourselves."

Sagel stared at her boots. There was no other way.

"This could work," Sagel said, a smile stealing across her face.

"Of course," Daniel said. "Trust us, Sage."

Exhilarated by their newborn plan, they sped up into a jog. They reached the stable at a sprint, though there was no casual banter as they entered the barn.

"How many horses will we use?" Sagel asked.

"Well, there are four crates and four horses, so, I guess

we'll bring them all."

"What about Ola and Alo? They're not ours to use."

"Their owners are in Starling city," Daniel replied.

"Oh, well in that case…," Sagel said.

Daniel crooned to Gordon as he filled his trough with hay.

"We'll feed them first. Can you feed Galah?"

"Okay."

"What about Wisle?" Sagel asked Dan, once all of the horses were munching.

"What about him?" Dan said, starting to gather lead ropes and bridles.

"He's another pack animal. We need as much help as we can get."

"He's barn sour. He probably won't even want to leave his stall."

"Still, Dan, we need him. We can coax him out," Sagel said, a little exasperated.

"We can try," Dan agreed.

They walked to the end of the barn and stepped up to Wisle's stall. His bottom was turned to them. Sagel cleared her throat.

"Wisle," She called.

The mule twitched his ears and snorted.

"At least he knows his name," Sagel said.

"What we need is a good bribe," Daniel thought out loud. "Let's start by feeding him."

As soon as Daniel placed the hay in the trough, Wisle turned and began to eat, not acknowledging the humans that fed him.

"Okay, I have an idea," Daniel said. "The feed trough is attached to the door, so if we open it while he's eating, he'll follow the door, and walk out of the stall, then we can tack him up."

"What will he do?" Sagel enquired nervously.

"Probably keep eating," Daniel said nonchalantly.

Sagel backed away, not wanting the mule to do something unexpected with her in kicking range. Daniel noticed her movement and smiled at her. He opened the door and, as he expected, Wisle simply followed the food, with no noticeable hesitation.

"There," Daniel muttered, relief flooding his voice, "no harm done."

With that he walked to the wall where the animal's tack hung, and took Wisle's harness off to tack him up. After they had Wisle geared up, they moved on to the other horses. Sagel had Daniel check her work. Daniel grabbed five long, heavy-duty ropes from the tack area and secured them on Wisle's back.

"So, how are we going to get them all down the mountain?" Sagel asked.

"Well, we can…um," Daniel started, thinking for a moment. He was holding the lead ropes for Gordon, Wisle, and Ola, while Sagel held the other two.

"Oh, of course," he said, pulling his hat tighter onto his head. "We'll each ride one of the horses, and tie the other three onto our saddles with their lead ropes."

"Okay," Sagel nodded. "Will the horses, you know, be alright with that?"

"Yeah, they all are really used to each other—well, except for maybe Wisle, but I'll tie him up to my horse so I can deal with him."

In the end, Sagel ended up on Balan, with Ola tethered behind. Daniel rode Gordon with Alo and Wisle behind. When Wisle tried to bite Alo, Alo backed and kicked him, unlike Gordon, who was not so aggressive. Since then, Wisle had been docile and quite submissive to the whole situation, only snorting in contempt once or twice. Sagel could feel her pounding heart settling back to its normal rhythm as the rode down the snowy road. Fortunately, Ola and Balan seemed to get along well; she didn't want to think about what would have happened if the two of them hadn't.

"Are we riding through town?" Sagel called ahead to Daniel, who led the procession.

"No, there's a faster route. We need to use the daylight. We'll ride up on the slope above town, and then down onto the main mountain road," Daniel thought aloud, nodding to himself and patting Gordon.

The village of Shinken had been built in a wide, shallow mountain pocket that sloped off gently onto the steeper side, and then down to the land below. A small and infrequently used trail had been cut into the ridge above the town by travelers in the early years of Shinken. Sagel had had no knowledge of the trail, but on one of their little expeditions, Daniel had brought her there. She had learned that Daniel knew more about the local landscape than any other child in the town.

The trail was only about two horses wide, and Sagel glanced frequently over the edge. It was a sheer drop down about twenty feet, and then the land began to slope down, eventually sloping into town. They could see the town's lights and chimney stacks not far below them. Relieved though she was to finally hit the main road, Sagel also began to feel a bubble of impending anxiety. This was it. Daniel turned on Gordon to smile encouragingly at Sagel, his eyes bright with excitement and strain. Well, at least she wasn't the only nervous one on this journey.

"Now we just ride down," Daniel said, scanning the road ahead, and easing Gordon into a very slow trot. Sagel tapped her horse ever so gently to start trotting, and Balan obediently picked up into a sluggish trot behind Daniel and his train. Much to Sagel's surprise, all the animals followed along with what the horses in front of them were doing, even Wisle.

Wind with a chilling bite whipped over them, and made the ride cold and tiring. Sagel pulled the top of her winter coat up over her mouth and nose, and yanked her hat down tightly around her ears. Her eyes stung with the tears of the thrashing wind, and her nose numbed. Never did they hit a perilous icy patch. None of the animals spooked or got out of their lines. Daniel turned regularly to see how Sagel was holding up, and smiled and turned around when he got a confirmation nod.

Sagel noticed that Daniel's nose was turning progressively pinker, but when she tried to motion to him to pull his jacket up, he shrugged and kept riding. The wind howled their entire journey, making conversation impossible. Much to their relief, the bottom of the road at last came into view. As she scanned rapidly for the crates, Sagel's heart began to pound. And then she saw them. The end of the road evened out onto a flat area that connected the steep mountain road to the highway that wound out into a hilly area that stretched all the way out towards the horizon. Four crates were lined up on the side of the road. Daniel turned to Sagel. There was no mistaking the relief glowing in his large, hazel eyes. Sagel grinned back, breathing out a long sigh, a cloud of white steam billowing from her mouth.

"Now what?" Sagel called to Dan, riding up beside where he and Gordon were standing. The horses had completed the first half of the journey without much excitement. They walked in line peacefully, only snorting occasionally, as if to remind the riders that they were still there.

"We—well," Daniel fumbled, looking from the crates and then back to the lines of horses and Wisle, "We use the ropes to tie the crates to their saddles, and tie their lead ropes together. One of us walks in front to lead the animals and the other walks behind to guide the crates."

Sagel looked at Daniel. "Did you just make that up?"

"No, Sage, it's taken me the whole trip down the mountain to figure it out! Elenry said we had to problem solve and she wasn't kidding."

"It sounds good. Let's do it."

Sagel dismounted Balan carefully, staggering briefly on her weary legs when she exerted her full weight. Grimacing, she bent her knees alternately, trying to work out the stiffness in her joints.

"Sage, look! They've got wheels!" he exclaimed. Breathing a sigh of relief, Sagel jogged over to see for herself. Each of the four crates was equipped with thick, black, metal wheels; there were eight of them on a crate—each wheel about five inches in diameter.

"How will we attach the horses' ropes to the crates?" Sagel wondered. Upon noticing metal handles on the sides of the crates, she figured they could probably tie the long ropes through them. Daniel saw them too, and gave the handles a pull, testing their strength.

"These look fine," he said. "We can just tie the ropes to these."

They tied the long ropes to the backs of the saddles and then threaded each rope through the steel handles. Finally, all the crates were secured to at least two horses, distributing the weight of the crates as much as possible. Despite the wind's bite, Sagel's face relaxed into a small smile, and her eyes softened. For the first time that day, she truly believed that they could complete the task at hand. Her forehead smoothed and the adrenaline in her veins receded.

"Okay," Daniel said, after double checking his knots. They couldn't take any chances, especially with the entire town's primary food source in their care.

Sagel's limbs had lost their stiffness, but the insides of her legs still ached. The two of them ducked under the ropes and up to the horses, where Daniel started gathering their lead ropes.

"I can pull and lead the horses first," Sagel said, taking the ropes from Daniel's gloved hands, "then we can switch off." She was inwardly hoping that she had given Dan the easier job, since he had already contributed so much to the task. It also felt good to be taking some initiative again. A slight bother was nagging at Sagel, for she was usually the one planning and making decisions in her and Dan's relationship, but in using the horses, she was forced to let Daniel lead the way, for his knowledge of the animals greatly exceeded hers.

"Sounds good," Daniel said, as he walked towards the crates. "Make sure you steer clear of any icy patches, or the crates might slide, or the horses slip."

Taking in the precautions, Sagel waited for Daniel to reach his position behind the crates, and then started walking. To her great relief, the animals all walked with force, pulling the crates without noticeable strain. They walked well together, creating a potent pulling force. Even Wisle walked without struggle. They went on like this for about fifteen minutes before Daniel called the parade to a stop, and jogged around the corner to claim the ropes from Sagel. Daniel was smiling, but puffing as he started walking.

To her dismay, Sagel found that she had indeed given Daniel the harder job, for pushing and guiding the crates from behind took much more force and concentration than leading the animals. Since there were four bulky crates to keep in line, Sagel found it best to push forward and slightly to the right on the crate that was nearest the edge of the mountain, so there was no way that the crates would slide of the edge, taking the animals, and possibly the pullers with them. A shudder ran up her spine as Sagel thought about that horrible possibility. It had taken them under an hour to get down the mountain, and they were now going significantly slower. Sagel tried not to think about the warm bed and food that would surely be awaiting her at home. The only other things to concentrate on were the crates, and Sagel decided that she should focus only on them. She remembered noticing that Elenry breathed deeply whenever things got tense, such as at the village meeting. Sagel started to breathe deeply in rhythm with her steps and pushes. Each breath she took grew heavier; she could feel her lungs protesting at the icy air that she was pulling into them.

With every step, her frozen limbs loosened. A surprise came when she realized that she could actually feel her toes, now that her warm blood was circulating through her body. Keeping track of time was another means of concentration that she tried, but she found that it was rather pointless; they would get there when they got there. Finally Daniel stopped walking, and the crates wheeled to a stop. The animals snorted and shifted their weight. The rest at the bottom of the mountain had rejuvenated them, but the long haul up was starting to wear on them.

Without being told or signaled, Sagel walked up past the row of crates and animals to reclaim the ropes. A sharp pain stung her left shoulder; probably from her hunched stance as she had pushed.

"We're about half way there," Daniel affirmed, rubbing his hands together, and then he turned and took his new position at the crates. Without conversation, Sagel bunched the lead ropes in one hand and continued the ascent up the mountain. She knew Dan was right, but she decided again not to try to mark the time, for that often made everything seem longer.

As she walked up the steepening road, shifting the bunch of ropes from one hand to another behind her, she let her mind meander down roads of its own. Images of lands unknown, the barren side of the mountain, and the journey that she hoped to make swirled in and out of her mind's eye. She imagined herself with Daniel and Elenry, braving a winter blizzard, holding protectively onto bottles of the life saving sap that Elenry had prophesized; and an image of them walking into the village and into welcoming arms, everyone applauding and hugging them for their brave and fruitful journey. But her mind wandered no more, for at that moment, Daniel shouted something unintelligible, yanking Sagel from her reverie.

"Daniel?!" she called back, alarmed.

"Sagel! Pull towards the mountain, now!" he screamed.

Two things happened at once. Sagel realized that the crates were slipping towards the edge of a drop-off, and Wisle brayed and took off into a full bolt, spooking the horses. All at once a wall of galloping creatures was running at Sagel. Gordon's shoulder knocked her sideways before she could dive out of the way. Fortunately, the force of their run pulled the crates through the icy patch on which they were slipping. Sagel was knocked towards the edge of the cliff, and slipped onto her back as her feet found and lost the icy patch. She began sliding down towards the crates that were speeding towards her faster than she towards them. She collided with the outermost crate, and the force sent her rolling over the edge of the mountain.

Chapter 19

The Glove

A silent scream rang in Sagel's mind.

Before she could slip off the edge, Sagel turned onto her side and reached for anything that she could grab. She grasped nothing but cold icy ground. Both of her feet were now off the edge, and dangling towards the dizzying drop below her. Frantically, she clawed at the ground, digging her gloved fingers into what little snow crusted the surface of the perilous patch. Nothing was holding her, and her feet could find no ledge to stand on. Farther she slid, until her hands were the only thing left clutching the edge of the cliff.

Then, like two steel manacles, Dan's hands clamped down on Sagel's wrists. He was leaning towards her, on his knees, which were as far away form the edge as his balance would allow.

"I got you," he grunted. Gravity fought against Daniel, pulling Sagel farther and farther down. Daniel switched his hold abruptly, making Sagel cry out. She was utterly unaware of the terrified tears that streaked her frozen cheeks. She was aware of little more than her seemingly imminent demise. The new hold that Daniel took was a brave one. Instead of holding onto both of her hands, he held onto one of hers with both of his. Sagel's free arm dangled like a frozen piece of wood nailed to her shoulder.

Slowly the hold he had slipped. He pulled fiercely as he tried to heft her up.

Something in Sagel's wrist popped.

A piercing cry of mingled shock and intense pain rang out across the snowy terrain bellow. The bad hand felt suddenly numb, and she knew that if her glove hadn't been so tightly tied around her wrist, she would not have been able to hang on to Dan's hand, and all one hundred and ten pounds of Sagel Bleudry would have plummeted. Crimson would have splattered the luminous ivory of the pristine winter blanket. But none of that would be so, because of a glove. A rush of adrenaline surged through her system, and she threw her good arm up towards Dan. Instead of catching Daniel, it caught the edge, and she gripped it with all of her strength. Just as Sagel had hoped, Daniel took her by the wrist of her clinging hand, and pulled back with as much force as was left in him. Both of them cried out as Dan fell backward, but to their immense relief, he brought Sagel up with him. She was pulled up on top of and then over him, both of them breathing and gasping hugely. Sagel rolled over, trembling.

"Oh, Sagel. Oh, I'm sorry, I'm so sorry, Sage," Daniel sat up, hovering anxiously over her shaking figure. "Sage? Sagel? Are you okay?"

A strangled mix between a whimper and a groan escaped Sagel's blue lips. Never before had she experienced this kind of pain.

"Sagel!" Daniel cried. "Can you hear me?"

"Yes," Sagel said through clenched teeth, "I can hear you."

Dan's mouth released and his eyes filled with warm concern,

though Sagel's face remained in the twisted grimace of pain. Daniel decided to say no more just yet; he could see the pain in his friend's face.

"Dan...," she gasped. "You saved me."

Slowly, Sagel sat up, propped by her good arm, though it shook like the rest of her body. A little color came back into her face.

"It was all I could do," Daniel mumbled, not used to being the hero, "you would've done the same for me."

"Of course," Sagel said, her voice breaking through the pain. She hadn't realized it but down her cheeks flowed warm tears, though they only stayed warm for so long until the bitter wind blew them away, leaving a cold trail behind. Gingerly, Daniel put his hands under her armpits and slowly raised her up. Sluggishly, her legs found their place under her, and to her relief, were stable enough to support her. Cradling the injured wrist seemed like the only thing to do, though even that small amount of pressure sent sharp pains through the injured arm.

Then Dan gasped. "The horses."

They set off, Daniel jogging up the road with Sagel hobbling along behind him. Running was absolutely the last thing that Sagel wanted to do. As they ran, Daniel kept turning around; each time he would apologize and promise that as soon as they found the horses they would try to do something about her arm. All that Sagel could do was nod and wince at what the pounding of her feet did to the pain in her wrist.

Daniel began to feel frantic. No longer did he look back to check on Sagel, who was falling farther and farther behind. He desperately repeated, "Oh please", as they covered distance up the mountain road. Then they could smell them. The earthy sweet smell of the Shinken horses was more comforting than Sagel had ever thought possible. Daniel's sigh was saturated with relief as he turned once more to look for Sagel who was a good twenty paces behind him. Tears of relief flooded over Dan's cheeks, and tears of pain brimmed out of Sagel's eyes as they approached the parade.

Five hoofed animals stood snorting and shifting toward the mountain wall by the road. The four crates were intact, from what they could see, though one of the wheels looked like it had snapped clean out of the wood.

"They're here," Daniel rejoiced. "Right here. Oh, thank you…"

He rubbed each of the animals' noses, pausing to hug Gordon around his thick neck. Sagel came to a stop by the crates, smiling with her own relief, though it was mingled with the pinched contortion of pain on her face. Meticulously, Daniel checked and rechecked all the ropes and knots on the horses and the crates. Though the pain was making concentrated focus difficult for Sagel, she tried to be useful by checking the wheels. All the crates were in good condition but the crate closest to the mountain's edge, which was now lacking one wheel; probably from the sudden jerk and speed that the horses had kicked up in their mad bolt.

At last, Daniel was done with his inventory, and stepped back to stand with Sagel. The pain in her arm was like nothing that she had ever experienced, though in truth, she hadn't experienced much in the way of pain. Every time a slight shift of position occurred in her arm, it felt like someone was popping the injured wrist in and out of its socket. Sagel preferred not to think of how she was going to fix it. Her first priority was to get back to town, and then deal with the arm.

"So…um," Daniel said, pausing briefly, "maybe I should push."

"Yeah, that'd be good."

The thought of pushing the crates up the long and twisting road was not a pleasant one for Sagel. Once again, the horrid flower of anxiety blossomed in her chest, its dark petals unfolding and flourishing in her imagination. New worries about the outcome of their suddenly misshapen adventure filled her thoughts. Would they pass Elenry's test? Were they up to her standards, even after their very close call with disaster? Pushing the thoughts as far from her mind as possible seemed to be the only thing that she could do. Focus her anxious energy on something more productive. Though the anxiety did her no good, it somewhat distracted her form the pain.

Without further ado, Sagel took the ropes in her good hand and began to walk. They were farther over towards the mountain side, and Daniel walked on the outside of the outermost crate, steadying and watching them cautiously. Surprisingly, the remainder of their fatigue inducing trek went quite smoothly. The horses continued, ever vigilant, up the road. Wisle was the only one to put up any kind of resistance, and that was in the form of snorting and head tossing. As the sun began to dip down behind the far horizon, a new, bitter freeze settled over the land.

Night's chill took hold of the mountain.

Not even the moon showed its face in the black abyss of the sky. No twinkling stars gazed down on the whitewashed landscape. Though it was not completely black, the shadow that the mountain cast across its south side made the road much darker. Only the faint pearly glow of the alabaster snow alerted them as to where the road was. A faint radiance began to softly resonate around the side of the next curve of the road, and every nerve ending in Sagel's body screamed in relief. Shinken.

Chapter 20

Release

As they slowly rounded the corner of the last curve in the mountain road, the light of the town washed its comfort across their exhausted parade. Never in her life had Sagel been more thrilled to see the little village. Not even after their harrowing journey up the mountain with Ebin in tow. If her arm hadn't been in so much pain, Sagel would have dropped to kiss the very ground of the village road. Sagel led the horses up the main road of town. Not many people were walking about that evening, but the ones who were gawked and whispered. Sagel and Daniel walked with their heads up and their eyes forward. Daniel walked up front with Sagel now that there was no need to keep the crates from slipping. To their relief, out of the five or so people they saw, no one approached them, but only nodded gratefully now that the village would be restocked with food. At the storefront of the little market in the center of town, Daniel untied the crates from the animals.

"Are they okay?" Sagel asked when Balan appeared to have fallen asleep standing as Daniel untied her.

"Yeah, they're just dead tired," Daniel said as he got through the last intricate knot.

"That makes all of us," Sagel said, yawning.

Daniel nodded in agreement and then turned back to Sagel, his large hazel eyes still anxious, but now with a hint of happiness.

"Are you sure you're okay?" Daniel asked.

"Yes, Daniel," Sagel said, her voice a little hoarse from fatigue and lack of use. "You—you saved my life." As she said these words, a sudden cloud of emotion engulfed her. The two most powerful feelings making up the reason behind her sudden tears were gratitude and love. Awkwardly, ignoring the stab of pain in her right arm, she put both of her arms around his neck and embraced him.

"Thank you."

Her voice was choked by tears, but she was sure that he understood, for he put his arms around her in return and muttered something.

"We better get the horses back," Daniel said, as they pulled away. It seemed harder now to stand by themselves after leaning on each other.

The walk back to the horse stable was dark and slow. They had left all four crates outside the storefront, where the manager of the store, Bailey Sinail, would find them in the morning. With the horses in tow, they trudged down the road towards the horse stable. All at once, Daniel turned to Sagel, his eyes glistening with power and excitement.

"We did it," he breathed.

"Yeah," she giggled. "We did."

Their pace quickened with this joyful realization. The sight of the warm barn was almost as welcoming as their first sight of the town. All the horses, and Wisle, were put safely in their stalls and given fresh feed and water.

Sleepily they walked the road to Elenry's camp, not speaking. They were far too tired to speak. A small but welcoming fire crackled and wavered cheerfully in front of the Medicine Woman's tent. She must have heard their crunching footsteps, for she was at the mouth of the tent, peering out at them as they approached. Arros was standing next to the shelter with a winter blanket draped over his vast back.

"Hello," Elenry said serenely. "How did you do?"

"We did it," they chorused.

"How did it go?" Elenry asked, after they were all sitting around the fire with hot mugs of tea in their hands.

Immediately, Daniel launched into a narrative of their experiences. His voice kicked up a notch from its tired cadence as he went further into their adventure. Throughout the entire retelling, Elenry listened. Her face remained soft and attentive through the entire story.

Daniel closed with a long sigh. Elenry smiled at them.

"I'm very happy with you both," she declared.

Both Sagel and Daniel watched her through sleepy lids. Though both of them were thrilled at her praise, they wanted nothing more than to return home to sleep.

"Now," Elenry said, straightening up and gliding towards Sagel, taking Sagel's bad arm in her hands very gingerly, "what do we have here?"

"Well, I heard a pop when it happened, and it really hurts every time-AHHHHHH!" Sagel screamed, as Elenry made one sharp tug; another popping sound following the pull. The intense pain was gone, sharp stabbing pains replaced by a dull ache.

"There," Elenry said. "You dislocated it."

"You fixed it?" Sagel asked, rubbing her wrist softly.

"Yes. It's almost as good as new."

Testing the pain, Sagel flexed the arm and wrist, wiggling her fingers and clenching her fist. Nothing hurt with significant pain, merely a dull throb leftover from the initial injury.

"Thank you," Sagel said, smiling gratefully at the Medicine Woman.

"You're welcome, Sagel," Elenry said, turning to her horse and removing his blanket. Immediately, Arros snapped to attention, standing straighter and facing Elenry.

"I will be taking you home, as I promised."

Without further conversation, Sagel and Daniel mounted Arros behind Elenry. Sagel's house was much closer, so they went there first. Sagel smiled at Daniel triumphantly as she dismounted and walked to the door. He returned a tired grin.

"Rest well, Sagel, and be at my camp by mid-day tomorrow," Elenry said, her voice smooth and encouraging. Sagel waved good-bye, happy that she now had painless mobility in both of her arms. Arros's solid hoof beats sounded off into the night towards Daniel's house as Sagel climbed the steps to her door.

She opened the door and exclaimed, "We did it."

Torren and Lorel embraced her exhausted body, helping her shrug out of her winter apparel. Her parents had waited up for her in the living room. Lorel had tried in vain to immerse herself in a book, while Torren had attempted to read a pottery catalogue. Their anticipation had gotten the better of them, and they had ended up twiddling their thumbs and making random conversation. Without remembering much of the process, Sagel ended up in her bed, pajamas on, face washed, and teeth cleaned.

"You can tell us all about it in the morning, honey," her father said, kissing her forehead.

"We love you, Sagel," murmured her mother, also kissing her before standing up and leaving her room. That was all Sagel saw before she blissfully fell into sleep's open arms.

Chapter 21

Circumstances

Dreams faded in and out all night. A dull gray light shone through her bedroom window, making a patch of gray on the floor. More snow had fallen the night before, and the temperature had plummeted even further. Low howling could be heard as the winter winds whipped at the mountain and through the village. Sagel woke up to the wind's moaning. Her eyes were blurry with sleep, and she found that her head ached. Her arm was still tender, but not nearly as fragile as they night before. Again and again she replayed their task as she dressed.

"Sagel?" A low voice said through her slightly opened door.

It was Nigel. His hair was sticking up in numerous places on his head and he was still in his pajamas, but his eyes were as bright and curious as always. Sagel took a step towards the door to open it, but an all too eager Nigel opened it wider and slipped in.

"What is it?" Sagel asked.

"Tell me all about it," he said quickly, sitting on her bed and watching her expectantly. "What did you have to do?"

Of course Nigel would be insistently interested in her adventures. The boy spent so much time *reading* about adventures, it was no wonder he was hungry for a real one. Sagel sighed. She knew that she would eventually have to describe their journey down and up the mountain, and she also knew that Nigel would press her for every last detail. Nigel nodded encouragingly.

"Can't you just wait for when I tell mom and dad?" Sagel said, ushering him off her bed so she could make it. "I really don't want to tell it four times."

"Please, Sagel?" he asked. His voice was not irritating or whiny, simply curious.

"Why do you want to know so badly?" she asked, fluffing her pillow and stepping away from the bed, still eyeing him.

"I'm curious," he said. "Why won't you tell me?"

"Because, I would rather tell it *once* to all of you!" Sagel snapped, rubbing one temple gingerly.

Nigel sighed, shrugged, and followed his sister from the room. The kitchen was still bathed in the dark haze of winter morning light. Sagel wondered how early she had gotten up. The little sun measuring instrument attached to the wall indicated that it was just past sunup. In other words, much too early. Sagel opened up the freezer and brought out a block of ice to melt, then lit the stove. Nigel shadowed her, looking desperate for answers. She pulled a pot out of the cupboard and placed it on the stove burner, putting the ice block in the pot to melt.

"Sagel?" Nigel asked, his voice small.

"What?" she sighed.

"Please?" he said simply, still watching his sister as she leaned on the counter top.

For a few seconds she merely concentrated on the pain in her head, trying to quell the ache. Once the ice had melted and the water had started steaming, she sat at the table. Reluctantly, she turned to face her little brother, and then began a recount of their long and strenuous journey. Nigel's eyes widened at certain parts, his jaw dropping in others. He was a good listener, only interrupting at the part where Sagel nearly plummeted to her death.

"And he saved you?" he asked, his voice full of mingled horror and awe.

"Yes," Sagel said, continuing without a break. She knew that she would hear an even stronger reaction from her parents when she told them of the dangers that she had faced. With this thought, she realized that telling Nigel first was helping her figure out how best to tell her parents, without frightening them so much that they might stop her from taking any more tests. She knew that they would be doubtful, even frightened for her safety. Daniel and she were in this now, and there was no way that they would turn back, especially with Dan's mother in the clinic. By the end of the story, Nigel's eyes were as wide as perfect, flat Nuntrefurs.

"So you passed?" he said, his voice hopeful, though his eyes were full of yearning.

"Yes…but we still need to pass the mental test," Sagel said, taking the boiling water from the stove and pouring it into her favorite mug. She took the pitcher of sap from the refrigerator, and poured a dollop into the hot water. Her thin brows furrowed as she pondered what they might have to do for the mental test. She only hoped that the test wouldn't have anything to do with counting and mathematical reasoning, which had always given her a hard time in school. Now that they were on break, she wished that she could go to school and have access to their plethora of books on Asthekia and other school subjects.

A door opened somewhere in the house, and a moment or two

later her mother and father entered the kitchen. Torren walked to his daughter, placing his hand lovingly on her head.

"How did it go?" he asked, his voice lively with interest.

"Tell us everything," Lorel said, walking to the freezer and bringing out some breakfast makings. "You have got to be starving. I'll make you a big breakfast."

"Thanks, Ma," Sagel said, her stomach growling.

Already her headache had begun to subside. She took a sip of her hot sap tea, enjoying the warmth that spread through her stomach and core. Torren sat in his usual chair and smiled at his daughter. Though Sagel could tell that Torren was eager to hear about her trial, just as her other family members were, she sensed a little trepidation as well. Moments later, Nova ambled into the kitchen, holding a little handmade doll. It took her a moment to recall what had been going on with Sagel, and for this break, Sagel was grateful, because Nova didn't bombard her with questions as Nigel had.

"Did you pass?" was all she asked, and looked impressed when Sagel said that she had.

"Wait, I'm almost done here," Lorel said. "I don't want to listen to the big adventure with sounds of the stove in my head."

When breakfast was placed on the table, the casual conversation among her family members dissolved, and they all sat watching her expectantly, even Nigel, who hoped he would hear even more about her experiences. Sagel sighed and took a bite of the sap soaked bread, gazing from face to face. And then she began.

The entire group tensed and stared open mouthed as Sagel sped through the description of her close call.

"You—you almost fell off the mountain?" Lorel asked, her

voice a mere whisper.

"Yeah, but Daniel was right there, and my arm is fine…."

"What did Elenry say about your arm?" Torren pressed, his brows creasing with worry and curiosity.

Trying to keep it as casual as she could, Sagel explained what had happened to her wrist, and how Elenry had easily corrected it. Lorel did not look appeased.

"You could have died."

"Ma, I'm fine. It was an accident, and it's over, we fixed it. Elenry wouldn't have sent us out if she had known we were going to be in any serious danger. It was my careless mistake, and I'll be more careful from here on out," Sagel said.

"Of course she would, Sagel," Torren interjected, "that was the point of the test— to see if you could in fact succeed without dropping the load off the mountain or dying. I thought you knew what you signed up for!"

"I know what I signed up for," Sagel retorted, her face crumpling with a grimace of annoyance. "I'm just saying that Daniel and I aren't stupid…we figured it out, and the next test shouldn't be that dangerous, because it's a test of mind."

Her parents exchanged glances.

"We're still going," Sagel said stubbornly.

"Of course you are, dear, we just need you to understand what danger this whole thing involves," Lorel said, her expression fixed with worry.

"I do understand. You don't need to worry," Sagel said. "We'll be safe with Elenry, and if we pass the other test then we can go." She spoke more to herself than to her parents.

From her closet she pulled the second of her two heavy winter coats. The first one was being washed and mended by Lorel, as it was stained and ripped from the previous night's journey. She pulled her hair up, something she rarely did. Only for school did she ever feel the need to tie her hair up, for it got rather irritating if her hair fell in front of her face when she was reading or working. Now she pulled her hair up because she felt it helped wake her mind up a bit. She looked at herself in the small mirror on her wall. It was strange seeing her hair pulled back. It wasn't so bad; she rather liked it. Without the curtain of mahogany, she could see her angular jaw line and high set, but thin, cheekbones. She didn't have much of a forehead, but it grew somewhat with the absence of hair cover. Without much gusto, she exited the room toward the living room, where she would bid her parents goodbye and make her way up to Elenry's camp.

"I have to go do the last test," she said, when Torren looked questioningly up from is book.

"Oh, of course," he said, as Lorel joined them in the small front room.

"Do your best," Lorel said, hugging her daughter tightly to her. Torren claimed her next, patting her on the shoulder as he released her.

"You'll do fine," Torren said, sounding surer of Sagel than she felt of herself.   Nigel walked in then, watching his sister with longing and a hint of jealousy. Sagel was happy that Nigel wasn't going. Not because he would be a nuisance, or steal her glory or anything like that. She was happy because she would fear for his safety. Already she feared for her own, and they had completed only one perilous test.

"Um, I'm not sure when I'll be home," she said uncertainly.

"That's fine, but ask Elenry to escort you home if you finish after nightfall," Torren replied. Lorel nodded, reassuring Sagel that they were fully supporting her. Nigel was still watching Sagel, looking like he wanted to wish her well, or give her a hug. But Sagel knew that he was too stubborn to do that, especially when he was being left out of the thing he wanted most.

With that, Sagel smiled, cocking an eyebrow.

Reassuring smiles followed her to the door.

After a silent but deep breath, Sagel opened the door, stepping out into the frigid jaws of winter. The warmth of the house was lost behind her as she shut the door. Down the porch steps she went, her legs moving automatically as her mind whirred into gear. Reviewing various facts that they had learned in school took all of her concentration, which was a nice break from the gnawing anxieties that had eaten away at her through the morning.

The creaking had grown infinitely worse in the trees around her house; walking down the road was like being surrounded by a wailing chorus of mournful beings. It was too eerie to even review the capitals of the continents with the voices of the ailing forest swirling in her ears. The breath in her chest quickened and her heart sped, overactive imagination intensifying the growing fear. Never had she been so grateful to enter the Stretch. Silence enveloped her, and she sighed in relief. Sagel inwardly scolded herself. Getting all worked up over trees—trees that groaned. Still, trees, nonetheless. A normally willingly imaginative soul, she now willfully pushed all imaginings from her mind and noticed, with relief, that her headache was completely gone. As she hurried down the snow packed road, tucking the hood of her jacket more tightly around her icy ears, she tried not to let herself fall into the land of unnerving fantasies.

No sun shone through the veil of clouds. Something tugged

at her attention. She suddenly felt that she should go to Daniel's house before she went to Elenry's camp. It was not mid-day yet, and she had at least thirty minutes before Elenry would be expecting them.

A shiver ran up her spine as she saw the town. Much to her disappointment, the usually comforting lights and smells of the village were not very noticeable that day. The houses had fewer lights shining from the windows, and the stores looked indifferent. The streets were eerily empty. A small cluster of somber townspeople was standing in front of the clinic—some leaving, some coming, and some just standing about. As she passed the clinic front, she couldn't help but steal a glance at the unnerving sight. At least five or six people were standing in front of the door; some coughed, but most were silent.

Briefly through a front window, she glimpsed inside the clinic. People rushed about, nurses and patients moving from the front room to the back. Galah was carrying a tray laden with small wooden cups. Sagel was sure that the cups were full of tree sap.

Snow had fallen heavily the night before, packing the streets with a new layer of white powder. As she walked, she imagined that the snow had healing properties, and that all who wanted to be well would only have to walk barefoot through the magic white dust. If only her imaginings had any semblance of reality. She tried not to think of Shinken's situation as she walked up to the Carson's home.

Daniel's house had not a light in it. Trotting up the walk, Sagel hurried up to the door and knocked softly. No one came to the door, so she tried once more, a little harder this time. Footsteps trudged on the other side of the door, and Sagel took a step back from the front door as it opened.

Michael stood before her. Down his cheeks ran veins of tears. Scruffy stubble speckled his jaw line. Michael's were eyes pink, and rimmed with red. Sagel couldn't help a stifled gasp.

"What is it?" she asked, her voice cautious as she expected the worse.

"Gone...she's gone, and now he is, too," his voice was a hoarse whisper, and more tears beaded up in his eyes, defying the rims that held them back.

"Oh no," she breathed, feeling a lump forming in her throat. Louise had been a second mother to her. Fond memories of Louise taking her and Daniel by the hand and walking them up the road to Sagel's house in the warmer months swam before her. She remembered Louise bringing little berry flavored ice cubes out to them as they ran dizzying circles around the grass behind Daniel's house.

"Where is Daniel?" Sagel asked suddenly, sickening dread taking hold of her.

"With Elenry," he said simply, as fresh tears blazed new trails down his pale cheeks. She took a step toward Michael, and opened her arms and hugged him. He was still for a second before returning her embrace. She felt a shiver run through him as he stifled a sob. She herself was doing everything she could not to break down herself.

"You'd better go," Michael said finally, releasing her. "Daniel's already there."

Sagel nodded quickly, turning and walking down the snowy path from their house. The door was already shut, as Michael retreated into the sorrow wrought home.

A swirling breeze tousled her dark pony-tail across her shoulders. Tears brimmed over as she hiccoughed sobs. It hadn't been like this when Gwenoth died. Not even close. If Gwenoth's death was a bee sting, then Louise's was the amputation of an extremity. Another choking sob grasped her by the throat, and her breath came quickly and shallowly. The road wound underneath her as she walked, though she was only vaguely aware of where she was going. She cringed at the thought of telling her parents. But maybe they already knew. Perhaps her mother or father would run into town for some errands, and pay a visit to Michael, only to learn the news themselves. Sagel willed it to happen this way, for something about telling them herself put a crushing weight on her chest.

Roughly wiping the tears from her face, Sagel was surprised to find that she was already at the mouth of the Stretch. Before she went any further, she stopped to prepare herself mentally for what state Daniel might be in. As she tromped through the deep snow of the healthy forest, she heard soft voices above the crackling of a hearty fire. She broke through the trees to find Daniel and Elenry sitting across from one another at the fire. Daniel's eyes were cold and red. She did not know what to say.

"Hello, Sagel," Elenry said, her voice smoother, but her eyes weary.

"Hello," Sagel replied quietly, relieved that her voice did not crack.

"I'm sorry," whispered Elenry.

"Thank you," replied Sagel through cinereous orbs.

No more words were needed. A sudden wave of paralyzing dread flooded her system. How were they going to test now? All of this seemed horribly unfair. Sagel felt ashamed. Her best friend's mother was dead, and all she could think about was whether or not they would still test.

"I will not rush either one of you into anything, but I need to know if you still wish to test," she said, passing Sagel a mug of hot sap tea.

Sagel looked at it disdainfully, but took a long drink. She hesitated before she replied, and looked anxiously at Daniel, who had not even turned to look at the Medicine Woman. He did not answer, and somehow Sagel felt like he was waiting for her to answer first.

"Yes…I—I still wish to test."

Elenry nodded, peace coming to her eyes. Sagel watched as the woman's attentive gaze trained itself on Daniel.

"No."

Sagel froze. Never had that word cut her so deeply. Slowly she turned her head towards him, listening intently for anything he might say. Surely she had misheard.

"I can't…leave my father."

Blood flooded Sagel's chilled face. Whom she was really angry at, she was not entirely certain. Hot tears clambered from her eyes and down her cheeks, screaming defeat and disappointment as they streaked her flushed face.

"I…I just can't," Daniel's watery voice filled every corner of Sagel's mind. His father—of course, his father. But how could it be, that the one person who wanted nothing more than to experience the unknowns of the world around him, would suddenly give it all up? After convincing her to embark on this seemingly impossible journey, after gaining her commitment to this mission, after saving her life, he was giving it up. She could not accept it. It was as if a wonderful game had suddenly come to an end and she had lost everything. Like the end of her childhood had come early with the surrender of her childhood companion.

"P-please, Daniel," she whispered, feeling like a little girl pleading with a stubborn parent.

He shook his head as tears rolled down the cold-flushed swells of his freckle dusted cheeks. A blush of mingled embarrassment and anger washed her face, and she turned her gaze to the snow at her feet. Then Elenry was there, her arms snaking around their shoulders in a protective embrace. She said nothing at first, but was merely there as the two of them sat in muddled silence. Had Sagel done something to Daniel to change his mind? It most certainly was the death of his mother. If Lorel had been taken by the disease, surely Sagel would abandon all attempts to risk her own life on a breakneck journey to bring home the cure. That had to be it. Even so, she stewed in the simmering anxiety of her thoughts and inward wonderings. Did she still want to go? Would she go alone? Could Elenry and she do this thing together, with no one else?

Chapter 22

Family Time

Silence pressed them into themselves. Sagel squirmed restlessly and looked at Daniel, willing him to say something. As badly as she wanted to try to persuade Daniel not to back out, she knew it wasn't the time. She had to let him mourn.

After a long meditation in the flames of the fire, Elenry smiled to herself and told Sagel to come back the next morning as soon as she was up and ready, and then Elenry would give her the test of mind. Daniel looked to be at war with himself as they made their way to the road. To go or not to go? In truth, Sagel felt no more anger towards her friend. How horrible it would be to lose a parent. How truly horrible. Fresh tears budded along the dams of Sagel's eyes, but she refused to let them overflow. More for her own sake than Daniel's; she was much too weary and shocked to handle another crying jag.

Suddenly Daniel stopped walking. They were on the road on the edge of the center of Shinken. Sagel's heart jumped, readying herself for anything that he might say or do.

"I'm sorry, Sage," he said, his voice no more than a whisper. Slowly he raised his head, looking pitiful, "I didn't want to do this to you…I-I just can't go. My father has no one but me. No one. He cried all night, and hadn't stopped when I left this morning. I can't leave him. I just can't. It doesn't feel right…I'm so sorry." Fresh tears were trickling down his cold-bitten cheeks.

"Daniel, I'm not angry with you. I really am not. I'm sorry, too. I have *no* idea what you must be going through. Please don't feel guilty…I'm not angry."

"I'm sorry…" Daniel whimpered, his arms hanging loosely. He seemed to have no more expendable energy to even lift his heavy hands.

The winter chill swirled around them, mixing with the sorrow that seemed to hang everywhere in the air.

Daniel was one of those people who once barraged by his own guilt, would simply wallow interminably in it, waiting for someone to pull him out. Sagel could tell that it was going to take awhile for Daniel to fully accept that he wasn't to blame—for anything.

"Maybe we should have left earlier…gotten the cure sooner. Then she would have been okay," Daniel sobbed.

"Daniel, don't you blame yourself!" Sagel said, putting her hands firmly on both of his shoulders and holding back determined tears. "You are not to blame for your mother's death. It wasn't your fault, and there was nothing you could have done to help her."

Sagel could almost see a tangible veil of black guilt enfolding her friend.

"I just don't know what to do," Daniel hiccupped.

"You don't need to *do* anything but stay here, be with your father, and stay healthy."

As Sagel assured her friend, she found herself already letting go of any last remnants of anger that had lingered, waiting for an opportunity to spring.. She had felt abandoned and deserted, but the awful fact of his loss made her own reactions seem trivial.

Daniel stepped backwards, wiping the moisture from his cheeks before the frosty air froze the tears to his skin. After clearing his throat a couple of times, he managed a very weak smile, just barely lifting the corners of his thin mouth. Silently, they turned back towards town. Daniel's house loomed ahead. Not wanting to disturb Michael, Sagel said goodbye to Daniel on his doorstep. A lump formed in her throat as she recalled the wonderful afternoons that the duo had spent sitting on Daniel's rug, sipping various seasonal drinks provided by Louise.

"Thank you, Sage," sighed Daniel, looking more fatigued at the moment than anything else. Sagel couldn't help but wonder if Daniel had actually been there when Louise had died. If he had seen the light go from her eyes and the breath leave her chest for the last time…. Pushing that thought aside, Sagel smiled at Daniel, her gray eyes growing soft and her cheeks flushing with color as she realized how completely forgiving and accepting of his decision she had become. It was strange as she walked home through the quiet village. Emotions swam confusedly through her head. One minute a pocket of acceptance would envelop her, and the next she would walk into a brief inferno of abandonment and resentment.

One old car that belonged to the village grocer putted along through the snow slowly, but the windows were fogged, obscuring the driver. The clinic seemed to be the most populated area in the village. A steady stream of people could be seen moving about inside.

Her step quickened as she passed the crowded building.

Not even the Stretch could draw Sagel's preoccupied attention. The usually perceptive girl was now fully immersed in a world of her own, where the dark and light aspects of her personality had it out to see which would supply the final feeling towards all of this. Dark pushed an aggressive resentment that easily overtook the acceptance, but light was quick to send out powerful compassion. It went back and forth like this all the way to her front doorstep.

Upon walking into her familiar surroundings, comfort blossomed in her chest. A mellow fire crackled in the fireplace on the far side of the sitting room, and the little reading lamp by the comfortable reading chair was turned on, adding to the soft light emanating through the room. Warmth from the fire and the sheer good energy of her home warmed her chilled bones, and momentarily placated the storm of her emotions.

In the chair sat Nigel, curled up with his sketchbook in his lap. He appeared to be hunched over something very detailed, as his face was taut with concentration. Suddenly aware of her presence, he looked her up and down, confusion plain on his features.

"What's going on?" and then, more excitedly, "did you pass?"

"No," Sagel sighed, "I didn't take the test yet."

Before her ever inquisitive little brother could deploy his barrage of questions, Sagel broke into a shortened recount of the morning's happenings. Nigel sat wide-eyed upon hearing about Louise. Before long, both Lorel and Nova had joined them and were listening quietly as Sagel repeated it all for them. Lorel gasped and brought her hand to her mouth, tears forming quickly in her eyes.

"Oh dear…dear, dear, dear," her mother whispered. "Michael must be in a state."

More tears fell as her voice broke and she stifled a sob. Nova had been holding one of her dolls by the torso, but left it forgotten on the living room floor as she went to sit on the couch and snuggle beside her mother. Sagel too sat with them, placing a hand on her mother's back and rubbing her shoulders gently. This had been the part that she had dreaded most. While Sagel had loved Louise and had sought her out as another mother figure, Lorel and Louise had grown as close as sisters. They had shared their lives and families with each other. Louise had introduced foreign but delicious Earth recipes, and Lorel had broken out the oldest and most complicated concoctions passed down in her family. They had grown gardens, children, and love with one another.

"So, Daniel's not going?" Nigel asked.

"No," Sagel replied.

"So there's no one to go with you?"

"No," Sagel said again. She knew exactly what he was thinking.

Nigel said nothing more, but instead stood up from his comfortable post and walked off towards his bedroom, turning at the last minute back to Lorel.

"Should I get Dad?" he asked.

"Y-yes," Lorel sniffed, trying to gather herself together. "Yes, that would be good. Thank you, Nigel."

"Where is Pa?" Sagel asked.

"Out in the pottery shed," Nova piped up. Nova loved her father's pottery and would often help him paint simple designs on small vases or plates. She had her own little treasure of discarded pottery pieces that she had painted herself.

"Your father thinks that after this is all over, his customers from Starling City will be excited to see his new pieces," Lorel said, standing from the couch and touching both of her daughters' heads. The muscles in her face tensed, as did her mouth. "If either your father or I fall ill, you children will go to stay with Michael."

Michael was loving, and was a good father. Still, Sagel knew that she and her siblings would become horribly homesick, and pine for their parents. Sagel blinked back tears and swallowed the expanding lump in her throat. Nova looked at her mother anxiously.

"But you *won't* fall ill," Sagel stated, the all too familiar anxiety grasping at her once again. Lorel knew her daughter well enough to know that when Sagel tried to take control of reality, it was the nerves talking. She bent to kiss her eldest girl's forehead.

"Just keep putting out good energy to everyone," Lorel finished, and with one last look at her daughters, she straightened and headed for the kitchen to brew sap tea.

Sagel leaned back against the couch, trying hard not to think of anything but the gentle crackle of the fire and her intake and output of her breathing. This meditation worked for awhile, until she heard the backdoor open to let her father and a draft of winter chill in. Voices of her parents drifted in from the kitchen as Lorel explained what Sagel had told her. Not wanting to hear the story again. Sagel sat up as quickly as her tired body would allow, and then made for her room, stepping carefully through the sea of doll clothing and accessories that littered the floor around Nova.

"Don't step on anything!" her little sister gasped as Sagel's ankle scuffed one of her little finger sized dolls. How amazing it was that even in the midst of all of this drama and illness, Nova could still find refuge in her own world of make believe.

Before she could take another step, Sagel's heart lightened as she remembered something. The one place that she had always been able to truly lose herself in her own little wonderland of solitude was the creek. Nestled into her rock she could daydream and float into the sanctuary of fantasy. Yes, it would be cold, but she could bundle up and perhaps take a thermos of sap tea to warm her insides. Once in her room she donned yet another layer and then dragged a brush through her tousled hair. Simply performing these necessary tasks made it easier to suppress her anxiety. She found herself smiling inwardly as she headed for the kitchen, already planning her afternoon by the frozen creek.

Sagel hadn't taken two steps when she heard a sharp and meaningful knock at the door. Her pulse quickened as she course-corrected in that direction.

"Who is it?" Nigel called as he jogged up behind her. Nova padded behind the pack, still clutching her favorite doll.

Torren warily opened the door.

Chapter 23

Of Mind

Elenry smiled softly, the corners of her full lips barely turning upward.

"Hello, Elenry," Torren said.

"Hello, Bleudrys. I apologize for coming unannounced, but this is important," Elenry said quickly.

"Why don't you come in," Lorel offered. "It's freezing out there."

Elenry nodded gratefully and stepped inside.

"Thank you, Lorel," Elenry said, letting her ebony cloak fall from her back and into Lorel's hands. It shimmered curiously with the movement.

"Do you need anything?" Torren asked.

"Yes. But let's start with your ears."

The family watched her uncertainly.

"I'm not giving that lady my ears," Nova whispered to Lorel, stepping back from the Medicine Woman.

They all laughed, the vague tension clearing.

"Let's all sit down," Torren smiled, leading everyone to the couches.

Nova climbed up into her father's lap, and proceeded to watch Elenry for any signs of ear thievery. Elenry sat down next to Sagel, crossing and then uncrossing her long legs.

"I'll just get to the point then," Elenry began, "I'm not sure how much Sagel has told you about matters concerning Daniel…"

"We've been informed of everything," Torren responded at once, nodding slowly.

Lorel stifled a sigh, nodding along with her husband.

"What happened was dreadful, but it happened just the same, and he decided for himself that he was unwilling to continue testing for the impending journey, which has left us all in a bit of a bind," Elenry said. "Sagel, however, has informed me that she still wishes to proceed with things as planned."

Sagel nodded vigorously to both the Medicine Woman and her parents.

"To that I am as grateful as ever. But alas, if we wish for this to be a successful journey, we will need one more person to accompany us. If not to help with whatever the cosmos throws at us both physically and spiritually, then to help pack equipment, and hopefully the cure. Also, in my vision, two other people accompanied me."

"Is there anything else that she needs to do besides the test of mind?" Torren broke in, his brow creasing.

"No," Elenry replied quickly, "she has done everything that I have asked of her wonderfully, and if she passes the test of mind then I would be much obliged to bring her with me, as we have agreed…but I have come here to ask something of Nigel."

Nigel started, his eyes widening and the corners of his mouth twitching, eyes sweeping among the adults in the room.

"I have come to ask both of your permission to allow me to test him, as I see no one else as willing or as fit as he to accompany Sagel and me—assuming they both pass the remaining examinations."

"He's not going…I-I can't have two children gone," Lorel said at once. Torren said nothing, but sighed and pinched the top of his nose between his eyes.

"But Ma, please! I could help her—everyone! I could help, I *know* I could!" Nigel exploded from his chair.

"I implore you to allow this, Lorel," Elenry said gravely, her eyes holding Lorel's captive in their intense gaze. "Since no adult or anyone else has come to me, I need to turn to someone who is ready and willing to go."

"But he is so young! Too young for a journey like that. What if he fell ill? Or was injured? This is ridiculous!" Lorel retorted, forehead wrinkling as she clenched her fists. "Torren—say something!"

"Say what, Lorel?" Torren replied, lowering his hand from his face. "Say *no* to this village's last hope? Say *no* to our boy who is being handpicked by a Medicine Woman going on a journey that could potentially bring the cure back to us?"

Silence settled as Lorel's mind whirred for an adequate argument, but found only her fear of losing her son. Sagel bit her lip as she watched everything unfold. Nigel sat in the reading chair, feet planted on the floor, back straight, and hands fiddling.

"He's much less apt to fall ill if he is out of the village," Elenry stated, still holding Lorel's gaze. "I would look after him and Sagel. They are two strong beings. We must set aside the fact that they are children, and bring forward the fact that they are capable. The tests will prove it for sure, but just looking at them and being with them, I can see and feel that they are indeed ready for something like this."

"Please, Ma?" Nigel whispered, rising and standing before his mother.

Twisting anticipation coiled in Sagel's stomach as she looked from her parent's faces to her brother's.

The long silence was broken only by the sound of Lorel's sigh as she succumbed. Her eyes were still trained on Elenry's as she nodded. Nigel exhaled and then whooped, beaming as he twirled on the spot. Elenry stood.

"Thank you, Torren and Lorel. I understand that this is incredibly difficult for you, but seeing your children dying in the hold of the disease would be much more difficult. They will be safer out of the village," Elenry said, turning to Nigel and smiling at the boy. He smiled back and then hugged both of his parents. Sagel watched her brother and marveled at him. If he felt any fear of the journey, he did not show it.

"We haven't much time, as I wish to set forth on the journey the day after tomorrow at the latest. Sagel still needs to be tested for strength of mind, and I might as well test them both at the same time," Elenry said succinctly. "And as for Nigel's test of physical capability, I have decided that there is no time for it. I know that he is physically capable, and heals quickly, judging by the good state of his head."

Nigel's wound from the incident with Arros was nothing more than a fading red line on his forehead.

"Thank you, Sagel and Nigel," Elenry said to the children. She walked to each of them and passed both of her hands over the tops of their heads.

In Elenry's eyes there was true warmth and gratitude. An

outbreak of warmth filled Sagel's chest as the strong energy from the Medicine Woman engulfed her in a full tide. She could tell that Nigel felt it, too, as his cheeks grew even rosier and his eyes even brighter. Elenry's encompassing smile still shown over the Bleudry family as Sagel and Nigel bundled up in their winter cloaks. Sagel turned back to her parents before following Elenry out of the door and into the cold, smiling in the most reassuring way she could muster. As she turned, she was embraced by both of her parents, as was her brother.

"Take care of each other," Torren whispered into his children's hair.

"And remember, you don't *have* to do this," Lorel threw in, stepping back from her two older children.

"We *want* to," Nigel said simply, echoing Sagel's thoughts exactly. Nova waved goodbye, imploring eyes watching as her siblings cleared the doorway and stepped out into the winter morning.

They heard their sister's voice from behind the door, "Is she going to take their ears?"

The siblings jogged to keep up with Elenry. Ahead lay the Stretch. Nigel felt no fear as they walked into the frosted forest. No longer did he see Shadow Shades lurking behind every other tree. Nightmares had left the Stretch to live in the dying trees and villagers.

"Do not get me wrong. I know from just being with you two that you are both intelligent," Elenry began, kneeling in front of the empty fire pit and striking two fire stones over dry kindling she had just laid in the ashy depression. Sparks showered the firewood, igniting orange and red flames on the thin sticks. "I do not know much about whether or not you react astutely in trying situations. I need to test your reaction times, and how you think on your feet."

With that, she vanished into her tent, emerging a moment later with two sheets of beige paper and two pencils. The paper used in Asthekia is much stiffer than that used on Earth, making it easy for one to write on their laps or soft surfaces without breaking through the paper. Elenry gave both of them a sheet of paper and a pencil, and then stepped back to add larger logs to the small blaze.

"I will now describe a situation that needs solving, and you will have two minutes to write down the best possible solution. Do not consult one another, and know that it is not a race between the two of you. Just finish within the allotted time period."

Their hearts fluttered with nervous expectancy as they readied themselves to listen and write. Nigel could feel the blood drain to his hands, leaving him a little light headed. Sagel's hands were quite cold, and she chewed her lip.

"Relax. All you need to do is your best," soothed Elenry, moving the large pieces of wood into the hottest part of the fire with her foot.

"Imagine you are playing on the bank of a raging river with your younger sister, Nova, when a Geruck approaches. You don't know what it wants to do. How do you respond?"

As Elenry painted the grim picture, Nigel's mind began to whir. He imagined Nova and himself situated happily on a boulder by the stream. A fierce and famished growl breaks into the melody of the creek. A wolf-like creature slinks out from behind a bush, its jaws laced with froth and its eyes wild with hunger. Gerucks cannot see well as they rely almost solely on their fantastic sense of smell. If he were to somehow lure it into the water, all smells would be dampened and they would have a chance to escape while it was swept away, without even its nose to help it.

His chaotic script flew across the paper as he plotted how his sister and he would stand at the lip of the boulder, and when the Geruck leapt at them, they would jump sideways, letting it slip and fall into the water. Fuzzy, black spots appeared across the paper, but stayed even after he looked away to try and clear them. With a sudden draw of alarmed breath, he realized that he had stopped breathing. Nigel let his shoulders fall from their lifted position, and looked at Elenry who was standing behind the fire, watching them intently. She nodded at Nigel when they made eye contact, and then turned her attention back to Sagel.

A solution was slower coming for the girl, who had only a minute and a half to come up with a plan. Sagel tapped her pencil on her head while she chewed her lip. Her breath was ragged and loud as she tried to relax enough to clear her head. At school they had been taught about the various dangerous and benign animals that inhabited the mountains. Of course she had been more in-terested in the less fearsome animals, as in truth, anything that ate meat frightened her. The problem now was that she could not recall whether or not the Geruck was blind or deaf. If it was blind, then perhaps they could sneak away in the river, masking their scent with the water. But if it were deaf then it would have no problem watching them walk away and quickly following after them. She was quite sure that the Geruck was in fact deaf, and could see just fine.

When she was just a small child, a dog in Starling City had chased her, and she had run from it. Torren, after rescuing his daughter from the excited canine, had explained that it was never a good idea to run from dogs or animals of any sort, since then they might see her as frightened prey and make a deadly game out of chasing her. Instead, she was to bow to the potentially threatening animal, sending it signals of love and peace, either verbally or with her mind. This seemed like a good way to go about it.

With relief at this solution, Sagel jotted down her answer and some reasoning behind it.

"Done," Sagel sighed, smiling up at Elenry.

"Very good," Elenry stated, pleased at the relatively short time it had taken them. A new wave of jittery energy took Sagel as Elenry swiftly collected the papers. While Elenry pored over the children's answers, the siblings exchanged glances.

Nigel's eyebrows were slightly raised and his mouth turned down. Sagel tried her best to relax her face, and offered a nervous grin at her little brother as they waited for Elenry to finish.

"Indeed, you are both very creative…and seemingly non-violent, which is a plus in most cases, including this one," Elenry delivered slowly, glancing once more over both of the papers. "As this was a made up situation, there was technically no 'right' answer, but both of your answers are very good. The Geruck would have been out of luck had it been hungry."

Sagel's heart leapt and Nigel let out an audible sigh of relief.

"The next question is not open to much divergence, as it does have a somewhat set answer," began Elenry, handing back the papers to the children. "Since you are both children of the mountain, I am assuming that your parents or teachers have instructed you on what to do in case of an avalanche. Is that correct?"

They nodded in unison.

"You have fifty seconds to write a brief outline of what to

do," Elenry said. "Go."

Pencils leapt to life as both children began explaining that if it was coming from far up the mountain, you were to run as fast as you could perpendicularly in either direction. Though it seemed like common sense to run straight down away from it, the force of avalanches is greater in the center of the wave of snow, and by moving far to one side you were more likely to run out of its path.

Thirty seconds was all it took for them to write, and Elenry smiled once more at their quick wits and speedy hands. Both children were less anxious about this answer, as their parents had told them time and time again about avalanches. As Elenry collected the papers, Sagel realized how much more at ease she felt since she knew that the correct answer was not subjective. Unlike so many of the questions and situations that the cosmos had thrown at her, this one at least had only one sure answer. The security of the question soothed her jumpy nerves.

Just a quick glance-over of each paper was all it took for Elenry to see that both of her examinees were well-informed about this mountain danger that could occur at absolutely any time in a mountain range as large and steep as the Seuthsai.

"Good, both of you," Elenry said quickly, crumpling the used sheets of paper and tossing them into the hungry fire. As the fire devoured them, they browned and then burst into flames. Sagel's anxiety seemed to momentarily go up in smoke along with the answer sheets, but returned when she pulled her gaze away from the entrancing flames to focus on the Medicine Woman.

"You have ten seconds to demonstrate what you would do if you were on a mountain summit and in danger of being blown off by a fierce wind. Go!"

As soon as Elenry uttered her start signal, Nigel dove at his sister.

"Get down!" he cried as the two of them fell to the snowy ground, holding onto each other and balling up as small as they could. Sagel was quick to follow her younger brother's orders, and was thrilled that he had done what he had. Neither one of them budged until they heard Elenry begin to laugh above them.

"Right, well, I think you two better get home," Elenry chuckled, beaming at the children, who stared at her uncertainly. Sagel bit her lip, as anxious as ever. Was this the moment that Elenry would deny them? The moment they would be sent home in defeat?

"You'll need to pack so we can leave tomorrow," Elenry reassured them, in better spirits than she had been in a very long time.

Chapter 24

Be On Your Way

Sagel's sack had a large and very inconveniently placed hole in it.

Though the Bleudry children had never travelled much, Sagel owned the old brown travel sack. It had been given to her by her deceased grandfather, who had loved to walk the mountainsides in his early years, and had been tickled by the fact that his eldest granddaughter shared his love of wandering. The problem was that it was so old and worn that a large hole gaped from the bottom of the bag.

Standing in the middle of her room, Sagel held the useless pack in one hand. The shock and joy of her and Nigel's success had yet to fade. Regular plumes of butterflies fluttered in her core, bringing smile after smile to her face. With these butterflies came the all too familiar anxiety. Would she prove to be useful on this vital journey? The only consoling words that she could offer herself were that she had passed both trials given by Elenry. She had passed fairly and truly.

"Dear, that aged bag will do you no good," Lorel tutted, stepping into her daughter's room.

"Would my school bag work?" Sagel wondered allowed, throwing the antique rucksack onto her bed and sighing with mingled frustration and amusement. How was she supposed to embark on a journey such as this one without adequate equipment?

"No, it's much too small," Lorel concluded. "Why don't you ask your father if you can use his? He's just in Nigel's room helping him pack."

Sagel nodded and set off down the hall, leaving her mother in her room. Lorel looked around her daughter's room, trying not to imagine what life would be like not knowing where her children were, or what they were doing. Again and again she told herself that by getting them out of the village and in the company of Elenry, they would be safer, as well as doing the village a great service. Yet every time she told this to Torren or herself, the nagging unknown slithered into her heart, bringing with it fear and helplessness.

Of the two parents, Torren was the more relaxed about the situation. It did not surprise him for an instant that his older children were completely capable of what the Medicine Woman had asked of them, and he was sure that they would be in good company with Elenry. What disturbed him was the prospect of Sagel and Nigel traveling through lands unknown to him. Sagel walked into Nigel's room, asked about Torren's rucksack, and his mind came back from the uncertain future to the present task of helping his children prepare to go.

Arros nudged Elenry's shoulder. The fire crackled softly as Elenry poured the horse's food into his feed bag and attached it to his nose. Like a dispersed thunderhead after a long storm, the constant worry that Elenry had harbored over the trials had finally abated. Now as she sat before the fire, she breathed deeply, letting herself drift from her body and into everything at once. She crackled with the fire and drifted with the falling snow. Winter drafts swayed her as it swayed the surrounding trees.

As she became one with everything, she called upon the energy of the cosmos to show her their path. Even though she had been wondering about this ever since her first forest vision, she had not wanted to ask until everything else was set into place, for she would not have had the required concentration for such a meditation. The days had gone by while she charged the question with her energy in order to receive the clearest possible answer.

Her curtain of hair quivered, and her hands became weightless, drifting into the air on the energy of all. Opening her eyes, Elenry let her head tip backwards as it was directed from the channeled power. In the luminous sky she saw dancers wreathed in green ribbons. They swooped and flailed with music unheard by the Medicine Woman as a dull throbbing light shone in their eyes and from their fingertips. Again she put forth her energy to the question of where they would go from the village, focusing on the diving beings. The throbbing light erupted. A shower of green filled the sky as it shimmered in emerald and jade veils. The Medicine Woman watched as a scene unfolded before her.

Four shadows shimmered as they floated towards a rock face. When they reached it they turned upwards, soaring not a foot from the mountainside. Then all was blank as the usual blanket of gray took the sky.

Daniel sat behind his father's desk and read a magazine from Earth. Michael had been busying himself at work all morning, and insisted that Daniel stay indoors. This would not have been a problem for the boy if he hadn't felt ripped apart by guilt and grief. He wanted nothing more than to run to Sagel's. To talk to her, to apologize again, to tell her how sorry he was and that he was confused and distraught. Most of all he wanted to get out of the house. Everything from the flooring to the bathroom sink reminded him of his mother. The house even smelled of her. The worst thing about the current situation was that Michael was adamantly not speaking about the death of his wife. Every time Daniel brought it up, or broke into tears over a sudden memory, Michael would pat his son on the shoulder and disappear into his room. If Daniel directly asked him about it or made an attempt at expressing his feelings, his father would shake his head and busy himself with something.

Daniel had never been so angry at his father in his life.

Along with the sizzling anger was fear that he would lose Michael to the same thing to which he had lost Louise. One minute he wanted to scream at his father, and the next he wanted to hug him and never let go.

At least he could sob freely when he was alone in the house. Haykyel had been going door to door all day, informing people that school was not to resume the following week as planned, as the illness was not officially contained, and having that many children together at once would be too dangerous for fear of spreading it further. Anyone who fell ill was to go directly to the clinic. As there were only three certified nurses on staff at the clinic, there was always quite a bit of waiting to be done before proper care was available. People had been told to stop going to the clinic for sap supplements, and were to wait for the nurses and village assistants to deliver their daily dosages.

Daniel sat back in his father's chair and flipped through the magazine without much interest, having read it many times before. Though Asthekia does not have magazines, even in metropolitan cities like Starling City, Daniel was the son of two Earthlings, and had been exposed to Earth literature and media throughout his life. Reading about the lives of Earth people like Jennifer Aniston and Kristen Stewart was a good distraction from life in Shinken for Daniel. He had never seen any of the movies they were in, and was often confused when the article writers referred to things like "mega-weight loss", or "the best beach bodies of the summer", but it was usually very amusing to read about the lives of the Earth celebrities.

Not knowing the state of the impending adventure was maddening for Daniel, especially since he was not going. At night Daniel lay awake pondering why he could not bring himself to leave the village in pursuit of the cure. Every time he fantasized about riding back into Shinken, bearing the cure in whatever form it was to come in—he usually envisioned bricks of frozen amber sap—he felt anger. Anger because his mother would not benefit from the long sought antidote. His limbs grew sluggish as he imagined climbing day and night over wild, unchartered ground. No longer could he bring himself to see the adventure and the wonder in the journey. All he saw was despair with his depressed father and the ailing, isolated village around him.

Everything sang that night. Wind gusted through the village and surrounding trees as the obscured winter sun set behind the mountains. Eerie twilight cloaked Shinken in milori blues and raven black shadows. In the midst of the orgy of shady colors, steady topaz lights shone from various dwellings. New snow held off for a time, temporarily satisfied with the bone white coverage of the landscape.

The Bleudry family had eaten and most were tucked into their beds, though none were sleeping. Nova was drifting and dozing in short intervals, but found herself imagining over and over again losing her elder siblings in one way or another. She had given them both extra hugs that night, and had given them both special rocks that she had painted in her father's studio that day. Lorel and Torren lay side by side in their double bed, fingers entwined on top of the covers. With all of the emotional hills and hurdles that they had cleared in preparation for their children's departure, they appreciated simply lying side by side silently with one another.

Nigel was nowhere near sleep, and didn't expect to drop off anytime soon. With his rucksack packed and repacked, he no longer had anything of great purpose to do. Ripples of exhilaration went through him like an incoming tide. The only thing to do now was to lie on his back and stare out of the closed window into the surrounding dusk. In the room next to Nigel's, Sagel sat leaning against the wall across from her window, a pillow under her as padding. Torren's rucksack was filled with two long sleeve shirts, a pair of long pants, a knee length skirt, an extra pair of shoes, and various undergarments.

Elenry had recommended that they pack light, as they would be carrying their own belongings. Aside from the clothing, Sagel had packed a few hair ribbons and her brush. As for food, Elenry had told the children not to worry, and that she would be taking care of the provisions. Sagel wondered if Elenry would buy goods from the town store, or if she had her own supply. Either way, she worried that they would not be able to bring enough for however long the journey would take. At times Sagel wished that she could be more like Nigel; he hardly seemed to feel anxiety, or at least he did not express it. Sagel climbed into her bed then, not bothering to draw her shades, as it was too dark outside to make a noticeable difference. Surprisingly, she fell asleep almost instantly.

Shinken saw the pale winter sun for the first time in days. The morning began as it usually did for most of the inhabitants. Without school, the healthy children of the village were left with ample free time to play in the snow and relax; other than that, things ran as they normally did.

Though it was early, Elenry was already standing at Haykyel's door, waiting for him to answer her knocks. Arros stood just off the front yard's foot path, snorting at the packed snow in front of him.

"Elenry, what brings you here in this early hour?" Haykyel inquired upon opening the door. He was dressed in dull gray pants and a long sleeve shirt to match. His face had become increasingly haggard since the last time Elenry met with him, with more prominent frown lines and a tightly set mouth.

"I bring you good news," Elenry spoke with a smile. "I have tested and chosen two worthy members, and they will be leaving today with me in the pursuit of the antidote."

"Who? Who have you chosen?" Haykyel asked, with a new light in his gentle eyes.

"Sagel and Nigel Bleudry," she stated.

All remnants of excitement and relief drained from the Town Head's eyes, and his mouth grew even more worried.

"But-but they are children!" he exclaimed.

"You are correct," responded the Medicine Woman. "Though

they are young, they have both proven themselves capable and willing to participate. There is no other choice, as no one else has offered me their services. This village can be saved, if you trust Sagel, Nigel, and me. Furthermore, you heard me tell my vision at the meeting."

After a moment's pause, Haykyel surrendered his gaze, which had been fixed unhappily at the ground before him. Looking at Elenry, he nodded, licking his lips and sighing.

"You are right, Medicine Woman," Haykyel breathed. "As always, you are right. I placed my full trust in you as soon as you agreed to see young Gwenoth, and I trust you now every bit as much as I did then. Just do whatever you need to do. I will stand behind you as Town Head."

Despite the palpable anxiety emanating from Haykyel, Elenry could see that he was relieved. Elenry passed both of her hands over his head and said a blessing.

"I suppose I should gather the town in light of the wonderful news," Haykyel sighed, traces of a smile braving his stiff lips.

Breakfast was a bit of an ordeal in the Bleudry household. Because they were so excited, neither Sagel nor Nigel wished to eat anything, uniting under a rare brother and sister front in the hope that their mother would cave if they banded together. Lorel was not so easily swayed. A smart mother such as she knew that her children would not do well setting off on a journey with stomachs full of nothing but nerves. She didn't let them leave the table until they had each had a piece of berry and sap bread and a bowl of porridge made from the special Asthekian grain, Tulush seed.

Though he did not admit it to his mother, Nigel felt noticeably less nervous once he had eaten. But food could not take the edge off the impending sadness that he was starting to experience about leaving his parents and younger sister. As Torren reminded his children about the various dangers of the mountain, while they were finishing up breakfast, Nigel clung to his father's every word, remembering the varying cadences and pronunciations in Torren's speech. The boy knew that that night, when he and his two traveling companions were sleeping alone on some unfamiliar mountainside, he would want to remember the voice of his beloved parents. Similar feelings ran through the hearts of all of the Bleudrys, who all seemed rather reluctant to so much as be in a different room than the others.

Now the family gathered in the front room; both Sagel and Nigel were dressed and rucksacked. Sagel wore her favorite pair of black pants and a green long-sleeved top, made by Lorel, under her warmest of winter coats. Nigel too had black pants, with a comfortable brown top under his overcoat. Identical expressions of mixed excitement and anticipation filled their faces as they stood before their parents.

"We will walk you to Elenry's, of course," Torren said, making his voice light.

"I want to bring them!" Nova chirped, taking Sagel's hand in her right hand and Nigel's in her left. Ordinarily, Nigel would have pulled away in annoyance, but now he squeezed his little sister's small hand lovingly.

"Of course you do. We'll all go," Lorel replied, ushering her brood towards the door before donning her coat.

"Oh!" Sagel exclaimed as they piled into the back of the car. "Do we have time to stop by Daniel's? I want to say good-bye."

"Yes, we do. It isn't even midmorning yet," Torren nodded as they stepped out into the frigid day

They had hardly made it down the driveway when Haykyel drove up in front of them, his loudspeaker blaring from the top of his vehicle.

ALL HEALTHY INHABITANTS OF SHINKEN ARE TO MEET AT THE VILLAGE COUNCIL HALL IMMEDIATELY FOR A MANDATORY MEETING. IF YOU ARE ILL IN ANY WAY YOU ARE TO STAY INDOORS AND AWAIT A DESIGNATED TOWN MESSENGER TO COME AND PERSONALLY FILL YOU IN!

Sagel felt a kind of relief, as she was quite sure that the meeting was being called to announce their departure, and the hopefully fast-nearing end of the strange plague. It was as if by having a collective meeting that their journey would be made official. Somehow it made her feel better knowing that at least some of the town would be there acknowledging the beginning of the ordeal. Other cars crept down the street in front and behind them as their fellow villagers made there way to the Town Hall. There couldn't have been more than five or six cars in total, as a great number of people fell under the category of 'infected', and would have to await the designated messenger. Twenty people at most could be seen walking towards the meeting hall.

"It's really happening," Nigel breathed, sitting between Sagel and Nova in the backseat. Sagel nodded and smiled to herself. They were really going. The tests were completed, their bags were packed, and soon they would be trekking onto the unknown slopes of the mountain's body.

Haykyel and Elenry stood in front of the great, painted doors of the town hall, which were still shut. Then Sagel remembered the rule about not gathering inside closed spaces in large groups.

While the group of villagers slowly grew, Sagel peered around to look for Daniel, spotting him at last standing with a miserable-looking Michael. Ice enveloped Sagel's heart as she took in her best friend's appearance. Hazel eyes showed the color of used dishwater, matching the color of his unkempt hair.

"Daniel?" Sagel called lightly.

His head snapped towards her voice, eyes scanning hopefully for a face to match. When their eyes met they both started towards each other, smiles creeping into their faces. Sullenness that had plagued Daniel receded. They shared a short hug and Sagel sighed in relief at the strength that Daniel demonstrated in their quick, tight embrace. He felt alive.

"Sagel, I'm so sorry I haven't come to see you…I haven't left the house for awhile," Daniel explained.

"Me, too. I've been busy, with the tests and the journey," Sagel replied. "Please don't apologize anymore."

Daniel, who had just been about to express his apologies in regards to his cold feet, smiled sheepishly at Sagel—how well she knew him. Instead he just nodded.

"I-uh-please, be careful, Sage."

"I will Dan…I will. And when we bring home the cure I will tell you all about the far side of Mt. Aarotte. Are you still keen on going sometime if it looks good over there?" Sagel giggled, hoping to make Daniel at least crack a smile of humor, and not of apology or guilt.

"Sure…just because you're going without me doesn't mean that I won't drag you back one day…we still need our adventure," Daniel smiled. "And look after Nigel. Hopefully you two won't kill each other."

"Yeah, if a rogue band of Shadow Shades doesn't kill us,

sibling rivalry surely will," Sagel said, throwing a glance back towards her family, who were motioning to her to come back. Lorel and Torren smiled at Daniel, and then walked over to them, both of them noticing Michael and heading over to console and talk to him.

"Hey, Dan," Nigel piped, trembling from the cold wind and his burning nerves. "Sagel, we should go talk to Elenry—to check in."

Sagel nodded at her little brother, and then turned back towards Daniel, who smiled at them both.

"We'll say goodbye later," Sagel said, already anticipating the moment when she would part from her friends and family.

The siblings made their way through the thin and solemn crowd to the doors, where Elenry stood, flanked by Arros and Haykyel. Upon laying eyes on the children, the Medicine Woman smiled, nodding in approval as she appraised their attire. Haykyel was dressed in his usual robe that he wore for important town functions, a deep maroon cape that draped around his shoulders and down to his ankles. Snaking yellow designs embroidered the fringes, looking like little flowers springing out of fresh Earth. Never before had Sagel and Nigel seen the robe up close.

"So here are the young adventurers," Haykyel said, stepping forward and placing his left hand on Nigel's shoulder, and his right hand on Sagel's. Both children bowed their heads respectfully. At once the subdued murmur of the crowd died away, and Sagel could feel all eyes on them.

"On this brisk morning, we call you here in light of joyous news. Medicine Woman Elenry has tested and selected two fine villagers to accompany her on the journey that we hope will bring the cure to our village. No one can help us at this point but ourselves. We are all quarantined and forbidden to enter any inhabited cities or villages off this mountain, and we have been offered no advice from Starling City. Today I can tell you that we are making a step towards our recovery," Haykyel addressed the crowd, who listened silently and intently. Haykyel stepped back and gave Elenry the center of attention.

Elenry scanned the crowd and spoke slowly, "As you know from our last gathering, I have been working these past few days with the brave people that have stepped up to accompany me on this journey. Now I stand before you and am happy to say that Sagel and Nigel Bleudry will be venturing out with me in search of the cure." A ripple of conversation went through the sea of hunched shoulders and raised eyebrows.

"I know that they are children," Elenry continued, "but they fulfill my vision, no one else has offered themselves, and they are two very capable and worthy people."

"They're so young!"

"Their parents will be so worried."

A woman at the front of the crowd addressed Elenry directly and sharply, "Who's to say you will not just abandon them in the wilderness and desert us all?"

Haykyel raised his hands and gazed meaningfully over the crowd, putting a hold on the rally of questions. Elenry continued, unperturbed.

"People of Shinken, I know how frightened you must be, how angry you are to be almost completely helpless in this situation, and I assure you that I will *never* desert you or the Bleudry children. As a Medicine Woman and magical being, it is my duty, purpose and intent to bring aid to those who cannot be helped by other means. I will not leave until a cure has been found and brought to you."

The audience looked dubious, but did not lack the energy to voice more doubts.

"How can we be absolutely sure that you will come back?"

"You will be sure when our journey is fulfilled, and the cure is brought to you. Until then, you will just have to trust in our way," Elenry said.

Many looks were exchanged among the people before Elenry.

The same large, determined woman spoke again. "You are taking something of ours, two of our children. We should keep something of yours until you return."

Many villagers nodded and muttered in agreement.

Elenry said nothing, but stood watching the villagers, neutralizing her own energy as much as possible in order to give the villagers complete freedom of choice in this matter. She knew that, in spite of Haykyel's consent to her plan, the combined voice and sentiment of the villagers could sway him and stop her.

She looked directly at the woman and spoke evenly, "What would you have?"

The woman pulled herself up to her full height and faced the Medicine Woman. They looked at each other for a long moment. Elenry could feel the strong, positive intention of the woman that was, at the same time, soaked with fearful caution. The woman finally answered, "Leave your horse in the village, and we will trust you to return with the children and the cure."

"Arros is my companion. He is part of my magic and power. He is no ordinary pack animal."

Glances were exchanged as the villagers shifted uncomfortably.

A man in another part of the crowd said, "And this is no ordinary journey, Medicine Woman. Our lives are at stake, and two of our children are leaving. I agree with the demand."

"We could supply you with another pack animal," said Albert Felik, the owner and maintainer of the horse stable. "You could take Wisle."

Sagel inwardly groaned at the thought of taking Wisle, the headstrong mule. He had pulled his weight bringing the crates up, but he was old and stubborn. Arros's back was twice the size of his. How could they expect to bring large enough quantities of the cure back to the village?

Elenry sighed and looked to Haykyel, who looked apologetic. He studied the snowy ground. As much as he wanted to accommodate Elenry, he knew that in order for her to have the villager's trust, she had to leave something of value in their possession. He could see no other alternative but her horse.

The Medicine Woman stroked Arros's nose. Her heart ached at the prospect of parting with her horse. She knew that in order to succeed in bringing peace to the ailing village, she would need trusting energy from its inhabitants. While separating from Arros's magic might affect her energy, lacking the support of an entire village would make conjuring and channeling impossible. Arros knew this, too, and nuzzled his mistress' shoulder and neck to reassure her. In her mind she apologized, and when she looked into Arros's dark, clear eyes, she knew that it would be alright.

"I will have to do it without you," Elenry whispered to her four legged partner.

Arros snorted softly and stepped towards her, brushing his fuzzy lips in the nape of her neck. With that, Elenry turned back to the crowd.

"I accept your terms, and would greatly appreciate taking another animal in Arros's stead."

The crowd started and then relaxed at her complete acceptance. Even the withered elders, all bundled up in thick handmade robes and coats saw Elenry in a different light. Albert nodded slowly, smiling thinly at Elenry. The woman at the front of the crowd relaxed and bowed slightly toward the Medicine Woman.

"Albert, would you fetch Wisle and his tack so that they can depart?" Haykyel requested. Though Albert was at least seventy years old, his gate was strong and his mind sharp. He turned and made his way up the road without another word.

Wisle was led to the Town Hall by Albert, tacked and packed with Elenry's traveling gear, and restrained several times before he stopped twisting back and trying to bite the people near him. Elenry had dealt with difficult animals in many situations, and being a Medicine Woman, she had always had a way with animals, particularly those with hooves. She could tell just by looking at Wisle that he was a frustrated animal. He had never lost his native strength or intelligence, but his owner had treated him as useless for a long time. Wisle was bitter and resentful. When she read into his energy she could see nothing but discomfort. He was also lonely for the company of other humans and animals, but had been kept inside so long that he had become seriously barn sour. She breathed evenly and deeply beside him and assured him that this trip both needed him and would be greatly to his liking.

And then came time for good-byes.

Lorel and Torren held their children as close to them as possible.

"I can feel that you will be fine," Torren said to his son and daughter, kissing them both on the forehead and sighing back an onslaught of tears. Lorel was less inhibited, and cried freely as she brushed her hands along the planes of her children's cheeks, marveling at their beauty and strength, and dreading how much she was going to miss them. After reassuring the Bleudrys that their children would be well looked after, and thanking Lorel and Torren once again, Elenry said her own silent goodbye to Arros, stepping back to stand with the newest addition to the journey, Wisle, who was now standing still, facing the road out of town.

The villagers watched as Sagel and Daniel embraced one last time, and both Sagel and Nigel walked towards Elenry.

"You are ready," Elenry said quietly to the children. They both nodded rather numbly. And as the foursome turned and walked up the road in the direction of the mountain side, Haykyel said aloud:

"Ebe noey ruoya yawal."

Be on your good way.

Chapter 25

Nook

"I can't see the village," Nigel puffed, his lashes frosted from the cold that had settled on the mountain.

"Indeed," Elenry nodded, turning back and gazing down through the thinning trees in the approximate direction of Shinken. Elenry, Sagel, Nigel, and Wisle had been walking for just over thirty minutes, and already their view of the village was obscured by the forest and small hill that rolled off the mountain side like a dew drop from a leaf. If they had been up higher, they would have been able to look down at the little pocket in which Shinken was nestled. Now all that told there was civilization close by were three thin plumes of gray smoke drifting lazily into the white of the lowering clouds above.

Sagel felt a sharp pang of sadness at the fact that they were putting so much distance between themselves and her parents, sister, and warm bed. But she shook it off to the best of her ability, since this was just the beginning of what could be a very long separation.

Wisle was much tougher than he looked. At first Elenry had been concerned about whether the old creature could handle climbing a steady slope through trees and over rocky ground. So far he had, only snorting every so often. They had trekked up the schoolhouse road, and then followed a trail up around the large rock behind the school. Then they had picked their way left and slowly up the ridge on an old road cut onto the side of the mountain. Elenry felt that their route corresponded to the interpretations she had made from her visions. Now there were many more barren, sickly trees, but the ground was leveling off somewhat, though it still led upward towards a small summit.

All the while, Sagel had been itching to ask where they were going to go once the hill ran out and they reached the top. While Sagel wondered, Nigel tried to replace his fear and homesickness with exciting thoughts about what would lie ahead and not with what would happen if they were unsuccessful. Nigel was very good at completely snuffing out unpleasant thoughts.

"You will soon see what is at the top, Sagel," Elenry thought aloud.

"You know," Sagel said, amazed once again at Elenry's second sight.

Elenry led the group, holding Wisle's lead rope loosely. The sky grew larger and clearer as they neared the peak. Elenry crooned to Wisle and calmed him each time he threw his head or snorted, stroking his nose and noticing, in spite of herself, that it was not as smooth as Arros's.

Nigel picked up the pace, crunching up the remainder of the incline to the summit. Sagel watched as her brother stopped cold, his hands falling to his sides and his shoulders relaxing. As she, Elenry, and Wisle reached the top moments later, Sagel felt the breath leave her chest and her lips part.

Sprawling country greeted them as it rolled ever onward.

Smaller peaks rose below them, though they were far below the height of Mt. Aarotte. Sagel realized then how high up they really were. Beyond the dwindling peaks was a site that Sagel had never seen in her life.

"What are they?" she whispered aloud.

"Those, Sagel, are the Meya Grasslands," Elenry replied. Snow-frosted hills spread out as far as the eye could see. Elenry fondly pictured the emerald expanse of summer green that it would become in warmer months. Many times had she ridden Arros down the meandering trail that wound through the country's gentle inclines and declines.

"Is that where the cure is?" Nigel asked distractedly as he continued to soak in the new vista.

"I do not believe so, Nigel," Elenry responded. "The place that both Sagel and I saw in our visions was a place of great trees and dense undergrowth. The Meya Grasslands are exactly that—grasslands. Few trees grow there, however lush the hillsides and flowers are."

"Why don't trees grow there?" Sagel enquired. They had learned little about what lay north of the Seuthsai mountain range, as most people from Shinken seldom traveled north.

"The soil is mostly volcanic ash. It will grow grass, but it has too few nutrients to grow trees," Elenry said. Sagel's curiosity about the lay of the land was partly assuaged, but she knew that Elenry would not want to use energy on random geography lessons. Sagel was going to have to focus and accept many things that she did not fully understand.

As a chilling wind arose from the summits below them, Sagel wrapped her cloak more tightly around her. Half the day had passed since they had left the village, and the hazy winter sun and its companion moon could be seen sluggishly crawling through the heavens. Above them to their right towered the three high, jagged peaks of Mt. Aarotte. Sagel was relieved that their visions had not depicted any mountain climbing. Not any steep, rocky ascents, anyway. Elenry led Wisle behind her as she walked to the right of where the two children were standing. Nigel gazed around, surprised again at how far up they had come and finally realizing that all his fantasies about making this trip had contained a solid core of truth. Behind and below them lay the edge of the ailing forest. The ground between them and the stunted trees at tree line showed only the snow-packed tops of occasional shrubs and the angular forms of large rocks. To their left, the summit ridge abruptly cliffed off, giving way to a deadly drop to jagged rocks and pinnacles below. To their right, the ridge turned into a shelf. The north side of the shelf sloped more gently down and away from the main body of the mountain, and appeared maneuverable if they were to go carefully.

The Medicine Woman slowed her approach to the shelf. The distant, sheer face of the snow dusted mountain wall loomed above them as they found the beginning of Elenry's route, and made the small group feel even smaller. In completely unfamiliar territory, Wisle had stopped resisting Elenry's leading and coaxing, and was completely attentive to the snow-covered, rocky ground. Sagel nodded encouragingly to Nigel as they caught up to Elenry. Edging closer to the beginning of the mountain's slow decline, Sagel felt that the trip was really beginning.

"We'll need to go single file down the trail," Elenry said, turning towards the children. "I will go first to make sure the ground is safe to walk on, and then Nigel will come behind me. Sagel, I want you to lead Wisle behind you."

Sagel's stomach turned uncomfortably. Wisle could be unpredictable, and though he had been walking in an agreeable manner for Elenry, she was a strong Medicine Woman with a gift for communicating with animals. Even with the sweetest of animals, Sagel was wary.

"You'll be fine," Elenry coaxed, feeling the anxiety of Sagel's silence. "Hold the lead right under his chin so he feels secure, and lead with your left hand so you are closer to the mountainside. He shouldn't give you any trouble. He's a good boy." Elenry patted the mule.

"I'll be fine," Sagel declared, stepping up beside the mule.

"Very good," Elenry smiled, giving Wisle a pat and moving her hand so Sagel could take the lead rope. Wisle threw his head, and then settled, his ears back. The familiar cautiousness took over Sagel, and she stood stiffly beside Wisle as Nigel walked ahead of them to follow Elenry.

"Talk to him, Sagel," Elenry said, "He will not hurt you."

"Good boy," Sagel whispered to the mule. "You're a good boy."

Wisle did not throw his head or snort contrarily, but relaxed his shoulders and swiveled his ears to the front.

The shelf that they had come out on funneled into a path-like formation, which gradually wound some way down the mountainside. Sagel could not see where it ended or became flat, as it disappeared around the flank of the mountain. How she wished she could tell Daniel and her family of this curious, treeless land. The cold sun cast ill-defined cloud shadows on the white and black speckled scree that sloped steeply up on their right. Close to the sun, the moon faded in and out of the white clouds like a slowly blinking eye. 'The Barren side of the

Mountain' was a well-earned name, as aside from the trees that they had left behind, vegetation was nonexistent here. They trod carefully, for the ground was uneven beneath the powdery snow. Occasionally, a few rocks would skip down the mountain in front of them, followed by showers of snow and sharp, ricocheting echoes. Sagel realized that she was listening to Wisle's hooves tramp across the ground and, besides that sound, there was nothing to hear but the footsteps of the three of them. At least at the creek, she could listen to the comforting rush of the water. Out on this mountainside, the silence was void.

The trail was no more than four feet wide, and when Sagel stole a glance down below, her head spun and her stomach clenched. Down, down, down it went, smaller peaks and hills rolling out like rogue waves from the mother sea of the mountain. Much to Sagel's relief, Wisle walked along beside her with no hesitation.

They continued in this fashion into the afternoon. The path that they walked widened in some places, and squeezed impossibly close to the steepening mountainside in others. Sagel's heart rate seemed to be connected to the state of their chosen path, speeding when the trail clung to the wall and slowing when it spread out from the mountain.

Nigel occasionally glanced back at his sister and Wisle behind her. As he put more distance between his town and himself, he began to grasp the gravity of the journey. Small pains started to ache in his feet, and his shoulders were beginning to throb from carrying the unfamiliar weight of his rucksack. The additional weight of homesickness for his parents hung heavy on his heart, making his feet trudge. Fear burdened his nerve endings while making his adrenaline rush uncomfortably. He was glad that no one could see his face, as his brow was puckered and his lips tight.

Of course, Elenry did not need to see the children's faces or body language to tell that they would need a rest soon. The Medicine Woman could almost taste their feelings as they washed from behind her. As she made her way carefully along the gradually descending path, she wondered with a bit of apprehension whether or not the two young souls could make it. Had the villagers been right? Had Lorel been absolutely correct when she said that they were too young for such an endeavor? These unfavorable prospects gnawed at Elenry, and she had to slip into a sort of walking meditation to quiet her sounding nerves. Another obvious predicament to consider was their sleeping arrangement. Surely they could not all sleep comfortably and safely on the side of an actively sliding mountain. Not to mention Wisle, who would need to be fed and tied up over night as well as brushed and warmed up.

The Medicine Woman let her mind wander from empty meditation to the vision that she had seen back in her camp—how she had risen up through the air, following a trail unknown. Something in her confidence about their path had changed. Doubt had nested in her heart, but she did not know what she could do to affirm that their current path was the one that they needed.

Elenry stopped suddenly, rooting her feet to the spot. A sudden crack rang out across the valley, making both Sagel and Nigel stop and gasp behind her. Wisle whinnied in fright and threw his head. Sagel tightened her grip on his lead rope, stepped closer to him, and held his head down so he would not rear up. She whispered quietly in his ear. A shift in the trail had frozen them in their places.

"Don't move," Elenry whispered.

All of a sudden, the trail beneath their feet began to slide down the mountain. Wisle slid before Sagel, pulling the rope from her hands as they tumbled and slipped down the snowy incline. Nigel tried to dig his hands into the snow and rock enough to stop gathering speed, but the ground he grabbed moved with him. Never before had Elenry been in a situation like this, and all she could do was try to fall without injuring herself. More snow began to sluff off behind them and in front of them, creating a small avalanche.

Without warning, the slope came to an end, becoming a small cliff that the group slid over, all crying out as they fell into a great bank of freshly avalanched snow. Though the snow was softer than the rocks, it was not very comfortable to land in from a twenty foot drop. Elenry could not breathe at first when she hit the snow bank, and sat very still for a minute or two as her breath came painfully back to her. Nigel had been a little luckier, and had slid off the other side of the snow bank when he hit, his momentum preventing him from coming to such an abrupt stop. Wisle had landed on his side and rolled off the same side as Nigel. He was unhurt, though he was paralyzed with fear as he stood trembling beside a sprawling Nigel. The load on his back had shifted, but had not broken loose. Sagel, like Elenry, had landed on her back, and was now panicking in her lack of breath. As soon as Elenry had regained her composure and ability to breathe, she went to the girl.

"Calm down," Elenry whispered, taking Sagel's rucksack off her back. "Just breathe normally and you will be fine."

Sagel could hear Elenry's words, but in her panic she could hardly make sense of them. Her vision began to tunnel due to her rapid and shallow breaths, but returned to normal suddenly when the air rushed back into her lungs. Elenry drew her hand away from the girl's sternum when she saw that Sagel was breathing normally.

"Thank you," the girl gasped, sucking air hungrily into her lungs, which were now tingling with a foreign warmth. "Nigel?! Where's my brother?"

"I'm here!" Nigel piped from the ground below.

Sagel smiled with relief, as did Elenry. Nigel scrambled up the snow bank after paying a quick glance to Wisle, who was standing stalk still, his shoulders as tense as ever and his eyes fixed with fear. As soon as Nigel was in reaching distance, his sister pulled him to her.

"You're okay," she sighed, letting him go after a moment.

"Of course I am," he burst out, overwhelming relief coming in the form of uncontrollable giggles. Sagel watched him for a moment before melting into joyous hoots herself. Before long Elenry was giggling, clutching her aching sides and letting the laughter flow.

The three of them sat atop the snow bank laughing for a few minutes more, shedding the stresses, fears, and worries that had been plaguing them up until that point. At last Elenry stood up, brushing snow and small pebbles from her cloak and pants. In one swift movement, she slid down the snow bank and landed on her feet, walking towards Wisle. The Asthekian mule stood still, watching Elenry approach him. The Medicine Woman crooned to him gently, putting her hands out in front of her with her palms welcomingly upwards. He did not step away from her. Elenry rested her hands on his shoulder and chest, patting his neck gently as he relaxed to the kind touch. Nigel too slid down the snow bank, though not quite as gracefully as the Medicine Woman had.

Sagel was about to slide down herself and join the group below when her immediate surroundings caught her attention. They were situated on a mountain shelf. It continued outwards about twenty feet before cliffing off into another sheer drop. Beyond the cliff of the shelf sprawled the land, which was now more detailed as they were much closer to the foothills than they had been before.

"How high up do you think we are?" enquired Sagel, brushing the snow from her cloak and legs after her slide down the bank.

Elenry did not pause in her calming of Wisle, who was beginning to relax, judging by the way his eyes had less white around the iris, and by how his taut shoulders were now more lax. She kept stroking his long nose as she answered.

"I'd say about two thousand feet, perhaps more," she replied, scanning the mountainside and smiling.

Nigel looked as if he were about to walk out to the edge of the cliff, but then thought better of it and stayed put, shifting his weight from leg to leg.

"We might as well stop here to eat and rest," Elenry said, taking Wisle's lead rope off and digging a feed bag from the depths of one of the saddle bags. She filled it with hoovar—a grain for horses and mules—that she pulled out of another sack.

Up until then, Sagel had not been paying any attention to her appetite, and was rather surprised to feel that she was quite hungry. Nigel needed no extra prompting, and quickly sat down with his rucksack, digging out the lunch that Lorel had packed for him. Sagel sat next to her brother, fishing out her mother-made lunch. Elenry was about to take out food for the children, but realized that they had already begun eating.

"I see your mother has you all set for the first meal," she said, smiling at both of them in turn as she sat beside them, holding a small bag of dried Churkey meat. The siblings returned her smiles, nodding as they tucked into their sandwiches.

"Now you see how dangerous the mountain can be," Elenry commented. "And how helpful."

Nigel cocked his head, swallowing quickly before speaking. "How was sending us down that drop helpful?"

Elenry laughed out loud, taking a bite of a bit of Churkey.

"Look up there, to the left of where we fell," Elenry said, pointing up at their old trail. The children's eyes followed her finger and saw with great horror where they would have ended up. The trail continued on about fifty feet, snaking slowly around a sharp corner where it abruptly dropped off.

"You see, we would have had to turn around, as there is no way to get down from that point without a nasty fall into that steep valley."

Elenry was right, as all that lay below the sudden end of the path was a deep and precipitous valley of rock, snow, and ice.

Sagel looked up to Elenry, who was smiling at her knowingly. Something about the way Elenry perceived and seemed to see through people's minds was comforting. Sagel felt this perhaps because there was no need to conceal difficult or embarrassing thoughts, as the Medicine Woman would intuit them anyway.

"Elenry, may I ask you something?" Sagel said, putting down her sandwich.

"You may ask me anything, though I may not answer," Elenry replied.

"How did you become a Medicine Woman?" This particular question had been floating about in Sagel's mind since the day she had first met the healer. Of course in school they were taught briefly of the Medicine People and their origins and customs, but no one had taken the subject very seriously, as it had barely interested the children at the time when it was taught back in the healthier days of the secluded village.

Nigel leaned forward, naked curiosity painting his features.

"An interesting question, though the answer is not nearly as intriguing," Elenry said, pausing a moment to eat more of her lunch. "I was born in a very small village. Even smaller than Shinken. It's called Nook...or *was* called Nook, as I do not know whether or not it exists any more."

"Why wouldn't it?" Nigel asked.

"When I was a child there were no more than thirty people living in Nook. You see, it was a seaside village, positioned right on the edge of a cliff. I daresay it was a very strange place for a village. Very dangerous. When the storm season came, the weather turned hellish, as there was no protection from mountains or even tide pools or an ocean reef. The rock that Nook was built on bore the full force of the angry ocean in every storm. In the seasons of pleasant weather, the village was primarily a fishing village, and people fished the waters for small golden creatures called Ferril."

"I've never heard of Ferril!" Nigel exclaimed.

Elenry only smiled at Nigel and continued with her story.

"My father was a modest fisherman, who worked all the fishing season long out in a small boat, pulling in enough fish for my mother to sell at the village exchange market, and enough for us to have dinner on the table every night. You see, Nook had never been influenced enough by the modernized world to use money. Everyone fished, grew vegetables, made bread, or produced other useful things, and on one day every week there would be an exchange market in the center of the town where everyone would barter their goods for other people's products. An old woman, perhaps of sixty or so, lived only two houses down from us, and as far as anyone knew, she did not produce goods of any kind. But every market day people would go to her house bearing the best of their crops, carvings, bread, and fish, in hopes that she would help them.

I do not remember whether or not she had a proper name like you and I have, but I do recall that everyone called her Relae, which means healer. The first time I was brought to her, I had a vicious cough, and my mother had worried about me so much that she had given herself a headache. My father loaded up a basket with the largest of the fish he had brought in that day, as well as a coat that my mother had made for the cold months. Relae's house was unlike any other in the village. It's amazing how vividly her little dwelling is etched in my mind…," Elenry paused to take a bite of Churkey. She chewed as the children also continued to eat.

The Medicine Woman took a long drink of water from a flask, and then proceeded with her story. "The exterior was normal enough; walls made of stone and a roof of orange bricks made by the village people themselves, out of a type of clay that is native to that coastline. Anyway, the inside was unique. Every patch of wall—and I mean every—was covered with plants and herbs and strange smelling sea vegetation. The ceiling was painted sky blue, though no one ever knew how she managed to get it that color, as there was nothing natural to the land in that area that would have turned anything blue, and especially not sky blue."

Sagel and Nigel had become so engrossed in the story that they had stopped eating completely. Even Wisle, who was standing over by the snow bank, pricked his ears in Elenry's direction.

"When my mother and I knocked on the door, it swung open instantly, as if Relae had been expecting us. She was common looking enough. She had long brown hair that was streaked silver with age, and her face was broad and sharply featured, like most everyone else in the village. But her eyes—," Elenry stopped abruptly, breaking the spell that she had cast over them.

"What about them?" Sagel whispered, leaning in closer.

"They were odd…a subdued sort of gray encircling obsidian centers. It was the type of gray that the sky might turn if it wanted to depress the land below. Not vibrant or particularly beautiful. As I said before, they were odd, though not because of their color."

The Medicine Woman sat back for a moment, as if recollecting and organizing her thoughts for the next section of her tale.

"Every once in awhile, I would detect something in her pupils. A sort of…flash, for lack of a better word. A flicker, yes, that describes it much more accurately."

Both Sagel and Nigel looked at each other, their eyebrows raised and their eyes wide. On many occasions they had both seen this legendary flicker in Elenry's eyes. The Medicine Woman, as perceptive as ever, looked encouragingly at them, "What is it?"

The children exchanged glances in silence.

Sagel began, "Well…I don't know, I mean I suppose it could have been a trick of the light, but— "

"It couldn't have been," Nigel interjected.

"No, you're right…light wouldn't have done that," Sagel concluded. "Well, I guess I speak for my brother as well. We've both seen a flicker, or something like a flash, in your eyes."

Elenry did not say anything immediately, though Sagel could

have sworn that she could hear the healer's mind whirring away.

"Good. You're both learning," she finally said.

The three sank into silence, each in his or her own thoughts.

"Would you like to hear more?" Elenry finally asked quietly.

"Yes!" they chorused.

"Ah, you two are a wonderful audience," Elenry said cheerfully before she continued. "Well, Relae seemed to know what was wrong with me before my mother could get a word in. She had my mother sit in this great soft cushion chair near the window with a grand view of the sea—not that any of us were deprived of that view— and gave her a draught of maeweed to calm her nerves. I was led to a little room off the kitchen, which was at the other end of the small cottage. I couldn't tell you exactly what was on the shelves in that room, but the smell was absolutely intoxicating. I daresay I have used many of the same ingredients in my own healing practices, but the way she had them all lined up and displayed next to each other was magnificent. So, down I sat on a little stool by a work table—at this point she had still not addressed me directly—and just watched her. Now, I know this is going to sound silly, but you must remember that I couldn't have been more than ten turns around the sun, if that, but I remember being scared stiff that she was going to poison me and use me as fish bait.

You see, it was a rather common fear among the fifteen or so of us village youth, that Relae was a crazy old woman who didn't like children. I do not know how the tale got so out of hand, as many of my friends had been in her company and lived to tell their stories. Relae was the usual person that we vilified, as she was so peculiar, what with her lack of ordinary work and production, her silent demeanor, and her unexplained powers. We would

— 266 —

go through phases when we were sure she was a scheming witch from the Wanderlands out to get us."

"What are the Wanderlands?" Nigel asked.

"The Wanderlands is the north most region of Kovraantic," Elenry replied, not missing a beat. "And as far as we know, they are completely uninhabited and extremely dangerous, since no who has ventured in has ever made it out to recount their journey."

"Wow," Nigel breathed. "Does anyone know what happened to the people who went in there?"

At this point, Sagel was getting a little irked that they had strayed from the story, though she knew better than to try and stop her overly-curious brother until his slough of questions had run dry.

"Many people have asked that same question. Unfortunately, none of them were ever seen from or heard from again once they seriously pursued an answer."

"But what if a great group of explorers, or scientists—"

Elenry held up her hand, still smiling at the boy, who instantly quieted.

"I wish I could tell you more, but I have told you all I know on the subject," she said softly, her voice firm.

"There I sat, waiting for her to brew some frightful poison, or send spirits of dark energy and power to haunt me. She went to one of the exquisitely organized shelves on her packed walls, and pulled a small blue stone from a glass jar.

"Suck on this," she told me, handing me the stone.

"But it's a rock," I answered.

"It is medicinal. Your cough will be gone by morning if you suck on it for about an hour."

I held it, and felt a dark, painful energy surrounding it, so I pretended to put it in my mouth, and then I pocketed it. I did all of this with her back turned. What made me do this I did not know, though I can safely say this was when my second sight surfaced for the first time. As soon as I pocketed the blue stone, I felt her change. Her eyes softened, as did her whole demeanor. She turned to me, smiling for the first time since we had arrived.

"You knew, young one," she whispered.

"Knew what?" I asked her.

"You were right not to suck the stone," she nodded, taking it out of my pocket and replacing it in its jar with the others like it. "Had you taken it, your body would have started shutting down. In a few minutes, you would have been dead. I gave it to you because I knew what you would do with it. No ordinary human, no. If you were, you would have taken it. Taken it without question. Of course, I had an antidote that I would have given you if you had taken it, and you would have been fine. I do not poison children and use them for fish bait. You felt it, didn't you?"

I nodded, because I *had* felt 'it'. I did not know what 'it' was, but I was relieved that she understood what I would not have been able to explain. She patted my cheek and I felt a strange energy somewhere between harshness and tenderness. I remember being speechless.

"You're a Medicine Woman," she said.

I had no idea what a Medicine Woman was, and even if I was, I was doubtful that she would have known by the short time she had spent with me. Soon, I learned that Relae did not need much time to understand people better than they understood themselves. I grew up in a village where there was no school. All of us young people started working around the house as soon as we could hold simple tools. My father taught me to fish, my mother taught me to hunt birds, and other basic necessary skills like cleaning and cooking and such. If you had told me then that great mountain ranges like the one we sit in now existed, I would not have been able to imagine it. I knew only Nook. Only the simple ways of our people and village. Of course our village traded with traveling merchants, but they were usually so tired and hungry from travel that they hadn't the energy to enlighten us about the world that they had come from.

Of course, Relae was quick to explain the basics of Medicine People, and to inform me that she herself was one. Then, she did the most amazing thing. She walked over to me and placed her left hand on my chest, and her right hand on my throat. Suddenly an intense heat took over the two areas. I just sat there, amazed as the soreness and the mucus left my windpipe and chest. And that was that. She had healed me.

After that, she went to my mother, recounting our extraordinary exchange. My mother was taken by surprise, as she had never considered our family anything out of the ordinary. I must tell you I do not think she believed Relae, and thought that she was just an old woman desperate for an apprentice and would say just about anything to get one. I jumped in then, excited by the prospect that I might be a healer, and told her exactly what had happened in my own words.

It was a few days later, after much discussion among my parents and Relae, that I packed a small bag of clothing and went to live with Relae. I was still allowed to spend time with my parents in the evenings, for I could not bear to part with them completely at that age, but I spent all of my other time with Relae, helping her with her work. I learned to mix draughts, identify healing plants and lethal plants, to collect wild foliage to use in simple spells and energy conjurings.

News spread fast in the small village of my new position as apprentice Medicine Woman. But with the excitement and fame came ridicule. My friends became frightened of me. Some were still civil, and regarded me with a sort of respect that I was a magical being, but others would have nothing to do with me. Relae let me help out and work with the simpler cases that came through; the head colds, small lacerations, stomach aches, and other such ailments. As there were not many people in the village, no serious illnesses ever took hold of Nook's inhabitants. That is, until one day when Nook was plagued with an illness unlike anything we had ever known."

Sagel and Nigel exchanged excited glances, and Elenry responded at once.

"I'm afraid it wasn't the same disease as the one plaguing Shinken. It did not start off as aggressively in its symptoms, though it spread much more quickly, if you can believe it. We had nearly the entire village lined up to receive Relae's treatment, as I was told to stay out of the way of the illness. I suspect that Relae did not want me to contract it in case my young immune system could not handle it. In those weeks that Nook ailed, I spent my time down on a beach about two miles west of Nook's cliff. I swam, fished, and drew in the sand. Every night I would make my way back to the village at nightfall, treading the well worn path through the sea grass and eroded rocks. One morning I awoke to Relae shaking me awake, her rough hands prodding my shoulders urgently.

"Go early," she told me as soon as I had completely returned from the dream realm of my sleep.

"Why? What is wrong?" I asked, seeing something ominous

in the irises of her mysterious eyes.

"This day is dawning a sick one," she replied, ousting me from my warm cot. "Go to your beach and do not come back until I send for you."

The grave tone of her usually serene voice frightened me more than the illness ever had. First I wanted to see my parents, but she said no, and told me that she would stop me if I tried. With that, I dressed, holding back tears as I dressed and left my village. I sat in the gray sand before the ocean for hours and hours, staring at the horizon but not seeing it. All I saw was death. I knew that something horrible was happening in my village, though I could not say what. So I sat, emptying my mind and psyche like Relae had taught me, trying to calm the waters of my being and understand what my sixth sense was telling me. But I was young and I was too anxious about my parents and Relae to meditate. Finally I could take it no more. I ran back to Nook, beginning to sob even before I saw reason to. I did not need to *see* it, you see, as I could *feel*.

Creeping down the main path, I searched for life in the village. But there was none. No movement, no voices of my neighbors and family. Nothing. I went straight to Relae's cottage and found a group of about ten people inside, all dying, clutching their chests in their futile attempts to breathe, or already dead, the air completely squeezed from them. Relae was not among them, and neither were my parents, much to my relief. The other twenty or so villagers were dead or dying in their homes, or on the road connecting the village buildings and small square. I found my parents lying peacefully in their beds. They could have been sleeping had it not been for their still chests and absent pulses."

Both Bleudry children wore expressions of mingled horror

and pity at Elenry's stark account.

"As I stood in the doorway of our little bungalow, I heard her calling—Relae running through the village, shouting my name. I somehow broke my grief-induced paralysis, and ran to her voice, shouting her name back. She was uninfected, though she had been in the epicenter of the illness and death. But I could have cared less how she had survived, for that moment I only sobbed in her arms as she held me there in the village square, our audience only the expired friends and family littering the ground. We left the village after she packed a large backpack of essentials, taking the merchant road to the lands that had always been a mystery; a frightening unknown to a young village girl. I had never wished to see anything else but the safe confines of Nook. I had never been more than three miles away from the village square. What a shock it was to leave it in the state it was in. In the state I was in."

Elenry stopped her story, her voice ringing with finality. Sagel looked away when she observed the thin trail of a single tear rolling down her cheek. Nigel followed suit, taking a sudden interest in his rucksack.

"I'm sorry about...everything," Sagel said.

"Thank you, Sagel," Elenry replied, her voice unwavering. "I, too, am sorry for unloading that onto you two. As if you needed any more talk of disease and sorrow."

"Don't be sorry. It was interesting—not the *good* kind of interesting," Nigel added. "What I mean is, it was good to hear."

"I understand what you mean, Nigel," Elenry assured him with an amused smile.

"But how did you—how did you cope?" Sagel asked, intrigued and a little frightened by the story.

"I had no other choice. It was either cope and go along with whatever direction the stream of my life took me, or fight the current and be miserable," Elenry explained. "Of course, Relae helped a great deal; comforting me, brewing soothing drinks, and singing familiar tunes of our village. It was not easy, not at all. Every night for the first four or so months after we left I cried myself to sleep, and then some nights after that. As I matured and aged I learned many ways to accept and let go of my sorrow and other difficult feelings."

"How old are you?" Sagel asked.

"That is an interesting question," Elenry laughed. "The truth is, I do not know. I lost count after my thirty-second birthday. But I would postulate that I am somewhere between thirty-five and forty."

Sagel smiled at Elenry's response. She had never met anyone who did not know his or her age; this made Elenry even more timeless.

"It must be nice, not knowing your age," Sagel thought out loud.

"Why is that?"

"I don't think I'd like it very much," Nigel countered.

"Well, it seems like so much revolves around what age we are. As if age is the only thing that matters. The *only* thing that can qualify us. If you didn't know how old you were, you would be free from everyone's expectations. And your own expectations," Sagel explained, piecing her thoughts together as she spoke.

"I see what you are saying," Elenry answered, "and I agree. A number does not dictate what we can or cannot do," Elenry said. "Did you know that on Earth, men and women are encouraged to retire from work at a certain age?"

"Why? If they can still work, and if they still enjoy it, then why would they stop?" Sagel wondered. Nigel nodded in agreement to his sister's questioning.

"Because their society is governed by the notion that one's age is more important than one's ability. One's 'status' is the deciding factor in what work they do, what food they eat, and what beds they sleep in."

Nigel and Sagel thought in silence about what Elenry had said. Both children were brought up in a village where the old worked until they could not work anymore or until they grew too bored of their job. If they grew bored of their present occupation or hobbies, they would move onto something new. When they grew too old to do the jobs they once did, they would then retire to their homes, where family, friends, and neighbors would come to help them with chores, or just spend time with them.

"Then what do they do when they retire?" Nigel asked.

"I do not think that all of them retire, but I suppose that those who do sit around gathering dust," Elenry offered.

"Strange," Nigel shrugged, his sister nodding in agreement.

"What happened once you left Nook with Relae?" Nigel pressed.

"I would love to tell you more now," Elenry answered, standing up and beginning to pack up, "but it will have to wait for the next meal. Now we must walk."

Chapter 26

Downwards and Onwards

Elenry seemed invigorated by the lunch and the story-telling. Her stride grew even longer, and her eyes brighter and more determined. Wisle walked faster, his hooves planting and unplanting themselves in the snowy ground. The siblings trotted along down the slope. Though Sagel felt empowered by their faster pace, her feet ached. Nigel fell behind, and Elenry slowed to accommodate his shorter legs. From the first path far above them, the mountain had looked much steeper than it actually was, to the relief of the party. The ever changing sky now showed a shocking blue. Clouds swelled on the fringes of the horizon, adamant to move in by nightfall.

Sagel replayed Elenry's story in her mind. Part of her did not want to know more of the deeply sad story of their guide; imagining an entire village falling to the ravages of a horrible illness made her heart race and her hands grow cold. How hard it must be for Elenry to find herself in this situation again, even though she was so much older and bound by her vows as a healer. Is that why she was so determined to stay? Though she did not like to admit it to herself, Sagel knew that had she been in Elenry's situation, she would have left long ago. That horrific night when Gwenoth had passed away would have been enough for her to flee.

Elenry had a tight hold on Wisle's lead rope as he did a sort of side step down the slope. He had amazing balance for his age. Their course felt right. The Medicine Woman had never been this hopeful or positive about their journey until now. Unfortunately, she was the only one with any deep feelings of inner peace in the group. The children stumbled more often. Over the whispering wind, Elenry could hear their labored breathing. She let them stop for water often.

The only thing that changed around them was the ground that passed under their feet. Clouds stayed at bay on the edge of the sky, snow glistened in pearls in the afternoon sun, and a light breeze played over the steep mountainside. Beyond the mountain slope, Elenry could see where the smaller hills sloped down into a steep valley. She could not see what lay beyond the slopes, but there did seem to be some sort of pocket in the land. This brought a smile to the Medicine Woman's face. It would be a good three to four day trek, but Elenry was confident and assured by a force greater than her eyesight that that valley was the place they needed to go.

"Look out and far," Elenry said, stopping her descent and pulling back gently on Wisle's lead rope to stop him.

"What?" Sagel asked, scanning but not seeing. Her eyes began to water as a rising wind washed icily over her face.

"There!" Nigel cried, motioning toward the valley and pulling his hat farther down over his ears.

Following Nigel's finger with her gaze, Sagel saw it.

"That's it," Sagel whispered, making it more of a statement than a question.

"What did you say?" Elenry called, leaning her ear towards Sagel.

"That's it," she said more loudly.

"Yes, it is," Elenry answered with finality.

"How can we be sure?" Nigel wondered. "Uh—I guess we'll just see when we get there."

Elenry smiled back at him.

"How long will it take us to get there?" Sagel continued, feeling a new energy. It was a kind of drawing sensation that made it difficult for Sagel to pull her gaze away from the dark crease in the white expanse.

"Three days at least, and that is only if we go steadily," replied Elenry.

"Let's go," Nigel piped, grinning from cold ear to cold ear.

They continued again down Mt. Aarotte with their energy renewed and their hope rekindled. Snow billowed around them on an aggressive wind that now plowed through the sky, ahead of the clouds, whipping down on the mountain.

Their pursuit of the valley was slow, as Elenry would not allow them to hurry down the mountain. The excitement made Nigel want to run down the snowy expanse. Nigel and Sagel occasionally made animated conversation and speculations about their newfound destination, though their talk died as soon as the wind picked up, drowning out their voices like water diluting a dollop of sap. Elenry would stop every so often to scan the horizon. Sagel always followed her example when the Medicine Woman did this, and was concerned to see the swelling clouds beginning to seep across the sky, darkening as they moved.

"Is something coming?" Sagel called over the droning wind.

"Indeed," Elenry said over her shoulder, patting Wisle as she took in more of the sky.

Cold had finally found its way through Sagel's layers of clothing and was making her shiver lightly. She bundled tighter, decreasing some of the chill. Nigel, in front of his sister, pulled his hat further down over his ears and speeded up after Elenry, who had begun walking again. Twilight came with the drop in temperature, slowly relieving the exhausted winter sun. The moon disappeared behind a rolling, black cloud, illuminating the edges with silver light, and then vanishing entirely.

Snow flurried and the flakes lashed through the sky before blowing to the ground, with the wind ever present. Sagel had to wipe the dry bits from her eyelashes every few minutes, and rub her numbing cheeks. Once again, Sagel's thoughts returned to Shinken. What were her parents doing? Perhaps her father had retired to his chair after a long day of painting. Nova might be playing in her own world of imagination and dolls. Lorel could be sipping a mug of tea and reading one of her many books, or discussing her day with Torren in the living room. Thoughts of her warm bed taunted her when she remembered that they would soon be laying their heads on their knapsacks in Elenry's tent.

Nigel felt as though they had been plodding along for ages, but judging by the look of the land, they might have not moved at all. Only the foothills, growing larger and more distinct below them, assured him that they were actually making progress.

"We will need to make camp here," Elenry called through the wind song. "It's far too dark for us to hike any farther."

"How will we set the tent up on the slope?" Nigel enquired, setting his knapsack down and crouching to rest.

"I do not believe we will get much use out of the tent on such a slope as this," Elenry commented, also removing her pack. She brought a small stake from one of the saddle bags and drove it through the snow into the hard ground, and then tied Wisle's lead rope to it. "This wind will whip away any tent put up tonight, so we will have to burrow into the mountainside and tuck the cloth of the tent around us."

If the children had been with anyone other than Elenry, they would have been frightened, but now they just nodded. Sagel was still worried by the prospect of burrowing into a mountain, especially after they had experienced how unstable this land could be. How would they stay warm? All of these nagging thoughts ran through the girl's mind as she helped Elenry clear snow from the slanted ground. It was nice to use her arms as opposed to her legs. The movement got her blood moving, and she could feel herself warming marginally. A depression began to take shape before them, big enough for the three of them.

"Right, climb in," Elenry instructed, removing and unfolding the canvas tent shell that would have looked much more welcoming had it been set up. Sagel took one last look at the sky, watching as the moon peeked through a brief break in the massive storm clouds.

The tired children obeyed, clambering over the small wall of snow, rock and dirt left from their digging. As they bivouacked in the snow shelter they heard Elenry rustling around in the saddle bags. Sagel's stomach grumbled remarks about food. Nigel was too tired and homesick to even think about his empty stomach, and he snuggled closer to his sister.

She slid her arm behind his shoulders and pulled him closer. A shuddering sigh to match those of the wind ran through Nigel as he stifled impending tears.

"Cry Nigel—I'm scared too," Sagel whispered. Nigel let go, allowing a few warm tears to slug down his reddened cheeks.

They both must have fallen asleep, as they were startled awake when Elenry lifted the flap of the tent roof and climbed in, bearing a small sack of something. They ate their bread and dried Churkey quietly, too tired to make conversation, even about Elenry's story. Outside, the wind dumped rattling handfuls of snow onto the tarp, and then swept it clean with buffeting howls. Elenry knew that it would not be wise to start a lengthy story in the midst of their exhaustion. There was just enough room in the little shelter for the three of them if they all curled up. Finally, even the wailing wind could not rouse them from their slumber. Wisle, who was sleeping beside the shelter, did not like the relentless gusts, and hid his head beneath the tent flap.

Morning spread cold and dim across the Seuthsai range. Nigel was the first of the siblings to awaken, not surprised to find that Elenry had already woken. Since they had all slept in their clothes and snow attire, Nigel climbed out of the shelter as soon as he was able, having to wait for some soreness in his legs to subside.

There was Elenry, pouring hot tea into a mug, a small teal blaze before her. The boy stepped rather timidly towards the fire.

"It is a soul reading fire," Elenry explained, handing him the first mug and fishing in the cookware sack for another. "I had to use it to light what little kindling I brought; to give it a bit of a boost."

"Whose soul is it reading?" Nigel asked, as mesmerized as Sagel and Daniel had been upon first gazing into it.

"No one's, at present," Elenry said, setting Nigel's steaming cup down in the snow beside where she crouched. "You have to place your hands into the flame for it to get an accurate reading."

"What? Wouldn't you burn?"

"Not in this fire."

"Wow," Nigel exhaled, taking off his gloves hopefully. "Can I try?"

"Of course," Elenry answered. "Simply place your hands into the center of the flame, and wait. I will read what different colors or formations the fire shows for you."

Without further questions, Nigel plunged his hands into the licking flames, wincing ever so slightly and then grinning at the tingling sensation.

"Amazing," he giggled.

The fire leaked from one color to the next, all rather smudged together and undefined before finally settling on orange and crackling merrily.

"What does that mean?" Nigel whispered.

"That you are a merry soul, undeterred by cold," Elenry paused when the fire dimmed, its flames simmering to a feeble glow. "But you let your curiosity prevent you from seeing what is right in front of you."

Nigel removed his hands from the fire and it crackled back into a dull teal.

"What does that mean," Nigel asked, "what is right in front of me?"

"Think about it, Nigel. You just asked me a question. Can

you see what is right in front of you?" Elenry asked, proceeding to make a simple breakfast identical to their dinner the night before.

While Nigel puzzled over his reading, Sagel stirred within the shelter, eventually emerging.

"I'm not sure it's possible, but I think it got colder," she announced, crouching beside Nigel and wincing as her joints cracked and moaned.

"My sentiments exactly," Elenry smiled, handing Sagel a mug of tea.

"This isn't sap tea," Sagel commented after sipping the brew.

"No it isn't," Elenry confirmed. "It is steeped from the leaf grown on a special bush that is found in the southern valley country of Thous Avaykwathorel. It's called Palar leaf, and it is very good for boosting your immunity."

"Why did you not give it to the people in Shinken?" Nigel asked.

"Because there was not nearly enough to go around among even five people, and it does not cure the illness or hold it at bay," Elenry answered.

"How do you know?" Nigel pressed.

"I gave Gwenoth two mugs of it and nothing happened." Elenry then snapped, "There was nothing else I could do."

Nigel averted his gaze to the fire once more.

"I apologize," Elenry said quietly. "I should not have taken out my frustration on those who have so valiantly volunteered themselves."

"It's alright," Nigel answered.

Elenry sighed, "We are all hungry and rather chilly, so let us eat and then walk. I will continue my story during our next break."

The two of them nodded in contentment at the Medicine Woman.

Sagel turned towards the valley out below them and gasped. "We can't see a thing!"

Nigel groaned. A dense wall of cloud and fog encased the land below them. He could see a ways down into the foothills, but their once panoramic view of the country and the destined valley was now completely blotted out.

"What will we do now?" Sagel asked Elenry, setting down her mug.

"We will continue on as we have before. Do not fret, you two, as I only planned for us to use this day to get down the mountain and onto the flatter lands. We will take a longer rest for the night, and then the next day we will hopefully complete our journey in a long trek to the valley. We need not much visibility for this first day, as we can only go down," Elenry said calmly. Along with a developed ability to see through her physical surroundings, she had much keener eyesight than either one of the children, and could see where in the foothills they would aim for to have the safest descent into the valley.

"What if we get lost?" Nigel queried.

"Then we will have to find ourselves again," Elenry answered.

In the following two or so hours, they picked their way down the decline in a painfully slow manner. Elenry could feel that the land was rather unstable. One wrong move and they could be riding a wall of snow to their deaths below. Elenry tested and prodded the ground before her with her feet and sometimes hands before taking a few cautious steps onto the apparently safe area, and then she would start with the next few feet of ground. Sagel was in back again, leading Wisle.

After yesterday's slide, he was much more wary of the ground beneath him. Every time they stopped to let Elenry probe, Sagel would pat him and whisper in his ear. Before long, her neck ached from craning to his ears, so she just spoke out loud. Both children gazed often at the slowly clearing fog. Since they had began their day's walk, the formidable mist holding them to the mountain had subsided some, but the weak winter sun had not been strong enough to burn it all off before midday.

Suddenly, the steep slope leveled off slightly, ending in another sort of ledge. The mountainside seemed to be composed of high rises of sheer cliff, random, broken ledges, and smoother slopes like the one they had followed down. Elenry stopped and turned towards the children.

"We'll break for lunch," she said, smiling when Sagel and Nigel broke into excited grins. This promised more of her story.

Wisle looked toward the edge of their small terrace tensely. Elenry scratched his ears and spoke softly; he snorted and then settled on his weary feet, shutting his eyes and lowering his head to rest. How she missed Arros. The Medicine Woman pushed these longing thoughts from her mind; they would not contribute anything but distraction to their journey.

Elenry went through their food bag, removing their usual meal and giving the children their lunches. She pulled the tent tarp from a saddle bag and laid it on the ground like a picnic cloth. Sagel and Nigel took a load off of their knees and sat on the tarp, happy to be out of the crouching position and off the snow. The wind silenced as they waited for Elenry to continue her story. Peaking the children's anticipation, Elenry took her time as she readied herself for her tale. She first settled herself, took a few mouthfuls of her food, chewed slowly, swallowed, breathed deeply several times, and then began.

"Relae and I left Nook on the main road. It was not particularly hot or cold, as I remember—a comfortable temperature for traveling on foot. Keep in mind now: Nook is in Sekamorathai, which is a much larger continent than Thron Avawkwathorel. Also, know that Nook is almost on the most southern tip, far away from any major city, but the road we traveled was well worn from all of the tradesmen and travelers who used it.

I believe that by now it has been paved and lined with more cities and developed villages. Actually, I hear it is a favored travel destination among the northern dwelling folk who long for warmth and sea air. When I was a child, it was still considered a remote part of the country, home to the small and the simple.

Relae walked at a slow speed, painfully slow, but ever steady. Why, she could probably have gone all day and all night with only bits of rest here and there had it not been for me. The country there was flat with small rolling hills. The sea was always to our backs, fading farther and farther behind us—this was also very strange for me, for I had never been in a place where I could not see the ocean. She put up a shelter for us every night and had breakfast waiting for me in the morning. We walked all day, occasionally stopping so she could pick plants from the road side, to relax in the shimmering green fields, or to bathe in a stream. Animals there were small and harmless—well, most of them. There was a bird called a Shelbee that had talons the size of your head and a beak to match. It likes colorful objects and dove at us if we wore anything of flamboyant color. Being a young girl from a sea-side village, all I had was colorful clothing, as did Relae. While we walked in the Shelbees' territory, we had to don brown shawls to deter the shrieking birds." Elenry paused, smiling ever so slightly at the memory.

"If ever I asked where we were going, Relae would just shrug, smiling to herself. This drove me mad. I pleaded with her, tried to bribe her into telling me. I so longed for some sort of security, some sort of finality, or some inkling of promise in my forever changing situation. The old Medicine Woman was too clever for me. She was trying to keep the reassurance that I longed for most from me so that I would mature enough to reassure myself. This is a skill that takes some people a very long and hard time to master.

Around the sixth day of our trek, I stopped asking and accepted that my tired feet would carry me wherever we were going and there was not much I could do to change it unless I wanted to carry on by myself in another direction. I suppose she was also trying to teach me acceptance. As we trailed inland, the scenery changed drastically. The barely-noticeable foothills stretched upwards into grand knolls, each covered in trees and vegetation of all sorts. By then, the sea was a distant memory, invisible in any direction no matter how high we climbed.

Relae spoke to me more and more as we went; mainly she commented on various plants and their medicinal properties, or told me odd little tidbits about what to do in emergency medical situations. Sometimes she would quiz me by pointing to a plant off the trail and asking for its name and purpose. Sometimes she asked what it smelled like. In turn, I grew to talking to her more. I told her of my old friends or stories about the sea that my father had gifted me with on stormy nights by the light of our fireplace. She nodded occasionally, soaking everything in and storing it somewhere that I could not see. When food ran low, we substituted what we did not have with various plants and animals from the lands surrounding the road. She taught me about roots, edible flower blossoms and stems, and how to skin and cook small mammals like Willbs and Fifes."

"What are those?" Nigel interjected.

"A Willb is a small brown creature that is blind and therefore very easy to catch, and a Fife is a tiny white mammal that squeaks, though it is harder to catch because it is not blind.

I remember well the first building—well, structure—that I saw in those ten days of walking. It was a large cottage made out of a dark wood, unlike the stone structures of Nook. It had wide windows on the front and sides of the house whose frames were white with painted, red flowers. Relae was as curious as I was, so we picked up the pace. A sign hung above the door, bright and welcoming. Keep in mind that this happened many years before the Earthlings came to Asthekia, so nothing was written in their alphabetic script. This sign was written in Haviia, the main old language of Southern Sekamorathai. Nowadays, the only two languages you hear are Sdrawkcab and English, with only a few small villages who speak the old dialects. Anyway, the sign said 'Mungereie', which means restaurant."

"Did you stop and eat?" Nigel interrupted, too engrossed in the story to notice that Wisle had just knocked over his barrel of huvar and was now snuffling around in the snow beside Nigel.

"Yes we did. It was the best meal either of us had had in days. The food was delicious with roasted meats and sweet fruits and nuts. All local, of course. The food was very strange to us, for we did not have any nut or fruit trees near Nook. The only fruit we ever had was brought by tradesman two or three times a year, and it was always either hard and unripe, or rotting. This fruit was perfect. The couple running the roadside establishment was eager to hear our story and about where we had come from, for they had never even heard of Nook. And I was amazed that they had never even seen the sea. Over an hour or so of eating and talking, we gathered that the closest town was Kulkatry, about ten miles north. The fastest and safest way would be to keep following the road we were already on.

I would have loved to stay longer in the comfortable, clean little restuarant, but Relae said that we must keep going, as she wished to get to Kulkatry before nightfall. So on we went, our canteens filled with cool water and our knapsacks packed with fruit, nuts, and dried meat. I cannot say why, but when we stepped away from the roadhouse, satiated with good food and love, I had to fight with myself to keep the tears from pouring down my cheeks. Relae, who never missed a thing, must have sensed my emotion, because she hugged her arm around my shoulder once and then continued her steady pace toward Kulkatry.

"What will you do in Kulkatry?" I asked her once I had regained enough control to speak without crying.

"You mean what *we* will do," she replied, smiling at me, her small crowded teeth glistening. "I will continue my work and serve the ailing, and you, Elenry, will help me. I will teach you the ways of the Medicine People: show you how to save someone's life, how to let them die if that is what needs to happen, and much more. We will start over, child."

I was stunned, to say the least. I half expected her to leave me with a nice family in Kulkatry and then continue her wandering.

"Can I stay with you?" I asked, just to be sure.

She laughed, a low chuckle of delight, "Of course, Elenry. Where else would you stay? We know no one in that town. You are under my care.'"

So for the next ten miles I pondered what I would learn, who I would meet, and how I would heal them. The landscape changed even more then, the road climbing from small knolls to rugged hills. Ragged gray stone jutted through the earth like spurred bone, and our road became more uneven and pot-holed than before. At last we came to the top of a small, exposed summit and the hills began to slope downwards. We could see the town of Kulkatry, at least three times the size of Nook, nestled in the rough hands of the hills."

Sagel and Nigel watched Elenry intently, willing her to go on, knowing that it was in vain. They were right.

"Finish eating now, and we shall continue our journey, not mine," Elenry said, returning to her lunch. "Perhaps I will tell some more at our evening meal."

The foursome contentedly finished their lunch and then walked onward and downward.

Snow began to fall silently, limiting their visibility even more. The ground they walked on smoothed from jutting rocks to snow-packed, pebbled ground. Elenry led them on down the mountain hoping to gain more visibility as they lost altitude. As she predicted, the white haze thinned and began to clear.

"I think we'll make it," Sagel said hopefully, pulling her hat back from in front of her eyes.

"I won't make any promises, but we certainly have a fair chance," Elenry replied.

Sagel felt like she was holding her breath for the rest of their descent, hoping that nothing would happen to delay them from striding off the volatile slopes of the mountain. Wisle grew restless, throwing his head and snorting more often than he had that morning. Elenry finally took his lead rope from Sagel to calm him. A wave of disappointment bristled through the girl. How she wished she could assuage animals like Elenry could.

They rested here and there, only long enough to crouch in the snow, rest their weary legs and drink some water. Elenry had set a course that took them east of the foothills where the mountain flattened gradually into a plain. As they came closer and closer to the bottom of the mountain, trees unlike any Sagel and Nigel had seen started to crop up in thicker and thicker groups.

"We're here!" Nigel breathed, running ahead down the last twenty feet of inclined land to where the trees at last made the outskirts of a forest.

The trees were thicker than those up on the mountain and would take two full grown men to put their arms all the way around one of them. The bark was a pearly white with charcoal grooves like blackened scars. Thick branches started to jut out about ten feet up the tree, and held no leaves, just small, twiggy extremities.

"Yes," Elenry said, stopping and gazing around the forest, taking in everything. "We did, didn't we?"

Sagel and Nigel whooped and laughed and danced in a circle of triumph.

"It has gotten late," Elenry remarked, patting Wisle calmly.

The children looked up from their celebrations to appraise the sky. No star twinkled, no clouds rolled, and no moon or sun watched. Dark, evening sky glared down, and they lowered their gazes.

"We'll camp here," Elenry said, beginning their night-time routine. Sagel and Nigel helped pitch the tent by tying the tarp to the posts and the stakes that Elenry had pounded into the ground. The children went to gather firewood while Elenry finished setting up their campsite.

When a fire was blazing, with a large pot of melting snow suspended over it, and they were seated with their dinner, they began discussing what lay ahead.

"So now we just walk to the valley?" Sagel asked.

"That's right," Elenry said. "Of course, it will be much safer and quicker than our perilous descent, but we will be walking through forest. We will have to be more careful to stay on our course so we do not miss it entirely."

"How will we do that?" Sagel questioned, wanting to stop talking and eat but too curious and anxious to do so. Nigel, on the other hand, happily downed his bread and dried Churkey.

"Fret not, Sagel, tomorrow I will teach you," Elenry said.

"Will you teach me?" Nigel asked, surfacing from his food.

"Yes, I will teach you both."

Before anything else was said, they all dove into their dinners.

"I can't believe we made it!" Nigel sighed a few minutes later, more talkative now that his stomach was full. "No injuries, no epic battles, no Shadow Shades—I mean…uh, well, nothing *bad* happened."

"Right you are, and not one Shadow Shade," Elenry smiled, her voice tinkling playfully.

Sagel laughed at her brother, "Shadow Shades? You *still* think that they exist?"

"No. Well, you never know…," Nigel grumbled, blushing.

"Shhhh…hush now," Elenry whispered. "You'll scare away the story."

"Oh!" Nigel cried happily, before Sagel clamped her hand over his mouth.

Before resuming her tale, Elenry made sap tea for all of them. They sat in silence for awhile, letting the heat of the mugs warm their hands. Then, Elenry began.

"I was most curious about coming to a new village, though since I had never left Nook, I expected Kulkatry to be just like my old home. In many aspects, I suppose it was similar. The people wore the same sorts of clothing, worked the same kinds of jobs, and spoke the same language. Women wore the same summery dresses or skirts, the men wore the same light pants that only went down to their knees, and the children wore dresses, skirts, shorts, and tee-shirts of the same sort as those in Nook. I must have been around nine or ten, so little things like clothing and food interested me greatly. Relae, on the other hand, just wanted a place to live and work.

She paused and they all drank deeply and sat a moment in silence. Then she continued. "The people of the town accepted us well enough. The adults brought us food and set us in a small, empty house near the center of town. Ah, yes, the houses were also similar, though instead of orange clay, it was white. Relae was quick to tell me that I would need to stay close by in case she needed me. This was not hard for me, for, truth be told, I was frightened of Kulkatry. It was much bigger, the people were faster, and the food was much richer and stronger. Everyone spoke loudly and you had to pay for things you needed with white rocks. This was the first time I had ever used money. Whether or not Relae had ever used money I do not know, but she was very quick to catch on to the patterns and ways of it.

Business started slowly. Very slowly. Once or twice a week

we would have a sufferer come in with a runny nose, or a painful rash. Relae would fix them up, I would watch, and they would pay us in white rocks, the amount depending on the severity of their condition. As our stay lengthened, more and more townspeople came to us. I became hungry for the knowledge of healing, and Relae seemed eager enough to feed my new passion. She would stay up late into the night with me, explaining the secrets of medicine and meditation, or reviewing chants and potions and healing mixtures. Sometimes, I would wander through Kulkatry. People were kind enough, but everyone had their own jobs to do; besides, I was just a child. I tried to engage people, but sometimes I would say things that scared them. For example, if a woman I was talking to had broken her favorite plate that morning at breakfast, I would express my condolences, though I had not been there to witness it, nor had I been told about it. Once a man had lost his wife the night before, and I brought him a flower to show my compassion. Any time these strange occurrences happened, the people would look at me. They would stare at me, frightened by my second sight, and yet, relieved and curious.

Some even sought me out when I was walking about, telling me about there problems or consulting me on small medical maladies. I told them what they needed to do, be it a tissue for their tears or a touch for their sore muscles, and sent them on their way, free of charge. Relae did not like this. When I came home one day, after seeing a woman about her painful kneecaps, and giving her the directions for mixing a curing potion, I found Relae waiting for me. She explained that good Medicine People did not give out their potions. Nor did they give free consultations.

"Are you angry?" I asked her.

"Not at all, Elenry," she said, putting her hot hand on my

cheek. "I am just teaching you the ways of our people. Everyone makes mistakes, but it is your own job to learn from them and do right next time. Even great healers need to buy food."

This ended my walks, for I did not think that I could deny people my services. The other village children steered clear of me, for I was the 'stranger from a distant land whose village had died'. Though I would not admit it to Relae then, this saddened me deeply. I had no close friends my own age. But the years rolled on, and we did good business.

Almost every day it seemed that I was exposed to a new ailment, or a different broken bone that I would then learn to mend or heal. Relae would watch me work, commenting on and complimenting my work. It got to the point where she would stay in the back sitting room reading or meditating, or just sleeping and I would take the clients. I hated taking people's money, and I even started giving the clients discounts, or if it were a brief visit, I would not charge them at all. Somehow, Relae found out and had yet another talk with me.

"Are you angry with me?" I again asked, staring at my feet.

"No...no, I am disappointed," she said, and somehow that was worse than anger. "I hoped you would *learn* from your mistake. I expected you to, Elenry. We need to buy our supplies and pay for the things of our own lives. When we first arrived in Kulkatry, people gave freely to us. But now, we work for our bread. No one gives us those things for free anymore."

"I'm sorry Relae," I whispered, "I won't do it again. I've learned. But it just doesn't feel right to exchange money for health."

She did not answer me

Oh, how eager I was to please her. It pained me not to have

her absolute approval. A few nights after that, I asked her a question that had been pressing on my mind for quite some time. The question had come up in bits and pieces, like a puzzle I was trying to solve, and then I finally realized that I needed to ask it out loud, to Relae.

It was evening. Warm summer rain battered our windows outside as we sat in our modest living room. I set down the potion book I had been reading and turned to Relae.

"How did you become a Medicine Woman?" I asked.

Relae had been sewing up a hole in a pair of my pants, and continued to sew as if she had not heard me. I waited a few moments, watching her lithe hands dance with the needle across the fabric.

"Relae—"

"I heard you, Elenry," she said, her sewing undisturbed.

I sat across the room from her until she finished fixing my pants, wondering all the while what was going on inside that head of hers. Finally, her eyes rose to mine, the skin around them crinkling as she smiled.

"I became a Medicine Woman the very same way that you are becoming one," she said, the smile never leaving her face. "I was born as one."

She was about to stand, but I was not done with her, "I mean, how did you find out that you were one? I found out when I met you and you tried to give me the rock."

"I see," she sighed, relaxing back into her living room chair. "You don't want an answer. You want a story."

I grinned at her and nodded eagerly.

Relae spread her hands on her knees and breathed so deeply that I could almost feel the air rushing to her. Then she began,

"I was born in Nook. My father was a furniture maker, and my mother was a fulltime child-maker. I had five older brothers. All of them are dead now of old age." Relae paused to pick her nail. "My father made furniture to bring to the market, which was much smaller back in my day. There were only twenty or so people in Nook then—it was like living in a very large family. You see, I was a small child and weak from birth. I was almost always ill with colds or fevers. One night, I heard my parents whispering in their bedroom about how they did not think that I would survive until adulthood. That night I wept silently in the room I shared with two of my brothers. I resolved then to survive my childhood and become a strong, healthy young woman. I hadn't the fun that the other children in the village had, for I was always kept home by my mother, who was convinced that I was too frail to exert myself as much as my peers.

I spent a great deal of time working with my mother—I cooked, cleaned, washed clothing, played by myself in my room, or just in front of our cottage where my mother could keep a safe watch on me. Sometimes she would have me rub her back, for with all the work she did around the house, she was prone to aches and pains. When I was eight years old, my mother started letting me play with my brothers by the sea. I was not to go in the water, as they could, and I was not to run, scream, or wrestle. My oldest brother, Rawin, was very protective of me. Yes, he was well trained by my mother. He told all of the other village children to stay a safe distance from me so they wouldn't infect me with their germs. Rawin was a big, strong boy, built like my father, so no one dared to cross him. The other children left me alone. I became known as the 'Nucta Palesh' of the village."

"The fragile fruit," I breathed, for we were speaking in my native language.

"Yes. The fragile fruit. At age fourteen, Rawin was told by my father that he was no longer to play with the children, as he had to begin his work as my father's apprentice. As sad as my brother was to essentially leave his childhood behind, he was proud to work as a young adult. That also meant that I would have more freedom without my brother's constant presence. He was as conscientious as my mother, and now, I had one place that I would not be constantly protected." She paused and seemed to be struggling with something in her memory. I felt as though she was weighing whether or not to go on, to tell me something of more importance. After all, what she had said so far didn't tell me anything about how she had become a Medicine Woman.

She read my thoughts. She said, "Medicine People start as ordinary people, Elenry. You need to know that. You yourself one day will help ordinary people to discover that they are not so ordinary."

Sagel and Nigel looked at each other. Every nerve in Sagel's body tingled as she looked at her little brother. She looked down at her own long, graceful hands, and felt that they were good for more than eating and playing.

"In time you will find what else they are good for," Elenry said quietly.

The Medicine Woman took a sip of her cooling tea and smiled at Nigel, who was poised in anticipation for the rest of the story, which she continued. "It was a stifling, summer day, and I went with three of my older brothers—Garreo, Rilon, and Daeshin— down to the little beach not two miles from Nook. The very same beach that I sent you to."

My stomach clenched at the memory of waiting anxiously as my village perished just up the path. Relae nodded slowly and continued.

"I played with Daeshin, who was only one year older than I was. We built and drew in the sand while Garreo and Rilon roughhoused at the edge of the water. They took to flinging wet sand globs at one another, and before I knew it, I was splattered as well. At once Daeshin and I joined the fight, giggling and shouting as we pelted each other.

Something released inside me as I joined my brothers in normal, childish play. I shrieked and laughed, and ran, my skinny legs flailing and my dark hair streaming wildly behind me. A building euphoria made my hands tingle. For once, I was not the 'Nucta Palesh'. No longer was I breakable, or sickly. I was a child, and that was all that mattered.

Our battle died away, at last, and my brothers went to the edge of the sea to wash themselves. I followed suit, bending and scrubbing the sand from my skin. As I scrubbed, I realized that the sand was not going to fully wash away unless I completely immersed myself in the water, so I waded out into the gentle sea.

"What are you doing, Relae?" Garreo shouted, starting out towards me.

"I'm washing off. I'm fine," I called back, dunking my head in the shimmering blue.

"Mother will be furious to see you wet like that," he groaned, "and it will be my fault, because I'm the oldest."

"Say I fell in," I replied, floating onto my back.

"She'll be mad that I let you."

"You'll figure something out."

Rilon and Daeshin joined me in the water, but Garreo stood

fretting on the beach. We made a game of seeing how long we could hold our breaths under water. I lost every time, being as small as I was. A strange thing happens in the ocean." Relae paused to take a long breath.

"What was it?" I asked eagerly.

"You start off hanging just at the shore, and the more you play and jump around, the farther out the water takes you. Unless you are very wise about the sea, you may not notice it. Being a seven year old child, I was by no means wise about anything.

"Come out, you three! We need to go home for dinner," Garreo yelled from the beach. I looked up at him and noticed how much further away he was than when we had first started playing. My brothers started swimming in immediately, but I, drunk with my newfound freedom, decided to dunk my head one more time. I lay my head back in the water to wet my hair, and momentarily lost my balance on the ocean floor. I stepped back and stepped off the underwater shelf of the beach. All of a sudden I was flailing, my feet searching frantically for something to stand on. I remember screaming for help once before I went under. A powerful ocean tide ripped me from the shore and started to pull me out to sea. I surfaced for air once more, long enough to hear my brothers screaming for me.

Something happened then. I understood that unless I saved myself, I was going to die. The tingling in my hands that I had felt on the beach peaked suddenly, and in my fast-slipping consciousness, I felt them begin to pulse. Without thinking, I brought my hands to my chest. Suddenly, I could breathe. My eyes focused in the bright ocean world around me, and I realized that I was floating only five or so feet from the surface. My hands pulsed harder as the energy flowed from them into my chest. The aqua blues swirled around me as I gazed upon the ocean floor. It was like a dream. I began kicking my feet, and propelled myself to the surface. I hung there, my head just out of the water and my legs kicking as I treaded water. I was exhausted, but any time I felt that I could not go on, I simply brought one hand to my chest, and I was replenished. It felt like I was there for days before a boat with villagers rescued me.

They hauled my tiny frame into the small craft as the crowd waiting anxiously on the beach cheered. My father and Garreo were in the dingy with two of the village fishermen, and held me close to them all the way back to shore. Of course, my mother was sobbing on the sand, and shrieked joyously as she pulled me from the boat and into her frenetic arms. I tried to explain to my family how I had survived, but they attributed it to good luck, not to the special energy that I insisted I had felt and had saved me. They told me that the spirits of the ocean had kept me alive and afloat, and that I only imagined that my hands had pulsed be-cause I was so sick from lack of oxygen. I became confused and frustrated. What they said made some kind of sense, but it was not—it was definitely not—what I had experienced. I decided that talking about it to anyone was useless. So when I was alone, I tried for hours at a time to make my hands pulse again so I could show them. Finally, I got my chance.

It was one day at breakfast when my right hand began to heat up. Slowly, my left hand began heating as well. Before long, they were both pulsing. I showed my mother, who said that all she could feel was intense heat. As usual, she saw it as something dreadful, and thought I had a fever. A day or so later, she was the one that fell sick. She said that her muscles ached and her head throbbed. She could not get enough water, and was perpetually thirsty. My father tried to nurse her back to health, but she only got worse. Her head ached so much that she could not open her eyes. When my father had taken enough time from his work, he told me that I would need to care for my mother. I agreed, and went to her bedside.

"Relae…rub my back," she whispered. I obliged, placing my hands on her weakened, shivering body. All of a sudden, the pulsing that had been in my hands for the past few days intensified to the point where my mother started from the heat of my touch. I kept my hands there for a very long time.

"What is…what is that—so hot. Don't stop that, Relae. It is helping…," she murmured. Finally, exhausted, I let my hands fall away. I sat for a moment, and felt my hands return to normal.

All of a sudden, my mother sat up, her eyes clear and face bright.

"I feel much better," she said to me. She took my hands and studied them for a long time, turning them over so that she could look closely at the palms and the backs. She began to cry.

"What is it, Mother?" I gasped, hugging her anxiously.

"You are a healer," she sobbed, holding me close to her. "Our village has not had a healer since I was a small girl. He passed away before you were born, and there has not been another one since. Oh, this is wonderful."

During the next few days, the news spread through the village that I was a healer. People flocked to our house, bringing food and specially brewed drinks, all for the exchange of my healing touch. Some came with sore backs or injured arms. My parents were thrilled, but also rather shocked that their sickly little girl was now a healing being. I did only hand healing until I was eleven, when a Medicine Man passed through our village. His hair was curly and silver, but his back was straight and his body was muscled and young. He was weary from traveling, and my parents offered him a home and food in exchange for his teaching me the ways of medicine. He stayed and taught me as I have taught you until I was nineteen, when he left our village. I do not know why he left, and I missed him sorely. He had complained that a negative energy sometimes hung around him when he was in our village, so I concluded that he left to clear himself of what burden plagued him in Nook."

"Did you ever see him again?" I asked.

"Never…but I did ask him, one day, shortly before he left, the same question you asked me."

"Which question, Relae?"

"How did he become a Medicine Man."

"Did he tell you?"

"Yes. He came from a family of Medicine People. It was passed down to him by his parents and grandparents on both sides. That was all he told me."

"What did you do after he left?"

"I started my own practice as a young woman, and I worked from my family home until the day that our village fell to the illness." After she finished, she went to bed, leaving me to ponder all that my mentor had told me. I was enamored by Relae's epic tale, and felt closer to her than ever before. We continued our little business in Kulkatry, but all the while, I felt something in our relationship changing.

The sun revolved, years passed, and then I became sixteen sun revolutions old. That is when I left."

Silence punctuated with the diminished crackles of the fire filled every pocket of air.

"And that is where I will leave you tonight," Elenry said, breaking from her story telling voice to her conversational cadence.

"But you can't stop there!" Nigel cried, stifling a yawn with his hand.

"Just a little more," Sagel agreed, her eyes drooping.

"I thank you two for your attention, but I insist that you to go to bed, for you are both going to collapse into the flames before long, and then I will have to teach you the procedure for healing burns, Sagel."

Sagel's eyes lit up.

"You would teach me?"

"Perhaps. But not tonight. You both—we all—need to sleep now."

Elenry quickly checked Wisle's knot that tied him to the tent stake before holding the tent door open for the children and then climbing in herself. Nigel fell into sleep almost as soon as his eyes closed, but Sagel spent a good while taming the anxious beasts that growled and tossed in her mind. Shinken, Nook, Medicine People, parents, death, trees, sap, school, Daniel, her bed...everything under the sky seemed to visit her thoughts before she fell asleep, but when she finally did begin to fall into sleep, nothing but the sound of Nigel's steady breathing filled her head.

Late that night, Sagel surfaced briefly from a black, dreamless slumber. She lifted her head slightly and looked around the tent. Elenry sat up by the door of the tent, a dim candle by her feet. She was writing something on a slip of paper. Sagel remembered no more, for she was pulled back into sleep's empty embrace.

Chapter 27

Fahrien Forest

The children were awakened by the sound of Elenry preparing breakfast. Sagel crawled out of the tent, gazing up at the forest around her. Nigel followed behind, rubbing his eyes sleepily. Above them, the sky shone a pale blue through a web of branches. The temperature had not changed from the day before, but now a soft breeze breathed around them. On the eastern horizon, the sun and moon had begun their climb, throwing soft, morning light across the sky.

"Good morning, travelers," Elenry said, passing them each their usual mug of hot liquid. This morning's concoction was sweet and milky.

"Where's Wisle?" Sagel asked suddenly. The mule was not tethered to the tent post as he had been the night before.

"Wisle is gone," Elenry said simply.

"What?" Sagel said.

"How?" Nigel cried.

"When I climbed out of the tent this morning, he was gone. I looked for him around the forest close by, but he was long gone," Elenry said. "He must have left during the night

— 304 —

or early this morning while we were sleeping. His tracks go back the way we came."

"But our stuff—"

"Not to worry, Sagel," Elenry cut in. "I completely un-tacked him last night. The only thing he had on was his saddle blanket."

"Where do you think he went?" Nigel asked.

"I have a feeling that he has started back to Shinken."

"Wow," Nigel breathed. "I hope he makes it."

"Wisle is a tough animal. I think he will," Elenry said. "Drink up, while your drinks are warm."

"How are we going to carry all the gear?" Nigel gasped.

"We will distribute it among us. I'll carry the heaviest load, but all of our loads will be heavier from now on," Elenry explained.

Sagel's face grew long as she said, "Then, that means we'll be going slower."

Elenry smiled, "Slower, but on mostly level ground."

They sat quietly, sipping their beverages and adjusting their minds to their new condition.

"What is this?" Sagel finally asked, taking another long sip. "It's delicious."

"That is ahi powder in hot water with sap," Elenry answered, sipping from her own mug before passing them their plates. "Ahi powder is not uncommon, in fact, your mother probably has her own bottle. It is just a sweet thickener from the Ahi plant."

They ate in silence, hungry from their walk yesterday and their long night of sleep.

"I apologize for the monotony of our meals; I am sure your have noticed that they have been exactly the same," Elenry said, smiling dryly. "I find that consistency of food is best when everything else is inconsistent, just to keep your body as happy as can be."

"What if your body gets bored?" Nigel asked.

"Better bored than ill. Today will be a long one, because I have a feeling that if we push long enough, we will make it to the valley."

"Really?" Sagel asked happily. "That would be wonderful! I never imagined we would get here this fast."

"Neither did I, but at the pace we've been going, and the lovely conditions today, I think we can make it. I don't think we'll stop long enough for me to tell a good story, so how about if I finish off the saga now while we eat?"

"Yes, that sounds good," Sagel replied, smiling and sipping her drink.

For once Nigel said nothing, but smiled at Elenry and listened.

"Let's see, where did I leave off?" Elenry paused.

"You were in Kulkatry, and you got in trouble for healing people for free, and then you turned sixteen, and you left," Nigel said quickly.

"Oh yes. So I turned sixteen. Relae said that she considered me an adult then, and that she would trust me with more responsibilities. She began teaching me more difficult potions and chants. I practiced late into the night so that the next day I could perform them as best I could for her. There came a day when she did not teach me a new spell. I was not troubled by this, and was relieved, in a way, because that would give me time to practice and perfect the many I had already learned. The weeks went by, rolling into months, and then three months. I asked her one day at breakfast if she would teach me anything, and she did not answer me directly. She said that I knew enough to be a wonderful Medicine Woman. I did not realize it then, but she did not want to admit to me that she did not have any more to teach me. I learned quickly, and soon, I could perform the healings as well as she could.

The day I left started with a young boy. A woman named Sabita brought her six year old son in because he had been lethargic for the past threes days. He had not eaten anything since his chronic exhaustion began, and would only drink small amounts, when coaxed. Relae said that she would take this patient, because she sensed it to be something more serious. She did the routine body scan with her hands as she chanted. I stood over the boy's shoulder, mopping the sweat off his forehead from the intensity of the ritual. In the middle of his chest, Relae's hands stopped. She found a malignant mass that had started in his stomach and had spread all through his digestive track. She tried to suck the negative energy out, to push it out, and to massage it out. She meditated on it and concocted a very difficult and rare draught for him to drink to try and flush the poisonous growth out. Her attempts were futile.

"I cannot heal him, Sabita," Relae told his sobbing mother. "He is too far gone. He cannot be saved. I am sorry Sabita. You have to let him go, now."

"Wait...no," I said, stepping up to the tableside. "I can heal him."

Relae was doubtful, and tried hard to get me to give it up and let him die peacefully, but I knew that I could save him. I let my hands fall close to his stomach, and then I let all of the energy of the cosmos run through my hands and into him. He convulsed and then grasped his stomach, screaming and crying. Relae almost stepped in to stop me, but I held her back, physically held her back. He threw up. What he vomited was black and stinking, congealed and slimy. The poison was gone from him. Relae charged them double what she would have normally charged for a case like his, and poor Sabita paid the price.

That night Relae was very quiet, and I became frustrated. I told her that I wanted to leave, and that I did not agree with her ways of charging people money for their health. She said that that was the only way one could live, and when I pointed out that she could make a good wage charging reasonable amounts instead of charging absurd amounts to become rich, she became angry. Relae said that I was young, inexperienced, and no good at anything else but healing. I said I was going to leave, and that I would not let her keep me there." Elenry's eyes froze in a hard sheet of ice, and then melted into sorrowful warmth.

"She tried to convince me to stay, and I told her that I would sleep on it and decide in the morning. She must have been exceptionally tired from the day's happenings, for I was able to sneak out before sunrise. The only things I brought with me were my backpack full of clothes, and a pouch of my white rocks I had earned when she started paying me small shares from every healing I helped in.

I had it in my mind to go off on my own, far away from Kulkatry and Relae, and start my own healing practice. Over the next six months, I walked and hitched short rides all the way to Konakiak, the largest city in Sekamorathai. There I acquired Arros from a man I healed who did not have any money to pay me. In those days, I told all of my patients that they could pay me however much they wanted to depending on how they liked my services. It is truly amazing how much money I made from grateful people, and how much people are willing to give when they are grateful for their good health. Nowadays I have a slightly higher fixed rate, but with the modern medicine of hospitals and clinics, I do not have as many jobs as I had in the past. I have been traveling around Asthekia by boat and horse ever since. I do not like charging people, but I must eat and feed Arros. That is all."

The siblings breathed a collective sigh of finality.

"The end?" Sagel said.

"The end," Elenry replied.

"Thank you, for telling us all of that," Sagel said.

"Yeah, thanks," Nigel added, nodding slowly.

"You're welcome, and now I will attempt to teach you both something after we pack up."

The two children perked up, immediately starting to take down the tent and load their bags. With Wisle gone, all three of them had larger and heavier packs. Once they had their bags on their backs, Sagel and Nigel stood expectantly before Elenry.

"I do not have a map of this land, nor do I know exactly how we are going to get to the valley that we aim for. Though it might sound doubtful to you, you are going to have to trust me, and trust yourselves," Elenry paused. "Are you ready?"

"Yes," they answered, eyes alight with curiosity.

"We are going to find this valley by following our bodies," Elenry began. "We are going to let our minds become silent, and allow our bodies to take control of our travels."

"How do we do that?" Nigel asked immediately.

"Now, just listen to the sound of my voice, and do exactly what I tell you. Do not question it, and do not fight it, just let yourself do what I say," Elenry said, her voice taking on a slow, flowing rhythm, like a great, meandering river.

"Close your eyes…that's right, now walk."

The children began to walk, going in opposite directions.

"Make the first motion that your body wants to, now!"

Sagel lifted her arms and Nigel turned around to face the way Sagel was facing. Elenry smiled, happy with their responses.

"Now relax into your bodies. Feel every nerve ending, hair, finger, blood vessel, and muscle. Relax every one of your muscles. Breath from your lungs all the way down to your feet…that's it…very good. Now open your eyes slowly, at your body's pace, and then let go. Let it take you to the valley."

They began to walk, relaxing into their own rhythms. Elenry let her body flow and go with the energy. Her physical body took her in the same direction as her companion's bodies went. They seemed to float through the leafless forest. A cold, clear morning unfolded into an equally chilly midday, and then an even colder evening. They did not stop to eat lunch, for they felt no hunger now that they were outside their minds. Their bodies could go on what food they had eaten at breakfast, though they would all need to eat come nightfall. The cover of trees thickened around them. Gradually, they left the deciduous trees behind. Evergreens took over the forest until they were the only trees in sight as the land began to slope downward.

Late in the afternoon, with the sun and the moon no longer visible through the heavy tree cover, the spell was broken when a tall, cloaked figure stepped out from behind a tree. Sagel and Nigel broke from their walking trances and recoiled to stand behind Elenry, wary of this stranger. Elenry broke her spell more slowly, easing her mind back into sync with her body.

The figure before them was wrapped in a red robe with a heavy hood, and wore black pants and a black coat underneath. Around them, the trees stretched tall and thick, towering so far above them that they had to crane their necks to see their tops. A man's face came out from beneath the hood as he flipped it back to rest upon his thin shoulders. The man looked rather like he belonged in the trees with birds. His nose was long and thin, hooking over his pointed lips. His jaw was so narrow that it was a wonder he could eat anything besides seeds. By his sides his hands fidgeted.

"Welcome, travelers," he said, "to Fahrien forest. I will ask you to follow me now, for I know what you have come for. My name is Saivenn. You are Elenry, Sagel and Nigel."

Sagel and Nigel looked to Elenry, chilled by the man's accurate knowledge and unsure whether or not to follow.

"Let's go," the Medicine Woman said, falling in stride behind their lanky guide who had turned and was walking away from them.

Chapter 28

The Center

Elenry walked just in front of the children, scanning their new surroundings. The massive trees towered so high and made such a thick ceiling of branches and needles that there was hardly any snow on the ground, though it was still cold.

A great energy was there. Elenry felt her hands begin to heat. Sagel and Nigel exchanged glances. Both of them felt charged from head to toe. The spindly man who walked in front of them hummed a somber tune, full of lost loves and long winters; it wasn't a promising melody. Nigel was itching to ask where they were, where the cure was, if there was a cure, and much more. He held his tongue. Something about this place did not welcome questions. The forest spread before them so long and in such thickness that it felt like they were walking at night as opposed to early evening. They did not seem to be on a trail, but Saivenn walked with such purpose that he seemed to be pulled by some invisible force.

"What's that noise?" Sagel whispered to Nigel, unable to hold her own tongue any longer.

"What noise?" Nigel responded, confused. "All I hear is our

feet and everyone's breathing."

"That pulse," Sagel pressed. Every ten seconds or so Sagel heard and felt a low, humming pulse that seemed to ring through the forest. Elenry heard the girl, and looked back and nodded knowingly. She could feel and hear it as well.

"It is the energy of this forest," Elenry clarified, her smooth voice quiet and subdued, as if she were telling them a secret. "We are in a very powerful place."

"You are right about that!" piped the man over his shoulder, making them all jump.

"What is this place?" Elenry asked.

"This is The Center," the bony man said. "We've been waiting for you, Elenry."

"Why?" she asked suddenly.

"You'll come to find out in just a short time."

"You know my name. Why?" Elenry asked, her voice lowering.

Saivenn stopped and looked back at Elenry.

"No need to be dark," he cajoled, his pointy face dampening in fear.

"I will stop being dark when you stop being cryptic."

"I'm so-sorry, I cannot say anything as of now," he stammered. "It is not my place, you see."

Elenry nodded, "Then take me to someone who can say something."

The guide nodded jerkily and proceeded to lead them deeper into the forest, his pace quickening anxiously.

Sagel and Nigel trotted behind Elenry, not daring to speak. This place that had been their beacon of security now seemed ominous and difficult. Nigel turned to his sister, his tone as low as he could manage. "What are we doing?" he breathed.

"I don't know," Sagel replied, her shoulders tense and her stride choppy. "Just keep walking, Nigel."

Nigel's brow pinched and his eyes worried, "Will we find the cure?"

"I don't know," Sagel said through clenched teeth. "I know no more than you do. Keep walking and keep your eyes and ears open."

In the dark haze of the trees before them, Elenry could make out two cottages. They were constructed from a wood that was so brown it looked black, and the buildings both had roofs made of dark brown shingles. Their windows were small and curtained, with no soft light of any kind detectable in the dark windows. As they walked up to the houses, the three of them studied the place quickly, scanning left and right.

Beyond the first two dwellings was an entire collection of houses just like the first two. Each had matching shingled roofs and on the doors, insignias. The graphic on the black doors was white. It was two long, eel-like fish swimming around a leaf. The closer the houses were to the center, the more light the travelers could see in their windows. A few people sat outside their houses; meditating, chanting, reading, or writing. People in this place all wore red robes that wound around their whole bodies except for their heads, lower legs and feet. The women had their hair cut very short, so that it was no longer than the middle of their necks. Most of the men were bald. In all, they saw about twenty people in this strange little compound.

The center, and seemingly most important part of the village, was obvious. A small hut stood in the pupil of the compound's eye. There was a space of about twenty feet between the central hut and the other houses on all sides. Bluish smoke trickled upwards from its chimney, and the insignia on the dark door was even larger than its many matches; apparently the mother of them all.

"This is it," the man said with a shaky grandiosity.

"This is what?" Elenry asked dryly, her eyes dissecting every bit of the poor man's being.

"The center of The Center," he replied. "Please, please go in, Medicine Woman."

"There is no need to plead, Saivenn," Elenry said softly. "I mean you no ill energy."

With that, Elenry turned to Sagel and Nigel for the first time since they had met their wiry guide and nodded for them to follow. The stairs creaked under foot, and Elenry sucked in one deep breath before opening the dark door.

Eye-watering perfume engulfed them. Sagel and Nigel rubbed their eyes and Elenry concentrated hard on not coughing.

The room was full of different colored candles, some lit, some not. A fire was blazing in the fireplace, displaying an array of colors as the new entities walked into the room. The walls held many shelves that housed books and jars filled with herbs and dried plants. Above the shelves hung exotic plants and a few vividly colored scarves that whispered and swayed in a secret breeze. A stout woman with long hair stood in the front, right corner of the room. Her hair was an angry red that seemed to shimmer and dance even though her head was still. But what held their attention was what was in the center of the room.

"Welcome, Elenry, and children," said a voice from the center.

A woman with short white hair sat cross-legged on a crimson pillow. Her face was powerfully sculpted, but sagged with age. Her shoulders drooped and her hands were wrinkled and limp in her lap. Her robe was white and was fashioned exactly like the rest of the residents' robes. On her face she wore a grin that stretched her pale lips away to display small and crowded teeth. Sagel could not stop watching her eyes, for they were almost exactly like Elenry's. She could not put a color to them.

"Relae," Elenry said, her voice dry and wavering.

"Elenry," she said, laughing a deep, jolting cackle.

"How are you…what are—"

"Oh, treasure this moment, hold it close, my dear Elenry," she interrupted, lifting her head upwards and furrowing her pale brow. "So many years have come and gone, and I knew at the turn of every one that the next would bring me one turn closer to seeing you again."

Elenry walked to Relae and kneeled before her. Relae opened her arms and accepted Elenry into a long embrace. Finally, Elenry broke away and stood, backing up slowly.

"But what is this—" Elenry swept one hand slowly around her.

"This is The Center," Relae said flamboyantly. "The Center of the healing energy of this planet. Many years ago, I began to search for it, after dreaming of it. I knew that if I could find it, that I could bring complete, healing peace to this planet. The people who live here are all Medicine People who are willing to provide service to The Center."

"I was led here. Sagel and I were both led here by visions," Elenry explained. "I was in the village of Shinken, and it is suffering—"

"Yes, yes, I know all about Shinken. I have been dreaming of it for months. We have the cure, and we will give some to the children to bring back as soon as we are done here. About ten jars will do for the entire village."

"Jars of what?" Elenry asked, relieving both children of their mutual question.

"Of your long sought cure," Relae said, accenting her answer with a grand wave of her crinkled hand. "It is sap from the trees in Fahrien forest. It is charged with the energy of the cosmos that is so heavily concentrated in this area. We have tested it on many a sick person, and all of them healed perfectly, without any negative side effects, rebound symptoms, or discomfort."

"What kind of illnesses did they have?" Elenry probed.

"They were plagued with a myriad of ailments: coughs, malignant growths, negative feelings, vomiting, wheezing. I could go on but we might be here all night," Relae's smiled stretched further still. It gave Sagel the chills.

"You know of the illness that plagues Shinken," Elenry said slowly. "Can this sap cure it?"

"Yes. Yes it can," Relae answered, her expression deepening pensively.

"We tried to use sap to cure the disease, but it could not cure someone who had already contracted it."

"Yes, that is because it was not properly charged, due to the trees' lack of energy alignment with The Center," Relae said. "With this antidote, the people of Shinken will live in peace and health. As I said earlier, I will have ten jars of the sap made up and delivered to the children—"

"The children *and* myself," Elenry added.

"No. Just the children," Relae corrected, her pale finger waving at them.

"What do you mean?" Elenry said. Her voice was steady. Sagel and Nigel looked at each other, fresh fear brewing within them. Sagel shifted her weight to her other foot, trying not to bounce with anxiety. Her brother watched stonily as reality dawned on him.

"You have to understand this, Elenry: The Center is going to be the single most powerful healing location in all of Asthekia. Old medicine of the Medicine People will be combined with nature's power and the power of the cosmos. All three forces will work together to create such an ambience of health that people from all over this planet will pay to be healed here. Though we have the means to extract the sap and give it to people for a certain price, we also need the best Medicine People to live and work here. The longer they stay here, the more powerful they become as healers. You are the best I have ever known, my dear Elenry, and this place will not reach its full healing potential without you. You need to stay and help me—help Asthekia," Relae finished. She smiled proudly up at them.

"No."

"You do not have a choice, Elenry."

"I always have a choice, Relae. I will not be part of your greed," Elenry said, her voice controlled.

"Greed? No Elenry, not greed. I strive to help the people, not to, to— to indulge in greed!"

"But you do, Relae. I still remember your charging everyone who walked in your door a ridiculous amount for even the simplest of healings. I stayed with you because I learned from you, and when I could learn no more I left. I left because I knew you could teach me no more. I may not be good for much else than healing and animal caring, but I am by no means stupid."

Relae bowed her head, keeping her eyes trained on Elenry so that the magnetic intensity of her gaze probed deeply within Elenry's mind.

Elenry let out a strangled cry and clutched her chest, then breathed deeply and stood straight, staring down into Relae's eyes. Relae's smile metamorphosed into a grimacing snarl. Sagel and Nigel drew closer together, both fascinated and frightened by the intense energy surrounding the two powerful women.

"Elenry?" Sagel whispered, her voice cracking. Elenry did not respond to her.

"You horrible woman!" Elenry cried, brandishing her finger at Relae, who flinched. "You are a manipulating hag with a psyche so twisted and shriveled that even a brilliant healer like yourself could not save it. I know what you did, and I know what you are doing."

Savage tears of rage poured from Elenry's eyes.

"Yes, well, you were never supposed to know. I meant to protect you from it, to keep you in an unknowing realm while you and I helped the Asthekian people. It was always a plan for the good of the people," Relae said, planting her fist into her palm to emphasize her last sentence.

"You lie," Elenry said coldly, her eyes flashing a color that Sagel had never seen. It looked crimson red, but might have been deep, ocean blue.

"No, I do not lie."

"You lie about your killing off of an entire village, and then starting to kill off another one, and then you lie about lying," Elenry seethed.

"What?" Sagel and Nigel chorused in hoarse whispers. Elenry held her hand up in silence.

"I do not wish to see you any longer," Relae said, rising from her flat, red pillow. "Saivenn is just outside the door. He will take Sagel and Nigel to a guest cabin and see to it that they get their sap. They may rest for a few days and replenish their strength. Then they must leave." She turned to the children. "Tell your village that they are among the luckier ones, and that this is a token of The Center's love and protection. Say that they are welcome to come back anytime for any needed healings, but that they will have to pay from now on."

"Elenry—"

"No, Sagel," Elenry cut her off with commanding eyes.

Sagel understood and grasped her brother's hand, steering them both towards the door of the cabin and making their way outside to meet Saivenn. When they were gone, Relae unleashed a terrible grin onto Elenry, making the Medicine Woman's skin crawl and her scalp frost over with a suffocating film of terror.

"Sechia, show Elenry to her quarters and see to it that she does not wander from The Center."

Without a word or gesture, Elenry turned and followed the short Sechia, whose red hair billowed out like a thousand flags signaling danger.

Chapter 29

Choice

Saivenn stood restlessly on the porch just outside the cabin door; he had obviously listened in on the conversation and knew exactly what to do. Either that or he had been told before everything had taken place. He took one beady look at the children and smiled, his mouth pinched like a poised beak, ready to peck at any moment.

"So, on we go to your cabin," he chortled, walking down the stairs and starting off into his jerking pace once more. "I will bring the sap to you first thing tomorrow morning."

They followed him silently back the way they had come. At the edge of town, he led them up onto the porch of the very first house that they had seen.

"I will leave you here now to rest and replenish," Saivenn said quickly. "I will be here tomorrow morning with your ten jars of sap."

With a quick simper, he bowed his head and turned, heading off the porch and back towards the center of the compound.

The children retired into the dark cabin where they were out of sight and earshot.

"What are we going to do?" Nigel wailed, as soon as the door was closed behind them.

"I have no idea," Sagel said, slumping against the door and sliding to the floor.

"Why can't she just let Elenry go? She seems powerful enough to just do it by herself!" Nigel continued, pacing before Sagel.

"I don't think she wants Elenry because Elenry is a brilliant Medicine Woman," Sagel said quietly, holding back frustrated tears.

"Why else would she want her?!" Nigel cried.

"Well, there are two things actually," Sagel began, rubbing her face vigorously and then sitting up straighter. "The first is because she knows how much money she'll make when Elenry starts healing people left and right. The second is about her pride. Elenry left her once before, and she doesn't want her to leave again. It's like she wants to show her who's more powerful, or in control, or something."

"We'll figure it out, right?" Nigel asked solemnly.

"I don't know."

Sagel stood from the floor and observed the cabin. It had only one room, like Relae's. There was one small bed in the far corner, a table with one chair, and a red floor pillow. Three more chairs stood against the back wall. Sagel noted that the pillow was large enough to sleep on, since the bed was much too small to comfortably hold both of them. A moment later there was a person at the door. It was a lady wrapped in the typical red robe. She had short blonde hair and intense blue eyes. Flavi was her name, and she had a basket of food for them. Before she left, she lit a fire for them in the fireplace and left them candles for light.

The children ate, proclaiming form time to time how frightened or angry they were. The food was good, at least.

"You'd be a fool to run, Medicine Woman," Sechia said once they were at Elenry's doorstep. "This cottage is yours, not just for tonight, but for the rest of your stay here. It will be your healing house once people start coming here regularly, which will be very, very soon."

"And who would stop me if I meant to leave?" Elenry wondered dryly.

"The one hundred vigils who protect The Center," Sechia sniped. "They are all out in the woods surrounding this place. You probably passed a few of them when you came in."

"I need to speak to the children."

"Why is that?" Sechia asked.

"Because I need to give them instructions on how to get back to Shinken. They are far too young to be making the trip alone, but given the unfortunate circumstances, they have no choice," Elenry answered, her eyes locking onto Sechia's and repeating her words telepathically.

Sechia was silent and fixed. She breathed deeply and said, "Relae was right about you. Alright, I agree with that. You'll learn to love it here. You really will...er...well, I'll bring you to the children now."

Elenry smiled to herself and then followed Sechia through the village.

"I'll be waiting out here," Sechia said quietly, her muddy brown eyes appraising the Medicine Woman.

"Knock, knock," Elenry said, opening the door to the children's house.

"Elenry!" they chorused, abandoning their meal and running to embrace her.

"Are you free? Are we going back now? Did she let you go?" The barrage of questions was so thick that Elenry was unclear who had asked them.

"Slow yourselves," Elenry said, sighing as she pulled sadly from their embrace. "She has not let me go, nor does she plan to."

"Oh no," Nigel moaned, sudden tears filling his eyes.

"I must tell you more about what she has done in order to show you what a monster she is so that you will be more serious about fleeing here and not trying anything foolish to break me free," Elenry said calmly, laying a hand on each of their shoulders. "You can't do anything about this situation. That is the first thing you need to understand and accept."

They nodded glumly. Elenry led the children to their chairs and then brought one for herself to the table and sat facing them. Sagel's heart sank because she realized that they had no power to help Elenry. They had no control in this situation except for whether or not their village received the medicine it needed. Whatever Elenry told them, returning to Shinken with the ten jars of sap was their main focus now. This frightened her because she and Nigel were going to have to do it alone.

"When we were having it out in there, she showed me something with her mind. I do not know why she did it, though I have a feeling she did it to frighten me," Elenry sighed and continued. "All of those long years ago, my village perished in the grip of a horrible illness, not unlike the one that is gripping Shinken. I see now that she was behind the illness that destroyed Nook. She created it and spread it through horrible potions and dark meditations. I do not know how she did it, nor do I want to, but I know why. She saw that I was an extremely powerful girl who would grow to be an extremely powerful Medicine Woman.

I understand now that she has been planning this Center for a very long time, perhaps even before I was born. She had to isolate me, hence her killing off everything and everyone I knew and loved. She then took me into her care; feeding me, clothing me, teaching me, and mothering me. My leaving her after our little tiff was not in her plan, but she could not stop me then because I controlled my thoughts when I was around her, so she could not read my intentions. Then, I left in the night while she was asleep. I moved so quickly that I got out of reach of her powers.

She is holding me here because she wants to exercise her power over me; to put me in my place. She is also greedy for money, and she knows that the quality of my services will attract people who are willing to pay her a great deal of white rocks. She is greedy, jealous, and will stop at nothing to make her fame and fortune. I have also understood something about this place that I did not before, and it is absolutely crucial to the life of your village and the wellbeing of the surrounding area."

"What?" they chorused, their eyes glued to Elenry.

"This forest is not the sole source of its own healing energy. It is a lens that is channeling the healing power from the surrounding lands. It is sucking the healing energy and life right out of the mountains, villages and the people of Shinken. It is like a bloodthirsty insect with a great invisible proboscis. Relae is using the power of the Medicine People and her own powers to do this, but I believe that once the flow of energy into The Center is cut off, the Stretch in Shinken will have enough healing sap to cure everyone in the village and more. Once The Center, and Relae, stop sucking the life from the surrounding lands, everywhere will be a healing place, as it once was before this started. The trees died because they could not shield themselves from the cold with their own warmth; they hadn't enough life energy."

Nigel broke in, "Why couldn't she kill the trees in the Stretch?"

"I'm not sure, but my best guess is that the energy in the Stretch was so powerful before she attacked it that its powers could not be completely drained."

"But why would it be so much more powerful than the other trees?"

"You've lived there all your life. Hasn't the Stretch always been different?"

Nigel looked at Elenry a moment longer before falling into silence.

"Why did Relae single out Deagial and Shinken?" Sagel asked.

"Relae attacked Deagial to get to Shinken because she could see that I would be the one called to aid it. She knew that once I arrived in Shinken, I would end up here. She conjured all of the visions that we experienced, Sagel. She targeted you, Daniel and Nigel with a powerful spell that would push you to want to assist me."

"So, all that we did, all that we accomplished…we weren't really doing it?" Sagel said, her voice empty.

"Of course you were doing it! She only manipulated your internal motivation, but it was you who carried out the actions. Had you all not have been truly capable, intelligent, and strong enough, you would have failed miserably, possibly dying in the process of this whole perilous saga," Elenry said adamantly. The children smiled, their eyes sparkling with tears and gratitude.

"I don't understand it," Sagel said, once Elenry had stopped speaking. "I thought Medicine People were good."

"You are right in that assumption, Sagel. Medicine People are supposed to be good, but I do not think that Relae is good," Elenry answered. There was silence, both children soaking in the statement.

"What is she?" Nigel asked.

"She is a prisoner of her own darkness," Elenry said, holding up her hand before either of them could question or protest. "She is a very perceptive, very intuitive, and very aligned person. She can heal because she has learned the potions and the chants, but she does not have a healer's heart. I think she knows this, too, which is why she has surrounded herself with Medicine People. They are here because they have been fooled, or they are like her, or because they have been brought here under coercion by her vigils and helpers."

"What are her vigils?" Sagel asked.

"According to Sechia, she has one hundred people hidden in the forest to protect The Center from unwanted visitors and unwanted deserters. Now, before I leave, I must give you the instructions that will save your village."

Morning dawned with a dim light. The cloud-blotted sun strained to filter through the thick branches of the towering trees. Sagel awoke with a start, and then let her mind recall Elenry's instructions and prepare for what lay ahead. She rushed from her bed on the floor cushion and then woke her brother from the bed. They had both slept in their clothes. They ate a quick breakfast of leftovers and then put the rest of the food in their knapsacks. They left the house ten minutes after they had woken up and stepped with purpose through the snow and away from

The Center. They did not wait for Saivenn to bring them the sap.

As Elenry had taught them, they let their bodies lead them as they leaned into their strides. A weary smile lit Sagel's face when the dim forest light began to brighten, and the trees thinned and shrank. They were nearing the skirts of Fahrien forest.

"When will we meet them?" Nigel asked, breaking both Sagel and himself from their trances.

"Soon," Sagel replied, coming to a stop. "Elenry said to expect them when we are on the edge of the forest. It should be any time."

"Is she right?" Nigel asked after a moment of thought. He chewed his lip.

"What do you mean?"

"Is what we're doing right? Is Elenry right about all of this?" he continued.

"She said to trust her, Nigel," Sagel said. "That's all we can—look!"

They both stopped, grinning in awe and excitement.

About a quarter mile in front of them, a shape was coming into view. They could both tell that it was enormous, and moving towards them at a great speed. Something smaller rode upon it.

"Arros!" they cried running to meet the horse.

They ran at Arros and his rider until they finally met.

"Daniel?" Sagel said, stepping around Arros as the horse came to a halt and snorted.

"Oh!" Daniel exclaimed, sliding off the horse and embracing both Sagel and Nigel.

"I found you! I did it, you're here! You did it!" Daniel cried, his eyes flicking between them, a renewed sparkle present that had been utterly absent after his mother's death.

"You found us. You found us, Daniel!" Sagel said, still clutching her best friend.

"It was easy," he said, pulling away, still grinning from ear to ear. "I just got on Arros and let him take me. Elenry's note just said to let him run and he would take me to the place I needed to go."

"I don't understand. How did you know to come here?" Nigel said. "Elenry never said how you would do it, because she was taken away by Sechia when her time with us was up."

"Who's Sechia? Where is Elenry?" Daniel asked suddenly.

"Never mind Sechia, and we'll explain everything on the ride home, but how did you know to come here?" Sagel pressed.

Daniel raised his eyebrows and began, "I was at the barn three days ago feeding the horses—no one had really been feeding them because of the illness and such, and Wisle walked in. I was really excited because I thought that it meant that you three had come back, but then I saw the note on him. It was Elenry writing to whomever got the note, and she said that you would be coming with the cure, but that you would need Arros and someone else to come and meet the three of you in Fahrien forest. Then she wrote that Arros would know what direction to go and that all I would need to do was just get on him and let him go. I packed a bunch of food for me and Arros, and warm clothing, because the note said to, and then I just rode."

"That's amazing," Sagel said. "Oh."

"What?" the boys said.

"I know when she wrote that note," Sagel said, gasping in with her sudden realization. "The night before Wisle supposedly ran off. I woke up in the middle of the night and Elenry was writing on something, but I was too groggy and just went back to sleep without asking her about it. I didn't remember it in the morning. That must have been the note she was writing. Oh!"

"What?" they cried, leaning towards the excited Sagel.

"And Wisle was so homesick that of course he would go back to the barn, and Elenry knew that," she finished, relaxing back into her normal tone of voice.

"So, where is she?" Daniel asked again.

"Let's ride and talk, we need to get back to Shinken as soon as we can," Sagel said, pulling herself up onto Arros's saddle blanket and then offering her hand to her brother, who climbed up and sat behind her.

Daniel nodded, took off his backpack and handed it to Nigel, and then climbed up in front of Sagel, taking the reins and steering Arros back the other way towards Mt. Aarotte. Arros pulled in the opposite direction, throwing his head towards Fahrien forest.

"Arros," Sagel said gently, "Elenry said you needed to bring us home. She said you will see her again."

After another moment of resistance, Arros bowed his massive head and began trotting in the direction of Mt. Aarotte.

"You got the cure, right?" Daniel asked.

"We didn't have to get the cure," Sagel said, holding onto Daniel as Arros began his steady trot. "The cure will be in Shinken."

Elenry woke not long after the children had departed. She dressed in her warm white shirt and pants and then wrapped herself in the deep red shroud that Sechia had left on her bed the night before. Her dark hair was pulled back in a tight ponytail. She ate breakfast quickly, running through her plan over and over again, fool-proofing all the time. She meditated and sent positive energy to the universe.

The Medicine Woman easily found her way back to the center of The Center, and ascended Relae's porch steps. She knocked on the door and waited. Saivenn walked by on his way to perform his duty of sap collecting for the children, though they were long gone by that time. He flicked his gaze to Elenry, and upon deciding that her actions were innocent, he turned his attention back to his task. Elenry touched the box in her pocket as she waited.

"Who is it?" called Relae's low voice.

"It is Elenry, here to discuss some ideas for The Center." As Elenry stood, waiting in the silence that she had expected, she aligned all the powers of her mind with Relae's desire for ultimate healing power.

"Elenry?" Relae asked, her voice a little stronger.

"Yes. I have returned."

There was a pause, in which Elenry focused on Relae's greed, and then Relae's now excited voice urged, "Come in, dear, come in!"

Elenry opened the door and stepped in, then shut the door behind her. She focused on the shelves and recited to herself all that they held.

"I knew you would come around, Elenry," Relae said, turning from the bookshelf she seemed to have been perusing. Her physical wellbeing had deteriorated greatly since Elenry had left all those years before. Her formerly square stance was now drooping and wobbly. When she turned she had to clutch the shelf for support. She walked to Elenry, but wobbled so badly that she looked in danger of toppling to the floor.

"Sit Relae, sit. You don't want to tire yourself," Elenry said, taking the woman by her elbow and leading her to her floor pillow. Relae stiffened at the touch and flushed, and then allowed Elenry to lower her gently onto the pillow. Elenry stepped back and stood, head bowed respectfully but eyes continuing to move slowly across the shelves. She knew that her mind had to be full of Relae, and nothing else.

"So what has changed your mind?" Relae asked peevishly, as if she had won an argument.

"I just realized that you were right," Elenry began, seeing each and every jar, book and plant in her mind's eye. "People who deserve to be healed should be healed. Fahrien forest is quite a wonder, and I believe that it will be a successful place of healing."

"You do, do you?" the old woman said, her eyes searching for something, but not finding it.

"I meant all that I said," Elenry explained. Then, with a sweep of her hand, she said, "You have gathered a treasure house of healing here. It is so strong that last night I was gifted with thoughts that kept me up nearly all night."

"Tell me, my dear," Relae crooned, relaxing into her pillow.

"As I said, this place will certainly heal people that would not otherwise be healed, but there are some things that need to change. I don't expect you to agree with some of my thoughts, but I hoped that with your being of such a powerful mind, you could help me whittle my thoughts into plausible actions."

"Of course I can, Elenry, and of course I will," Relae said, smiling up at Elenry. "Make yourself comfortable here on my pillow. I wanted to say that I did not intend for yesterday to go so bitterly. I actually expected you to be more open to my plans, but now that you have come around I can see that all is forgiven."

"Yes, Relae, I forgive you. I forgive you for everything, and I apologize," Elenry said, pulling a small box from her pants pocket. "Oh, I almost forgot! I brought these for you."

"What are these lovely morsels?" Relae said, opening the box. Inside were nested in neat rows small red balls with slightly crusted exteriors that looked like hardened sugar. Relae picked one up cautiously, held it up to the light from the fireplace, and examined it closely. "It is very interesting, and it feels—" turning it over and over in her hand—"strong."

"You have not lost your touch, Relae. They are indeed a wonderful little healing and energizing supplement. I began working on them following a potion for strengthened immunity that you yourself taught me. I had a strong hunch and decided to add an unlisted ingredient. It turned out to be so effective that I produced many of them, a whole pot full of these little balls. I take one every day, and I have not been sick in years. A person need swallow only one."

"I'll take one now," Relae said, rolling the ball in her crooked hand. "As you can see, I am a bit weak." She looked at the red balls in the box again, a smug smile of pride painting her face at the fact that she had scored such a gift, and that her potion had been used to make it.

"It will strengthen you," Elenry added, her eyes flickering to the top shelf that she described silently to herself—*jar of ahi powder, three red books, one potted root plant.*

Relae held the ball for a moment before her open mouth, and then placed it on her tongue. She allowed it to rest there as she examined it through her interior senses. Closing her mouth slowly, she sucked it slightly and then swallowed slowly, her aged throat working to get it down. She coughed softly and then smiled.

"See there, not a problem…thank you Elenry," she said. "Now, about your plans?"

"The plans can wait," Elenry said, breathing out through her mouth, and focusing now only on the red ball doing its work inside the body of her former teacher.

"No, Elenry. I want to hear them now. I've been waiting so long for you. I really do think I should hear them," Relae stopped mid sentence, holding her hand to her head. "Oh dear."

Elenry sat up straighter, watching Relae intently.

"I feel so relaxed. Your potion is so soothing."

Elenry smiled and patted Relae's hands.

"I am very sleepy," the old woman said. "I do feel so much like sleeping…soundly…peacefully."

"Yes, you look as though you deserve a long, peaceful rest. You have worked so hard and accomplished so much. Rest should be your reward," Elenry said, taking one of Relae's hands. "Why don't you lie back…your drowsiness will pass soon. You won't feel any pain."

Elenry became aware of the tears that she might have shed years ago and relaxed, dry-eyed as they did not come.

"What's happening to me?" Relae's voice was fainter and more garbled.

"Just lie back, Relae, just rest now," Elenry whispered, helping her fall back onto her pillow.

"Yes, I'll just close my eyes for a minute, and then you can tell me your…plan…pla…."

"Rest now," Elenry said, squeezing Relae's cold, limp hand and looking away from her face out of which all life had slipped like the last drop of a melting icicle.

The Medicine Woman stood up and away from the pillow, stowed the box of red balls in her pocket, and then left the dead, old woman and her cottage.

Elenry began walking to Sechia's house. She was going to explain everything.

With Arros's steady gait, the journey home was short and uneventful. It took the children only two and a half days to return to Shinken. The first half day of their ride had been devoted to explaining every little detail of their experiences with Elenry, including all that had happened in The Center. Daniel had been enthralled, 'wowing' and 'woahing' every so often.

Daniel had left without telling anyone, because that is what Elenry's note had said to do in order to have the simplest departure. When Michael and the rest of the town had discovered that he was missing, they became distraught. No one could leave the village, but they had searched the surrounding land and forest, finding no trace; Arros's hoof prints had been covered up by a recent snowfall.

The children bivouacked twice on the mountainside, huddled under a blanket that Daniel had packed. Arros crouched beside them and helped keep them warm with his intense body heat. The horse was comfortable with just his saddle blanket for cover.

Sagel thought often about Elenry as they rode up the mountain. Before Elenry had bade them goodbye on the night they last saw her, she had told them that all they needed to do was to set Arros free with all of his tack as soon as they got back to Shinken. On the second day, something changed in the atmosphere. The energy on the barren side of the mountain was charged with a positive aura. A great wind blew for about an hour. It was so strong that the children had to stop and wait it out. This wind was no ordinary wind, however; it danced and sang all around them, whistling tunes and chants that they could hear rise and fall in the gusts.

All laughing in relief when the wind had finally passed, they knew that the energy that Relae had locked up in The Center had been redistributed around the surrounding land. Elenry had cut off the proboscis.

Both Sagel and Nigel had asked her whether or not she would return to Shinken, but she said she would not make any promises. They implored her, begged her, and cried, but no matter how much they insisted that they would miss her, she did not give them an answer. Sagel understood now that Elenry was not the kind of person who formed attachments with places and people. She went where the cosmos took her. No one knew where the Medicine Woman had been before Shinken, and no one would know where she would end up afterwards. Though it saddened her, Sagel accepted this about Elenry.

Chapter 30

Shinken

"There!" Daniel cried, pointing down from the summit that was nearest to the village. It was noon of their third journey day, and they had finally topped the rise above the village.

After joyous whoops and a few secret but relieved tears from Sagel, Arros snorted and then began a quick descent through the trees towards Shinken. Around them, the forest was strong. The trees stood straighter than they had ever seen them, and their bark was a deep, healthy brown.

The children rode into Shinken, shrieking and laughing to the townspeople. Villagers poured from their doors, pulling the three children down from the horse and hugging them. Sagel had explained as simply as she could what the cure was, and a few healthy villagers had immediately gone to fetch fresh sap from the Stretch that would now cure the ill and prevent further contagion. Lorel, Torren, and Michael had to push their way through the crowd of celebrating villagers to reach their children.

"You did it," Lorel said, over and over again, holding her children so tightly that they struggled to breathe. Torren held his family, including Nova, who had finally run through the legs of the crowd and was now hugging her siblings' waists.

Michael and Daniel embraced, and Michael smiled at his son when they finally released their gripping hug.

"Thank you, Daniel," he said. "Your mother would have been pleasantly surprised."

"Yeah, she would have," Daniel said, hugging his father again.

"I love you, Daniel."

"I love you, too."

In the next week or so, Shinken began to heal. Everyone who was ill was told to stay home and take hourly doses of tree sap. Improvements started happening within a day or so, and deaths stopped altogether. In total, twenty-three people had perished. The children told Haykyel and their parents all that had happened, and Haykyel decided that it would be prudent for them to tell the village at a meeting. The children were received with love and gratitude; a complete turn around from the doubtful, frightened attitude of those who had seen them off. Everyone was shocked at the story, which Sagel and Nigel told together. Daniel told his part of the story, reading Elenry's original note to the village. The children were honored and received ceremonial blessings from Haykyel, as well as special crystals with Shinken's insignia on them.

Within a week or two after the meeting, things had gone back to normal. People on the street still greeted the elder Bleudry children and Daniel with great warmth, and when school started again, their classmates held them in special regard, good naturedly grilling them for details about their journeys.

Arros rested for a night in the stable after they returned, ate, slept and was then set free, fully tacked by Sagel and Daniel. Nigel would have been there, but Lorel had wanted him to stay home. She had been keeping all of her children very close to her since they had returned.

"Can I say something, Sage?" Daniel asked as they walked back towards Shinken after they had set Arros free.

"Sure," she said.

"I am sorry that I backed out on you…but I think I was supposed to," Daniel said. "I don't know how it worked, but it was like the cosmos or whatever wanted me to…or something like that."

"I think you're right," Sagel replied.

"And you know that that didn't count as our big trip to the other side of the mountain."

"Daniel!" Sagel cried.

They laughed as they walked the winding road to Daniel's house, where they would sit on his carpet and try to decide what they would do for the rest of the day.

Icy winds blew through Shinken the next winter, but all they brought was the promise of snow.